Jack

Stan

Best Wishes for your
life after *[illegible]*

WAR AND BETRAYAL

From Manzanar to Dachau

A Novel

Jules F. Bonjour

Second Print Edition
ISBN-10: 0692424431
ISBN-13: 978-0-692-42443-8

The photo on the back cover is a compilation of two photos. The one of the little boy was taken by Russell Lee in 1942 for the Farm Security Administration. The photo of the entrance to Manzanar was taken by Ansel Adams in the fall of 1943.

Book cover design by Ezra Barany. Front cover photo credits: Barbed wire by Eugene Sergeev; Flag (without the swastika): Igor Stevanovic; Constitution: Onur Ersin.

Book Layout by Beth Barany.

For all those who will face the next challenge.

Have courage.

Bon courage.

CONTENTS

FOREWORD

The past is never dead. It's not even past.
    —William Faulkner, 1951

This novel was written as a cautionary tale. Even those countries with long-standing adherence to due process and the rule of law can succumb in times of crisis and abandon those principles. When they do, they leave the innocent, the weak and unpopular minorities with no protection against injustice. This is what happened to the Jews after France was defeated by Germany in 1940, and in the United States to those of Japanese ancestry after Pearl Harbor.

Now that living memory of those times is rapidly coming to an end, it is important that we are reminded of what happened so the next time, and there will be a next time, the mistakes of the past are not repeated.

    Jules Bonjour
    Berkeley, California
    January 2015

NOTICE

Headquarters
Western Defense Command
and Fourth Army

Presidio of San Francisco, California
May 5, 1942

Civilian Exclusion Order No. 41

1. Pursuant to the provisions of Public Proclamations Nos. 1 and 2, this Headquarters, dated March 2, 1942, and March 16, 1942, respectively, it is hereby ordered that from and after 12 o'clock noon, P. W. T., of Monday, May 11, 1942, all persons of Japanese ancestry, both alien and non-alien, be excluded from that portion of Military Area No. 1 described as follows:

> All of that portion of the City and County of San Francisco, State of California, within that boundary beginning at the intersection of Presidio Avenue and Sutter Street; thence easterly on Sutter Street to Van Ness Avenue; thence southerly on Van Ness Avenue to O'Farrell Street; thence westerly on O'Farrell Street to St. Joseph's Avenue (Calvary Cemetery); thence northerly on St. Joseph's Avenue to Geary Street; thence westerly on Geary Street to Presidio Avenue; thence northerly on Presidio Avenue to the point of beginning.

2. A responsible member of each family, and each individual living alone, in the above described area will report between the hours of 8:00 A. M. and 5:00 P. M., Wednesday, May 6, 1942, or during the same hours on Thursday, May 7, 1942, to the Civil Control Station located at:

> 1530 Buchanan Street,
> San Francisco, California.

3. Any person subject to this order who fails to comply with any of its provisions or with the provisions of published instructions pertaining hereto or who is found in the above area after 12 o'clock noon, P. W. T., of Monday, May 11, 1942, will be liable to the criminal penalties provided by Public Law No. 503, 77th Congress, approved March 21, 1942, entitled "An Act to Provide a Penalty for Violation of Restrictions or Orders with Respect to Persons Entering, Remaining in, Leaving or Committing Any Act in Military Areas or Zones," and alien Japanese will be subject to immediate apprehension and internment.

4. All persons within the bounds of an established Assembly Center pursuant to instructions from this Headquarters are excepted from the provisions of this order while those persons are in such Assembly Center.

> J. L. DeWITT
> Lieutenant General, U. S. Army
> Commanding

FRANCE 1790

LIBERTÉ EGALITÉ FRATERNITÉ

FRANCE 1940–1944

TRAVAIL, FAMILLE, PATRIE

WORK, FAMILY, FATHERLAND

VICHY FRANCE, SEAT OF THE FRENCH
GOVERNMENT AFTER OCCUPATION

Vichy Statute October 4, 1940

"Foreign nationals of the Jewish race may, from the promulgation date of the present law, be interned in special camps by a decision of the prefect of the department of their residence. A commission charged with the organization and administration of these camps shall be constituted within the Ministry of the Interior.... Foreign nationals of the Jewish race may at any time be assigned a forced residence by the prefect of the department in which they reside."

Vichy Statute July 16, 1941

Article 1: "The number of persons defined in Article 1 of the law of 2 June, 1941 admissible to be a lawyer ... may not exceed ... 2% of the total of non-Jewish lawyers inscribed at the Bar of each jurisdiction."

BOOK ONE

A SCRAP OF PAPER

Laws are silent in time of war.
—Cicero

CHAPTER 1

FRIDAY, DECEMBER 5, 1941

Oakland, California

The black Buick moved slowly through stop-and-go traffic toward the courthouse. Rain and the low marine layer covered everything under a gray shroud. The only color came from the blurry red taillights of other cars he could see through the windshield wipers, keeping time to Artie Shaw's music on the radio like a pair of metronomes. Jean-Claude reached inside the pocket of his raincoat for his pack of cigarettes. The car filled with gray smoke, which blended with the atmosphere outside.

He was going to be late—again. Judge Michael Kelly did not tolerate lawyers who held up proceedings in his court and would often hold lawyers in contempt for being late and lock them up for a few hours. This was especially true when appearing before him in the morning. One never knew when he might have had a bad night because he had too much to drink.

Jean-Claude looked at his watch. It was already 9:10. Court was to begin at 9. When he finally arrived at the courthouse, the only available parking place was the one reserved for the sheriff of the county. He took it and put his business card on the dash hoping it might keep his car from being towed. He pulled his hat down over his forehead, grabbed his briefcase, and ran for the entrance through the heavy rain, tossing his cigarette into the gutter where the rain water swept it away.

He entered through the heavy bronze and glass doors and made his way down the marble hallway to the bank of elevators. His gray suit, slightly rumpled because of the rain, still hung nicely on his broad shoulders.

Negroes operated the elevators and wore blue jackets with brass buttons and matching caps, just like in the fancy hotels on Union Square in San Francisco. As Jean-Claude approached, the door to one opened. It was Percy's elevator. Percy knew every lawyer by name and by looking at the morning calendar posted in the clerk's office he knew which courtroom each lawyer was to appear in on any given day. He had been there many years and was considered an institution.

"Missa Bonnay, Judge Kelly is gonna eat you alive," Percy said. "You is late again."

"Thanks, Percy, I am well aware. Look, do me a favor and take these over to Judge Golden's courtroom," Jean-Claude said as he took off his raincoat and hat and handed them to Percy. "Ask his clerk to keep them for me until I'm finished in Kelly's court. I don't want to walk into his courtroom dripping water all over the place. Tell her I'll be over there later this morning to pick them up."

"Sho will. I'll also tell 'em if you don't get there by noon to send somebody to get you out on a writ."

"Good idea." Jean-Claude smiled and nodded in agreement. "I don't want to sit in his holding cell all day."

"Seventh floor," Percy said as the elevator door opened. "Good luck," he called out as Jean-Claude quickly walked down the long corridor. When he reached the double doors of Kelly's courtroom he felt a sudden rush of adrenaline. His hands grew cold and his heart rate increased. *No matter what Kelly says or does, just stay calm.* He pushed open the door and went in.

There was spectator seating on both sides of a center aisle that led to the well of the courtroom. As he walked down the aisle his attention was focused on Kelly, who sat on the bench beneath a large American flag, glaring at him.

"Well, Mr. Bonnay, you have finally decided to grace us with your presence," Kelly said, looking up at the big round clock on the wall. "It is now 9:27. That makes you twenty-seven minutes late. I need not remind you this is the second time this week you've been late. If we weren't in the middle of a preliminary hearing, I'd put you in custody right now, but since there is a civilian witness you have also inconvenienced, I'm going to wait until the end of the hearing to decide what to do with you."

"My apologies for keeping the court and the witness waiting," Jean-Claude said, looking directly at Kelly. He kept his tone respectful, his voice calm. He was relieved he hadn't been put into custody on the spot.

No need to offer excuses for being late, because no excuse except death would justify being late to Kelly's court. The apology was more for the witness's benefit since he didn't want to alienate a critical witness.

His client was a young Negro charged with strong-arm robbery—snatching a purse from an elderly lady in Berkeley. She could not identify the person because he had come up from behind. The purse was never recovered. The only witness was a woman who claimed to have been walking toward the lady and saw the person as he jerked the purse from her shoulder and ran past her. She was the witness who was going to testify.

"Bailiff, bring Mr. Bonnay's client in from the holding cell," Kelly said in his deep voice. "And keep the cell warm because Mr. Bonnay may be joining him after this hearing is over." He was not smiling when he said it. "Let's get started. Counsel, state your appearances for the record."

The DA rose to his feet. "Mario Antonelli for the People.

We are ready, Your Honor."

Antonelli was once a very good trial lawyer, but now with his best years behind him and retirement approaching, he was handling smaller cases without a great deal of enthusiasm.

Jean-Claude stood. "Jean-Claude Bonnay for the defendant, William Lewis. We are ready," he said in a strong voice.

"I doubt you're ready, Mr. Bonnay, but nonetheless we shall proceed. Mr. Antonelli, call your next witness."

Jean-Claude ignored the remark and focused on the witness who was about to testify. "The People call Stephanie Stevenson to the stand."

Stephanie Stevenson walked to the witness chair from the back of the courtroom where she had been seated. Jean-Claude hadn't noticed her when he'd entered as his attention had been focused on Judge Kelly. As he turned in his seat at counsel table to see what she looked like he was stunned. She was about five feet ten. Her shoulder-length brown hair and her high cheekbones gave her an aristocratic look. She wore a conservative tailored gray suit that appeared to be very expensive, but did not disguise her well-proportioned figure. As she passed by him on her way to the witness stand he observed that she looked every bit as good from the back as she did from the front. She sat down and crossed her legs, showing off her black and white spectators.

Jean-Claude was immediately attracted to her. He was single and beautiful women always got his attention. He tried to see if she wore a wedding band, but she had her hands folded in her lap. If she wasn't married, he was going to use his time during cross-examination to get to know her.

The clerk swore in the witness. "Do you swear to tell the truth, the whole truth, and nothing but the truth, so help you God?"

"I do."

The clerk continued. "Please state your name for the record."

"My name is Stephanie Stevenson."

Antonelli began his direct. "Miss Stevenson, how old are

you?"

"I'm twenty-six."

"Are you employed?"

"I am. I am the assistant curator at the University Art Museum in Berkeley," she answered in a clear, firm voice that showed no signs of nervousness. She sat straight in the witness chair and focused on Antonelli.

She's going to be a tough one, Jean-Claude thought.

"How's your eyesight?"

"It's excellent."

"So, on the morning of November twenty-third at around eleven, do you recall where you were?"

"Yes. I was walking down Bancroft Way in Berkeley."

"Did you observe anything unusual at that time?"

"Yes. A man ran up behind an elderly woman who was walking toward me and grabbed her purse." Her voice grew in intensity as she relived the experience.

"Were you able to get a good look at the person who took the woman's purse?"

"Yes. He ran right past me."

"Do you see the person who took the purse in the courtroom?"

"Yes, I do," she said firmly.

"Would you point him out, please?"

She paused for a moment, looked at the defense table, pointed at the defendant, and said, "He's the young Negro sitting next to his lawyer."

"Let the record reflect that the witness has identified the defendant," Judge Kelly added, making sure the record reflected it was Bonnay's client who was identified.

"I have no further questions. Your witness," Antonelli said as he glanced at Jean-Claude and sat down.

Jean-Claude hesitated a moment and looked down at his notes before getting to his feet to begin his cross-examination. The pause had nothing to do with preparation, but was to allow Stevenson to get a good look at him before he turned his attention to her. He was twenty-eight years old, six foot three and considered handsome by most despite his prominent nose that set him apart from the ordinary. He told people it marked him as decidedly French.

He walked slowly to the lectern, facing the witness. They made eye contact. She folded her arms and glanced down. He thought she blushed. "Good morning. Is it Miss or Mrs. Stevenson?"

"It's Miss."

That answers that. "My apologies for keeping you waiting."

"It's not a problem. I had a hard time getting here myself due to the weather," she said and regained eye contact with him.

"But unlike you, Mr. Bonnay, she was able to make it here on time," Kelly said with a smirk.

Jean-Claude ignored him and went right to his cross-examination. "How long have you been the assistant curator at the Museum?"

"This is my first year. I started in September."

"Are you from this area?" Jean-Claude tried to make her relax by asking his questions in a conversational rather than a confrontational tone.

"Objection, Your Honor. Irrelevant," Antonelli said.

"Your Honor, I just want to determine how familiar she is with the area where the robbery took place," Jean-Claude said, frowning. "It goes to the accuracy of her identification."

"I'll allow it, but I caution you, Mr. Bonnay, do not waste any more of the court's time with a lot of irrelevant questions." Kelly then turned to the witness. "You may answer."

"No, I'm from Connecticut."

"I assume you went to school there?"

"Yes. I went to elementary and high school in Greenwich, Connecticut and to Vassar College for my degree in fine art."

"Were there any Negroes in your classes in elementary school, high school, or college?"

Antonelli rose to his feet. "Objection, Your Honor. What does this have to do with her identification?"

"It could have a lot to do with it, Your Honor," Jean-Claude responded. "If you haven't had a lot of experience around Negroes it can make it difficult to distinguish one from another, especially if they are young." Jean-Claude was aware that Kelly had often made the statement when referring to Asians that it was hard to tell one from another. He hoped he felt the same about Negroes.

"You may answer the question," Kelly said. "Objection overruled."

"No, it was a private school and there were no Negroes," Stevenson said. "I think there was one or two at Vassar."

"Did you have any Negro friends or associate with any Negroes?"

"Well, yes. We had a maid and a houseman when I was growing up. They were both Negroes."

"Is that it? Is that the extent of your association with people of the Negro race?"

"Yes, I believe so."

She's obviously East Coast old money, sophisticated, well educated, not to mention good looking. Interesting.

"Let's talk about the day of the incident," Jean-Claude said with a smile. "Did the grabbing of the purse take you by surprise?"

"Oh, yes. I was startled. It was the last thing I expected."

"Did it happen fast?"

"Yes, very fast. It happened so fast. I was in a state of shock."

"Less than five seconds?"

"Yes, I guess so. I immediately thought to myself I had better get out of his way so he doesn't take my purse."

"So, in addition to being in a state of shock, you were also concerned about your own property?"

"Yes."

"And for your personal safety as well?"

"Yes. I was more shocked than frightened, but yes, I was concerned. I just wanted to get out of his way."

Jean-Claude shifted gears. "Let's describe the man you saw. How tall was he?"

"He was taller than me, and I'm five ten and a bit shorter than you."

"I'm six three, so six one perhaps?"

"That sounds about right."

"Did you get a look at his face?"

"Yes. Briefly."

The questions and answers were coming quickly now. He had a rhythm going. The witness was reacting rather than reflecting.

"Was he dark-skinned, light-skinned, or in between?"

"Well, that's hard to say. In the art world color is very nuanced. What is dark to one may be light to another. So I don't know how to answer the question."

"Let's do this. Close your eyes and take a moment to try and visualize the man you saw that morning. Try to remember his face. I know it happened quickly, but it created an impression. Have you seen the movie *Gone with the Wind?*"

"Who hasn't? It was wonderful." She smiled as she closed her eyes and unfolded her arms. The barrier was coming down.

"You remember Prissy, the young maid?"

"Yes, I remember her well," she said, eyes still closed.

"How would you describe the color of her skin?"

"She was light-skinned."

"Was the man you saw light-skinned like her?"

"No, not that light. He was quite a bit darker."

"Now open your eyes." Jean-Claude turned to his client. "Mr. Lewis, please stand up."

He turned back to Miss Stevenson. "Now look at my client. Does he have the same color skin as the man you saw that morning?"

She paused for a moment and looked directly at Lewis. She frowned and looked a bit puzzled. She then glanced back at Jean-Claude. "No," she said. "He is light-skinned like Prissy. The man I saw had darker skin."

"Is he the same height as the man you saw that morning,

"No. He is shorter than the man I saw." She uncrossed ㅡ
legs and began to shift nervously about in the witness chair.
This is going quite well, Jean-Claude thought.

"Did the police subsequently arrive and question you?" Jean-
Claude asked.

"Yes. They said they had caught the man, and he was in a
patrol car around the corner. They asked me to come and
identify him."

"What happened when you got to the patrol car?"

"They asked me to take a look and tell them if this was the
man I saw. I hesitated for a second because it all happened so
fast. But they said they had caught the man, so I was pretty sure
he was the one."

"Did you say he was the one because the police said they had
caught the man, or because you were sure he was the one you
saw?"

She thought for a moment, tipping her head from side to
side as if she were pondering the alternatives. "It was a
combination of both. I was pretty sure, but I believed the police
would not make a mistake."

"Given all of the above—the brief period of time to observe,
the fact that you were shocked and apprehensive, the fact my
client is a light-skinned Negro and under six 6 feet tall, and the
police told you they had the man before you were asked to
identify him—can you be absolutely sure as you sit here today
this young man is the person you saw?"

Jean-Claude kept eye contact with her and she with him. She
paused, appeared to take a deep breath, then turned and looked
at Kelly. "Your Honor, I don't think that's the man," she said.
"I think I have made a mistake."

Jean-Claude continued to stare at her, not changing the
expression on his face. She didn't acknowledge him but instead
continued to face Kelly.

"Young lady, everybody is nervous when they testify in
court," Kelly said, peering at the witness over his glasses with a

look of skepticism. "Mr. Bonnay has asked you a lot of questions and he may have confused you. So take your time and think about it, then give us your answer."

Thanks, Kelly, you asshole. Jean-Claude stared at Stevenson, willing her to make eye contact with him, but she continued to look at Kelly.

She sat back in the witness chair, took another deep breath, tightened her lips, and said, "Your Honor, I'm now sure."

"Good," Kelly said with a look of satisfaction. "You're sure your initial identification was correct." It was not a question. It was a statement.

She didn't hesitate. "No, Your Honor. I'm sure he is not the man."

For a moment, everything in the courtroom went silent. The clerk stopped writing at his desk. Antonelli sat up in his chair. The bailiff smiled, but sat totally still, and Judge Kelly had a pained look on his face. Jean-Claude did not change his expression. He knew from experience it was best to let the scene play out without any show of emotion on his part.

"Mr. Antonelli, I assume you have some redirect," the judge finally said.

Antonelli glared at the witness. "Yes, Your Honor. I do." He rose to his feet while speaking. "You testified on direct that you were sure the defendant was the man. Now you say he is not the man. Which version is the truth?" he asked, his voice tinged with anger.

Jean-Claude jumped up.

"Objection, the question assumes she was lying when she just could have been mistaken."

"Objection overruled." Kelley said with a slight smile on his face in anticipation of how the witness was going to deal with the question.

Stevenson didn't need Jean-Claude's suggestion as to how to answer. She looked directly at Antonelli. "I didn't lie. I just made a mistake. The lawyer made me realize that. It all happened so fast and I was frightened. I just made a mistake, that's all." Jean-Claude could tell from the determination in her voice she was not going to be intimidated

Jean-Claude kept his eyes on her the whole time, but she never looked at him.

"I have no further questions," Antonelli said with a look of disgust. He could have gone on a great deal longer trying to bring her back to her original identification, or at the very least made her very uncomfortable. But he wasn't going to waste his time trying to rehabilitate a witness who now had no credibility should she ever change her mind and testify at trial. He wasn't giving up much. After all, it was only a purse snatch.

"Mr. Antonelli, do you have a motion?" Kelly asked.

"Yes, the People move to dismiss in the interests of justice," Antonelli said with a note of contempt in his voice.

"Very well. The case is dismissed. The defendant is discharged from custody. Miss Stevenson, you may step down. You're free to go."

Jean-Claude watched her as she left the stand and walked past him toward the back of the courtroom, but she didn't acknowledge him.

I guess she wasn't that impressed. Oh, well. I won the case. That's the important thing. Kelly then brought him back to reality.

"Mr. Bonnay, we still have the little matter of your contempt of court for being late. I was going to put you in the holding cell for the rest of the day. Instead, given the fact you might have just saved an innocent man from prison, I'm going to give you the option of paying twenty dollars or doing six hours. If you choose to pay the money, don't leave the courtroom until you have given it to the clerk." With that, he walked off the bench.

Jean-Claude began to put his file in his briefcase when the clerk turned to him. "It's pay-up time."

Jean-Claude stuck his hands into his pockets. Empty. "Eddie, I left home in such a hurry, I don't have any cash on me. Can you lend me twenty bucks? I can get it back to you this afternoon."

"I'm sorry, Jean-Claude, I would if I could, but I don't have it." Eddie shook his head.

Jean-Claude stood there, wondering how he was going to occupy the next six hours in the holding cell. *Maybe I can hustle a new client while I'm in there.* It was the best idea he could come up with, but it did little to ease his frustration.

"Mr. Bonnay."

Jean-Claude heard his name being called from the back of the courtroom. He turned and saw Stephanie Stevenson standing by the rail that separated the audience from the well of the courtroom.

He paused for a second then walked over to her.

"I'm sorry I put you through that," Jean-Claude said, attempting to appear sincere.

"Don't apologize. I want to thank you for saving me from making a big mistake," she said as she extended her hand. "I'm now sure he was not the man. I was too influenced by what the police said."

Jean-Claude grasped her hand and felt paper pressed against his palm. When he looked, he saw it was a twenty dollar bill.

"No, ma'am, you don't have to do this," he said, putting up both hands as if to say stop, but still holding on to the twenty.

"I know, but I'm grateful you saved me from making a terrible mistake."

"Thank you. I'll pay you back, I promise."

"I know you will." She smiled.

"Wait for me. I'll be right back." Jean-Claude walked back to Eddie and gave him the twenty dollars.

"Man, you are one lucky guy," Eddie said with a sly smile. "You get your client off and a beautiful woman bails you out of jail. This is the stuff legends are made of."

"I know. I want you to tell every lawyer you see what happened," Jean-Claude said and pointed a finger at him as if giving an order, then winked. "Just don't let Kelly know."

He turned and walked back to Stevenson. "Listen, I need to know how to get in touch with you so I can return the money."

She handed him her calling card. "Here. It has my address.

Just mail me a check."

"I have a better idea." He stuck her card in his pocket. "Do you like big band music? Artie Shaw is at the Claremont Hotel a week from tomorrow. Would you like to go? I could give you your twenty dollars in person if you can wait for it."

"I'd like that," she said with a smile.

"Great."

"My phone number is also on the card I gave you. Call me and let me know the time." With that she turned and walked out of the courtroom.

Jean-Claude could not take his eyes off her as she walked out. "I will. I'll call you," he said loudly as he raised his hand to wave good-bye, but she was already out the door.

He left the courthouse so excited he completely forgot his raincoat and hat that Percy had taken to Judge Golden's courtroom. Fortunately the rain had stopped and his car had not been towed, but it had a rain soaked five-dollar parking ticket on the windshield. He swore and stuffed it in his pocket. The morning had cost him twenty-five dollars, but it was money well spent, he thought as he lit a cigarette and pulled away from the curb heading toward his office.

CHAPTER 2

SUNDAY MORNING, DECEMBER 7, 1941

Berkeley, California

The Matsumoto family gathered around the radio in their living room listening in total silence. They stared at each other in shock and utter disbelief. Japan had just attacked Pearl Harbor. The reporting was sketchy at first, but then came in greater detail. The destruction was horrific. The death toll was high and mounting. Mas Matsumoto, Japanese born and patriarch of the family, sat on the sofa, his face frozen. He attempted to conceal the conflict he felt as he dealt with the realization his native country, which he still loved, had just attacked his adopted country where his children had been born and they all called home. He fought to control his anger over the attack and the fear of what he believed would be life-changing consequences for his family.

His wife, also born in Japan, sat on the sofa beside him, weeping. Sarah, their oldest daughter, tried to console her mother, but could not keep her own tears from coming. Katy, her younger sister, sat motionless except for her hands, which trembled. Ken, age twenty-nine, an accomplished architect and their only son, nervously paced around the room, then appearing to have heard enough, went into the kitchen to pour some tea.

When Ken returned to the living room, Mas turned off the radio. He stood up and with arms folded looked at his family. "Japan has brought shame upon us. We are all going to suffer because of it," he said through clenched teeth.

"Hold on," Ken said, raising his hands. "Nothing is going to happen to us. We have done nothing wrong. People know us. They buy plants and flowers from our nursery. We are their neighbors, they are our friends." Ken looked at each of them as he spoke. He seldom contradicted his father, but he believed he was wrong.

There was a brief pause then Mas spoke again as if he hadn't heard his son. "Things are going to change. Our lives are going to change, but whatever happens, we will survive." He had a fierce determination in his voice. No matter what was to come, he wasn't going to let the events of the day destroy his family.

All they could do was wait to see what the reaction was going to be. In the meantime, Mas told everybody to stay inside.

Earlier that morning, just a few miles away from the Matsumotos' home, Jean-Claude was looking forward to his Sunday ride in the Berkeley hills on his Peugeot bike. It was one of the few possessions he brought with him when he and his father immigrated to the States from France fifteen years before. Bike riding was one of his passions. After his ride, he would usually relax over breakfast with the Sunday paper.

Berkeley was rimmed with hills and miles of trails that ran along the ridges and through forests and canyons. Because of recent heavy rains, Jean-Claude chose a paved path that tracked the rim of the hills and provided one of his favorite views—the bay on one side, and the Diablo Valley on the other.

The ride relaxed him and helped him think. He thought about Stephanie Stevenson and the prospect of seeing her next weekend excited him. Call it chemistry, call it lust, call it love at first sight—whatever it was, he couldn't get her out of his head.

While he was thrilled about the prospect of seeing her again, something nagged at him. Turning her testimony had been so easy. Of course, he could attribute it to his masterful cross-examination, but he knew from experience getting a witness to change their mind about identification while testifying was very difficult. Lewis had never confessed, but he hadn't given Jean-Claude a good explanation as to where he'd been at the time of the robbery, either.

Did she lie because she wanted to gain favor with him? Had he become the pursued rather than the pursuer? But why should he diminish a great courtroom victory with such thoughts? He should assume she told the truth. His job was to defend, not judge. That was Kelly's job.

The rain of the past week had stopped and the sun was shining. He breathed in the crisp, rain-cleansed air. Even though it was December, the temperature was in the low sixties—a perfect morning for a ride.

He looked out at the San Francisco Bay as he rode along the ridge. The Golden Gate, the Bay Bridge, and San Francisco glistened in the sunshine. The view was spectacular. It was quiet and peaceful. He could not know that 2,400 miles due west a catastrophic event was about to take place.

Jean-Claude rode for about an hour and a half. When he returned to his Buick and headed home, he was drenched with sweat and felt relaxed.

He lived in a brown shingle house about a mile east of the Berkeley campus. He'd lived with Bernard, his father, before he returned to France to join the Resistance in July of 1940, shortly after France fell to the Germans.

The house held many fond memories. His father, a professor of European languages at Berkeley, had often entertained his colleagues from the university with multicourse dinners he would prepare accompanied by fine French wines from his cellar. Jean-Claude was frequently invited to join.

Following dinner, intense animated conversations often stretched into the early morning hours as the house filled with cigar and cigarette smoke. The more wine and, later, brandy that was consumed, the louder and more heated the conversations became. The talk usually included opinions about politics and always some discussion whether Communism was the wave of the future. They also discussed the Great Depression, the rise of Hitler and fascism in Germany, and the resulting anti-Semitism. This was the intellectual diet Jean-Claude was raised on.

The conversations left little doubt that Bernard was an ardent Communist and violently anti-fascist. He vowed that if Germany ever invaded France again he would go back and rejoin the French army where he had served with distinction in the last war. This was exactly what he had done, except it was the Resistance he joined, not the French army, which had been left in disarray by Germany's victory.

The one exception to the dinnertime conversations about politics involved a professor at the law school who was a good friend of his father. He had been a prosecutor before he joined the Berkeley faculty, and would regale those around the table with stories about his exploits in the courtroom. It so captured Jean-Claude's imagination he decided he wanted to be a lawyer.

He opened the front door of his home and went into the living room. Once inside, he turned on the large console radio so there would be music while he read the paper and had his coffee. It was 11:30 a.m. Suddenly, the music was interrupted. He couldn't immediately process what he heard, but the gravity of the news caused him to sit down.

"We interrupt this program for the following announcement. At 1:07 Eastern Standard Time, the Empire of Japan attacked the naval base at Pearl Harbor in Honolulu, Hawaii. Preliminary reports are that there have been heavy casualties and destruction of many ships that lay at anchor. This attack was clearly planned well in advance and executed with numerous planes launched from carriers off the Hawaiian coast. As reports come in and more is known, regular programming will be interrupted to bring you updates."

Jean-Claude didn't believe the announcement at first. Could it have been a dramatization like the Orson Welles radio show from several years before announcing an alien invasion that had panicked everybody?

It didn't take long for him to realize this was no dramatization. It was real. Pearl Harbor had been attacked by the Japanese. He continued to listen to the reports as they came in. The news got worse as the day progressed. The casualty figures began to mount as the scope of the devastation became known.

The magnitude of the violence and deaths shook him. He'd lived through the last war as a child in France and it had devastated him emotionally. For three years he lived day to day not knowing if his father, who was fighting on the Western Front, was alive or dead. In the waning days of the war, his mother was killed when an unexploded bomb went off as she was walking down the street in her parents' village in Alsace.

Underneath his brash exterior often exhibited in the courtroom lay insecurities born out of that trauma; insecurities that came to the surface during times of extreme stress. The news made him feel empty and brought back all his fears from the past. His hands grew cold and his mouth went dry and he felt vulnerable and very alone. The house, that had just moments before stirred warm memories, now felt lonely and cold just like he did. He now feared the worst for his father.

He didn't want to be alone. Not this day. Not this night.

He thought about calling friends, but he kept coming back to one name: Stephanie Stevenson. He didn't want to think any more about the events of the day or his father. He just wanted to escape and be with someone. She could be that someone.

He found her card, hesitated for a moment, took a deep

breath, then picked up the phone and called her.

"Hello?" a woman's voice answered.

"Is this Stephanie Stevenson?"

"It is. Who is this?"

"It's Jean-Claude Bonnay. We met in court on Friday. I wanted to call you to tell you I don't know if the dance at the Claremont is still on for next week, but I want to assure you I intend to repay your money." He paced around the living room with the receiver pressed to his ear with one hand, a smoking cigarette dangling from his lips as he held the cradle with his other hand. He tried to sound cool and calm given what had just happened.

"How good of you to call." She sounded pleasantly surprised to hear from him. This gave him courage. "I'm not a bit worried about the money, but I am very worried about what has just happened. The news is terrible. Do you think we are going to be attacked here?"

"I don't think so." He spoke in a reassuring voice. "I think we are well out of range of their carriers, but if they are headed this way, I'm sure we'll get plenty of warning."

"I'm still nervous," she said, her voice trembling. "I just spoke to my parents on the phone and they want me to take the next plane or train home. I told them I would wait and see. I'm not the type of person who runs at the first sign of trouble, but I want to be smart too."

"Not to worry. There may be air raids, but I'm sure there is nothing imminent. Perhaps we could have dinner together tonight? It might make you feel more secure to be with someone." He took a deep breath.

"What makes you think I'm not with someone already?" she asked.

How dumb was that? Now she believes I'm a jerk for thinking she has no one to be with.

"I'm sorry. That was presumptuous of me. Of course, you must be with friends, or a friend, or someone," he said, wanting to get off the phone as soon as possible to avoid further embarrassment. "I'll call you later in the week once things have settled down."

"You were right. I'm not with anyone and I would feel better if I weren't alone. I'm concerned about going out, however. It is still too uncertain out there. Why don't you come here for dinner? I'm not the greatest chef," she said with a nervous laugh. "But I'm sure I can put something together."

"You say the time and I'll be there." The previous calm that had characterized his voice gave way to an excitement he couldn't disguise.

"How about seven?"

"Seven is perfect. I have your address. The Regillus, right?"

"Yes. I'll let the doorman know you're coming so he'll let you in. It's apartment 512."

"See you at seven."

He put the phone down and let out a whoop. His self-confidence returned. His excitement over the dinner invitation had put Pearl Harbor and the fate of his father out of his mind but as he hung up his thoughts returned to the events of the day and to his father. During the past several months, concerns over his father had increased to the point he wanted to go to France but he had made Jean-Claude promise not to follow him. He told him, You are an American now and this is not America's fight. But Jean-Claude knew today's events would change everything. It was going to be America's fight and he no longer felt bound by the promise he had made. Freed of the promise, he made an instant decision. He would go to France and join his father. He felt a sense of relief. He was going to do something in response to the tragic events of the day. He would fight back. He would go to war, but first he had to get ready for dinner.

After he took a shower, he went down into his father's cellar to pick out some wine. He selected wines from the Northern Rhone near Lyon where he had grown up: a Côte-Rôtie for the red and a Condrieu for the white. Even though he didn't know what Stephanie was fixing for dinner, he knew these two wines would go well with anything, or they'd be great by themselves.

His father would have a fit if he knew he was taking them, because they were two of the best in the cellar. He realized it was a selfish act but he couldn't help himself. One of his shortcomings was that he often put himself first and in this case he didn't want to show up to Stephanie's empty-handed. Times were too uncertain, he rationalized, to allow good wine to sit and not be enjoyed. He wanted to make a good impression. He hoped his father would understand.

CHAPTER 3

DINNER AT STEPHANIE'S

The Regillus, located next to Lake Merritt, was the most expensive and elegant apartment building in Oakland. Jean-Claude had always wanted to live there and promised himself someday he would.

He wanted to buy some flowers, but all the stores were closed. On his way to her place, he stopped off at Our Lady of Lourdes church, which he attended on those rare occasions he went to Mass. It was just on the other side of the lake from her apartment. He felt it might settle him down. His thoughts were still racing from Pearl Harbor to his father to dinner. He was agitated and had chain-smoked for most of the day. He needed to calm down or the evening would not go well.

Mass had ended hours ago, but the church was filled with parishioners probably there for the same reason he'd come—to pray for the men and women at Pearl Harbor. To pray for the country.

He went up to the altar and lit three candles—one for the memory of his mother, one for his father, and one for the men

22

and women at Pearl Harbor.

The prospects of the evening had an intoxicating effect. Being in the church was very sobering, which was good. It put the two events of the day into perspective. He sat with his hands folded, his head bowed, and his eyes closed. He could smell the soft scent of incense surround him. It brought back memories of his early childhood when he and his father would attend Mass together after his mother died. It had brought them closer.

He opened his eyes, took comfort from all the others in the church, and no longer felt lonely. His thoughts returned to the present, to Stephanie, and to the evening ahead that was full of promise.

He arrived at the Regillus a little before seven. The doorman let him in and showed him to the elevator. He rode to the fifth floor and rang the buzzer of apartment 512. He could feel his heart rate increase as he waited.

Stephanie opened the door. She was more beautiful than he remembered. She wore a long black dress. It was not form-fitting, but displayed her figure perfectly with just a slight show of cleavage in a tasteful yet sensual way. She wore a necklace of flat gold. Her hair was up, revealing two gold earrings. She carried a faint scent of lavender. For a second, he couldn't speak.

"I brought some wine," he said, awkwardly shoving it at her. "I hope that's all right."

"It's fine. Put it on the dining table and fix yourself a drink. I still have some work to do in the kitchen," she said with a surprised smile. She stepped back from the door and ushered him in.

The apartments at the Regillus looked very European with high ceilings and crown moldings. The windows in the living room were tall and spaced in such a way that they provided a panoramic view of the lake from which he could see the courthouse. A fire in the fireplace gave off the aroma of burning oak. An expensive Persian rug covered the dark hardwood floors, and the furniture was upholstered in French fabric. He knew it was French, because he had seen similar fabrics in the homes in France.

She certainly had good taste and some money behind her. People didn't live like this on an assistant curator's salary.

He walked over to the bar and browsed her selection. He wasn't much of a hard liquor drinker. Wine was a different story, however. He had been taught that wine was a vital part of life, to be savored, and consumed slowly over a good meal. Liquor was for getting drunk. He poured some scotch into a glass and added lots of water and ice.

"Can I fix you something?" he called out.

"Thanks. I'm fine. I have to keep my wits about me since I don't do that much cooking living by myself."

There was a phonograph next to the bar and a selection of records on the shelf above. Some big band albums, but mostly classical.

His mother had trained as a classical pianist and had records of piano concertos, which she would play on the wind- up phonograph in their living room with him by her side. The records were scratchy, but the beauty of the music came through. These were some of his happiest memories of childhood. He pulled the album of Beethoven's 5th piano concerto from the shelf. It had been one of his mother's favorites and one of his as well.

"Can I put on some music?"

"Of course. I don't have much of a variety. I tend to like classical music mostly. But please help yourself."

He selected the side of the album with the second movement. He put the record on the turntable and set the needle. The beauty of the music always moved him.

"Jean-Claude, I love that piece," Stephanie said from the kitchen.

He smiled. "What are we having for dinner? I'll open a bottle of wine."

"Lamb chops."

"Good, the red should go fine with the lamb." *It will be more than fine. It's perfect.* He found a corkscrew on the bar and pulled the cork out. The tip was dark red, almost black, but the rest was white. No leakage. The smell on the tip of the cork was magnificent—like burnt oak tinged with pepper.

Stephanie had set the table with sterling silver on a white tablecloth.

"Come sit down," she said as she came into the dining room with a platter of lamb chops surrounded by some small potatoes and green beans. He helped her with her chair as she sat down.

"Lucky I had the lamb chops in the fridge. There's a little grocery store around the corner run by a Japanese man, but it was closed. I guess he was afraid of what people might do." She sounded sincere but not overly concerned. "Do you think he'll be all right? I mean, are people going to attack him?"

It was the first time he had thought about Pearl Harbor since he had arrived, a measure of how the evening had become a welcome distraction. "I think he will be okay. They are good people and the ones I know are loyal." He took his own chair. "So far, there's been nothing against Germans or Italians living here despite what's going on in Europe. So I don't expect there will be any ill will toward the Japanese, but you never know. This was a direct attack, a sneak attack. That could make a difference."

"It was certainly a treacherous thing to do," she said and flipped her napkin in the air before placing it on her lap. "It doesn't speak well for them as a race."

Jean-Claude ignored her comment about race, not wanting to start the evening off with a disagreement. Instead he said, "Smells delicious. Shall I pour the wine?"

"Please do."

He poured two glasses of the red.

"Help yourself," she said. "It's not fancy. I hope you like it."

"I'm sure I will," Jean-Claude said as he took a lamb chop

and a generous portion of vegetables and passed the plate to Stephanie. He then raised his glass. "Let's drink to a better day because this one has been terrible."

Stephanie raised her glass and touched his. She took a sip and sat back in her chair. "My God, what is this?" she exclaimed. "It's not from California. It has to be French. It's magnificent. Let me see the bottle." She reached across the table and held up the bottle to read the label. "Côte-Rôtie? I've never heard of that wine before. It's delicious. Where did you find it on a day like today?"

"That's a long story."

She smiled and leaned in anticipating she'd hear something about an obscure wine store he knew somewhere in town. "Well, the night is young and we're not going anywhere, so let's hear it."

"I was born in France near Lyon where these wines are from."

"You're kidding," she said. "You were born in France? How wonderful." Her eyes sparkled with excitement and she smiled broadly. "Your English is perfect. You have just a trace of an accent." She took a bite of her food. "I love France. I spent a year there after college and studied art at the Sorbonne. I would suggest we converse in French for the rest of the evening, but my French is very rusty and I don't want to embarrass myself."

"No bother. I prefer English anyway. The less I'm reminded of France these days, the better."

"It's terrible what's happened." She took a sip of the wine. "Why did your family come to America?"

"I came with my father when I was twelve." He paused for a moment and glanced down at the food. This was always the hard part, telling someone his mother was dead. He raised his head and looked at her. "My mother was killed in the final days of the last war."

Stephanie gasped. "How terrible."

"I was five. I cried until I swore I'd never cry again." He stared down at his hands, unable to look at her.

26

"I am so sorry. How hard that must have been for you," she said, gently touching his arm.

After a few seconds of silence, he regained his composure.

"Was it her death that caused you and your father to come to the States?"

"In a way. My father was a professor of European languages at the university in Lyon. He went back to teaching after the war, but he was never the same. He had survived the gas attacks and the mayhem of the war, but he never recovered from Mother's death."

"He must have loved her very much."

Jean-Claude paused. "We both did."

"Do you have brothers or sisters?"

"No, and he never remarried. So it was just the two of us. We got pretty close after she died." Talking about his childhood always made him feel uncomfortable. He shifted his weight in his chair and took a bite of food.

"So how was it that you came to the States?"

"My father had been an officer in the French army and was friends with an American officer he served with. They kept in contact after the war. He encouraged him to move to the States and get a fresh start. So when, a few years later, Berkeley offered him a visiting professorship, he accepted. He wanted to leave the memories behind. We came and never left."

"As I said, your English is perfect. You must have an ear for languages."

"Languages were my father's passion and he wanted me to speak more than French, so he taught me English and German. He not only taught me the languages, but how to speak them with the correct accent. He's a perfectionist. He said they might come in handy someday. Anyway, the wine came from his cellar."

"I would very much like to meet him and thank him personally for this wonderful bottle of wine," she said, lifting her glass as if she were toasting him.

"He's not here." Jean-Claude put down his fork and lowered

his head. "He's gone back to France. Soon after France fell, he went back to join the Resistance. I haven't heard from him for quite a while." He glanced up and looked at her, his concern visibly showing in his face.

She must have sensed the change in his mood. "What an awful thing to have to go through. I feel so badly for you, not knowing and all." Her voice was warm and sympathetic. She reached across the table and touched his hand a second time.

"Now that the Japanese have attacked, we will be in the war in Europe soon. When that happens, I'll get to France somehow. I want to find him."

Neither of them ate very much, because the conversation had taken such a serious turn they didn't want to interrupt it. That didn't stop the consumption of wine, however.

"Haven't the Germans divided the country and left some of it free to be governed by the French?" she asked, obviously changing the subject.

He shook his head. "That's a joke," he said with scorn. "Vichy is a puppet government. They're as bad as the Germans."

"How can that be? The Germans are awful."

"Vichy has passed anti-Semitic laws that are as bad as the ones the Germans have enforced in other occupied countries. The difference is they are French laws enforced by French officials." He stopped eating altogether. Instead he took a large swallow of wine.

"The Jews seem to always bear the brunt of things. There is so much anti-Semitism." She took a sip of wine. "It's terrible. Of course, you and I wouldn't feel it, not being Jewish." Her indifferent tone suggested she felt what was happening to the Jews in Europe was of little consequence to her.

Jean-Claude hesitated. He thought for a minute. If they were ever going to have a meaningful relationship he had to tell her and tell her now. They made eye contact.

"My mother was Jewish," he said in a matter-of-fact tone looking directly at Stephanie.

Her head jerked back slightly and she blinked. Her gaze focused on the food on the table as she rotated her wine glass with her fingers.

There was a moment of strained silence.

"So are you Jewish?" she asked in a tentative voice as she looked up and regained eye contact.

"My father is Catholic and I was raised Catholic because of the anti-Semitism in France. Anyway, does it bother you that I'm half Jewish?" He watched carefully to see her response.

"No, no," she said, sounding slightly defensive. She leaned back and shifted her weight in her chair. "I must confess. My father, who is a banker in New York, is rather anti-Semitic. I grew up hearing him rant about the Jews. But I am not like that. No, it doesn't matter to me." She looked at him, and it appeared her brown eyes softened as she spoke. "I would like you no matter what." She sounded sincere, then smiled and took another sip of wine. So did he.

Jean-Claude paused before answering. Normally he would not express his feelings for a woman until he had known her for a while. He always guarded his emotions, especially when it came to relationships. But these were unusual times.

He decided to take a chance. "I have to confess I haven't stopped thinking about you since Friday. Even today with all that's gone on, I wasn't able to get you out of my thoughts. That's why I called you." The words rushed out as if he feared they might stop coming in mid-sentence. He took a deep breath and a big swallow of wine and then another. "I can't believe I said that," he said, shaking his head.

"Are you just saying that to be nice because I said I liked you, or do you really mean it?" She leaned forward and looked him in the eye.

"I know today is an emotional day and I don't share my feelings easily, but I meant what I said. I think you're special."

"That's sweet," she said, smiling with a gleam in her eye. "Even though you think I'm special, don't count on anything more than a kiss good night, and maybe not even that."

"I didn't say it because I wanted something. I said it because I meant it." He was somewhat offended she thought he might have had an ulterior motive.

"Well, I don't know where this is going, but I'm looking forward to finding out," she said, smiling again. "We better finish eating before it gets cold."

"I'm sorry. I've been talking too much about myself and not paying enough attention to you and the wonderful dinner you prepared."

"Don't worry. I didn't want you to stop. It's such an emotional story. Thank you for sharing it with me. Anyway, you know everything about me already. You found it out during your cross-examination." They both laughed.

They finished dinner and the red wine and moved into the living room taking the bottle of white wine with them. They sat down in front of the fire. Jean-Claude took out his cigarettes and offered her one.

She put her hands up. "No, thanks, I don't smoke. They won't tell you, but they're bad for you."

"I know. I've heard the same thing. I still want one. Is it okay?"

"If you must. Now tell me about this wine."

He lit the cigarette, took a deep breath, exhaled the smoke, and sat back.

"It comes from Condrieu, a little village on the Rhône River. The winemaker is one of my father's best friends."

"I'd love to visit there someday."

"Unless things change, that will never happen," he sadly told her. They finished the bottle while they talked well into the night.

When it was time to say good night, she walked him to the door. He put his arms around her and kissed her, not passionately but with feeling. She kissed him back. He hoped it was because she had feelings for him. But then maybe it was just the wine.

CHAPTER 4

JUDGE STANLEY GOLDEN

There are some judges who are special. They are revered by both prosecution and defense. In order to be deserving of this type of affection in a profession where affection is often in short supply, you have to be part rabbi, part priest, and part judge. And most important, people have to trust you.

Stanley Golden was such a judge. At seventy-two, he provided wisdom like a rabbi, heard confessions like a priest, and dispensed justice like a judge. And he was trusted. On the bench he was Judge Golden, off the bench the lawyers knew him simply as Stanley—which was not a sign of disrespect, but rather of affection, and he encouraged it.

Jean-Claude knew Stanley was a devout Jew, not an orthodox Jew, but one who believed deeply in his faith. He ruled based on the law, but often with his own unique interpretation given what he believed was a just result. When someone objected, his response to them was simply, "I'm the judge." It was the law according to Stanley, and because his judgment was proven right the vast majority of times, few challenged him. Those who did got sent to Judge Kelly.

Stanley became Jean-Claude's mentor from the time he tried his first case before him as a young public defender. Stanley brought him into his chambers at the end of the trial and told him, "You got some rough edges but you got talent. I'll give you some advice. The only way to make a name for yourself is to get a lot of trial experience, then leave the public defender's office and start your own practice so you have a chance to get the big cases."

Stanley introduced Jean-Claude to Irving Stern, who had been Stanley's partner before taking the bench. Irving offered Jean-Claude space in his offices and after a few more months in the public defender's office, Jean-Claude took Stanley's advice, accepted Stern's offer, and opened his own practice.

Over time, Stanley became Jean-Claude's friend as well as his mentor. He would frequently stop by the judge's chambers in the late afternoon on his way home and have a cigarette, talk law, and gossip about what was going on around the courthouse. They loved to gossip.

They would often have lunch together at the Claremont Hotel where Stanley gave him advice on life and the law. He was an expert on both. They became close enough that Jean-Claude shared with him the truth about his Jewish heritage, something he rarely did. This cemented their relationship. When Stanley heard Jean-Claude's mother was Jewish, he sat back, slapped his thigh, and let out a big laugh. "I knew it. I knew that *schnoz* of yours wasn't a French nose."

Stanley instilled in Jean-Claude the belief he could make a difference in the lives of the people he represented. Defending the weak, the poor, and the despised against the power of the government was the highest calling in the law, even though it was not the most lucrative.

Stanley had emigrated from Russia to escape the anti-Jewish pogroms at the end of the 19th century. The oppression of the Jews had made an indelible impression on him, resulting in a profound distrust of government. Stanley also fervently believed the justice system was the best and last barrier to the abuse of power by government, but that it could become vulnerable to corruption.

Stanley's chambers in the mornings were legendary. They were the congregating place for the criminal bar, both defense and prosecution. Even other judges would drop in from time to time to "consult" with him. For an hour before he took the bench in the morning, his chambers had an open door to everyone. His advice was free to anyone who sought it.

As Jean-Claude entered Stanley's courtroom Monday morning he was greeted by Julie, the judge's clerk of many years.

She said nothing about Pearl Harbor, but looked irritated. "Whadaya think this is, a cloakroom?" she grumbled.

"Courtroom or cloakroom, Julie, you are the best," he said, trying to soften her up because he sensed her irritation at having to keep his wet hat and raincoat over the weekend. "I had to put it somewhere. I couldn't go into Kelly's courtroom dripping water all over the place. After court, I just wanted to get out of there as fast as I could, and I forgot to come by. Please forgive me," he begged.

"I heard you were late again. He probably threw you in the slammer," she said.

"I walked out with my freedom, a victory, and a date with the prosecution's star witness, who is a beautiful woman," he said, puffing out his chest.

"If I didn't know better I'd think you've been drinking Kelly's whiskey," Julie said with a skeptical look.

"I swear it's the God's truth. Just ask Eddie, and when he confirms everything I said, you can buy me lunch."

"That'll be the day. Go on, get outta here," she said with a dismissive swipe of her hand. "They're all gathered in his chambers. I'll buzz you in."

As Jean-Claude entered Stanley's chambers, he hoped

someone would mention his triumph in Kelly's courtroom on Friday. People filled the chambers and the air was thick with smoke. But no one said anything about Friday. He was practically ignored and felt disappointment, but given what had just happened the day before, it was understandable.

Stanley was holding forth sitting behind his desk, pounding his fist as he spoke. "See what I have been telling you all these years. See what's happening in Europe?"

His face flushed red with anger and he crushed a cigarette he had been smoking into the ashtray on his desk and lit another. "The courts become the instrument of the government's evil. Once the government corrupts the justice system, it's over— finished." His audience sat in rapt attention nodding in agreement as he spoke. Jean-Claude lit a cigarette. He'd heard Stanley's rant many times before.

"We were one catastrophe away from the same thing happening here, and that catastrophe happened yesterday." Stanley wagged his finger. "Look out. Things are going to change around here and change fast." His face was flushed with anger.

Silence filled the room for a moment as those listening reflected on his dire warning. Then the conversation shifted to the uncertainties of the future and how everyone's lives were going to be affected.

A young public defender's wife was pregnant with their first child and he feared being drafted. Another lawyer had a brother at Pearl Harbor and had no word as to whether he had survived. A DA with connections in the Attorney General's office in Sacramento said he had heard there was talk of putting Japanese, Italian, and German aliens in camps. Earl Warren, the Attorney General, was from Oakland, where he had been the District Attorney of Alameda County. He also headed up civil defense for the state. Any information, even rumor from that source, carried weight.

Another DA reminded everyone that in the last war, Germans had been harassed by vigilantes. "Some were actually lynched and they were white. Just think what's going to happen to the yellow bastards that live here."

"I agree," Stanley said. "Anybody who's not white and Christian is going to be vulnerable. Watch out when they start to screw around with the laws and the courts."

Just then Julie stuck her head in. "The presiding judge is sending us a case because he's gotten the all-clear to keep the courts running at least for today," she said.

"Okay, you guys clear out. Time to go to work." Stanley stood up, put on his robe, and started to walk into his courtroom.

"Let's go to lunch one day this week. There are some things I need to talk to you about," Jean-Claude said as Stanley passed by him.

"How about tomorrow?" Stanley said.

"That's fine. 12:15 at the Claremont?"

"You got a date. By the way, did you tip the hatcheck girl?" Stanley asked, smiling.

"No, but it's almost Christmas. I won't forget her."

"Better not, she has a long memory," Stanley said with a twinkle in his eye.

The crowd broke up. Jean-Claude gathered up his raincoat and hat and headed to the office remembering what Stanley said about the private practice of criminal law: Money has to be made so the overhead can be paid, but with any luck something will be left over to buy groceries.

CHAPTER 5

THE CLAREMONT HOTEL

Tuesday, December 9, 1941

The Claremont Hotel resembled a grand English Tudor mansion. Built in 1915, it stood on a hillside overlooking the bay just above the Berkeley Tennis Club. It was a commanding structure surrounded by beautiful gardens and large, towering palm trees. A porch spread across the front of the building on the side of the hotel facing the bay where visitors could take walks and admire the view of the gardens, the bay, the bridges, and San Francisco in the distance.

In the year before Pearl Harbor, the hotel had been painted entirely white, including its shingled roof. The white decor gave the hotel an ethereal quality, and at night with its lighted tower, the grand old building was majestic.

Although no longer a center for croquet, tennis, and badminton as it had been when it had opened, it was now a destination spot for the big bands who dominated the popular music of the day. Every Friday and Saturday night, one would headline. Artie Shaw was scheduled for December twelfth and thirteenth, the event Jean-Claude had invited Stephanie to attend. He seriously doubted this would take place. If it did, he and Stephanie would go as planned. If it didn't, after last night, he was going to make it a point to see her again soon.

"Good day, Mr. Bonnay," the maître d' greeted Jean-Claude. "Having lunch with the judge today?"

"Yes. Our usual table by the window if it's available."

"Of course. Right this way. I'll show the judge over when he arrives."

The maître d' guided him to their usual table with the spectacular view. On the entire west side of the dining room the windows offered a panoramic view of the bay and of San Francisco. The bridges seemed to link all the land masses, making them appear as if they were interconnected islands.

The view was particularly sharp that day. The sky was gray and overcast. A marine layer brought the ceiling down to where the clouds seemed to touch the tops of the tall buildings in San Francisco, framing the city like a black and white photograph. The two bridges were new enough that they still evoked awe every time he looked at them. But now, unlike Sunday morning during his ride in the hills, when he looked west he could only imagine the horror that had taken place at Pearl Harbor. He lit a cigarette and waited for Stanley to arrive.

"So, what's on your mind besides the fact we're facing Armageddon?" Stanley asked as he sat down and lit a cigarette.

"I was looking at the view across the bay and the two beautiful bridges and wondering how mankind can create such beauty and at the same time murder Jews and destroy Pearl Harbor?"

Stanley leaned forward and looked directly at Jean-Claude. "Good laws can keep evil under control in peacetime, but once there's a war, the good laws go silent and when that happens, man becomes the most dangerous creature on the planet."

Jean-Claude shook his head accepting the old Judge's wisdom. There was a pause, then Stanley said in an apparent attempt to lighten the mood, "I heard you had quite a morning in Kelly's court the other day."

"Yes. I fell in love during cross-examination."

"*Mazel tov.* Trying a case and courting at the same time. That takes *chutzpah.*" Stanley shook his head and smiled.

"But I have a problem."

"What's the problem?"

"I want to go to France as soon as possible to find my father."

"Perfect. Take your bride and go to Paris for a honeymoon."

"Very funny. We had dinner last night." He leaned forward. "Stanley, I have to tell you I've never felt this way about a woman. I don't want to leave her, but I want to get to France as soon as possible."

"So go to France. Take a boat, take a plane, join the army. Just be careful. Remember, you're a Jew."

"I'm Catholic," Jean-Claude shot back.

"You're a Jew. Your mother was a Jew, so you're a Jew." Stanley said emphatically.

"Okay, so if I get caught, I won't tell them I'm a Jew," Jean-Claude said, trying to make light of Stanley's comment. "I'm concerned that if I tried to go alone, I would get caught before I was able to find him." He paused to light a cigarette. "It's going to be a while before the Allies get back to France, so I don't know if the military is the answer."

Stanley nodded. "You still have that guy—the general your father knows? Contact him. He might have some ideas."

"I'm going to do that in the next day or so." Jean-Claude took a sip of water. "But that doesn't solve my other problem. I don't want to lose this woman. When I go, there is no guarantee she will be here when I get back."

Stanley picked up the menu. "There are no guarantees about anything anymore," he said with a note of sadness. "Better you enjoy her while you can. Accept things for what they are."

The rabbi had spoken.

The waiter came over and they ordered.

Jean-Claude changed the subject. "How are you doing?"

"Not too good. Stories are coming out of Poland about sending Jews to concentration camps. My sources tell me that once they get there, they don't come back."

"How good are your sources?"

"Very good. They're out of New York. They have a better pipeline there than we do. First it was kicking them out of government, then taking their property, now executions— bodies dumped into trenches. Women, children, old people. It's one of the few times in my life I feel helpless." Jean-Claude had never seen him so sad. "Washington is not doing a goddamned thing to help. They're not even willing to take the refugees." Stanley pounded the table with his fist. The water glasses shook, threatening to topple over. "What kind of government is it that won't take people in who are certain to be killed if they don't have a place to go?"

"Roosevelt is trying to remain neutral to appease the isolationists." He was trying to make some sense out of the government's inaction.

"Neutral," Stanley roared. "Never trust a neutral. You are either for me or against me. Neutral is just another word for coward and this government is a goddamned coward." Stanley had raised his voice, drawing attention from some of the guests seated nearby. He lowered his voice and continued, "Between the Japs and the Nazis, we're in big trouble. They have to be stopped. I don't think the Brits can stop them by themselves. You have to admire them—getting the crap knocked out of them night after night, but they don't quit like the French did."

Jean-Claude held his hands up. "Wait a second. Not all French quit. There are those in the Resistance who continue to fight."

Stanley put his hand on Jean-Claude's shoulder in a reassuring gesture. "I'm sorry. I got carried away and forgot about your father. But I'm concerned that until we get involved, it won't be enough to make a difference."

Just then the waiter came over. "Mr. Bonnay, you have an urgent phone call. Shall I bring the phone to the table?"

"Yes, thank you." He turned to his friend. "Stanley, excuse me while I take this."

The waiter brought the phone, which was tethered to a very long cord for just such occasions, and set it down on the table. Jean-Claude picked up the receiver. "Hello, this is Jean-Claude."

"Hi, Jean-Claude, this is Ken. Ken Matsumoto. Your secretary told me where you were. I'm sorry if I'm interrupting, but I need to talk to you right away." From the intensity in his voice, Jean-Claude knew it was serious. "My family is panicking and I need some advice. Can I come to your office today—this afternoon?"

"Of course. Take it easy," Jean-Claude said in a comforting voice. "Calm down. Nothing is going to happen to you or your family. Meet me at my office. As soon as I finish lunch, I'll come right over."

Jean-Claude hung up the phone and turned to Stanley. "That was Ken Matsumoto, a Japanese friend of mine. We went to school together. His family is starting to panic. He wants to talk about what going on. "

"Be careful," Stanley said. "There is going to be a backlash. You can't have a sneak attack that wipes out most of our navy and kills thousands without a lot of people getting very angry. You combine that with the racism toward Japs and something bad is going to happen."

"I've known them for years," Jean-Claude said. "This family is as loyal as you or me. They should be okay."

"Don't matter. In times like these, a Jap is a Jap, just like a Jew is a Jew. Hear me. It's racism driving all of this." Stanley leaned forward and looked around at the other diners. "Why do you think the Japs can't own land or become citizens or immigrate here anymore?" he said, lowering his voice so others wouldn't hear him. "Why do you think the Nazis are persecuting the Jews? It's racism. Mark my words. The Japanese are in for a rough time. All of them. Loyal or not."

Unease replaced Jean-Claude's cavalier attitude about what might happen to Ken and his family. It was a disturbing prediction. He didn't want to believe it, but Stanley was seldom wrong.

He didn't want to think any more about it so he changed the subject. "This is what I've decided to do," he said, returning to his personal problem. "I'm going to tell Stephanie I want us to be together for as long as possible, but as soon as I can get to France, I'm going. If she understands and accepts my decision, that's fine. If she doesn't, it will be the shortest love affair of my life." He attempted to sound determined, but his voice wasn't very convincing.

"You're pretty smart for somebody who's only half Jewish," Stanley said with a chuckle. "Don't worry, if she doesn't work out there will be another one along soon enough."

"You can be so cynical at times," Jean-Claude said. "I've got to go." He called for the check. "I'll get this one. It's the least I can do for all the advice you gave me."

"You need to save your *shekels* for your honeymoon. I'll pay the check."

Jean-Claude got up to leave. "Stanley, I don't know what's going to happen. I don't think anybody does," he said. "No matter what, I want you to know how much I value our friendship." They shook hands. He smiled and walked out.

CHAPTER 6

THE CALM BEFORE THE STORM

Jean-Claude left the Claremont and drove directly to his office. On the way, he thought about Ken. He wasn't just another client, he was a friend.

Jean-Claude had just arrived from France, when on his first day in middle school, Ken had approached him and offered his friendship. He told Jean-Claude he looked like he was lost, like he didn't belong. Ken told him that he knew what that felt like. He and his sisters always felt like outsiders even though they were born here. They felt like Americans and acted like Americans. They just didn't look like Americans. Jean-Claude had never forgotten Ken's kindness.

When Jean-Claude arrived at his office, he found Ken Matsumoto in his reception room waiting for him. He immediately jumped up and gave Jean-Claude a big hug.

"Good to see you, Ken, it's been a while," Jean-Claude said, hugging him back.

"Good to see you too, Jean-Claude. Thanks for seeing me on such short notice."

"Any time. I knew it must be important given what just happened."

"Jean-Claude, my parents are very worried." His voice was edged with tension and he appeared anxious.

"Relax. Come in." Jean-Claude gestured toward his office, then followed Ken in. "Want some coffee or water?"

"No, thanks, I'm fine." Ken sat down in a chair in front of the desk and folded his arms across his chest. "Jean-Claude, what do you think is going to happen? My father is afraid he and Mom might get deported. Last night, rocks were thrown, breaking some windows in the greenhouse." He spoke rapidly, one thought tumbling out after another. "Some of our customers are talking about not buying at the nursery and stopping the gardening service. I didn't think there would be any backlash. Now I'm not so sure." He leaned forward in his chair as if to add emphasis to what he was about to say. "We all think Pearl Harbor is terrible. We feel the loss just like everybody else. I still think we're going to be all right, but I wanted to get your opinion."

Jean-Claude looked directly at Ken and spoke in a calm voice. "The sheriff said in the paper today he will not tolerate any lawlessness against Japanese or Germans or anyone else. I know him. He means it. Law enforcement will protect you. Boycotting your business, that's another matter, but I don't believe that will happen. I think only a small minority would do that since your parents own the best nursery in town. Everybody I know buys their plants and flowers from your parents."

Ken still looked concerned even after Jean-Claude's attempt to reassure him and nervously shifted his weight in his chair.

Jean-Claude took a cigarette from the pack on his desk, offering Ken one.

"Thanks, never started," Ken said as he sat back in his chair, uncrossing his arms and appearing somewhat more relaxed.

Jean-Claude lit up. "They can't be deported just because they were born in Japan," Jean-Claude said. "There has to be some evidence your parents pose a threat. We know this isn't the case. I don't think they have anything to worry about. You might suggest they do some volunteer work for the Red Cross or some organization that supports the troops."

Ken still didn't look convinced. "I hope you're right, but I honestly don't trust the courts or the government. They passed laws that no more Japanese could immigrate, and those that were here, like my parents, couldn't become citizens," he said. "So why can't they just as easily pass a law that says the ones who were not born here have to go back to Japan or get locked up until the war is over?"

"I don't think any laws like that will be passed," Jean-Claude said firmly. "And if there are, we have the courts to contest them."

"Sarah is a nurse and Katy is a teacher and I have my architecture license. We don't want to lose what we have worked so hard for."

"They can't do anything to you or your sisters," Jean-Claude said. "You're all citizens. You are more American than I am. You were born here. I had to be naturalized. All I can say is, I believe the justice system will protect you and I will do everything I can to make sure nothing happens to you or your family."

"It's been frustrating, Jean-Claude," Ken said with resignation in his voice. "I graduated at the top of my class in engineering. I was ROTC, commissioned a second lieutenant, did two years active duty, received an honorable discharge, went back to school and got a master's in architecture, and still couldn't get a job in a white firm. In a way it was a good thing because I started my own and I'm doing fine even though no whites will hire me."

Jean-Claude lit another cigarette to help himself stay calm as he became angry thinking about all Ken had put up with.

"I wasn't worried at first, but now I am. There's a lot of prejudice out there. Pearl Harbor could ignite things. A lot of folks out there believe we are the 'Yellow Peril' out to conquer the world or that we're just plain inferior." He began to get angry and stood up and paced. "No matter how hard we try, we can never blend in. We're just like Negroes. We look different and there's nothing we can do about it. They say we don't assimilate. You know why we don't assimilate?" He pounded the desk. "Because they won't let us assimilate." He sat back down in his chair, his shoulders slumped, and he let out a big breath having just gotten a lot off of his chest.

For a moment neither of them said anything, then Ken abruptly changed the subject. "I want to give you some money." He reached into his pocket as he spoke. "So if there's a problem, we can count on you to help us."

"That's not necessary." Jean-Claude put a hand up to stop him. "We can discuss money when and if the time comes that you need me."

"Will you come over to my house and, perhaps this Sunday for dinner, explain all of this to my parents and sisters?" Ken asked. "I know you could reassure them like you did me, and it would make them feel a lot better."

"Sure, I'd be happy to. It would be nice to see your family again. It's been a while," Jean-Claude said. "Do you think your parents would mind if I brought a friend to dinner? I met this girl and I want to spend as much time with her as I can."

Ken smiled broadly. "No, please do. I would like to meet her. Do you think you've finally found the one?"

Jean-Claude shrugged. "I think so, but with all the uncertainty, I don't know where it will lead. What's with you? How come you're not married?"

"I was seeing a girl for several years, but marriage was not possible, so we broke up," he said, looking frustrated.

"Your parents didn't approve?"

"No, she was white."

Jean-Claude winced. "Shit. That law is outrageous."

"I hope yours works out. She better be white," Ken said, smiling.

"She's white, but I have an uneasy feeling she's a little anti-

Semitic."

"Well I'm not sure how you can be a 'little' anti-Semitic, but here's what we'll do. We'll go fight in the war to defend America's right to continue to be racist and anti-Semitic." He was only half joking when he said it. "Sunday dinner is at one," he said as he stood up to leave. "See you then."

They shook hands. Ken was very strong physically and had an iron grip that Jean-Claude had forgotten about. His memory was quickly refreshed.

"Feel free to call me if anything happens," Jean-Claude said. "I'll see you on Sunday."

"Thanks, Jean-Claude. I feel better. I knew I could count on you," Ken said as he turned to leave.

After Ken left his office, Jean-Claude scribbled "Matsumotos, Sunday at one," on a notepad, put out his cigarette, and called Stephanie to see if she was available to go. He wanted her to accompany him because he wanted to be with her, but he also wanted her to meet them so she could see what decent people they were and correct her notion that the treachery of Pearl Harbor was because of race.

CHAPTER 7

SUNDAY DINNER

December 14, 1941

Stephanie told Jean-Claude she'd be delighted to go with him to meet the Matsumotos. He reminded her of her concern about the Japanese race being treacherous. She said she'd studied Japanese art and respected Japanese culture and her comment was a reaction to what had just happened at Pearl Harbor and not because she was prejudiced against their race. She sounded sincere so Jean-Claude had no concerns she or the Matsumotos would be uncomfortable during their visit.

They arrived promptly at one o'clock. Jean-Claude hadn't been to the Matsumoto home for several years. As they approached the front door, he thought back to the times he had visited there when he was in school.

They lived in a Craftsman-style bungalow, popular at the beginning of the century in Berkeley and Oakland. It had a large porch that extended across the front of the house that was filled with flowers and plants. Next to the house stood the nursery and next to it, a large greenhouse.

On the front door hung a sign that read, "All Are Welcome." Jean-Claude knocked. Several minutes later, Mas Matsumoto, Ken's father, opened the door. He had short gray hair and the leathery face of a man who'd spent most of his life in the sun. He had the same stocky, muscular build as his son.

He bowed. "Welcome. Welcome, Jean-Claude. We are honored to have you in our home again. We have missed seeing you."

"I have missed you too. Mas, this is my friend Stephanie," Jean-Claude said.

Mas bowed. "We are honored you have come to join us for dinner."

Inside the Matsumoto home, the first thing Jean-Claude noticed was a picture of the Japanese emperor hanging over the fireplace. He'd probably seen it on other occasions, but had never paid much attention to it. It hadn't had the same significance as it did now. He frowned. It concerned him. To a stranger, this picture could be an immediate sign of disloyalty.

As they entered the living room, Mrs. Matsumoto greeted them with a worried look. She spoke very little English. Jean-Claude remembered her as always having a warm smile, but there was no smile today.

Jean-Claude gave Katy and Sarah, Ken's two sisters, each a hug and introduced them to Stephanie. They were both single, in their twenties, and still lived at home. They were attractive, well-educated, and had careers. They looked very concerned.

After some small talk, they all sat down at the dinner table. Mrs. Matsumoto brought food from the kitchen and placed it in the center of the table, family style.

During dinner, Ken and Jean-Claude got caught up. Stephanie and Ken's sisters hit it off right away and talked as if they were old friends. Mas sat quietly and listened while Mrs. Matsumoto spent most of the time in the kitchen when she wasn't bringing food to the table and clearing the plates. She made sure everyone had enough to eat.

Toward the end of the meal, there was a lull in the conversation. Mrs. Matsumoto rejoined the group at the table. Mas stood up and began to speak. Everyone stopped eating and listened.

He spoke slowly and in a soft voice, but his presence commanded respect. "I came to the United States by myself in 1900 from a village near Hiroshima when I was twenty." As he spoke, his eyes grew bright and he stared straight ahead as if he were being transported back in time reliving the experiences. His family knew the story, but they sat with rapt attention as did Jean-Claude and Stephanie, who were hearing it for the first time.

"I lived in the Salinas Valley. I worked as a farm laborer. I could outwork anyone. The pay was low, but I saved. After a few years, I was able to rent a piece of land so I could grow my own vegetables and flowers and sell them to the local markets.

"I saved some money and sent word home that I wanted a wife. I sent a picture of myself. My family arranged for a girl from Hiroshima to come to the United States and marry me." He turned and nodded toward his wife. "Together we worked and saved and raised a family, then decided to move here. Better opportunities. Better schools." Mas paused for a moment then continued.

"I saved enough money to buy a house and the land for the nursery. I had to put them in Ken's name. I could not own land. I was not a citizen. They would not let me be a citizen." There was no bitterness in his voice, just resignation.

"We are loyal Americans and believe Pearl Harbor was wrong. We all believe that," he said, looking at each of his children who nodded in agreement, then at Jean-Claude and Stephanie. "Japan has dishonored us and we are going to suffer the consequences." His expression was grim as he spoke.

"I am very proud of my children and what they have accomplished," he said with a satisfied smile. "It has not been easy for them, but they have succeeded. This is the strength of my children. This is the strength of America. I don't want them to suffer."

He paused and everyone remained silent to ensure he was finished. When he lowered his eyes and sat down, Ken brought up what had to be on everybody's minds. "What do you think is going to happen, Jean-Claude?"

Jean-Claude didn't hesitate. Hesitation could have conveyed uncertainty and he wanted the Matsumotos to trust what he was about to say. "I believe that everything's going to be all right," he said. "The Attorney General of the United States, the highest law enforcement official in the government, said that every effort would be made to protect the Japanese from discrimination and abuse. The head of the FBI also said that there was no law that allowed for citizens to be picked up and moved out of the area without proof of some law violation. I feel confident we can rely on what they say.

"The laws will protect you. I believe you are safe and should go on about your business normally. If there is a chance to show your loyalty by doing volunteer work to aid the war effort, I suggest you do it. These are difficult times, but I'll be there to help you if it becomes necessary."

Katy and Sarah looked relieved. Mrs. Matsumoto with her limited English probably didn't understand much of what was said, but she could sense her daughters' relief. Mas, the stoic, said nothing. He would wait and see. Ken gave Jean-Claude a pat on the back as a sign of appreciation.

Jean-Claude then looked directly at Mas. "Mas, I mean no disrespect, but you ought to take the Emperor's picture down. It could cause a problem if an outsider should come to the house and see it."

Mas paused for a moment, took a sip of tea, not acknowledging Jean-Claude's suggestion. Then he stood up. "Please come with me," he said to Jean-Claude. "You come too, miss." He gestured to them to follow.

Jean-Claude and Stephanie followed as he walked to the rear of the house and passed through the kitchen. He stepped out the back door and walked along a path that led through the nursery to the greenhouse.

Despite the chill in the air outside, the interior of the greenhouse felt warm and humid and had a musty, but pleasant, smell of soil and vegetation. It was quite large and lit by fluorescent lighting, which cast an iridescent, purplish glow. Rows of camellias were in full bloom with pink and white flowers that added color in contrast to the monotone green of the other plants.

Mas led them to the rear of the greenhouse and stopped at a large table filled with miniature trees in ceramic pots. He pointed to them. "These are bonsai trees. I make them. I give them to customers as gifts. They take many months to create. It takes much patience as they grow very slowly," he said and picked up a small plant. "You must shape the limbs with a thin strip of wire with care and precision. No two are alike and they can live to be very old. The roots are strong but they must be cared for every day. There is stability and security in these trees."

He lowered his head for just a second as if in prayer and then put the bonsai back on the table. "They bring enlightenment and peace. They give us a sense of harmony and well-being. I know that no matter what happens, we will be like the bonsai—we will survive."

There was reverence in the way Mas spoke about the bonsai. He was a very strong man and the fact that he drew strength from a miniature tree suggested he felt there was something truly spiritual about them.

"Jean-Claude, my wife and I are old. We have lived our lives and will accept whatever happens, but if people turn against us, please, Jean-Claude, protect my children." Mas was not one to express his emotions outwardly, but the anxiety in his eyes conveyed his concern.

"I will, Mas. You have my word." Jean-Claude extended his hand to cement his commitment. Mas shook hands then bowed to show his appreciation.

Jean-Claude and Stephanie followed Mas back into the

house, paid their respects to Mrs. Matsumoto, and thanked her for the wonderful dinner. They said good-bye to Ken and his sisters.

"Please call me if you want to talk more," Jean-Claude told them as he was leaving.

Jean-Claude and Stephanie climbed into the car. "I hope you're right," Stephanie said as they drove away. "The law can be very unfair at times."

"Not to worry," he said with slightly less authority in his voice than when he was reassuring the Matsumotos. "Things will be fine." But in the back of his mind he was thinking about what Stanley said at lunch: the Japanese are in for a rough time.

CHAPTER 8

THE TIDE TURNS

Late December 1941

It had been almost three months without word from his father and Jean-Claude was growing increasingly concerned. He should have received some contact from him after Pearl Harbor given the momentous event. But still there was nothing. He made up his mind that day in the wine cellar he was going to France to find him. He didn't know the best path to take, but he was not going to wait any longer before making a decision.

Bernard and General Randy Scott had become friends during the last war and had kept in contact over the years. Whenever Scott went to the Presidio in San Francisco on military business, he and Bernard would get together and renew their friendship. He was a two star general stationed in Washington and while Jean-Claude had had no contact with him for several years, he felt Scott's relationship with his father was strong enough that he could call and ask for advice.

It took several calls and navigating several layers of military bureaucracy, but he finally got through.

"General Scott, this is Jean-Claude."

"Jean-Claude, good to hear from you," the general said. "I've been concerned about Bernard. Have you heard anything from him?"

"I haven't heard anything for months and I'm worried," Jean-Claude said in frustration as he lit a cigarette.

"I'm not surprised. Things are getting pretty nasty over there," the general said. "You probably know he called me before he left and told me he was going back. I advised him to wait and let me see if I could arrange some cover for him. He said he wanted to go right away and that he had pretty good connections on the ground."

"You know how headstrong he is. There was no stopping him once the Germans invaded. General, I want to go to France and find him. Can you help me?"

"Let me make some inquiries about Bernard first and see what I can find out. We have contacts with the British who keep in touch with members of the Resistance." The general paused. "As far as helping you get to France, I would strongly advise against going back on your own. It's pretty dangerous, especially in the Lyon area, and you don't have the training Bernard has. It would be better if you went back in some military capacity."

"Do you have a suggestion?" Jean-Claude asked.

"Let me think about it. I'll get back to you as soon as I find out something about your father."

"Thanks, General. This means a lot to me. I'll wait to hear from you."

"Glad to help. You know how I feel about Bernard."

Two weeks later he got a call from Scott.

"Jean-Claude, I haven't been able to find out anything about Bernard," the general said, sounding exasperated. "The Nazis have clamped down and so has the Vichy government and it's difficult to get any word out. I believe if anything had happened to Bernard we would have heard about it because he's such an important figure in the Resistance. Unfortunately I can't confirm anything."

"Thanks for trying, General. It looks like I'm going to have to go and look for him myself."

"Let's talk about that. I can arrange for your enlistment. I'm pretty sure, given your fluency in French and German and familiarity with the area, I can get you into a new special unit called the OSS, which the president has just set up. They will train you and then drop you into France. We need people on the ground that we can rely on to get information about troop strengths. We just can't count on information from the Resistance." He sounded more serious than usual. "Hopefully once on the ground you'll be able to find Bernard. I have to warn you, you won't be in uniform so if you get caught you would not have the protection of the Geneva Convention. What do you think?"

Jean-Claude paused several seconds before answering. "You mean I would go back as a spy?" He hadn't considered that possibility.

"We don't call them spies anymore," the general said. "We call them special ops. But if you're caught and they find out who you are, they would treat you as a spy and you could get executed. You may want to think it over before making a decision."

"I do have a problem doing something right away," Jean-Claude finally said. "I have agreed to represent a Japanese friend of mine in the event there is an attempt to force his removal from his home. I don't know what that will require but for the moment I can't give you a firm time commitment."

"You say he's Japanese? That's a pretty gutsy thing to do," the general said, sounding skeptical.

"He's a friend. I've known him since high school and I know he's loyal. Will this present a problem if I represent him?" Jean-Claude wanted to know if this would prevent him from accepting the military option, if that's what he decided to do.

"I don't think so. Here in Washington we're more focused on the Germans than the Japs. Just keep the military out of it and don't represent any Nazis." The general chuckled. "Let me know when you've made a decision and I'll have someone get in touch with you to start the process."

"Thanks again, General Scott. Please let me know if you hear anything about my father."

"I will."

Jean-Claude hung up the phone, sat back in his chair, and lit a cigarette. He thought about what the General had proposed as the reality sank in. *My choices are pretty limited. I can go back as a spy and risk getting shot or on my own with a greater risk of getting shot or I can stay here and be safe. Maybe going back to France isn't such a good idea. I need to talk to Stanley.*

The next day, in the late afternoon after court, Jean-Claude stopped by Stanley's chambers as he often did. It was just the two of them, smoking and talking. He always ran big decisions past Stanley.

"I called my friend the general, and he said there was some new unit he thought he could get me into that might be able to get me into France," he said, watching for Stanley's response.

Stanley lit a cigarette, stared at him, and said nothing.

"He said they would train me to be a spy and then drop me in to collect intelligence. He said once I'm there maybe I'd be able to find my father."

"*Oy.* A spy?" Stanley exclaimed in disbelief. "What are they going to do, dress you up in a spy costume so no one will recognize you?"

Jean-Claude blew smoke toward the ceiling. "Christ, I hadn't thought about that. I was twelve when I left France, but I'm sure there will be people who will recognize me. I'm glad I didn't give him an answer. I told him I had to wait until this situation with the Matsumotos is resolved. I'm having serious second thoughts about going back."

Stanley remained silent for a moment then said, "These are times when we have to take risks. There's too much at stake to do nothing." He was looking directly at Jean-Claude as he spoke.

Jean-Claude didn't respond but moved on to what was foremost on his mind. "I'm getting more worried about what's going to happen to Ken and his family. Every day the news gets worse. Japanese atrocities in the Philippines." Jean-Claude lit a cigarette, got up, and started pacing. "The war in Europe is going badly. Air raids around here are scaring the hell out of people. Commercial vessels are fired on by Japanese submarines off the coast. The governor says some Japanese have been communicating information to the enemy. Worst of all, the military is talking about moving them from the coast to the interior." He shook his head. "Biddle seems strong, so the Justice Department should be able to prevent it, and I think we can count on Warren, but he's running for governor, so who knows?" He rubbed the back of his neck to relieve the tension that had built up.

"So why am I not surprised?" Stanley asked. "I told you once the drumbeat started, they were in trouble. You think that's bad? Read this." Stanley handed him a newspaper. "It was in the *Tribune* yesterday."

Jean-Claude began to read the article. Halfway through he sat down and crushed out his cigarette.

> It was learned that on Thursday, Friday and Saturday of last week the Germans rounded up 6,000 French and foreign Jews in Paris for deportation to Eastern Europe. The group included some of the wealthiest and influential Jews in Paris. Two of them were former presidents of French courts. The French police aided in the roundup.

Jean-Claude crumpled the paper and clenched his teeth. "I can't believe French police did this. It makes me sick."

"That's what happens when there is total collapse." Stanley

frowned. "You either collaborate with the conquerors or get annihilated."

"The Nazis aren't forcing them to do these things. In one of the last letters I got from my father, he told me the Vichy government is doing these things on their own."

"What I am really upset about," Stanley said, getting red-faced, raising his voice as he leaned forward, "is Roosevelt not doing a goddamned thing about it. He's afraid of making this a war to save the Jews." There was a moment of silence. He took a breath and changed the subject. "So what's with you? How's the *shiksa?*" Stanley crushed his cigarette in the ashtray and lit another.

"She's fine. That's the problem," he said, rubbing his hands together. "I don't want to give her up."

"There are times when you have to make tough choices. Be careful. When you're in love or upset, you don't make good decisions, and you're both."

"I don't know what I would do without your wisdom," Jean-Claude said with a smirk.

"If not from me, then who?" Stanley shot back.

"Everything is messed up," he said, frustrated. "You're right. I'm not thinking straight. I need to clear my head." He rose and walked toward the back door. "I'll see you later. I'm gonna go for a bike ride." With that he abruptly turned and walked out of Stanley's office.

"You can ride, but you can't hide," Stanley called out after him, trying to be humorous.

"Yeah, but at least I'll burn off some of the anger," he said, not seeing the humor as he headed for the elevators.

Jean-Claude was still angry when he got home and the anger depressed him. He was angry because he was conflicted. He'd thought he had it all worked out. He'd help the Matsumotos, go to France, find Bernard, then come home and marry Stephanie.

Now the reality of his situation hit him. If he went to France there was a chance he wouldn't find Bernard and a good chance he might not come back. His selfish side told him, stay home. Be safe. His honorable side said, go to France, find Bernard, and fight the Germans. Eventually he would have to make a decision, but not now. He changed his clothes and headed for the Berkeley hills and a long ride.

Two hours later he was back home and in the shower. He felt better, or at least calmer, but still conflicted. After his shower he went down in the cellar and got a good bottle of wine.

It was the best painkiller available.

CHAPTER 9

THE MILITARY PREVAILS

January 1942

T hings were changing rapidly. The tide was turning in favor of removing the Japanese from the coast and Jean-Claude grew concerned he had misjudged the situation. He needed to get reliable information so he could prepare the Matsumoto family if removal was ordered, and prepare himself to go to court to prevent it.

Paul Fitzgerald, a friend and classmate from law school, worked for the Justice Department in Washington. The closer he could get to the decision makers the more accurate the information, and these decisions were going to be made in Washington, not Oakland.

Jean-Claude knew Fitzgerald well enough that he felt comfortable reaching out to him. After several attempts, they finally connected on the phone.

After some preliminary pleasantries, Jean-Claude got to the reason for his call. "Paul, I've been friends for years with a

Japanese American fellow. He's a citizen. His parents are not. He and his family are very worried about possibly being forced to leave their homes and sent to a camp. I'm going to represent him in the courts if removal is ordered so I need to know what's going to happen."

"Well that's probably not the smartest thing to do, given all the anti-Japanese sentiment in your area but then you were always kind of a maverick," Paul said. "You're going to get a lot of publicity. Aren't you worried about what that will do to your practice, not to mention your reputation?"

"I plan to go to France as soon as the case is over and by the time I get back the whole thing will probably have been forgotten. Regardless, I would represent him because he's a good person and a good friend and he's loyal. I know that."

"What the hell do you want to go to France for? Things are terrible over there."

"My father is over there fighting with the Resistance and I want to join him."

"You've bitten off quite a bit." Paul chuckled. "I admire you. Personally, I think it would be a mistake to remove any of them, especially citizens, unless there is evidence they pose a threat." He paused, took a long breath. "Listen, whatever I'm about to tell you has to be off the record, and whatever I tell you today could change tomorrow. That's how fast things are moving. Understood?"

"You have my word."

"Biddle said right after Pearl Harbor protecting the civil rights of the Japanese was his priority. His heart's in the right place, but he's only been attorney general for a short time, and he's not a Washington insider like Secretary of War Stimson. Stimson carries a lot of weight so Biddle often defers to him but he has assigned two of our brightest deputies to handle the negotiations with the War Department. Stimson has assigned his assistant secretary John McCloy to do most of the negotiating for them. He's a tough old son of a bitch and because the War Department represents the generals in the negotiations it's going to be a tough slog. Do you know who General DeWitt is?"

"I've heard the name," Jean-Claude said, "but I don't know anything about him."

"He's the commander of the eight Western states headquartered at the Presidio in San Francisco. A report just came out from the presidential commission established to investigate the causes that led to the disaster at Pearl Harbor. They said it was due to the lack of preparedness by the military commanders. Now the whole military high command on the West Coast is telling Stimson they want all Japanese removed from the coast," Paul said with concern in his voice. "DeWitt is leading the charge. It's a classic knee-jerk reaction driven by a desire to cover their asses."

"It's also paranoia driven by racism," Jean-Claude said. "There's not been a single act of sabotage, no evidence of a fifth column, no rush of Japanese to return to Japan since Pearl Harbor." He took a deep breath. He was clearly getting irritated. "I assume citizens are safe."

"I'm not so sure. The cries from the generals are that they all have to go. They say you can't tell the loyal from the disloyal no matter whether they are aliens or citizens and there is no time to sort it out."

"That's bullshit and you know it," he said, irritation growing. "They're doing screenings in Hawaii and letting most of them go back to work, for Christ's sake."

"I know. It gets worse," Paul said. "The military also wants us to authorize searches of houses and buildings without a warrant where they think there might be something that could aid the Japanese war effort. No probable cause, just a suspicion. I think Biddle may order our office to take the position in court that a mere suspicion is enough and no warrant is necessary. Everybody is scared out of their wits and nobody wants to be blamed for another Pearl Harbor."

"So what is your best guess as to what's going to happen?"

"This is strictly confidential." Paul lowered his voice. "There are meetings going on in San Francisco right now between our lawyers and the lawyers from the War Department. DeWitt is there, and he is hammering away saying there isn't a merchant ship that leaves one of our ports that the Japanese don't know about, implying there is a fifth column feeding them information. This has got everybody scared because there have been some merchant ships fired on by Jap subs off the coast of Carmel and Eureka. Our lawyers have pushed back and are taking the position that any removal based on race alone would be unconstitutional. I don't know how it's going to end. Ultimately it will be up to the president. But I would tell your Japanese friend to prepare for the worst."

"So what good is the Bill of Rights," Jean-Claude said in exasperation, "if it can be ignored when things get bad?"

"I agree. What they didn't teach us in law school is that there is a little asterisk next to the Bill of Rights that says, 'Caution, the above may not apply in time of war.'"

"That's not very reassuring." Jean-Claude lit a cigarette and took a deep puff. "It's during a crisis we need them the most. Anyway, Paul, thank you for the information. I will keep it confidential. Can I call you from time to time to get an update?"

"Sure. Call me on my direct line. Tell the long-distance operator you want Washington D.C. Kensington 7-6709."

"Thanks again, I really appreciate it."

"Good luck. Stay safe."

"I will," he said and hung up.

In early February, Jean-Claude learned from local press accounts about developments that would virtually seal the fate of the Japanese. DeWitt and Attorney General Earl Warren met, and Warren told him there was bipartisan support for removal. Warren said that all Japanese, alien and citizen alike, had to be removed.

Jean-Claude was incredulous. *How could he believe this? It's politics and paranoia.* It was an ominous sign.

Now fearful that things were moving inexorably toward removal, he called Paul Fitzgerald again.

"I was wondering when I was going to get a call," Paul said.

"Warren has crossed over," Jean-Claude said. "The press is stirring up public opinion. DeWitt is in the papers every day saying they have to be removed. I don't like how this is going."

"You're right to be concerned. We have word that Stimson went to the president to advise him on the situation. Stimson is still skeptical that removal of all Japanese based on race is constitutional, but he was getting so much pressure from the generals, he felt he had to advise the president. We hear Roosevelt told him to do whatever he thought best and he would back him up with an executive order. I'm afraid it's out of our hands."

"Isn't there anything your department can do to stop it?" Jean-Claude was now very concerned that removal was an inevitability. It caused his head to spin.

"I don't think so," Paul said, resignation in his voice. "We've done all we can do. Frankly, there's a real split in our office as to what's best to do. There are a lot of lawyers around here who think it would be best if they were removed."

"They are asking the wrong question," Jean-Claude said emphatically. "It's not what's best to do; it's what's right to do."

"Unfortunately in time of war, it's what's best that drives decisions," Paul said.

"I assume before any order for removal is issued, there will be reviews of individual cases so that the loyal Japanese will be allowed to stay. That's the least they are entitled to."

"One would hope so, but I'm not so sure," Paul said. "The generals say the situation is so dire there's not enough time for that. I think we will know very soon what the final decision will be. Call me in a day or two. I may know more."

"Thanks again. I'll call you."

Two days later, on February eighteenth, Jean-Claude called

Paul again. "What's the status?" he asked.

"The news is not good," Paul said. "We were told Stimson finally decided to go with the generals. He feels they know best how to protect the country. He's had the lawyers in his office draft a proposed executive order allowing the military commanders to take whatever steps they deem necessary, including removal to protect the West Coast. McCloy told Stimson, 'If it's a question of the safety of the country the Constitution is just a scrap of paper.'"

"You've got to be kidding. 'Just a scrap of paper?' Where'd he go to law school?"

"Harvard," Paul replied.

"They must have taught him the version of the Bill of Rights with the asterisk." Jean-Claude said sarcastically. "We'll fight this all the way if they don't give us a chance to prove our loyalty before they order removal."

"After Biddle heard this he immediately went to see the president to ask him to reconsider," Paul continued. "The president told him he was going to do whatever Stimson decided. The president said he shared the concerns about removing citizens, but said we were at war, things had to be done to protect the country. After he left his meeting, Biddle said the Constitution has never greatly bothered any wartime president. We expect an executive order to come down any day. When this is over we'll have a drink and look back on the decisions that were made, good and bad, and see how it all turned out."

"I could use a drink now. Thanks again for keeping me informed. Let's keep in touch." They hung up.

Jean-Claude leaned back in his chair, wondering how things could have gotten so bad. He lit a cigarette. *Well, nothing has happened yet. Maybe Paul got it wrong.*

The next day, February 19, 1942, President Roosevelt issued Executive Order 9066 giving the military the authority to remove any persons from the West Coast they deemed a threat. Several weeks later, Congress unanimously passed legislation making it a misdemeanor to disobey any order issued by the military pursuant to the executive order. It was now a crime to refuse to relocate when ordered to do so.

All the great defenders of civil liberties—Warren, Biddle, and finally Roosevelt—gave in to the fears spawned by the military, the pressure from Congress, and the groundswell of public opinion. Now 110,000 people—citizens and aliens—were subject to removal from their homes, by force if necessary. It was done in the name of national security, but in reality, it was done because of wartime paranoia and racism.

Ken Matsumoto was smart and very well informed. He understood what was going on. He had back-channel access to Japanese American sources that told him removal was now inevitable, but now there was a law that could be challenged in court.

Jean-Claude and Ken constantly ran through different scenarios as to what action they would take if removal without a hearing was ordered. Jean-Claude believed there would be time to ask the courts to intervene before any removal took place. He was certain the courts would not allow removal without some process to distinguish the loyal from the disloyal.

However, Stanley's prediction proved right. The Japanese were in serious trouble, but it still remained to be seen if the courts would protect them or if the Constitution was just a scrap of paper like McCloy said. The next few months would be telling.

CHAPTER 10

MOVE 'EM OUT

February To May 1942

Jean-Claude met with the Matsumoto family at their home shortly after the law was passed making it a crime to disobey an order from the military for removal. It wasn't a meeting he looked forward to but at least now he had something that could be challenged in court.

He sat with the family in their living room and shared what he knew. "It may be that the military will issue orders for your removal to the interior. I don't know yet what they intend to do, but you should begin to plan in case you have to move." He paused to look at Mas, then Mrs. Matsumoto, Ken's two sisters, and finally Ken. "I want to tell you how sorry I am I misjudged what was going to happen, but we can fight it in court and we will." He wanted to sound defiant, but feeling he had let them down, he could only muster a determined stare.

Ken's two sisters hugged each other and fought back tears. There was little he could do to comfort them. Ken paced the living room probably to relieve his anger, but, most likely in deference to his father, said nothing. Later, in private, he told Jean-Claude he felt they were being treated like trash—like criminals, tried and convicted without a review of their loyalty, but he couldn't say that in front of the family.

"There will be no fight in court," Mas said. "If such an order is made we will follow it." Respect for authority was the way he was raised. "We must make plans," he said, turning to his family. "If we have to go, we must rent the house and make sure the plants and flowers don't die." Unlike his son, who was pacing nervously, Mas stood straight with his arms folded and spoke in a firm, commanding voice. "I will call the Botanical Gardens at the university and ask them to take as many plants as they can. I will give the flowers to the cemeteries and hospitals and the rest to whoever wants them. The plants must not be left to die."

The girls began to cry, but said nothing. It was clear they would obey their father. That was the way they had been raised.

Jean-Claude knew Ken was not going to submit. He was an American citizen and had been an officer in the United States Army. He wasn't going anywhere without a fight. He and Jean-Claude had already decided they were going to go to court and fight any order for removal, though they weren't going to bring that up in front of Mas. It would only add to an already stressful situation.

Mrs. Matsumoto didn't understand the words, but Jean-Claude could tell from her subdued expression she knew what was happening. She looked down at her hands and said nothing to contradict her husband. All they could do was wait to see what would happen. They would show patience. They would stay strong. They would be like the bonsai.

"I will do everything I can to help," Jean-Claude said. It was the only thing he could say but the words didn't make them feel any better. The Matsumotos were already preparing for the worst.

In late April, two months after the executive order was signed, DeWitt issued proclamations posted in public buildings, on storefront windows, and on telephone poles all over Oakland and other cities in the Bay Area. They ordered Japanese to be in their houses by 8:00 p.m. and not to leave until 6:00 a.m. the next morning, and then not to travel outside of a five-mile radius of their homes. The proclamation made no distinction between citizen and alien and provided no process to appeal the order.

In May, another proclamation followed. It established zones that had to be evacuated within forty-eight hours. All residents in those zones were told all they could take with them were the clothes on their backs and what they could carry. The Matsumoto family was in one of the zones.

All those being relocated had to dispose of their personal effects as best they could. Pets were not allowed and if no home could be found, the pet had to be destroyed. Many had to sell prosperous businesses on short notice at a great loss. Despite this, the overwhelming number of Japanese who were ordered to evacuate did so peacefully and without protest, despite the personal losses.

In the three months between the signing of Executive Order 9066 and the issuance of the proclamation ordering removal, there hadn't been one act of sabotage. Stretching justification for removal to its maximum absurd extent, a prominent lawyer from the War Department was quoted as saying the very fact no sabotage had taken place to date was a disturbing and confirming indication that such action will be taken in the future. Hearing that confirmed Jean-Claude's belief that war hysteria and racism were the driving forces behind removal.

The preceding months had been stressful for everyone. The Matsumoto family lived in a constant state of uncertainty. When would they have to move? Where would they be moved to? Would they be able to stay together as a family? Their greatest fear was that they would be separated.

Jean-Claude was also under stress preparing for the upcoming court battle and living with the unresolved question of whether he would go to France. During it all, he and Stephanie were spending a considerable amount of time together and the stress began to take its toll on their relationship. Subtly at first, then more directly, Stephanie made it clear she wanted to get married. She said she didn't care if they had an uncertain future or if they might have to be apart for a considerable period if he returned to France. She wanted to get married.

Jean-Claude's response was the same each time. "Things are too uncertain to make permanent plans. If I do go to France, I don't want to leave a widow behind if I don't come back." But in the back of his mind he worried it might have been the urgency and uncertainty of the times that made him fall for her so fast. He had some lingering doubts about her and maybe that was the reason he didn't want to commit, or maybe it was simply the fear of commitment itself, something that had plagued him in the past. Each time the subject was raised he would close up and become uncommunicative, then she would bury her frustration and drop it.

This created tension especially because Stephanie wouldn't sleep with him. She said it was because she wanted to wait until they were married. It made for more than a few frustrating evenings. However, Jean-Claude accepted it. He didn't want to pressure her. The thought even crossed his mind that she might still be a virgin, but he was resolved not to be forced into marriage just to have sex.

The time for the Matsumotos to leave their home finally arrived. Jean-Claude and Stephanie went to help them move. Everyone in the family was on edge. They tried not to show it but he could feel it. He could see it in their faces and in their body language. There was little conversation, just robotic movements loading things into boxes, pausing sometimes to consider and reflect on the item being packed away.

Boxes were piled high in the living room. Mrs. Matsumoto sat on the sofa going through personal items she had brought from Japan. There were photographs of her family and letters she had kept from them over the years. This was the family history from her childhood. She took each one and looked at it slowly before carefully packing it away. At one point she began to cry, but then caught herself, regained her composure, and continued the task of packing her life's memories into a box.

Ken said she was worried they would be lost while they were gone, even though they had made arrangements with a Caucasian friend to store their things in his garage. She told him if the pictures were lost, it would hurt more than having to move.

They found a nice couple to rent the house, and Jean-Claude arranged for Irving Stern to collect the rent and put it in his trust account. Stern would send it to them if they needed it and make sure the property taxes were paid.

The nursery truck and the car would be kept by a client of Jean-Claude's who owned a used car lot and who promised not to sell them. Jean-Claude made sure he would keep his promise by telling him if he sold the vehicles, the cops would somehow find out about all the stolen cars he had fenced.

The proclamation stated that all residents of the military zone where the Matsumotos lived were to report to Tanforan Race Track in San Bruno within forty-eight hours. Tanforan was to be an assembly point and only temporary until they could be transferred to their permanent facility.

Jean-Claude decided he and Stephanie would drive Mr. Matsumoto, his wife, and the two sisters in their cars. Ken would not go because he would be detained. Jean-Claude in his Buick and Stephanie in her DeSoto helped the Matsumoto family load what little they were allowed to take into the trunks of the two cars. They said their good-byes to Ken. Mrs. Matsumoto and her daughters cried. But Ken and Mas remained stoic, showing no emotion. Mas never said a word to Ken about his decision to fight the removal order; however later, Sarah wrote him from Tanforan that Mas was proud of his decision. This made Ken feel better because he never wanted to disappoint his father.

The drive to San Bruno only took forty-five minutes. It was just across the bay from Oakland and just south of San Francisco. Jean-Claude took Mas and Mrs. Matsumoto and Stephanie took Ken's two sisters. Jean-Claude's initial attempts to start a conversation failed. Tense silence filled the car for the rest of the trip. When they arrived at Tanforan, the Matsumotos were directed to an assembly center where they were checked in. Military police were everywhere. It was crowded, but orderly.

Jean-Claude and Stephanie were not allowed inside the assembly center. When Jean-Claude protested, saying he was their lawyer and wanted to accompany them to the housing unit to inspect it, he was told if he didn't leave the restricted area, he'd be arrested. So they had to say their good-byes at the gate.

He wanted to hug them, but mindful of their traditions, he bowed to Mas. Mrs. Matsumoto also bowed, but then Jean-Claude instinctively gave her a hug. Her body became rigid, then just as quickly relaxed, and she hugged him back. Stephanie hugged the daughters. All four women wept. Jean-Claude and Mas remained unemotional. At least outwardly.

Several days later, Jean-Claude found out about the conditions at Tanforan from letters Ken received from his sisters. They and their parents were housed in horse stalls that had been washed down, but still smelled of manure. The toilets were located some distance from the stalls in outhouses and the food served in a massive dining hall was terrible. Mrs. Matsumoto felt humiliation at the lack of privacy in the toilets.

The letters went on to say there was nothing to do during the day except hope they would be sent to their permanent facility soon so they could get out of the horse stalls. The letters said Mas was getting depressed because he was powerless to do anything about their conditions but that they had accepted their situation and vowed to survive.

Ken was furious after reading the letters. He went on verbal tirades against the government. Jean-Claude knew he hated that he couldn't go outside or to his office because if he did, he could have been arrested for violation of the removal order. He wanted to begin the legal fight immediately. Jean-Claude attempted to enlist the aid of the ACLU, who he believed would be deluged by many Japanese who wanted to protest their removal in court. They could all join in one lawsuit. There would be strength in numbers.

The following week, Sarah called Jean-Claude at his office and told him they were going to be moved out of Tanforan the next day. They were going to Manzanar in Southern California in the high desert, about 230 miles northeast of Los Angeles. They would be going by train from San Bruno. Jean-Claude immediately called Ken with the unsettling news.

There was no hesitation on Jean-Claude's part. He and Stephanie were going to the train station to say good-bye. The next day as they drove to San Bruno they asked each other questions for which they had no answers: "How could it happen here? Was this any different than what was happening in Europe to the Jews? What were the camps going to be like? Were they going to be treated like prisoners?"

When they arrived, they tried to approach the departure platform, but were prevented by armed military police. The train looked ready for boarding, so they walked over to a pedestrian bridge that overlooked the tracks. They looked down at the people below, hoping to catch a glimpse of the Matsumotos.

The people stood in long lines, hundreds of them. They all looked weary. But there were no protests or resistance, just resignation. They stood next to the few bags they had been allowed to bring. The men were dressed in suits and hats, and the women had chosen their finest dresses and coats to wear. They wore their finest not because of the occasion, but because they could only take the clothes on their backs, and they wanted to save their best.

Jean-Claude could see they all had tags attached to their clothes. They were being treated like baggage. He felt a surge of anger. He clenched his jaw as he glared at the spectacle below.

Standing guard on the platform were uniformed soldiers at parade rest; one hand behind their backs, the other holding a rifle with a fixed bayonet. Other soldiers stood on the platform, checking names from the tags and noting them on a clipboard.

Then there were children. Lots of children.

Jean-Claude saw a little boy who couldn't have been more than four standing next to one of the soldiers on the platform. He barely came up to his hip. The little boy looked up at the soldier with a puzzled expression. He obviously didn't understand what was happening. Jean-Claude understood what was happening, he just couldn't believe it. He didn't want to believe it. But there it was right in front of him, hundreds of people calmly and silently waiting to be transported to a concentration camp. Jean-Claude thought he would never see a sight like this in the United States.

Some people had already boarded the train. Jean-Claude could see a group of young children leaning out of a window. One of them waved an American flag.

The scene appalled him. He resolved to fight the removal with everything he had. He looked at Stephanie. Tears were streaming down her face. Even though he showed little emotion, he had to bite down hard on his lower lip to keep from flying into a rage over what he was witnessing.

"I didn't see the Matsumotos, did you?" he asked quietly.

Stephanie shook her head, too emotional to speak.

They drove back to Oakland in silence. Ken had asked him to come by the nursery on their way back.

When they arrived, Ken asked Jean-Claude and Stephanie to

come with him. They made their way to the greenhouse. It was ghostly inside with most of the plants gone, but it still had that purplish iridescent glow. They followed Ken to the back and there on the table Jean-Claude saw a single bonsai plant.

Ken picked it up and handed it to Jean-Claude. "My father wanted you to have this. He said it will give you peace and keep you strong."

Jean-Claude took the bonsai from his friend. The events of the day almost overwhelmed him but he managed to keep his composure. He, Stephanie, and Ken walked back to their cars. Ken and Stephanie talked quietly. Jean-Claude said nothing. He was still too angry to speak.

Jean-Claude dropped Stephanie off at her apartment. He'd had enough stress for one day and was glad he wouldn't have to deal with the tensions of their relationship that night. He and Ken drove back to his house. Ken was staying with him and wanted to talk more about what had happened at the station, but all Jean-Claude would say was that things went peacefully and they got on the train safely.

Ken persisted. This was his family. He wanted to know.

Jean-Claude told him how his family and the hundreds of others were treated like baggage while waiting peacefully to be shipped off to a camp somewhere in Southern California to an uncertain future.

It was too much for Ken. He asked Jean-Claude if he had any wine or whiskey in the house. Jean-Claude accommodated his friend by going down to the wine cellar. He brought back two bottles. Wine was a good thing. Neither of them would have been able to sleep without it.

Several hours later they both passed out.

CHAPTER 11

THE LEGAL BATTLE

July 1942

T he next morning, Ken sat in Jean-Claude's office with his arms folded across his chest. He was still livid. "Let's go. Let's get this goddamned case in court." Jean-Claude knew he was in no mood to wait. Ken wanted the fight to begin.

"We've got to get you arrested first." Jean-Claude lit a cigarette and calmly inhaled. "Once you get arrested, we get into court."

"Arrested? Do you mean I have to sit in jail the whole time we're fighting the case?" Ken's anger now turned to annoyance.

"All depends on the judge we draw. A few might let you out, but I'm afraid most would keep you in." Jean-Claude leaned forward and stared at Ken. "We have to be prepared to fight the case from inside. I'll make arrangements to surrender you and let the U.S. attorney know, so he can go to the grand jury and get an indictment. Once there is an indictment, we will file a writ of habeas corpus challenging the legality of the curfew and the removal."

"When do we go?" Ken asked, his knees bouncing.

Jean-Claude held up a hand to slow Ken down. "I have been waiting to hear from the ACLU to see if we could join in any lawsuits they were filing. So far we're the only ones who want to fight it."

Ken didn't appear surprised since he'd told Jean-Claude he had heard from his contacts in the Japanese community that the general consensus was not to fight the removal for fear of a backlash that could result in violence.

"It looks like it's just going to be you and me. In a way, I'm glad. We can do it our way without being dictated to by the ACLU or anybody else."

Ken unfolded his arms and appeared to relax a bit. "Jean-Claude, I really appreciate what you're doing. I know I'm frustrated and haven't been the easiest client, and I know my case could hurt your reputation. You'll probably lose clients because of me."

Ken opened a brief case he had brought with him and removed a large envelope. "My father gave me this to give to you. He's been keeping cash buried in the yard for years for emergencies. He wants you to have it. I know you said we would discuss money when the time came, and I think now is the time."

Ken handed Jean-Claude the envelope. Inside were mostly small bills. They smelled moldy.

"There's a little over $2,500 in there," Ken said.

"This is too much." Jean-Claude handed the envelope back to Ken.

"No, it's not." Ken held up his hands, showing he wasn't going to take back the money. "He wants you to have it. If you are going to risk your reputation to defend me, you should at least get paid for it. Besides, I can't take it with me where I might be going."

Jean-Claude paused, then took a breath. "It's too much for what I am going to do. I think a thousand is fair. I will put the balance in Irving's trust account, the one he has set up for the rent money. It will be there whenever you need it. Don't worry about my losing clients," Jean-Claude said firmly. "If I go to France, it won't matter anymore." He paused and stared directly at Ken. "I want you to know I would have helped you even if I wasn't going. But I appreciate the payment."

"Just the fact you are willing to do this means a lot to me. We've been friends for a long time and I value our friendship." The two stood up. Ken gave him a hug of appreciation.

Two weeks later, Jean-Claude and Ken walked into the Oakland city jail at 9:00 p.m. The desk sergeant and Jean-Claude knew each other.

"You here to see a client, Jean-Claude?" the sergeant asked, looking up from his paperwork.

"No, I'm here to have you arrest my client."

The sergeant looked at Ken. "I got a feeling it has to do with that Jap fellow standing next to you."

"Your powers of observation are remarkable."

"So what's up?"

"This is Ken Matsumoto. He's a friend of mine and also a client. Its 9:00 p.m., an hour after he is supposed to be home because of the curfew. He is also in the zone that was supposed to report for internment two weeks ago, and he is refusing to go."

"Come on, Jean-Claude," the desk sergeant said with feigned pleading. "You and your friend go home. Come back tomorrow when somebody else is on the desk."

"We want to do it tonight," Jean-Claude insisted. "Look, all you have to do is book him then call the U.S. marshals. I've already notified the U.S. attorney we are surrendering, and they have alerted the U.S. Marshals Office to come pick him up as soon as he is in custody. Then they'll take him to federal court in San Francisco. Very simple."

"Simple for you. A lot of lousy paperwork for me."

"Come on now. This is going to make the papers. You'll look like a hero." He waved his hands through the air to signify the newspaper headlines. "'Oakland police sergeant arrests Jap who refuses to observe curfew and report to a camp.'"

The desk sergeant thought for a second. "Yeah, that sounds good. I'll have one of the jailers come up and start the process of getting your boy booked."

Ken was taken to a holding cell where he would remain until the U.S. marshals came for him.

Three days later, the U.S. attorney advised Jean-Claude an indictment had been returned and a U.S. marshal would pick up Ken and bring him to San Francisco to the federal courthouse the next day for arraignment and a detention hearing. Jean-Claude immediately filed a writ of habeas corpus. The legal battle was about to begin.

CHAPTER 12

HABEAS CORPUS

September 1942

The federal courthouse at 7th and Mission in San Francisco was completed in 1905, and was only one of two buildings south of Market Street to survive the 1906 earthquake and fire. Perhaps fate spared the courthouse because it was a marvelous example of Renaissance architecture. The courtrooms were opulent. It was like trying a case in a palace in France or Italy. The judges' chambers had wood-burning fireplaces, perhaps to soften their attitudes, which could, at times, be imperial and dictatorial, and at other times relaxed and friendly. One judge would invite counsel into chambers for a brandy while the jury deliberated, yet another would hurl invectives at a lawyer for the slightest misstep. It all depended on the judge one drew.

The case was assigned to Judge Anderson Clayton, who had been nominated by President Coolidge after serving on the San Francisco County Superior Court. Clayton fancied himself a legal scholar and frequently boasted he'd only been reversed once by the court of appeals, and that was on a ridiculous legal technicality. He wasn't the judge who invited counsel into chambers for brandy, but he wasn't a tyrant either. His personality ranged somewhere in between.

Jean-Claude felt they could have done worse. At least Clayton would listen to the legal arguments. He had to realize this was a landmark case, perhaps destined for the Supreme Court. The judge was certain to issue a lengthy written opinion, which would serve as the basis for Ken's appeal if they lost.

At 9:00 a.m. on July 16, 1942, in courtroom number one, the court clerk called the case of *United States v. Kenneth Matsumoto*. "All rise," the court clerk cried out. "The United States District Court for the Northern District of California is now in session, the Honorable Judge Anderson Clayton presiding. Calling the case of *United States versus Kenneth Matsumoto* CR-42-96."

Ken was brought in from the holding cell in handcuffs and leg irons. Jean-Claude was outraged at this but said nothing. The case had to get off on the right note, and a battle over handcuffs and leg irons was not a good place to start.

"Please state your appearances for the record," the clerk commanded.

Both attorneys stood.

"Alfonso Bonaventura, assistant United States Attorney for the government."

"Jean-Claude Bonnay for the defendant Kenneth Matsumoto." Jean-Claude felt a surge of adrenaline, tightness in his stomach, and his heart rate increased. These were good things. They helped him focus.

Ken was arraigned on a two-count indictment alleging violations of the curfew order and failure to report as directed. He entered pleas of not guilty to both counts. Jean-Claude then asked to address the issue of releasing Ken on bail pending the hearing.

The judge nodded that he could proceed.

"Your Honor, my client is a U.S. citizen, a graduate of U.C.

Berkeley, has no criminal history, and voluntarily presented himself for arrest, proving he is not a flight risk. Neither is he a danger to the community—" That's as far as he got before the judge interrupted him.

"How do I know he is not a danger?" His voice rose in volume and intensity. "Isn't danger to the community the very issue in this case? Isn't that the concern which led to the signing of the executive order and the issuing of the proclamations implementing it?" He sounded blatantly hostile. "He could be a saboteur or passing messages to the enemy. How do I know? What I do know is how to ensure he's not a danger. Request for pre-trial release is denied. He is remanded to the custody of the U.S. marshals."

He slammed his gavel down adding emphasis to his emphatic denial of Jean-Claude's motion for bail. Jean-Claude felt it best not to continue the argument. Being denied bail didn't come as a surprise. Jean-Claude had expected it. The hostility concerned him though. It did not bode well for a successful outcome. What happened next did surprise him, however.

"Now let's deal with your writ," the judge went on. "I note that the U.S. attorney has filed a reply so we will now proceed to argument on the merits."

Argument? Now? He had assumed a date would be set for a hearing sometime in the future. Federal judges managed their own calendars and set the dates for hearings, but to move to argument immediately was unusual.

"Mr. Bonnay, you may proceed," Clayton said, peering down at Jean-Claude as if to measure his reaction to the surprise at having to proceed to argument immediately.

Jean-Claude stared back at him. Argue now or in two weeks, it didn't matter. He was nervous, but prepared. It was a good thing. It would move the case along faster. He began with his strongest argument in a confident voice.

"Your Honor, I have set forth our arguments in the writ, but I wish to reiterate our reliance on the 1866 U.S. Supreme Court case *Ex Parte Milligan*. I don't see how the government can get around the language in *Milligan*.

"The Milligan court held that only by an act of Congress could the writ of habeas corpus be suspended and that no military action could be taken except under martial law conditions. *Milligan* states clearly that martial law can never exist where the courts are open and in the proper and unobstructed exercise of their jurisdiction." Jean-Claude was speaking from memory and only briefly glancing at his notes to make sure he hadn't forgotten anything. He kept eye contact with the judge, which was a little disconcerting since the judge was glaring at him.

He continued in a firm voice. "Military rule cannot arise from a threatened invasion. The necessity must be actual and present, the invasion real, such that it effectively closes the courts and deposes the civil administration."

Jean-Claude paused, looking for a reaction from the judge, whose expression did not change. "It is clear martial law has not been declared and my client has been detained by a military order without a hearing while the civil courts are open. Our case fits squarely within the holding in *Milligan*. The writ should be granted." He had ended on an emphatic note and felt good about his presentation.

It would be interesting to see how Bonaventura was going to get around *Milligan*, Jean-Claude thought as he sat down.

The judge looked directly at the federal prosecutor. He had a very serious look on his face. "Mr. Bonaventura, at first I was of the belief this writ was frivolous. I am no longer of that opinion. You should be prepared to respond to the defendant's argument, and I want you to pay particular attention to the *Milligan* decision. We will resume at two o'clock," the judge said and pounded his gavel.

The clerk cried out, "All rise" as the judge walked off the bench.

Resume at two? What kind of bullshit is that? He jams me to argue right away and then gives Bonaventura four hours to prepare his rebuttal. Well, he'll need it. Milligan is right on point. But that might signal that we have a chance. These were , Jean-Claude's thoughts as he left the courtroom. It was a long shot. The country was at war and the military felt there was a threat if all Japanese were not evacuated from the West Coast. What judge could stand up to that kind of pressure? Would he dare to overrule a presidential executive order and a criminal statute passed unanimously by Congress? Doubtful. He would find out at two o'clock.

During the noon recess, Jean-Claude visited with Ken in the holding cell.

He leaned against the gray cement wall of the cell. "If that's a taste of what's to come, we're in for a tough time," Ken said, most likely referring to the judge's order detaining him.

"I agree." Jean-Claude lit a cigarette. "We knew it wasn't going to be easy. This guy is tough, but he will make a good record on the legal issues. If we lose the writ, I'm concerned about the sentence he might impose if we plead guilty," Jean-Claude said, walking slowly back and forth in the cell thinking out loud. "We have to show him you're loyal to the United States and don't pose a threat. If we can convince him of that, he may go easy on the sentence. There's only one way we can accomplish that."

Jean-Claude drew heavily on his cigarette and exhaled. "We will not plead guilty. We will demand a jury trial and you will testify," he said firmly. "That's the best strategy. You will almost certainly be found guilty, but that's the only way I can educate the judge as to the kind of person you are."

"Whatever you say. You know what's best and I trust you."

Jean-Claude crushed his cigarette beneath his shoe and called for the jailer to come and let him out.

At 2:00 p.m., Jean-Claude reentered the courtroom and was shocked to see that it was packed with lawyers from the office of the Judge Advocate General's office at the Presidio, all in uniform.

What a cheap shot. Nothing more than an attempt by Bonaventura to intimidate the judge. Jean-Claude was angry, but it was a sign Bonaventura was concerned about the outcome.

"Hello, Jean-Claude. How are you?" It was Sam Neufeld, a former prosecutor Jean-Claude had tried cases against in State court, but was now in the military. He came striding up to him smiling.

"Neufeld, this is bullshit. It's a clear attempt to intimidate the Court," Jean-Claude said, his jaw tightening.

"It's a public courtroom," Sam said with a wry smile. "Anybody can attend. And these guys clearly feel they have an interest in the outcome, so they want to see what happens. By the way, we have a surefire way of getting you off the case—we can have you drafted." His smile turned into a smirk.

"You can take that threat and shove it up your ass." Jean-Claude was not amused or intimidated. "When and if I go in, it won't be in some candy-ass outfit like the Judge Advocate General's Corps." He turned and walked to the well of the courtroom and took his seat at counsel table. He was angry, but before Bonaventura began his rebuttal, he had regained his composure and felt ready for whatever was to come.

"All rise, the United States District Court for the Northern District of California, the Honorable Anderson Clayton presiding, is now in session. You may be seated," the clerk said.

Bonaventura began with a bold strategy. He had to do something in the face of the *Milligan* case, which was clearly against him. "The dissent in *Milligan,* particularly Justice Chase's dissent, is the better reasoning, Your Honor, and it is the position we urge the Court to take."

That took some balls. Asking a district court judge to overrule a Supreme Court case based upon a dissent. Jean-Claude breathed a little easier since dissents were almost never adopted by trial courts, especially when it involved a Supreme Court decision.

"Justice Chase in his dissent said," Bonaventura continued, " 'Whenever the Congress or the President determine that such great and imminent public danger exists as justifies the authorization of military tribunals, the civil safeguards of the Constitution had no force.' "

He went on to cite a recent *Harvard Law Review* article in which the author not only supported the arguments made by the dissent in *Milligan*, but also the argument that the military had been putting forth: the unique racial characteristics of the Japanese made them more inclined to be loyal to their native country.

This was an argument Jean-Claude felt was racist and inappropriate and he objected. His objection was promptly overruled.

Bonaventura continued to refer to the article.

"I want to stress that the author agrees with General De Witt that there is a military necessity for removal," he said with authority in his voice to make up for the lack of authority the article should have carried.

Jean-Claude objected again. "Your Honor, there is no independent evidence for this assertion other than the general's belief that it exists."

"Objection overruled," the judge said in a dismissive tone.

Jean-Claude discovered later that the author of the *Harvard Law Review* article, a law professor at Stanford, was on active duty with the Judge Advocate General's staff when he wrote the article—something that wasn't brought to the judge's attention at the hearing despite the fact the courtroom was packed with his colleagues. Had it been brought to the court's attention it would have demonstrated the author's bias, but probably wouldn't have made any difference with the judge.

In rebuttal, Jean-Claude argued that a law professor is an academic voicing his views and can never have the full force and effect of a judicial opinion. Nevertheless, Judge Clayton appeared sufficiently impressed and he asked for a copy of the article so he could read it in its entirety.

"If there is nothing else, gentlemen, I will be prepared to rule at 1:30 tomorrow. Court is adjourned."

Jean-Claude was pleased the ruling would be quick. At least if he lost, he could begin the appeal process right away.

The next day, Judge Clayton took the bench promptly at 1:30 p.m.

"In my written opinion," Clayton said, "I have set forth the legal basis for my ruling. Rather than read the entire opinion, which I feel is thorough and reflects an appreciation of the constitutional issues involved, I will only read my conclusions."

The judge peered down at his opinion and began to read. "It must not for an instant be forgotten that since Pearl Harbor last December, we have been engaged in a total war with enemies unbelievably treacherous and wholly ruthless, who intend to totally destroy this nation, its constitution, our way of life, and trample all liberty and freedom everywhere on this earth." He paused and looked out over the packed courtroom probably to absorb what he perceived to be the overwhelming approval of his opinion. "I find that the technical interpretation of the due process clause offered as an objection to the curfew and evacuation orders should not be permitted to endanger all of the constitutional rights of the whole citizenry. Accordingly, the writ of habeas corpus is denied." He emphasized the word denied.

Judge Clayton looked up from his opinion with a pleased expression on his face and addressed Jean-Claude. "I assume that since there are no contested issues of fact, you intend to have your client plead guilty. If so, we can proceed to sentencing forthwith."

Jean-Claude replied immediately. "No, Your Honor, the defendant demands a jury trial."

The judge was taken somewhat aback given there were really no triable issues of fact. "Counsel," the judge said disapprovingly, "I do not look favorably on those who unnecessarily waste the court's time with frivolous motions or idle acts, such as asking for a jury trial in a case where there is no defense."

"My client demands a trial, which is his right, Your Honor," Jean-Claude said with determination. He stared at the judge.

"I am bound to honor your client's request, but I warn you not to make it a show for your legal position against internment. Those arguments have been made and ruled upon," the judge admonished. "The trial will deal only with the issues of whether he violated the curfew and failed to report for evacuation. Is that understood?"

"Yes, Your Honor."

"We will come back a week from today to pick a jury, unless of course you wish me to hear the case without a jury, which I urge given the predictable outcome of the case."

"No, thank you, Your Honor. We want a jury trial."

"Very well. Court is adjourned. We will reconvene one week from today at 9 a.m."

Jean-Claude didn't expect to win the writ, but he was upset about the judge's statement that the due process protections afforded by the Constitution should not be subjected to "technical interpretations."

"You mean like equal protection?" he wanted to ask the Judge but thought better of it.

John McCloy's position had prevailed. The Constitution was just a scrap of paper.

"You think I would let that old buzzard decide the case at a bench trial?" he asked Ken in the holding cell after court. The suggestion clearly irritated him. "I just found out he's a member of the Native Sons of the Golden West. These are the guys who have denounced the Japanese as posing a direct threat to the United States. This is why we have juries," he told Ken. "This is exactly why we have juries."

They had expected to lose the writ and now it was on to a trial. They would undoubtedly lose that too, but Ken would have a chance to testify and show he was a loyal American. Jean-Claude wanted to do everything possible to minimize

Ken's sentence. If he could convince the judge of Ken's loyalty and receive a lenient sentence, he would have achieved a lot. Stanley had taught him winning often means something less than total victory.

CHAPTER 13

THE TRIAL

It didn't take long to empanel a jury. Because the charges were misdemeanors, only six jurors were required, instead of the usual twelve. The judge did all the questioning for bias. All the prospective jurors were men which was fine with Jean-Claude as he believed women would be fearful of a Japanese man. The gallery was filled again with men in uniform. Jean-Claude didn't object because it would have sent the wrong impression to the prospective jurors who were also sitting in the gallery waiting to be called.

Bonaventura did not exercise a peremptory challenge accepting the first six, sending a message that he believed he had a winning case.

Jean-Claude only used one, on an active member of the army reserves. They had a jury in thirty minutes.

Bonaventura wore a dark blue suit that Jean-Claude assumed he reserved for his most important cases. From the lectern where the attorneys did their questioning, he called only one witness: the FBI agent who interrogated Ken after he was arrested.

"Agent Kilgore, did the defendant admit he willfully disobeyed the curfew order?" Bonaventura began, short and to the point.

"He did admit that to me on several occasions." The agent sat upright on the stand where he undoubtedly had been a witness many times. He had an air of confidence but did not seem arrogant.

"Did he also admit that he willfully refused to report for relocation to an internment camp?"

"Yes, he did admit that. He seemed quite proud of it." He appeared to smirk when he answered that question.

On cross-examination Jean-Claude asked only two questions. "Agent Kilgore, was Mr. Matsumoto cooperative with you during your interrogation?"

"Yes, he was very cooperative."

"Did he appear to be evasive in answering your questions?"

"No. On the contrary he was quite forthright. He seemed proud of what he had done."

"Thank you, agent Kilgore." Jean-Claude had begun to lay the foundation for his defense. Ken was an honest man who did what he did out of a genuine belief that removal was wrong. He was not a threat or a menace.

With that the government rested.

Jean-Claude was also dressed in a dark suit that had a vest. He had a pocket watch with a chain that hung between the vest pockets and was clearly visible. It had been given to him by his father when he passed the bar. It bolstered his courage.

"Do you intend to call any witnesses, Mr. Bonnay?" the judge asked.

"Yes, Your Honor, I do."

"You may proceed."

Jean-Claude called Ken Matsumoto to the stand.

Ken walked with his head erect, his shoulders back, looking confident as he strode to the witness chair and took his seat. He was allowed to dress in his own clothes for the trial. He'd asked

Jean-Claude to bring his dark suit, white shirt, and a blue and gold tie. He looked confident without appearing defiant. Jean-Claude felt he would do well.

The clerk administered the oath. "Do you swear to tell the whole truth and nothing but the truth, so help you God?"

"I do," Ken answered in a clear, strong voice.

Jean-Claude began his direct examination. "Mr. Matsumoto, are you an American citizen?"

"Yes. I was born here."

"Are you employed?"

"Yes. I am a licensed architect and have my own practice in Oakland."

"What is your educational background?"

"I have a bachelor of science in Structural Engineering and a master's degree in Architecture," Ken said in a confident voice while glancing at the jury. "I obtained both degrees from the University of California at Berkeley."

"While an undergraduate, did you participate in the ROTC program?" Jean-Claude nodded toward Ken indicating his approval at the way he was conducting himself on the stand.

"Yes. I received my commission as a second lieutenant upon graduation and served two years on active duty. I then served two years in the National Guard Reserves while I was getting my master's degree. I then received an honorable discharge."

"Are you prepared to serve again if called upon?"

"Yes. I have considered reenlisting." He looked out into the gallery at the men in uniform while answering the question.

"Do you speak Japanese?"

Ken shook his head. "Only a little. When I was in grade school my father sent me to Japanese school after regular school. There I learned a little of the language, but my Japanese is so bad my mother cannot understand me."

"Have you ever been to Japan?"

"No."

"Do you have any contacts in the Japanese government, either here in the States or in Japan?"

"No."

"Do you consider yourself a loyal American?" Jean-Claude kept a close eye on the jury while he did his questioning. He didn't detect any overt hostility. They all appeared to be listening intently to Ken's testimony.

"I do. I was born and raised here. I have served my country in the military. I would gladly do it again if called upon." This time Ken looked directly at the judge. "This is my home. I believe what the Empire of Japan did at Pearl Harbor was an atrocious act of cowardice. I hope they are defeated and will no longer pose a threat to us in the United States or anyone else in the world. I consider them as much of a threat to our way of life as the Nazis are."

"Thank you, Mr. Matsumoto. Your witness." Jean-Claude gestured to the prosecutor. He was very pleased with the way Ken conducted himself. But this would be the real test. How would he hold up under cross-examination?

Bonaventura rose slowly and moved to the lectern. He spoke clearly and asked direct questions. He was a good lawyer. "Mr. Matsumoto, would you allow for the fact that among the 110,000 people on the West Coast who are of Japanese ancestry, some may feel differently than you and sympathize with the Empire of Japan?"

"I suppose there might be some." Ken stiffened in the witness chair. "I don't know any."

"Mr. Matsumoto, given the fact there may be those in the Japanese population who wish us harm, wouldn't you agree that as a precautionary measure, at least until this crisis is past, everyone of Japanese ancestry should submit to relocation?"

"No," Ken said in a calm and measured tone, "because I believe there is a way that Japanese people can be screened before they have to be sent away from their homes, and those, like me, who are loyal can be allowed to stay." Ken stared directly at the prosecutor. "In Hawaii, the site of the most horrific destruction, only a small percentage of the Japanese population was put in camps. The rest were allowed to go about their business."

Bonaventura pressed on as if he hadn't heard the answer. "You agree, however, that the situation we face here on the West Coast is urgent and potentially very dangerous, and that we are vulnerable to fifth columns and sabotage?"

"Yes. I would agree there is a potential threat."

"Wouldn't you agree then, as a precautionary measure, relocation is the best way to guard against that threat?"

"No. There are precautionary things that can be done to determine who is a risk and who is not before locking 110,000 people up," Ken said.

Jean-Claude looked at the judge to see if he could detect a reaction. The judge sat stone-faced and motionless. He then looked at the jurors, who were still paying close attention.

"Mr. Matsumoto," the prosecutor went on, "were you aware that on the day you were arrested there was a curfew in effect?"

"Yes."

"Did you knowingly and willfully violate that curfew?"

"Yes."

"And on that same date, did you know you had been ordered to a relocation center at Tanforan Racetrack by the Military Authority?"

"Yes."

"Did you knowingly and willingly violate that order?"

"Yes, because I did not think it was a lawful order." He didn't appear defensive when he answered.

However, Bonaventura had gotten a confession and didn't need anything more.

Normally this would be the time for redirect, but before Jean-Claude could say anything the judge stepped in. "I have a few questions for Mr. Matsumoto."

Judges had the right to examine witnesses if they felt there was a need for clarification, but Jean-Claude wasn't prepared for his line of questioning.

"Mr. Matsumoto, what is Shinto?"

Ken paused and looked at Jean-Claude as if to ask if he had

to answer the judge's questions. Jean-Claude nodded that he should.

"Shinto, as I understand it, is the national religion of Japan."

"Do you adhere to its precepts?"

"No, I'm a Methodist."

"Are either of your parents of the Shinto religion?"

"Yes, my father and mother are."

Where is the old bastard going with this? Jean-Claude considered objecting because he believed the questions were irrelevant, but he didn't want to alienate the judge or make the jury think he was trying to hide anything, so he sat silent and listened with a placid expression on his face hoping it belied the frustration he felt inside. Small beads of perspiration began to show on his forehead.

"Did they have a picture of the Emperor anywhere in the house?" the judge asked.

"Yes, for years it hung over the fireplace."

"Doesn't the Shinto religion convey a divine presence to the Emperor?"

"I believe it does."

"And don't your parents believe that anything the Emperor says or orders has a divine quality to it?"

"Yes." Ken shifted his weight in the witness chair and clasped and unclasped his hands that he kept in his lap. The questions were totally unexpected and neither he nor Jean-Claude had prepared for them.

Hang in there. Don't get angry. Jean-Claude tried to convey the message by an encouraging nod.

"They are not citizens, are they?" the judge continued.

"No. They are prevented by law from becoming citizens."

"Are you bitter about this?"

"Not bitter." He paused, glanced down at his hands then turned and stared directly at the judge. "Just disappointed."

"Tell me, Mr. Matsumoto, where are your parents now?"

"They are in Manzanar, one of the concentration camps."

"Do you have brothers and sisters who are also U.S.

citizens?"

"Yes. I have two sisters. They were born here."

"And where are they today?"

"They are in Manzanar as well."

"They are not joining you in this protest against removal, are they?"

"No. My father is the head of the family. He believes in doing what his government asks him to do." He looked at the jury when he answered this question. "My mother and sisters follow his wishes. I chose not to because I believe it is wrong." He looked at the judge with a steely stare while answering this question.

"You took an oath when you became an officer in the army, didn't you?"

"Yes."

"Do you remember the words of the oath?"

"Some, but not all."

"What do you remember?"

"To obey the orders of the commanding officer upon proper authority in time of active service. Or something like that."

"It specifically says you will obey the orders of the president of the United States. So why don't you consider it your obligation to obey this order, which comes indirectly from the president, who is Commander in Chief of the armed forces?"

"Because I have an obligation to obey only a lawful order and I don't consider this order lawful. And I am not on active duty and my rights as a citizen are different than my obligations as a military officer." Ken continued to look directly at the judge as he answered in a firm voice.

Jean-Claude couldn't have put it better.

The judge paused. "Thank you, Mr. Matsumoto. Do either counsel have further questions?"

Both counsel said they had no further questions and rested.

Ken stepped down from the witness stand and walked to the defense counsel's table. He still had an air of confidence and a slight smile on his face. Jean-Claude smiled and nodded his approval.

That was a pretty good way to end it, even though the judge had injected issues into the proceedings Jean-Claude felt had no place. He chose not to do any redirect. It was time to leave well enough alone and move on.

"All right then," the judge said. "We shall proceed to final arguments. Mr. Bonaventura, you may begin."

Bonaventura walked over and stood in front of the jury. He was brief and to the point. He spoke without notes and looked at the jury, rotating his head so he could make eye contact with each juror.

"There is a criminal statute on the books and Mr. Matsumoto admitted violating it. He confessed on the witness stand. He has convicted himself out of his own mouth. It's as simple as that. Despite what you have heard about his background and his professed loyalty, you must, under these facts and the law that will be given to you by the judge, return a verdict of guilty. The issue here is not his character."

He paused and looked at each juror to make sure they understood, then continued. "It is whether he disobeyed orders to observe a curfew and report for relocation. He admitted he disobeyed both. You have no choice but to convict. Thank you." Bonaventura sat down and folded his arms in front of him suggesting he might not be as confident in the outcome as his argument would imply.

Jean-Claude had to be careful how he phrased his argument. Asking for the jury to disregard the judge's instructions and to vote their conscience was asking them to ignore the law. The judge would not allow it.

"Mr. Bonnay, you may give your summation."

Jean-Claude rose from his chair and slowly walked over and stood in front of the jury. He tried to make eye contact with each one before he began. He wanted every non-verbal, as well as verbal, communication to convey his sincere belief in what he was about to say. He spoke without notes.

He started innocently enough. "Gentlemen of the jury, you

have honored us by your service today in one of the most important cases to be tried in this or any other court in recent memory. You have been asked to serve during one of the most trying times in our history when our land has been attacked and our soldiers and sailors killed. It is a time where passions are running high. It is a time when we are all frightened and uncertain about the future. It is just such a time when you as a juror are called upon to render your highest service. You are asked to put aside your fears and prejudices, your preconceived notions about race or national origin, and render a true and just verdict." He paused and looked at each juror before continuing. "A true verdict is one that will allow you to go home after your service and find peace in what you did. You must be willing to say that if a loved one of yours were on trial, you would feel that a juror who reached your decision did the right thing."

Jean-Claude argued with intensity, but devoid of theatrics. He wanted the jury to understand he had a deep belief in what he was saying.

The jurors appeared to listen intently.

"You, the jury," he said, moving his finger so he pointed to each one individually, "are the last defense against a government that enacts laws that are unjust. The right to trial by jury does not exist in other countries and will undoubtedly not exist in this country if our enemies abroad are victorious. But an unjust verdict rendered out of fear is not one that serves to protect our freedoms. It is one step toward eroding them."

He turned and glanced in Ken's direction. "My client is a loyal citizen. He has stood by his principles. He has challenged this law because he believes it is wrong. He did what he thought was right, now he expects you to do the same. I trust you will." He paused and glanced once more at each juror. "Thank you," he said and sat down.

Bonaventura waived rebuttal. His decision was designed to show the jury he had total confidence in his case.

Had Ken's testimony turned the jury or at least one juror in his favor? Doubtful, but he hoped Ken's presence as a witness personalized him so that at time of sentencing the judge might be given to lenient treatment. Had he done enough to convince the jury to do the right thing?

In his instructions to the jury, Judge Clayton told them that the evidence was clear and uncontroverted. The defendant had admitted his guilt therefore there was no issue for them to decide, and they must return a guilty verdict. Jean-Claude knew this was coming, but it was still hard to hear. He had put his heart and soul into his final argument.

The jury went out at 1:00 p.m. By 3:00, they had not come back with a verdict. Jean-Claude's hopes were rising. Could there be at least one juror who did not want to convict? The verdict had to be unanimous. At 3:10 p.m., the jury sent word they had reached a verdict. They filed into the courtroom looking serious and tired.

"Mr. Foreman, have you reached a verdict?" Judge Clayton asked.

"We have, Your Honor."

"Hand the verdict form to my bailiff."

The bailiff took the verdict form from the foreman and handed it to the judge. He looked at it with no expression and handed it to his clerk.

"Madam Clerk," the judge said, "you may read the verdict."

The clerk read from the verdict form. "As to count one, disobeying an order for curfew, we find the defendant guilty. As to count two, refusal to report for relocation, we find the defendant guilty."

"So say you all?" the judge asked.

All the jurors nodded in the affirmative.

It was over. They had lost.

The jury filed out of the courtroom. None of them were smiling. One of them gave Ken a nod. He probably had been the hold-out.

Once the jury was out of the courtroom, Judge Clayton looked at Jean-Claude and Ken. Jean-Claude thought he detected some compassion in his face. It was probably just wishful thinking. He felt the hammer was about to fall.

"I am prepared to proceed to sentencing at this time." The Judge still had no expression on his face or tone in his voice. He looked at Ken. Ken rose to receive his sentence. Jean-Claude stood by his side. After an agonizing pause the judge said, while still maintaining his stern demeanor, "I sentence you to thirty days in federal prison with credit for the ten days you have already served. I will suspend the balance of the time pending a final determination of an appeal. Counsel, I expect you are going to appeal. This case certainly presents issues of significant constitutional importance. I will set bail on appeal at $2,500. Can the defendant make bail?"

Bail on appeal? Unbelievable. You old bastard. You do have a conscience. Jean-Claude couldn't believe what he was hearing, but immediately responded.

"Yes, yes, Your Honor, I have that amount in a trust account and can post it by 9:00 tomorrow morning," Jean-Claude said, ecstatic over the unexpected turn of events. He looked at Ken, who was also smiling broadly.

Bonaventura stood and began to object to the setting of bail and then for reasons that would soon become apparent sat down and remained silent.

"Very well. Bail must be posted with the clerk by 9:00 a.m. tomorrow. In the interim, the defendant is released from custody."

Jean-Claude gave Ken a hug. There was no automatic right to bail on appeal, and in a case where danger to the community was a major issue in setting bail it was a sure indication the judge had been convinced of Ken's loyalty.

This was a big victory. It meant he could stay out until the appeal had run its course, which could take many months or years. Jean-Claude began putting his papers in his brief case while Ken walked over to Stephanie, who was sitting behind them, to give her a hug.

Before he got to Stephanie, a uniformed MP approached Ken and commanded, "I have orders to take you into military custody. Turn around and put your hands behind your back."

Jean-Claude turned abruptly and confronted the military policeman. "The hell you are. This man has just been released on bail by a federal judge. You have no authority to do this," Jean-Claude said vehemently and glared at the MP.

Judge Clayton, who was starting to walk off the bench, also heard the MP and stopped in his tracks.

"I have my orders. He is not to walk out of this courtroom." The MP glared back him. "I am to take him into custody and deliver him to the nearest relocation center. And if you don't get out of the way, I will arrest you too." He put his hand on the butt of his service revolver holstered on his side.

The rule of law was now face to face with the butt of a gun.

Judge Clayton stood at the bench, raised his arms as if to protest, and opened his mouth to speak, but fell silent as both he and Jean-Claude watched the raw exercise of military power play out before them.

It was the imposition of martial law in a civil courtroom, exactly what the Supreme Court in *Milligan* held was unconstitutional. Judge Clayton could have summoned the U.S. marshals to confront the MP, but instead Clayton, a United States District Court Judge who had exercised total control over his courtroom during the entire proceedings, did nothing. He just turned and walked slowly off the bench. He was either unsure where the balance of power lay between his order and the military's, or he didn't want a violent confrontation in his courtroom. Whatever the reason, it was clear to Jean-Claude he was not going to intervene.

Ken was not going home. He was going to Tanforan.

Jean-Claude followed them out of the courtroom, yelling to the MP that he was violating an order of a federal judge and could be held in contempt. The MP ignored him.

In front of the courthouse a military police van was parked with its motor running. They were pretty rough when they loaded Ken into the back. Jean-Claude caught a glimpse of Ken sitting on the bench in handcuffs. He looked frightened. The

MP slammed the door and the van drove off.

Jean-Claude found out later they took Ken to the Presidio and then to Tanforan to await transport to Manzanar.

Jean-Claude could only watch with clenched fists and a rage that burned deep inside. What was happening in Europe had just happened here in America. He grasped Stephanie's hand and they walked slowly to his car. Both their hands were ice cold.

The state of justice in America was in deep trouble and Jean-Claude was helpless to do anything about it. The law had lost and the gun had won.

CHAPTER 14

PREPARING TO LEAVE

October 1942

Jean-Claude could do nothing more to help Ken and his family. The ACLU agreed to do the appeal. While he still didn't trust them completely, the lawyers at the ACLU were far more experienced in appellate work than he was.

Now he had to make a decision. Would he go to France on his own, accept General Scott's offer to enlist and go back as a spy, or stay home where his survival would be ensured? He needed to talk to Stanley. He never made big decisions without talking to Stanley.

He arrived at his chambers in the late afternoon, the time he usually stopped by. Fortunately, he was alone, so they could talk.

"You heard what happened in the Matsumoto trial?" Jean-Claude asked as he settled down in a chair and lit a cigarette.

"I heard Nazi storm troopers came and snatched your guy while the judge just stood there with his balls hanging out and did nothing." Stanley had a way of putting things in colorful, but accurate, ways.

"That's essentially what happened." He shook his head. "It was the worst moment I have ever had in a courtroom. I felt powerless. I was powerless. The guy had a gun. Words and laws don't count when the other guy has a gun."

"That's exactly right. That's why they have to be stopped."

"So I need your advice. Do I go back to France on my own or in the military as a spy? Or do I stay here and sit it out?"

Stanley didn't hesitate. "You don't have a choice. You have to go."

"What do you mean I don't have a choice?" Jean-Claude said, growing defensive. "I could go over there and find out my father's dead, and it would have all been for nothing."

"For nothing?" Stanley roared. "Listen *shmuck*, you're a Jew. They're out there trying to exterminate us." He slammed his fist on his desk and glared at Jean-Claude. "Those bastards have to be stopped and sitting on your ass here isn't going to get the job done. Join the army. You go to France. Go find your father. Go save some Jews. Be a *mensch*!"

Jean-Claude was taken aback by Stanley's forcefulness. He needed a moment to digest what his friend had said. "Stanley, I could get killed or worse," Jean-Claude said, his cowardly side taking over.

"Everybody's gonna die someday. When you have a choice as to how to die and one of the choices can make a difference in the way this war ends, you take it."

Jean-Claude paused. They continued to stare at each other.

"Here, look at this." Stanley handed him a recent newspaper article.

Jean-Claude began to read. "'Odessa, Ukraine. 19,582 Jews, most of them women, children and old people were deported to concentration camps near Balta. They were sent to the camps in cattle trucks. Those who died were taken off, their corpses piled in heaps, petrol poured over them, and the bodies burned before the eyes of their families. Eyewitnesses recalled that among those burned on the pyres were several who were not yet dead.'"

He finished the article and raised his eyes from the paper and glanced at Stanley, whose eyes were bloodshot, the stress having taken its toll.

"The military option is the best," Stanley said. "You'd never survive on your own. With some training and backup you stand a better chance."

"I don't know where you got your knowledge about survival training but it amazes me. Thanks for the advice as always. If I get killed, I'll blame you."

"Look, there has never been a time like this. The Nazis are coming at us from one side, the Japs from the other. We're on the brink. The world will never be the same if either of them wins." He paused and lowered his voice. "I don't want you to die. I just want you to do something to stop the bastards."

Jean-Claude bowed his head. "I know. I don't want to die either, or leave Stephanie." He paused then raised his eyes, looked directly at Stanley, and in a clear, decisive voice said, "You're right, I have to do something. I'll call Scott in the morning."

"You done good. I'm proud of you," Stanley said as he stuck out his hand to invite a handshake to seal the deal.

Jean-Claude looked directly at Stanley, nodded, shook his hand, then got up. "I've got to get back to the office. Thanks for the advice. I don't look forward to the prospects but I know it's the right thing to do." They said good-bye and he left.

On the drive back to his office he thought about the decision he'd made. There were many times in his life where he had made decisions because they were in his self-interest. Selfish decisions. But he also had a side that made him do the right thing. That's why he took on Ken's defense. That's why he wanted to go to France and find his father. That's why he would do what he could to defeat the Nazis.

Now he had to tell Stephanie he was really leaving. That would be difficult but it had to be done. It couldn't be put off. He would tell her soon but first he had to talk to Scott.

The next day he called. "General, this is Jean-Claude."

"Jean-Claude, it's been so long, I thought you might have decided against enlisting." The General was obviously happy to hear from him.

"I'm sorry it has taken me this long to get back to you. I had my hands full with the defense of the Japanese friend of mine. It lasted much longer than I expected." He took a deep breath. "But it's over now and I'm ready to sign up if the opportunity is still there. Have you heard anything about my father?"

"No. Unfortunately. I've not been able to get any information. I would have called you if I had." The general sounded tired. "I know this: if something had happened to him, we would have heard about it."

"Well, that's some consolation," Jean-Claude said, although he didn't feel it. "Is your offer still open?"

"A lot has happened since we last spoke. The OSS is now fully operational and is sending operatives into occupied countries. So if you are still interested, I can arrange for your enlistment at the Presidio and then I'm pretty sure, given your fluency in French and German and familiarity with the area, I can get you into an OSS unit." The general paused to see if Jean-Claude wanted to comment on what he'd just said. There was silence so the general continued. "You remember I asked you how you felt about going back out of uniform. No protections of the Geneva Convention. You could be shot or worse if you were captured, but it's the only way to get you into France now, absent going by yourself, which is not a good idea."

"I'm still interested and I want to get going just as soon as possible, but I need about six weeks to wrap things up. Is that okay?"

"I'm glad. Knowing you are Bernard's son, I had little doubt as to what you would do. The six weeks is fine. I'll send you the name of the person to contact at the Presidio to arrange enlistment. Call him when you're ready to go."

"Thanks, General."

"Great to hear from you, Jean-Claude. Glad you decided to serve. You'll be a valuable asset."

Jean-Claude sat back and lit a cigarette. There was no turning back now. The thought of what could happen to him made him anxious, but at the same time, he felt a rush of excitement. Stanley was right, this was a time when you had to put it all on the line. There would be no second chance.

He picked up the phone and called Stephanie. He wanted to make sure they were getting together that night. He had something important to discuss with her. They agreed to meet for dinner.

CHAPTER 15

AN INTIMATE EVENING

November 1942

"What do you have here?" Stephanie looked at the bottle of champagne he had with him. "Your father is going to be very upset." She smiled. "Are we having a celebration?"

"I just need to unwind." He knew when he told Stephanie he was really leaving, it was going to be a stressful night, and he would need some fortification.

"That's a mighty fancy way to unwind," she said as they sat down for dinner.

They hardly said a word to each other during dinner. "You're awfully quiet tonight. Still thinking about the trial?"

"Something else is bothering me." He lit a cigarette. He no longer asked permission although he knew it bothered her to see him smoke. "Remember Lewis, the kid I defended in the trial where you were a witness?" Stephanie nodded. "I learned several weeks ago he'd been arrested again for the same thing, a purse snatch. This time he confessed."

"That's awful," she said, appearing shocked.

"I didn't want to bring it up while I was in trial because I didn't want it to be a distraction. But now I need to know. Were you being truthful when you said he wasn't the one who stole the purse?"

She bristled. "I didn't lie. I really believed I had made a mistake." She sounded earnest. He wanted to believe her so he decided to let it go even though his doubts persisted. If he pursued the subject, the evening would end badly and he had more important things he wanted to talk about. "I'm glad," he said as he took another sip of champagne, happy to move on.

"I have something I have to tell you." They got up from the dinner table and moved into the living room, taking what was left of the champagne. "I called Randy Scott today and asked for his advice. He told me my best chance to find my father was to enlist and he would try to get me in an intelligence unit. They would send me back to Lyon posing as a civilian to gather intelligence."

"They want you to be a spy? That's crazy. They shoot spies." She took a deep breath and her eyes softened, filled with concern. "Are you going to do it?"

"I said yes. I told him I needed about six weeks. I know there's risk, but it's something I have to do."

She frowned. There was a long period of tense silence. Stephanie took another sip of champagne, as did Jean-Claude, each probably waiting to see who would speak first.

Jean-Claude shifted his weight in his chair, and lit another cigarette. Stephanie set her glass down and spoke first. "I knew this was going to happen sooner or later," she said with an edge to her voice. She handed him the ashtray. "Try not to spill ashes on the rug." Her voice had a tinge of irritation in it. "Don't you want to stay around and see what happens with the appeal?"

"It's best the ACLU does it," he said. "They have the experience and I don't want to wait. It could take over a year. I want to get to France as soon as possible."

She stood up and moved closer to the fireplace, putting

distance between them.

"Stephanie, this is something I have to do," he said. "If you say you want to end this now because I'll be leaving and don't want to get married, I'll understand." He forced the words, hoping she would say that wasn't what she wanted.

Instead she began to cry—an angry, frustrated cry. "You are so selfish, Jean-Claude. You say you don't want to marry me because you are going off to France. I don't believe you."

Her emotional outburst surprised Jean-Claude. He knew she would be upset, but the accusation came as a shock.

"You don't want to get married because you can't make a commitment. You're afraid of commitment because you don't want to get hurt, but you're really only hurting yourself. You rarely show your feelings to me or anybody else. You can be cold as ice." Tears were welling up in her eyes. "You never cry. Even at the train station when the Matsumotos were being sent off to a concentration camp you showed no emotion."

She had been angry before, especially when they had argued about getting married. But she'd never been this hostile. She'd never accused him of being cold or not showing his feelings or being afraid of commitment.

"I felt a lot of emotion at the train station. I just didn't show it. I told you why I never cry the first night we spent together. That's the way I've always been," he said. "I can't help it. That's the way I am."

There was a pause as they stared at each other. He put out his cigarette, got up from his chair, and walked over to her. He put his arms around her and held her tight. He feared he was losing her.

At that moment an emotional dam broke. All the feelings that had built up seemed to explode—the anger and helplessness he felt watching Ken being taken out of the courtroom in handcuffs, Ken's family being loaded onto a train like cattle, the fear that his father might already be dead, and the thought of losing her. It all came out as he held her. "I love you. I really do love you," he whispered in a voice she had never heard before. For the first time she felt he really meant it.

"I love you too." She sobbed, obviously sensing the change in him. "I want to spend all the time I can with you before you have to go."

Just then the air raid sirens sounded. "I better pull down the shades," she said, regaining some of her composure. "Give me a hand."

"Sure, but it's getting late. I'd better go." He used the sirens as an excuse to leave so he wouldn't have to deal with the emotional pain he was feeling.

"It's dangerous out there. That's why they sound the sirens." She sounded serious.

"No, it's not," Jean-Claude said. "It's just a drill. It's perfectly safe." Given the exchange that had just taken place between them, he was slow to get the significance of what she'd said.

"I don't think so," she said, gazing directly at him, a slight smile at the corners of her mouth. "You'd better stay the night."

For a second he didn't get it, but then he did. He didn't hesitate. "You're right. It's pretty dangerous out there."

"I'll be right back," she said as she walked down the hall toward the bedroom.

When he realized what might happen, old insecurities kicked in. He began to get nervous over the thought of having sex. The first time he was with a woman he would sometimes get overly excited and finish too soon, leaving his partner unsatisfied and frustrated. It was humiliating.

Stephanie came into the living room wearing a long silk nightgown. It was open at the neck showing quite a bit of cleavage. She took his hand and led him into the bedroom. They stood at the foot of the bed and kissed. She unbuttoned his shirt and took it off. Then loosened his belt and undid the top button of his trousers. She unzipped his fly and let his pants fall to his ankles. She then reached for him and began to fondle him. He was hard. He knew if she kept it up much longer the evening would be over.

"Let me go first," he said, gently loosening the sash on her nightgown.

She smiled in response.

He slipped the silky nightgown from her shoulders. She looked beautiful in the light of a candle she had lit. He gently laid her on her back across the bed and lay down beside her. The faint scent of lavender seemed to surround her body.

He stroked her hair and kissed the nape of her neck. "You are so beautiful," he gently whispered in her ear. He caressed her breasts and fondled her nipples while they kissed. Her breathing grew heavy, and she began to softly moan.

He kissed her nipples as he moved his hand up her leg and slowly began to stroke her inner thigh. He then began to massage her in the place he had learned to touch. She cried out with pleasure when he went down on her. As she grew more passionate she grabbed his hair and pulled him up.

"Take me, Jean-Claude. Take me now."

He lifted himself on top of her and went inside. He began to thrust.

"Harder, Jean-Claude, harder," she cried as she moved her body in rhythm with his.

After only a few thrusts, he came. *Oh God. Too soon.*

There was a long pause while they held each other. It seemed like an eternity waiting for her to say something.

"That was wonderful," she finally said, still a little out of breath. "So intense."

They continued to hold each other for another minute until she said, "I'll be right back." She jumped out of the bed and hurried into the bathroom.

He felt relief. Perhaps it was okay, even though it was over quickly, or perhaps she was just being nice. Usually he could tell. She seemed sincere, but the test would be if there was going to be a next time. One thing he now knew for sure, given her body language, she was not a virgin.

It had all happened so fast he'd never considered using protection or withdrawing. But now it was too late. He grew concerned.

"Stephanie, are you okay? I mean, do you think you might get pregnant?" He called out to her while she was still in the bathroom.

"No, I know my cycle," she called back, "and I am very careful. I am safe at least for the next week or so. Now is the time I could use a good French bathroom, though."

She came back into the room and lay down beside him. "Aren't you going to light up? That's what men usually do after sex."

"Usually, but not tonight," he said and looked at her. She was so very beautiful. "I don't want to change a thing. Not the smell or the light. It's perfect and I want to keep it that way."

"I felt your love tonight. I felt you really cared about me," she said as she stroked his hair.

He felt relieved. She seemed satisfied with the emotional connection. Whether that carried over to the sexual experience remained to be seen.

"Want a brandy? It's better than a cigarette," she said as she kissed him on the cheek and went to pour them a drink.

"Sure."

They both slept well that night. Champagne, brandy, and sex were a good combination. The thought of leaving for France was far from his mind as he fell asleep, but it was one of the first things he thought about when he woke up. There was no escaping the fact that things were going to change and change rapidly. Where that was going to leave their relationship was very much in doubt.

CHAPTER 16

SIGNING UP

November 1942

There was much to do in six weeks. He had several pending cases to resolve, he had to rent the house, and he wanted to visit the Matsumotos in Manzanar to say good-bye. Ken was there now, having spent less than a week at Tanforan.

His office partner, Irving Stern, said he would keep his office, and even though Jean-Claude offered to pay the rent, Stern adamantly refused. "That's the least I can do for somebody who's going off to fight the Nazis," he'd told Jean-Claude.

Jean-Claude contacted the university to see if there were any professors who might want to rent a large house on a long-term basis. An English professor and his wife and three children were looking for a larger home. Jean-Claude made the rent attractive. It was better to have the place cared for by a good tenant than to get maximum rent. The only stipulation was that the rent did not include access to the wine cellar. They said they had no intention of leaving Berkeley and would be glad to rent the house until he got back. He left the Buick with a former client with the same warning as to what would happen to him if he sold it.

All that took four weeks. The only thing remaining was signing up and a visit to Manzanar to say good-bye to the Matsumotos.

With some trepidation, Jean-Claude called the contact at the Presidio he had been given by General Scott. He knew once he enlisted there would be no turning back.

"Fifth Infantry Battalion, Staff Sergeant Anthony Rizzuto speaking. How can I help you, sir?"

"Sergeant, this is Jean-Claude Bonnay. I was given this number by General Randolph Scott and told to call."

"Yes, sir. I've been expecting your call. When would you like to come over?"

"Is the day after tomorrow too soon?"

"No, sir. We're open for business every day of the week including Sundays and holidays. I'll arrange to have you inducted when you arrive. It will take a few days to get you situated and get your orders. In the meantime, you can use the time to clean up your personal business. No telling when you might get back."

That was a reality check.

"Thank you, Sergeant. I will see you the day after tomorrow."

Jean-Claude hung up the phone feeling both exhilarated and anxious. He had difficulty getting to sleep that night.

The reality of what lay ahead finally hit him. He was going back to France with all of the unknowns that involved. He was leaving Stephanie and his law practice. He was putting his life at risk. It was overwhelming.

Two days later, Jean-Claude arrived at the Presidio and was directed to Sergeant Rizzuto's barracks. The sergeant was waiting for him.

"Hello, sir. Glad to meet you." The young sergeant saluted. Jean-Claude, not knowing how to respond, saluted back, guessing that was the proper thing to do.

"Nice to meet you too, Sergeant."

"Sir, I have been instructed to bring you over to post headquarters to see Colonel Williams. He's the post commander, second in command to General DeWitt. He said he wanted to meet you, probably because of your relationship with General Scott."

Jean-Claude followed the sergeant to the building that housed command headquarters at the Presidio.

Jean-Claude thought he might be treated differently than other enlistees due to his relationship with Randy Scott. He reminded himself he was nobody special and should act like any other recruit. He just happened to know a general who agreed to help him enlist. He was prepared for special treatment, but not the kind he received.

The colonel sat behind a large desk. He was in his fifties, obviously career military, heavily decorated, thin, and unsmiling. He didn't get up to greet him. Jean-Claude saluted even though he hadn't yet been sworn in, nor was he in uniform. Based upon his experience with Sergeant Rizzuto he guessed that must be the right thing to do.

The colonel did not respond. The expression on his face grew colder. "Sit down," he commanded in an icy voice.

"Yes, sir."

"You don't have to salute or address me as sir. You're still a civilian."

"Yes, sir, I understand that. I did it out of respect."

"Do you have respect for the military, Mr. Bonnay?"

The question took him by surprise. "Yes, sir, I do."

"Then why did you represent a Jap who refused to report for relocation?"

Jean-Claude thought for only a second. "Because I'm a lawyer and I was asked to defend him," he said with a bite to his voice.

"You didn't have to defend him. You wanted to defend him. Am I right?"

"That's correct. I did want to represent him. And I would do it again," he said and folded his arms across his chest as if to ward off the verbal assault.

"So do you consider that to be something a loyal American would do?"

"I resent you questioning my loyalty." He fought back his defiance. "I believed the order to put over 110,000 Japanese in camps was unlawful. I still feel that way. I believe what I did was an ultimate act of loyalty."

"You believe that was an act of loyalty to your country?"

"Yes, and to the Constitution." Jean-Claude unfolded his arms and leaned forward in his chair and looked directly at the colonel.

"You French are all alike," the colonel said with contempt. "You can't be trusted."

"That statement doesn't say much for your judgment," Jean-Claude snapped and immediately hoped he still maintained the protection of civilian status.

The colonel's face turned bright red. "I don't think we need men like you in the army and General DeWitt agrees. The judge in your case was angry about what happened in his courtroom and he let the powers in Washington know about it. It made for a difficult time for General DeWitt."

"I'm sorry for the general's inconvenience," Jean-Claude said in mock sincerity. "It was more of an inconvenience to Mr. Matsumoto to be handcuffed, put in the back of a van, and taken to Tanforan to live in a horse stall before being sent to a concentration camp. I'm glad the judge complained. I hope it will prevent something like that from ever happening again." Jean-Claude wasn't going to back down, even in a confrontation with the post commander on his first day in the service.

They stared at each other before the colonel broke the silence. "If you carried on like that while on active duty, I would've had you court-martialed. But you aren't, and I have my orders. You are to report for swearing in to Building G. Sergeant Rizzuto will take you over. You're dismissed."

Jean-Claude turned and walked out without acknowledging the colonel. He had saluted when he walked in, now he just turned his back side to the colonel and walked out. He felt that was enough to demonstrate how he felt about what had just taken place.

Rizzuto was waiting for him in the outer office, and became concerned when he saw the look on Jean-Claude's face.

"How did it go?"

"I'll tell you when we get back to your office," Jean-Claude said in a hushed voice.

As soon as they arrived back in Rizzuto's office, he asked again in an anxious voice, "So, what happened?"

"I was lucky to get out of the colonel's office alive."

"What did you do to piss him off?"

"I'm a lawyer. I defended that Japanese fellow who refused to relocate to one of the camps."

"You were his lawyer?" Rizzuto said with awe.

"You still want to take me over to get sworn in?"

"Yes, sir, I do. My parents are from the old country. Italy. There were rumors they were going to put Italians in camps. They called 'em enemy aliens. They said it's not going to happen now. But for a while they were really scared. So was I. Joe DiMaggio's father's been fishing around here for years. They won't let him go out in his boat anymore. Can you believe that? Joe DiMaggio's father. If they try to put Joltin' Joe in the camps, they're gonna have a revolution on their hands."

"I'm glad you know how it feels," Jean-Claude said to his unexpected ally.

"Yes, sir. I do. I hate Japs, but that don't mean those livin' here are all bad. Puttin' all of 'em in camps ain't fair but in a way they're lucky."

"How's that?" Jean-Claude wanting to understand what Rizzuto meant.

"Me, I got relatives all over Sicily. If they send me over there I'm likely to end up fightin' my cousins, or uncles. I love this country, but I sure don't want to have to fight any of my relatives. Your Jap friend don't have to worry about killin' any of his own people if he's locked up."

"I hadn't ever thought about that. I have relatives in France but most of them are Jewish so I don't think I'll have the same problem." Jean-Claude's quip was spontaneous and it surprised him how open he was about disclosing his Jewish heritage. He was finally coming to terms with the fact he was a Jew. Stanley would be proud.

"You a Jew?" Rizzuto asked somewhat shocked.

"My mother was Jewish but I was raised a Catholic," he freely acknowledged.

"You better take your rosary beads with you if you get sent to Europe. I hear they don't like Jews too much over there. By the way, you've been commissioned as a second lieutenant. How did you swing that?" Rizzuto asked.

"I have no idea. I'm sure it's the invisible hand of the general. It certainly didn't come from these guys."

Several hours later, Jean-Claude was sworn in with about a dozen others. Some draftees, some volunteers. They led him to the infirmary where he was given a physical. "Stick your tongue out, spread your cheeks, cough. You're okay. Next." Then to the quartermaster to get fitted with uniforms and gear. Then he was done. He'd walked in as a civilian and left as a second lieutenant.

Jean-Claude drove off the Presidio grounds. He had been given orders to go to the Alameda Air Station where he would catch a hop to Washington. He had five days before he had to report. He realized he no longer held his fate in his hands. It was an unsettling feeling.

CHAPTER 17

SAYING GOOD-BYE

December 1942

"Look at those mountains, Jean-Claude," Stephanie said. "Aren't they beautiful?" They were driving through the Owens Valley heading to Manzanar, the detention facility 230 miles northeast of Los Angeles where the Matsumoto family now made their home.

The mountains were magnificent, but the valley floor was desolate, barren, with little more growing than sagebrush. It was hot and dusty in the summer and now, in December, it was bitter cold. Manzanar means apple orchard in Spanish. Once the area had been fertile ground for agriculture, until the twenties, when Los Angeles diverted the water that fueled its growth. Then it became a wasteland.

As they approached the entrance to the camp, Jean-Claude knew immediately he was entering a prison. He had been to many. The camp looked like those low-level security camps in the county jail system, but was much larger. There were guard towers stationed at regular intervals around the perimeter fence of barbed wire. MPs with M-1s patrolled the streets. Guards in the towers were armed with machine guns.

The barracks appeared new and had been hastily built to accommodate 10,000 people. They were laid out in orderly rows against the backdrop of the majestic 14,000-foot Mt. Williamson. The location of the camp was at the base of the mountain that stood as both a real and symbolic barrier to escape.

A uniformed soldier greeted them at the gate and saluted Jean-Claude since he was in uniform. "Sir, how can I help you?"

"We came to see the Matsumoto family. I have made arrangements with the camp commander to meet with them."

"You said the name was Matsumoto?"

"Yes, that's correct."

"And your name?"

"Bonnay, Jean-Claude Bonnay. Lt. Jean-Claude Bonnay." He was not used to the title. He pointed to Stephanie. "This is my friend, Stephanie Stevenson."

"Yes, sir," the soldier said, looking at a chart. "I have you cleared for a visit. Go straight ahead and take the second left. It will take you to the administration building. They will call for them when you get there."

Jean-Claude nodded and drove on, following the guard's directions.

"Jean-Claude, this place gives me the creeps," Stephanie said, glancing around. "It's so desolate."

"And confining. Did he say to take the second left?"

"Yes. There, I think." She pointed to one of the many nondescript buildings similar in construction to the barracks except it had two stories and a sign on the outside that read "Administration."

They entered the building and identified themselves to the soldier at the desk, who had saluted Jean-Claude as they walked in. They were ushered into a conference room with a long table and chairs on both sides. They waited about thirty minutes. It was cold and drafty. Finally, the door opened and Ken Matsumoto walked in. He was thinner and his face was pale.

When he saw Jean-Claude in uniform he looked shocked, then frowned. No hug. No handshake. He remained standing. "So you're going off to war to fight for freedom and justice. Congratulations. Maybe you'll have better success overseas than we had in court." His voice was cold like the weather outside.

"That's no way to greet a friend. You sound bitter and you look like you've lost some weight," Jean-Claude said, taken aback by the reception and the way Ken looked. Ken hadn't even acknowledged Stephanie when he'd entered the room.

Ken remained standing, waving his arms as he spoke in an irate voice. "If you had to eat the garbage they serve here, you'd lose weight too. And who wouldn't be bitter?" He gestured at the bare wooden walls. "You should take a tour of this place. It's not a camp. It's a goddamned prison.

"There's no privacy." He shook his head. "My mother is humiliated. She has to sit on a pot in a room with twelve other women and there's usually no toilet paper. Families who are not related to each other have to share a room. It's boiling hot in the summer, and now it's freezing. And the wind. The wind blows dust into the rooms between the floorboards and through the knotholes in these flimsy walls. These tarpaper shacks have just been thrown together. To say they offend my architectural sensitivities would be an understatement. They're crap. They're chicken coops." Ken paced as he continued his rant.

When Ken stopped, Jean-Claude waited for a moment searching for the words to get their friendship back on track. "So what are you going to do? Maybe you should re-up, try to get your commission back. That would get you out of here."

Ken looked at him defiantly. "So I should go fight a war for a country that locks me and my family up without giving us a chance to defend ourselves?"

He paused and looked at Jean-Claude's uniform. "How'd you get those bars on your shoulders? You were never in the reserves. A reward for being a lawyer?"

"No, it came as a surprise." Jean-Claude spoke calmly. "I'm sure General Scott had something to do with it. They think I may have some special skill because I speak French and German and know parts of France pretty well. Joining up was the best way to get there so I might find Bernard. They are talking about dropping me in France in civilian clothes to gather intelligence."

"You're going to be a spy?" Ken looked incredulous, and almost laughed. "They shoot spies."

"That's what I said," Stephanie chimed in, obviously tired of being ignored.

Jean-Claude just shrugged. "Hey, it's a free ticket back to France. I couldn't turn it down." He then quickly changed the subject. "How's your family? Are they going to come over so we can say good-bye?"

"No. They are too ashamed. They're just surviving. My father is still depressed. They have stripped him of his pride. He has a menial job. Fortunately, they let him do his bonsais. My mother and sisters feel ashamed. They think they must have done something wrong to deserve this. They don't want to see you under these conditions." His testy attitude had returned.

"So what are you going to do?" Jean-Claude asked again.

Ken shook his head as he finally sat down across from Jean-Claude and Stephanie. "I haven't decided. I hate this place. Maybe I will try to re-up. Anything may become preferable to staying here." He turned to Stephanie. "You two married yet?" It was the first time he'd acknowledged her.

Stephanie's face turned red. Marriage was still a very sensitive subject and Ken had hit a nerve. "Hello, Ken. Thanks for saying hello," she said with a twinge of sarcasm. "Someday, maybe. Jean-Claude says things are too unsettled right now to make any long-range plans."

"Well, I have long-range plans. I've got to get back to designing a baseball field. I have to have it ready for spring training." Despite his attempt at humor, Ken obviously felt uncomfortable and wanted to leave. The meeting was clearly very painful for him.

"Ken, tell your father the house is still rented, and Irving Stern is collecting rent and putting it in a trust account in your father's name. He also has the rest of the money you gave me for your case. There are a few broken windows in the greenhouse, but it's still in one piece. Tell them it will all be waiting for them when they return. Here's the contact person for the lawyer at the ACLU who is coordinating your appeal." Jean-Claude handed him an envelope. "There are three others who went to trial, and they are appealing also, so you have company."

Ken took the envelope and stared at it for a minute. It seemed to transport him back to the trial and the experience they had gone through together. Ken's mood softened. He looked at Jean-Claude, who could see the softening in his eyes. "Take care of yourself, Jean-Claude. If they send you to the Pacific and the Japs capture you, tell 'em you're a friend of mine." He smiled and stuck out his hand. "I'm sorry for the way I acted. I'm just very frustrated. I'll always remember what you did for me and my family. I hope we'll see each other again."

Jean-Claude shook his hand. The iron handshake had softened a bit. He gave Ken a hug.

"However it turns out, you will always be my friend."

Ken hugged him back. "I feel the same."

Their emotional bond that had existed for years was still there. No matter where their lives might take them, Jean-Claude knew they would always remain close.

Ken turned to Stephanie, gave her a hug, and then walked out of the room.

Stephanie and Jean-Claude got back in the car for the long drive to Berkeley, still affected by seeing Ken so bitter and learning of the shame felt by his father, mother, and sisters.

Much of the drive was spent in silence. The subject of marriage wasn't brought up nor was his imminent departure for France. They were emotionally drained and didn't want to deal with any more stress.

The next day, Jean-Claude had one more good-bye. It was to Stanley. Since the stairs in the courthouse were rarely used he decided to take them rather than use the elevators. He was proud to be in uniform, but in the courthouse where he was so well known, he would have drawn attention and provoked questions—questions he wanted to avoid. He also had something he wanted to leave with the judge, and it would have caused a stir had he been seen carrying it.

After peering through the window to make sure court wasn't in session, he walked into Department Nine.

"Well, hello, soldier boy," Julie said, obviously surprised to see him in uniform.

"I've come to say good-bye to Stanley." He paused. "And to you too."

"Well, thanks for the afterthought. You still owe me for keeping your raincoat." She then buzzed the judge.

A moment later the buzzer rang back and she told him to go on in.

Jean-Claude walked into Stanley's chambers, where he had been so many times before. However, this time he knew he wasn't coming back anytime soon.

Stanley sat behind his desk holding a cigarette. He looked Jean-Claude up and down. "That's a mighty fancy outfit. Bet it cost you a pretty penny," he said with a gleam in his eye.

"They actually gave it to me. All I had to do was raise my right hand and promise to give my life for my country. I leave the day after tomorrow, so I came to say good-bye."

"They gave you a tree instead of a gun?" he asked, seeing the small bonsai tree Jean-Claude held in his hands.

"This was given to me by Ken's father. It's a bonsai. He wanted me to have it. He said it would give me peace and keep me strong. I can't take it with me where I'm going. I want you to keep it. You should water it once a day as a reminder of how the justice system screwed the Japanese." He put the bonsai down on his desk and sat down across from the judge.

"How's about you also give me a Jap flag to hang on the wall above it? That would really send a message." He chuckled. "They could call me the Jap-loving Jewish Judge."

"Come on, Stanley. Somebody besides me has to take a stand. If it symbolized what was happening to the Jews, you would take it in a minute. Everybody looks up to you. While I'm gone you can be the voice that keeps reminding people what's happening to the Japanese is wrong."

Stanley paused for a moment. "Okay, but you have to remember what we talked about."

"What's that?"

Stanley leaned forward in his chair and the expression on his face grew serious. He spoke very deliberately. "You have to stop those Nazi bastards from killing Jews."

"Stanley, I will do what I can, but I'm only one person," Jean-Claude said.

"One man can make a difference. I've always told you that. You've got to try. You and the other young ones are all we've got."

Jean-Claude looked into the old judge's eyes. "I promise. If I get the chance, I'll personally kill Hitler. Or at least one of his henchmen." He smiled. The judge did not.

"Can't you do anything at your end?" Jean-Claude asked.

"It's disgusting. Jews here are afraid of an anti-Semitic backlash if they make too much noise. The government won't do anything because there's still a lot of anti-Semitism, and they want to keep the public behind the war effort. It has to be a war to save us all from the Nazis and the Japs, and not just to save the Jews." He looked resigned. "So, I sit here helpless. I can do nothing. I send money, but that's about all I can do. That's why it's up to you and the others." Stanley ground his cigarette in the ashtray and lit another.

"That is the same frustration I feel about what's happening to the Japanese," Jean-Claude said. "They're in camps, and there's nothing I can do about it. I just got back from seeing Ken. It's terrible." He shook his head, remembering Ken's anger. "It's worse than the county jail. He's pretty bitter. It was sad to see him like that."

Stanley nodded. "I told you. So what's with the appeal?"

"The ACLU is going to do it. It will take months, maybe years. I can't wait around and it's better they do it."

"They're gonna lose."

"You're such an optimist."

"I'm a realist. Even the Supreme Court will buckle, if it gets that far." Stanley never made a prediction without a tone of absolute certainty in his voice.

Jean-Claude wanted to stay longer, but there was no more to say. He didn't want to get maudlin or sentimental. "I've got to go. I'll write if I get the chance, but it's unlikely given where I'm going." He took a breath. "Stanley, now that I'm really going, I'm starting to feel a little more like a Jew."

"It's about time." Stanley laughed. "You'll need to brush up on your Yiddish. When they capture you and put you in the concentration camp with all those Jews, you will need Yiddish so you can communicate." Leave it to Stanley to end on a note like that.

Jean-Claude started for the door, then he stopped and smiled. "Ken's got me captured by the Japs and you have me in a concentration camp with the Jews. I have a lot to look forward to. Maybe I'll just get lucky and catch a bullet."

Stanley got up from behind his desk, walked over to Jean-Claude, and gave him a hug. He'd never shown that kind of physical affection before. "You'll be back. I know you'll be back." He looked him in the eye with that familiar air of certainty.

Jean-Claude nodded in appreciation. "Remember, water the bonsai once a day," he said as he turned to walk down the hallway to the elevator.

He wasn't thinking about people seeing him in uniform anymore. He just wanted to get out of the building as quickly as possible so he took the elevator. It wasn't Percy's elevator. He was glad because he had already said his last good-bye for the day, although he was somewhat disappointed he hadn't run into

Judge Kelly so he could tell him what he really thought of him. One thing about going away and not knowing if you were ever coming back, you could say the things you always wanted to say without any fear of consequences.

CHAPTER 18

STEPHANIE'S SURPRISE

December 1942

Stephanie drove Jean-Claude to the Alameda Naval Air Station. His orders said to report there by 0900 hours. When they arrived, it was almost nine.

"Well I guess this is it," Jean-Claude said, wanting to say good-bye in the car.

They had said their good-byes over and over the night before between lovemaking and her tears. Now, he just wanted to be gone. He still had trouble expressing his feelings, and saying good-bye for what might be the last time made him freeze up. Stephanie wouldn't hear of it. "Not until I walk you to the plane or get as close to it as I can."

They got out of the car. Jean-Claude slung his duffle bag over his shoulder. They walked slowly to the terminal hand in hand and went inside. He approached the ensign at one of the counters. "I'm Lieutenant Bonnay. I have orders to go to DC."

"Yes, sir. Can I see your paperwork?"

Jean-Claude handed him the orders he'd received at the Presidio.

"Sir, your flight is departing in twenty minutes. You can store your gear here, and I'll make sure it gets on the plane. The gate is right through that door. I'm sorry, miss, but that door is as far as you can go. Security."

They walked slowly to the departure door.

"I guess this is really it," he said.

She paused and looked into his eyes. "Jean-Claude, I have to tell you something." She hesitated and took a deep breath, then looked into his eyes. "I'm pregnant."

He stared at her, stunned. After a second to gather his thoughts he asked in a gentle, but frustrated voice, "How long have you known?"

"Several weeks," she said softly, lowering her eyes as if afraid of what might come next. "And you decide to tell me just as I'm getting ready to get on a plane?" He gripped the orders in his hand and almost ripped them. He sorted through a wave of emotions. Frustration. Anger. Guilt. He took a step back from her to put some distance between them and glared at her.

"See, I knew you would be upset. I was afraid if I told you sooner, you wouldn't want the baby. I want this baby so badly. It's something I can hold onto until you come back."

"And what if I don't come back? I leave you with a baby who has no father." His voice shook with anger.

"Then I will always have a part of you with me. But don't talk like that." She took a step toward him. He didn't move.

It was finally beginning to sink in. Shock and anger gave rise to concern. He was going to be a father. He'd gotten a girl pregnant and like it or not, there was only one honorable thing to do. Marry her. He put his arms around her and held her to him. "Are you all right?" he asked. "Do you have a good doctor? Are you going to stay in Oakland? Do you want to get married?" That last question tumbled out of his mouth.

"Yes, I have a good doctor. Yes, I want to marry you. But I don't want you to marry me to make an honest woman out of me."

He hesitated for a second. "You know I would have married you when I got back. This is just sooner than I expected." It was an honest answer, but one that didn't answer her question. She didn't care. He was offering to marry her now. That was what she wanted to hear. That was enough.

"I'm going back to Connecticut to stay with my parents. I'm leaving day after tomorrow. So we won't be too far apart, at least initially. Before you leave for France, I hope we can get married."

The ensign ran up to them. "Sir, your flight is about to take off."

"I'll call you when I get to Washington," he said as they let go of each other.

As he walked through the gate, he turned and waved to her. She waved back. "I love you," she called as he walked toward the plane.

"I love you too," he yelled back, but his voice was drowned out by the roar of the plane's engines.

Once on the plane he had a chance to think. She'd said she was always careful. She must have known she could get pregnant. Did she trap him into marriage? Did it really matter at this point? What's done is done. She was pregnant and he was the father. If he didn't come back there would be a part of him left behind. He laid his head back and thought about it for a while. Even with some of his doubts about her, even with the pregnancy, deep down he loved her.

He smiled at the thought of becoming a father. Now all he had to do was survive. That was the last thought he had before he fell asleep. When he woke up the plane was on its approach into Washington.

CHAPTER 19

WASHINGTON

The morning after Jean-Claude arrived in Washington, he took a taxi to the Pentagon for his meeting with General Scott. On the ride over, he thought about the treatment he'd received at the Presidio and it still perplexed him. He had made Scott aware of his defense of Ken Matsumoto and it didn't seem to bother him. Yet Colonel Wilson and General DeWitt were more than a little upset. Was it because he was receiving the royal treatment from top brass in Washington or because he had chosen to defend a Japanese? Or both?

It really didn't matter what they thought at the Presidio. He just hoped it wouldn't affect his relationship with Scott, or the plan to go to France. He trusted Scott. Still, in the back of his mind, he wondered what kind of reception he was going to get. He decided he would bring the subject up and get it out in the open so he would know exactly where he stood.

When he arrived for the meeting, Randy Scott greeted him warmly. He looked very imposing in his uniform with all of his service commendations and two stars on his epaulets.

Scott introduced him to another officer who was in the room. "Jean-Claude, this is Colonel Littleton. He's assigned to the Office of Strategic Services, the OSS, the unit I told you about."

Jean-Claude saluted. "Pleasure to meet you, sir."

"I'm afraid we've still had no contact with Bernard. We think he's in the Lyon area, but our sources have dried up."

Jean-Claude lowered his eyes, disappointed. "Thanks for continuing to try."

Scott returned to his desk. "I've briefed Colonel Littleton on your knowledge of France, particularly the area around Lyon, and your fluency in French and German. He feels you can be very valuable in gathering intelligence on the ground, but as I told you on the phone, it's dangerous work." Scott looked at him intently, apparently trying to gauge his reaction.

Jean-Claude nodded then got right to his concern. "Before we get too deep into this, General, I have to ask you if my defense of the Japanese American will have any effect on my service." He looked from one man to the other. "I told you about the case when we talked on the phone and didn't think it was a big deal until I got to the Presidio. Apparently the post commander and General DeWitt are pretty upset about it."

Scott and Littleton glanced at each other and smiled.

"We know all about what happened at the Presidio," Scott said. "We've discussed it and we don't feel it's a problem. We're 3,000 miles away, but those guys have to live with it every day. DeWitt is okay. He just wants to keep the coast safe and cover his ass. As for us, we just want to defeat the Nazis." He glanced at the colonel then back at Jean-Claude. "Having your eyes and ears on the ground is a start in that direction. Anyway, we are not bothered by what you did. Actually, we admire a man who fights for what he believes in."

"That's good to hear. Thank you." Jean-Claude felt relief and he started to relax. "Mind if I smoke?"

"Go ahead." The general lit up as well. "Colonel Littleton will brief you on what we have in mind."

Like Scott, Littleton was also an imposing figure physically with broad shoulders and a thick neck. Jean-Claude estimated he was in his forties. Tall and a bit overweight, he looked like he could more than hold his own in a fight.

He spoke in a soft but intense voice with a slight southern accent. "There is going to be an invasion of the continent at some point. We aren't there yet, but we are in the planning stages." He pulled out some maps and set them on a long table. The general and Jean-Claude moved in for a better look. "The decision has just been made that there will be two invasions, one in the north, either France or Holland, the other in the south, either France or Italy."

Jean-Claude nodded while studying the map.

"We need as much intelligence as we can get on the troop strength of the Germans in the south of France, from Lyon to Nice. One of our potential landing sites is here." Littleton pointed to the broad expanse of coast from Marseilles to Nice on the map.

He glanced at Jean-Claude. Jean-Claude didn't react. He continued to stare intently at the maps. "We can't completely trust the information we get from the Resistance because they're factionalized and rife with informers and Communists. We've dropped some agents from England in there, but they speak French with an English accent, which is somewhat of a giveaway. We need someone like you who knows the language and the country—someone who can pass as a native and not draw attention. Someone we can trust. Do you still speak French like a native?"

Jean-Claude nodded his head. "Even after we came to the States my father and I spoke mostly French around the house."

"What do you think?" Littleton had been observing Jean-Claude while he spoke. He was trying to get a sense of Jean-Claude's reaction to see if he was up to the task.

Jean-Claude didn't hesitate. "Yes, I'm fine with it, General. Finding Bernard is very important to me, but you know my mother was Jewish. The Nazis and the Vichy government are doing terrible things to the Jews. I want to do whatever I can to defeat them."

Scott cut in. "Your first obligation is to your mission. That will help defeat the Nazis. As for Bernard, we don't know exactly where he is. We will drop you in the vicinity of Lyon and make arrangements for you to meet up with members of the Resistance in the area. It is quite possible they will know where he is. But there are no guarantees."

"I understand, General. I'm concerned about being recognized. I left there when I was twelve and I don't think my face has changed that much."

"We've considered that," Littleton said. "We've discussed plastic surgery to alter your eyes and nose, but we feel there is a less intrusive way. We've taken your driver's license photo and had an artist draw your face with a short-cropped black beard, dark eyebrows, and black hair. Take a look." He pulled out the touched-up photo from his briefcase and showed it to Jean-Claude.

He took it and looked at the photo. Jean-Claude shook his head in disbelief that his appearance could be changed that drastically by just a beard and black hair. "I hardly recognize myself."

"If you're ever recognized, we will try to get you out right away."

"What if there's not time to get me out?" Jean-Claude asked, his stomach tightening over concern for his own safety.

"We have contingency plans that will give you some choices." Littleton didn't elaborate.

"What do you think?" the colonel asked again. He obviously wanted to make sure Jean-Claude was still on board after having voiced some concerns for his safety.

Again Jean-Claude didn't waver. "I'm ready. But I'm no hero. I have no military training and I don't know how I would stand up under torture or the pressure of working in these conditions."

"Of course. Nobody knows until they have to do it," Scott said. "As far as training, we are going to send you to England. The Brits are way ahead of us in the espionage game. They have boot camps for agents at large country estates all over England where you will be trained by experts in espionage, self-defense, close combat, and gathering and sending intelligence.

"They will also teach you how to jump out of a plane. You won't be sent in until we feel you've been given the tools to survive. However, it's a dangerous assignment and in the end, survival will be up to you and your ability to stay undetected."

"Jumping out of a plane gives me some pause, but I guess it's better than walking in," Jean-Claude said with a smile that felt somewhat forced. "When do I leave?"

"We want you here for the next two days for an orientation, then we should be able to have you on a plane to London. In the meantime, I understand you have a lady friend in Connecticut you would like to say good-bye to," Scott said, smiling. "We have arranged for you to have a seven day pass after the orientation."

"Thank you, sir, and thank you, Colonel Littleton," Jean-Claude said, unable to conceal his excitement over the pass. "I won't let you down."

"We are glad to have you on board, Jean-Claude," Scott said. "If you are anything like your father, you'll be a real asset. Good luck."

He took a cab back to his billet. On the way, he again thought about the risk he was taking and the chance he wouldn't survive. He might never see Stephanie again, or his unborn child. His thoughts then abruptly shifted.

A seven day pass. I can't wait to call Stephanie. And he did as soon as he could get to a telephone.

CHAPTER 20

THE WEDDING

December 1942

"Stephanie, I have to stay here in Washington for another day, then I have a seven day pass." He called her from his billet, eager with excitement.

"Perfect! I've talked to my parents," Stephanie said, also bubbling with enthusiasm. "We can get married here in Greenwich. Nothing fancy. Just a few of my parents' friends and some of mine from school. They are so eager to meet you and are so happy they are going to be grandparents."

"Can you put together a wedding in that short amount of time?" he asked in amazement.

"Oh, yes. I've already started. Jean-Claude, I am so excited. We can go into Manhattan for our honeymoon. You'll love it."

"How are you?" he asked, concerned about her condition.

"I saw the doctor today. He says I'm doing fine. Everything looks good. Delivery in six months. I've started to show. Daddy said he is going to tell his friends I've been eating too much and gotten fat. He says I have to wear a loose-fitting wedding dress."

"Nobody's supposed to know you're pregnant? But they'll know soon enough."

"I know, but after we're married nobody will care. It's wartime. Certain things can't wait. Like having babies."

"I'm going to take the train to New York. What do I do then?"

"Just take a taxi from Penn Station to Grand Central, then the New Haven Line to Greenwich. It's only about an hour's ride." She sounded so happy. "I'll pick you up at the station. Call me from Grand Central and let me know when your train will arrive."

"You have it all planned out, haven't you?" he said.

"I've been thinking about nothing else since you left. It's going to be wonderful."

"I'll call you when I get to New York. I love you."

"Wonderful. I love you too."

Two days later Stephanie picked him up at the station in Greenwich in a Cadillac. He knew she'd come from money. He knew that from the decor at her apartment and her testimony at trial when she'd said she had servants while growing up. He just didn't realize how much money until they pulled into the driveway of her home.

It was a mansion—a mini Claremont Hotel with stately old-world architecture and a circular driveway surrounded by manicured gardens.

As the car stopped at the front door, a Negro dressed in a black suit came out and opened the door on the passenger side. "Welcome, sir. I will get your bags."

This is the world of WASPs, he thought as he got out of the car.

Stephanie's mother was the first to greet him. She embraced him and said how happy she was he and Stephanie were going to be married. She welcomed him into the family.

Her father came out minutes later and greeted him formally with what Jean-Claude felt was an air of disdain. But then, maybe that was just a false first impression, probably having to do with the fact that Stephanie had told him her father was anti-Semitic. Jean-Claude wondered how his being half Jewish was going to go over, or if Stephanie had even told her family.

"I'm Wallace Stevenson. Glad to meet you. We need to get acquainted, my boy," her father said, putting his arm around Jean-Claude's shoulders. "Stephanie usually brought her boyfriends home for a once-over. We have some catching up to do. Let's go into the library, shall we, and get acquainted?"

They walked through a large living room with beautiful chairs and sofas upholstered in the same French fabric Stephanie had in her apartment. They entered the library through heavy double mahogany doors. The library had three walls of bookcases and a large fireplace on the fourth wall. It smelled of aristocratic old-world wealth. "Would you like a brandy?" Stevenson asked as they settled into large leather chairs.

"Yes, thanks." Jean-Claude really didn't want a drink, but he said yes to be polite. "A glass of brandy sounds nice."

"Stephanie has told me a lot about you," Wallace said as he poured them both a brandy.

"Oh? What has she told you?"

"She says you are a lawyer, a criminal lawyer, and a damn good one. She says that was how you met—in a courtroom."

"Yes, she was a witness in a case I had."

"Won the case for you as I hear it," he said with some pride.

What's he talking about 'she won the case'?

"I think the facts won the case and Stephanie happened to be a witness," he said somewhat tartly.

"She said you two were attracted to each other right there in the courtroom. That's my Stephanie. She's a woman who knows what she wants and will do whatever it takes to get it." That statement piqued Jean-Claude's curiosity.

"Did she say what she meant by 'whatever it takes'?" Jean-Claude asked in a lighthearted manner. He sniffed the brandy and took a sip. "This is very good."

"It's vintage 1929. A very good year. She said she wanted to get to know you, so she helped you with your issue with the judge. Something about twenty dollars."

"Did she tell you anything else?" Jean-Claude asked as he reached in his pocket for his cigarettes. "Mind if I smoke?"

The old man nodded his approval and Jean-Claude reached for a silver lighter sitting on the table next to him.

"She said you were born in France, and your father has gone back to France to join the Resistance, which is most interesting. I hope he'll be all right. I hear the Resistance is full of Communists, and if they win, France will go Communist. That would be worse than being governed by the Nazis."

Worse than the Nazis? This guy is not only anti-Semitic, he's an idiot.

But if Stevenson was going to be his father-in-law, Jean-Claude should keep politics out of the conversation if possible.

"The Nazis get things done," Stevenson continued. "They keep the undesirables under control."

Jean-Claude could not let that pass. "The undesirables?" Jean-Claude asked in a non-confrontational tone.

"You know—the Jews. They aren't going to let the Jews control things like banks and the financial markets like they do here."

Jean-Claude reacted without thinking. "I guess Stephanie didn't tell you my mother was Jewish," he said in a steady voice, looking the old man in the eye.

What he saw was someone who appeared to have been hit in the stomach.

Stevenson coughed nervously. "No. No, she didn't," he sputtered. Then he paused as if to collect his thoughts. "I'm sorry, my boy, if I offended you." He sipped his brandy. "Have you and she thought about how that's going to affect your lives—I mean how you raise the child and things like that?"

How are we going to raise the child? Jean-Claude found it interesting this was the first thing the old man wanted to know. He was clearly thinking about his legacy. Stephanie said this would be his first grandchild.

Jean-Claude had to think about that one. He had never considered how the child would be raised, especially if he didn't come back.

"We never really discussed it. I was raised Catholic, but I don't go to church very often. I'm half Jewish, but have never practiced the faith. I guess she's Protestant. I never asked. We'll just make a decision about the child when the time comes," he said in a matter-of-fact voice. "Now that you have brought it up, I'm going to have a talk with her before I leave, so she won't have to make the decisions by herself." He was going to make sure the decisions were going to be his and Stephanie's and not her father's. Mr. Stevenson was clearly a man who liked to be in control.

"I know there are lots of rumors going around about what the Nazis are doing to the Jews." Stevenson changed the subject. "But they're just rumors." The old man was making an attempt to undo some of the harm of his initial statement. "They said the Nazis hated Negroes too, but they let Jesse Owen run in the '36 Olympics. Look how that turned out."

"It doesn't look like they intend to make the same mistake twice," Jean-Claude replied dryly.

"This isn't the way to start our relationship. Let's not talk politics or religion. I'm sure raising the baby won't be an issue and while you're away, Stephanie will make the right choices. Let's go back in the living room and meet the rest of the family," the old man said as he put his arm around Jean-Claude's shoulders and led him back into the living room.

Jean-Claude was introduced to the rest of the family and some friends who had come over to join them for dinner. The subject of religion and politics was never raised again during the time he was there. He was received warmly by family and friends who were particularly interested in his French heritage. He was the center of attention at dinner.

The wedding and reception were held at a private country club in Greenwich in another elegant, baronial building. It was decorated for the holiday season and had an old-world atmosphere he found warm and inviting. But it was obvious from the crowd it was a club only for the white and rich. He was sure if he could see its charter, it would have a covenant of exclusion for Jews and non-whites.

He hadn't been consulted about anything regarding the wedding even though he was the groom. The ceremony was to be Protestant. Since he didn't have a strong adherence to any faith, he didn't say anything. He just let it go. This wasn't about him. This was about Stephanie. This was what she wanted and the most important thing for him was her happiness.

Jean-Claude didn't have anyone for a best man, so her brother stood up for him. A nice fellow. Worked on Wall Street with his father, but didn't seem to have the same snobbish attitude.

The wedding went smoothly. The big reception area of the club was beautifully decorated for Christmas and the decorations were complemented by poinsettias, orchids, and camellias Stephanie and her mother selected. Mas would have been pleased even though he could never have been a member.

At the reception, her father gave a toast. "Jean-Claude has made my daughter very happy and that's all that matters to me and her mother. We don't care about anything else." Jean-Claude knew what the anything else was.

The old man raised a drink to toast him. "Jean-Claude, you will soon be going off to war, and we all wish you good fortune.

We know you will defend us well and return home to be a husband, and we hope someday a father."

The guests applauded.

Sooner than everybody knows, he thought to himself as he sat there smiling. He took another sip of champagne, which was excellent.

The reception ended with cake, more champagne, and dancing. Charleston for the old folks, and Glen Miller and Artie Shaw for the younger generation with an occasional waltz mixed in. Jean-Claude didn't request "Hava Nagila," although the thought crossed his mind.

After the reception, Stephanie's parents had arranged for a town car with a driver to take them into Manhattan to the Palace Hotel on Central Park South where they'd reserved the wedding suite for them. On the ride in, they sat side by side in the backseat of the town car. She asked him why he had to tell her father his mother was Jewish.

"He made some derogatory comments about Jews," he said in a matter-of-fact tone, "and I wanted to set him straight. Was he upset?"

"Let's say shocked. He had a lot to digest because everything happened so fast. He'll get over it. Anyway, I've told you it doesn't matter to me." She squeezed his hand.

Jean-Claude wondered why she hadn't mentioned it to her father, but decided to drop the subject. He wanted to talk about the child. "He did ask if we had discussed how the child was going to be raised. I know you don't like to think about this, but if I don't come back you can do as you think best so long as you tell the child who her father was and that her grandmother was Jewish. Agreed?"

"Don't talk like that." She started to cry. "You'll come back. You must come back. Oh, Jean-Claude." She hugged him close. "Let's not talk about this anymore, this is our honeymoon. Let's enjoy it. We need these memories to last us until we are together again."

The subject was not brought up again.

She said she would be staying with her parents in Greenwich. He said he would write her whenever he could, but that it would probably not be possible until he finished his mission. She said she understood.

The days together were wonderful. A light snowfall covered the entire city with a veil of white. They walked for hours, made love frequently, and gave thanks for the time they could spend together. But there was always a pall hanging over everything— a sense this magical time might be the last they would ever spend together. Her final words as they said their good-byes at Penn Station were, "Just write me when you can and think of me and the baby every day."

When their time together ended, he took the train back to Washington. With the exception of how he felt after his mother died, this was the saddest he had ever been. He left for England two days later.

BOOK TWO

RETURN TO FRANCE

War is the greatest plague that can affect humanity; it destroys religion, it destroys states, it destroys families. Any scourge is preferable to it.
—Martin Luther

CHAPTER 1

LA CHAPELLE

January 1943

The flight across the Atlantic was cold and long and included a refueling stop in Greenland. The air over the Atlantic was choppy. The C-47 rose and fell with the air pockets and constantly vibrated. It did nothing for Jean-Claude's confidence to hear that this northern route to England had only been in operation for a few months and they were losing about ten percent of the planes due to weather.

He got sick and felt tired and alone. The refueling stop in Greenland did nothing to alleviate his loneliness. If anything, the barren wasteland made him feel even more alone. He began to get those familiar feelings of vulnerability and inadequacy—the tight stomach, the cold hands, the negative thoughts about the future. What if he never came back, never got to see Stephanie again, or his unborn child?

And what about Stephanie? As the miles of separation rapidly increased and the glow of the honeymoon began to fade, he started to wonder about her again. Was she a good person? An honest person? Had she lied in court? Did she get pregnant just to trap him? Why didn't she tell her father about his mother? But he soon realized whatever the answers were, she was now his wife and pregnant with his child, and he needed positive memories to hold on to. And he did love her despite it all.

He wanted to dismiss the negative thoughts, to clear his mind so he could concentrate on what lay ahead. A psychologist he once used as an expert in a trial told him that thoughts in the conscious mind are there because we allow them to be there. We can control them. We can change them. He knew it could be done because his apprehension over Pearl Harbor and the concern for his father that dominated his thoughts on that terrible December morning temporarily disappeared when he was invited to Stephanie's for dinner. It could be done. It just took discipline. He would have to do it if he was going to survive.

Once they began their descent into a small military airfield outside of London, he was focused on the present and the future. Stephanie and his doubts were no longer on his mind. He was ready for his return to France.

He was met at the airport by a British corporal who helped him gather his gear. They drove in a dark green military car for about forty-five minutes through terrain that changed from urban to farmland to woods. They turned up what appeared to be a private road. When they reached a clearing he saw a house that made Stephanie's look like an English cottage. It was imposing, majestic, and grand like the chateaus in France, but the architecture was definitely English.

They entered through the front door into a large foyer.

"I'll take your gear to your room, sir," the corporal said and grabbed his duffle bag. "It's the second door on the right at the top of the stairs. You need to get out of your uniform before dinner. There's a change of clothes in the armoire. For now, just go into the salon. Someone will be with you shortly."

Jean-Claude walked into a large wood-paneled salon furnished with overstuffed chairs and sofas. A huge fireplace along one wall with a crackling fire took the chill out of the air. Lovely pastoral oil paintings hung from the walls. The room was empty. He took a seat in one of the overstuffed chairs and waited.

Soon, an older man, perhaps in his sixties, walked in, smartly dressed in a tweed coat with a sweater underneath, knickers, and knee-high black riding boots. He wore wire-rimmed glasses and his hair was salt and pepper. His mustache curled and twisted into a point.

"Welcome, Mr. Bonnay, to Lord Montague's estate. He is off fighting in the African campaign, and he and his family have graciously offered their summer home for our training. I am Major David Longacre," he said in a crisp, aristocratic English accent. "I'm to be one of your trainers."

The major appeared to be very fit and every bit the English gentleman. "I fought in the second Boer war, and the last World War, so I have seen a lot of wars. It will be my job to help you survive this one.

"Dinner is at six 6 in the dining room," the major said. "There you will be introduced to your colleagues and given some background on the training. I will join you in the dining room for dinner. Please wait either here or in your room until then. The property has restricted areas, so don't go outside. Sorry to be so abrupt, but there are many things I have to do to get ready for tomorrow." With that, he was gone.

Jean-Claude was left alone in the opulent salon. He realized what had seemed so surreal yesterday was now a reality. This was not going to be like a trial where if you lost, you moved on to the next one. Here, if you lost...

He wouldn't let his thoughts go any further.

After a few minutes and seeing no one else around anywhere, he walked up the stairs to his room. It was sparsely furnished: a bed, a washstand, a small chest, and a hard-backed chair. He hoped the bed was comfortable. But then he wasn't there to stay in his room. He was there to learn how to be a spy and how to survive. He changed into the clothes that hung in the armoire. They fit. Somebody had done their homework.

Shortly before six, he descended the stairs and entered the dining room where a long table had been set for twenty-four with assigned seating. Almost every seat was taken. He found his name on a place card and sat down.

There were twenty-two men, including Longacre, and two women. There was one Negro who looked African, several men who were Middle-Eastern, and the rest were white. One of the women was quite large, the other was very attractive.

They engaged in polite conversation during dinner, but with a definite sense of formality. No one wanted to share too much about themselves, and given what had brought them together, this didn't come as a surprise. Jean-Claude sat between two Englishmen. The conversation felt superficial. Mostly small talk about the weather and sports.

They adjourned to the salon after dinner.

Major Longacre addressed the group. His manner was friendly, but when he spoke he sounded deadly serious.

"I want to welcome you and thank you for your service. You have volunteered for a dangerous assignment, but one that could have a significant impact on the outcome of the war. I must remind you your mission is secret. No one, not even your closest relatives, can know of your activities or whereabouts. You must not try to contact anyone." He looked around the room to make sure everybody got the message. Most nodded in agreement.

"Some of you won't make it through the training. That is no disgrace. It is tough, demanding, and sometimes dangerous. Those of you who do make it through will have the skills to succeed in a very hostile place but even with these skills you may not make it back. You may have to lie, steal, even kill in order to complete your mission and survive. You will have to compromise the values you have cherished your entire life because the success of the mission is what is important above all.

"Someday this war will be over and we will have won. You will be able to return to your normal lives and live by the rules again. You may look back and feel badly about some of the things you did. But you must always remember that if we had not succeeded, our way of life, the law-abiding moral way of life we have always treasured, would have been lost.

"I wish you all good luck. We begin at 0600 tomorrow. You will know what time to rise by a loud knock at your door."

For the next six weeks, Jean-Claude went through the most rigorous physical and mental training he had ever experienced. The physical was worse than a 100-mile bike ride in the hills, and the mental aspects made law school seem elementary.

The physical training required long-distance runs over terrain that was very difficult. Hills and trails were rough—full of rocks and forest debris. He was in pretty good shape thanks to his bike riding, but the other activities were new to him. They trained in rope climbing, gymnastics—special attention was paid to tumbling, because the instructor told them they might encounter times when they had to get out of the way of something or someone quickly.

There were also exercises in close combat. He was taught how to kill by coming up from behind, applying a stranglehold and a sharp twist of the neck. They taught him how to use a pistol with a silencer and how to follow a target, and how to lose a tail if he felt he was being followed.

He learned the elements of demolition and plastic explosives. There was an old railroad track that ran behind the property. He and the others learned how to misdirect signals and to set explosives to derail a train. The instructor stressed this part of the training.

"For some of you," he said, "sabotage will be one of the major functions of your mission." While Jean-Claude learned he should not engage in sabotage because he held more value gathering intelligence, it still interested him and he paid close attention to the instruction.

The classes were intense and included map reading, Morse code, use of carrier pigeons, still a valuable way of communicating even in modern warfare they said, fixing broken transmitters, and setting up and concealing antennae for radios. He was given a matchbox containing a miniature camera that could photograph documents even in low light.

Another part of the training consisted of instruction in the current customs of France, the current styles of dress, current events, and language including the latest slang and popular music and theater. His instruction focused on southern France and the area around Lyon. The instructor was from nearby Aix and complimented him on his French. She said she felt he would have no trouble passing as a native in Lyon.

Lastly, an instructor provided him with two sets of pills: one to keep him awake if he had to work many hours without sleep, the other to put him to sleep, permanently—within fifteen seconds of taking it. This pill would be used if he was captured and before the enemy had a chance to torture him. They would be given no weapons to take with them other than a mini pocketknife. Any firearm, if discovered, would give them away.

For recreation and relaxation, they played soccer. Even though the group was physically exhausted from the all-day training, the games were a welcome break. A team of RAF pilots came up from the airbase to play a team made up of fellow trainees. Jean-Claude had played soccer as a child growing up in France, and while he had not played for some years, he was a good athlete and the skills came back fairly quickly.

During one of the games, Jean-Claude got into an altercation with one of the pilots who fouled him constantly.

The fight only lasted seconds and consisted of a few wild punches, none of which landed. After the match, the two shook hands and had drinks together at the local pub. His name was Ian, and Jean-Claude found out he was one of the pilots who ferried men into occupied territory. They formed a wartime friendship—one that begins immediately, but can end suddenly.

The final phase of training dealt with learning how to parachute out of a plane.

For that they took him to a small airfield a short distance from the estate. There were two practice jumps: one from a stationary tower, the other from a plane. The tower stood 250 feet high. They hoisted him to the top, which took several minutes. The ride up made him queasy and his stomach churned. He began to feel sick. At the top they held him suspended for what seemed like forever. He vomited. The wind took most of the vomit, but some landed on his jumpsuit.

Finally his chute released and he landed safely. He felt embarrassment in front of the others because they had to endure the sight and smell of vomit for several hours.

Fortunately, the jump from the plane went better, but he was still nervous. The plane vibrated and he almost got sick again. His legs were rubbery as he stood in line waiting to jump. As he got to the doorway, he didn't look down. When he felt the tap of the instructor's hand on his shoulder, he jumped without hesitation. He landed without getting hurt. That gave him confidence he could successfully do it again.

Six weeks later, his training was over. He had let his beard grow and just before he departed one of the staff applied a dye that blackened the beard, his hair and eyebrows.

He was driven back to the same airfield outside of London where he'd landed. Upon his arrival, he was told to get some sleep because his drop was scheduled for 0200 the next morning.

Being told to get some sleep and sleeping were two different matters. He got a little, but not much. At 0100 hours he was awakened and told to dress. He had been given clothing during training that would allow him to blend in with the locals. He had been instructed to put his jumpsuit on over those clothes and take his parachute to the mess hall and get some breakfast. He ate what he could—some toast and black coffee, about all his stomach would tolerate.

At 0145 hours he strapped on his chute and boarded the plane. He didn't notice the pilot when he came aboard.

The C-47 took off at 0200. The night sky was clear with some light clouds over the channel, but all reports suggested the weather over southern France would be clear and cold—perfect for a drop.

Jean-Claude fidgeted with his pack as he sat on the cold bench. The engines made the bench vibrate and he felt he might get sick.

As he looked toward the pilot's compartment, the pilot motioned to him to come forward. Jean-Claude unfastened his seatbelt and used the side of the fuselage to brace himself as he staggered toward the front of the plane. Getting up helped his nausea. He was surprised when he recognized the pilot. It was Ian. He crouched down next to him.

"You better get me to where I'm supposed to go or I'll kick your ass the next time we play soccer," Jean-Claude teased.

"Be nice to me, mate, or I'll drop you into the channel." He then reached into a bag next to his seat and smiled as he removed a small holster on a belt that contained a miniature pistol. "I knew you were my passenger tonight, so I brought you a little something."

Jean-Claude smiled back, but looked perplexed when he saw the pistol. He didn't know if he should take it.

"I know they told you to go unarmed, but from what I hear from the lucky ones who do get back, it's good to have some insurance," Ian said. "Just in case."

Jean-Claude only hesitated a moment then took the gun and holster. "Thanks."

"It's called the Liberator .45 caliber. Only good for one shot before you have to go into the pistol grip for another bullet and it's only for short range—maximum seven meters. The Yanks just sent a bunch over to drop into France for the Resistance. I snagged one. Strap the holster to your thigh. Wear baggy pants and cut a hole in the pocket so you can get to it. It's loaded so make sure you keep the safety on. Hope you never have to use it."

"Me too." Jean-Claude said as he turned the small pistol over in his hand and examined its crude construction. "This thing looks like it was put together in a high school machine shop. You sure it works?"

"It works. I tested it. Better make sure the first shot hits the target. You probably won't have time to reload."

Ian seemed pleased he could give his friend some added insurance.

"By the way, I will drop you right on target. On clear nights like this, I never miss."

"You better not." Jean-Claude smiled. "And thanks for the going-away present."

"Cheerio. Happy landings," Ian called out and gave him a thumbs-up as Jean-Claude made his way back to the bench.

The jump sergeant called out, "Ten minutes to target."

Then the fear came. His hands went ice cold and began to shake, his stomach cramped. This was the point of no return. *Focus, focus. Control your thoughts. Channel your fears*, he repeated over and over.

He went over his mental checklist: Right after you jump, keep your knees and feet together, head down, elbows in, and hands on the sides of the reserve chute. Count: one thousand, two thousand, three thousand, four thousand. If there is no tug from the chute opening up, pull the handle on the reserve chute. If there is a tug, look up between the risers to make sure the canopy opened properly. Remember the reserve chute in case you get a streamer. Control drift by pulling down on the risers. Maintain stable body position while descending. Look down as you descend to get oriented as to where you are. Stay out of trees. Prepare for landing by keeping your feet together and bending your knees slightly. When you hit, do a landing fall like they taught you. Disengage from the harness straps as soon as you hit the ground. Quickly survey the area, then roll up and bury your chute, then get out of there.

He put the holster and gun inside a pocket in his jumpsuit. He got an adrenaline rush, which helped the fear subside. Adrenaline was good. It helped him shut all other thoughts out of his mind, except what he had to do once he jumped.

As they descended, the airspeed dropped. The red light above the hatch came on.

"Two minutes to drop."

The jump sergeant had opened the hatch and motioned for him to come forward. Cold air rushed into the cabin. The sergeant told him to attach his static line to a cable that ran down the middle of the plane. The sergeant checked it to make sure it was securely fastened.

Jean-Claude stood in the door, his eyes glued to the red light above him. His heart was pounding. He was ready. The green light went on.

Without hesitation, he jumped. An instant later he was falling through the night into occupied France.

He felt the canopy open, jerking him upward for a second. He looked above to make sure all the risers and suspension lines were aligned. He pulled on the risers to see if they adjusted the chute. They did. He twisted around in his harness to get oriented.

He was transfixed by the beauty of what he saw. By the light of the moon and local land lights, he could see the Rhône River, twisting through the valley, carving out canyons as it had done for centuries.

The moonlight gave an incandescent glow to the scene below. He needed to get an idea of where he was. He looked for landmarks. He wanted to make sure he landed on the plateau above the river and not on the adjacent hillsides that were terraced vineyards and very steep. He saw a large patch of lights to the north. That must be Lyon and on the other side of the river to the south a much smaller patch. That must be Vienne.

Tiny clusters of lights also dotted his side of the river. That could be Condrieu, which would be near his destination. Ian said he could hit any target on a clear night. Jean-Claude hoped he was right.

His destination was the small farming hamlet of La Chapelle, forty kilometers south of Lyon, across the river from Vienne, and above the wine-making village of Condrieu where the white wine he brought to Stephanie's came from. There was a safe house there where he was to rendezvous with members of the Resistance.

The ground approached rapidly. During his descent, he saw a church and a cluster of farmhouses. That could be La Chapelle, but he couldn't be sure from above. Now he had to concentrate on the landing. *Remember, drop and roll. Don't break something or get hung up in a tree.*

He saw what looked like a clearing below. The ground came up fast. It looked clear, no trees, and no concrete. He hit the ground and rolled, so the chute wouldn't collapse over him.

When he came to a stop he didn't feel any pain. He glanced around. In the moonlight he could see he had landed in a plowed field. Perfect for a soft landing. Now he had to find a place to bury the chute. His orders kept repeating themselves in his head. Bury the chute and your jumpsuit, so no one finds it. If they find it they will come looking for you.

The plowed field was not a good place. If it got plowed again the chute would turn up. He quickly gathered it up. After checking to make sure no one was around, he made his way to the edge of the field. At about 100 meters he came to a dirt road. On the other side of the road was a rock wall, behind it some dense underbrush. A good hiding place.

He climbed over the rock wall and stripped off his jumpsuit, dropped his pants, took the miniature pistol and strapped it to his thigh, and with his small knife cut a hole in his pants pocket.

He cleared the underbrush, took the small shovel out of his pack provided for just that purpose, and dug a hole about three feet deep. He threw in the chute and his jumpsuit. When the hole was about two-thirds full, Jean-Claude tossed the shovel in, and using his hands, filled the rest of the hole with dirt. He then covered it with leaves and vegetation. It looked good—not like somebody had been digging recently.

He climbed back onto the road, which ran north-south. The night sky was clear and he easily found the North Star. If Ian had hit the target, Jean-Claude had to head south, since La Chapelle was south of the landing site. He followed the road.

He looked for some landmark or familiar marking to confirm where he was. It was farm country. Even in the moonlight he saw no markers he recognized. The only thing he could do was continue to walk south and hope he was in the right place. He had to keep alert for farmers. Farmers got up early. Finally, the dirt road intersected a paved road. At the intersection there was a directional marker, which read, "La Chapelle, .5 kilometers."

He now knew where he was. He knew exactly where he was. Ian, he thought, you are a master.

CHAPTER 2

THE FARMHOUSE

He had been told the farmhouse where he was to rendezvous was small, about 90 square meters. The exterior was stone and the roof had alternating gray tiles. It had a broken brick chimney clearly visible, the distinguishing feature that would tell him he had found the right place. One side of the farmhouse faced north and looked out onto a meadow and to the valley below. This was the direction Jean-Claude had been instructed to use in his approach.

Though the night was cold, adrenaline and the exercise from digging and walking kept him warm. In the moonlight, he found the meadow easily. As he waded through the field of knee-high mustard plants, he could clearly make out a farmhouse with a broken chimney. He had found it.

He stopped when he was 200 meters away. He dropped to his knees, so he would be less visible. The adrenaline had started to wear off. He was very tired. He lay down hoping to rest for a few minutes before continuing on and immediately fell asleep.

The cold steel barrel of a pistol pressed against his neck woke him with a terrified jolt.

He was pulled to his feet and blindfolded.

"Do not speak. Walk slowly," a man said in French. The gun was now in his back. It felt like another man gripped his arm and guided him.

The speaker was clearly French, someone from the Resistance, or had he been betrayed by an informer? He hoped they were just taking precautions, making sure he was the man they expected. Still, his anxiety level increased rapidly. The perspiration from the walk to the farmhouse now felt cold on his back.

He tripped on what he thought might be a step. The man who held his arm kept him from falling. The stairs of the farmhouse, he suspected. Once inside, they removed the blindfold. It was pitch black. He couldn't make out anything.

Finally after a tense moment, someone lit a candle and held it in front of his face. Whoever was in the room could see him, but he could not make out anything except shadows of other people. No one said anything.

In the next moment, a second candle was lit in the room and the first one removed from his face. As his eyes adjusted to the light, he could see someone standing before him but his sight was blurry and it took several seconds for him to focus. Then it took him a second to process things because he couldn't believe what he was seeing. The man standing in front of him was Bernard, his father. A wave of emotion swept over him. "Papa," he cried out as they embraced each other.

They stepped back and stared at each other for a moment then embraced.

"Is this my son, the spy? I barely recognize you with the beard and dark hair," Bernard said, smiling from ear to ear.

"You've changed a bit too," Jean-Claude said in a teasing tone.

"You mean the gray hair and the wrinkles? This job ages you. How was the jump? You okay?"

"I'm fine. There were no problems. How did you know I would be here?"

"It was all set up through London with our contacts. We thought you deserved to be greeted by a familiar face."

Jean-Claude surveyed the room. Someone had lit more candles. He finally saw there were others in the small salon.

Bernard still had his arm around Jean-Claude's shoulder as he introduced him. "You remember Chantal? She was once your sweetheart," Bernard said and gestured to the only woman in the small farmhouse.

"It was not me who was his sweetheart," Chantal said, her arms crossed over her chest. "It was my sister, Natalie, he favored. But no matter. Welcome home, Jean-Claude."

He embraced her. Chantal felt rigid, tense. She was a petite woman with short brown hair. He remembered her, but as she said, he remembered her sister better. It was Natalie he'd missed most when he left.

Bernard gestured to a broad-shouldered man. "This is Michel, the assassin."

"Bernard, please. This is no way to introduce me to your son," Michel grumbled. "Assassin, mon Dieu." His voice was deep and his eyes were penetrating even in the dim light.

"Okay, you are the enforcer," Bernard conceded with a small smile.

Jean-Claude stuck out his hand, which was immediately swallowed up by Michel's huge paw. The enforcer stood at about six foot four and had to weigh at least 270 pounds. Michel had a thick black beard to go with a head of hair to match. He resembled Bluto, the villain in the *Popeye* cartoon series.

Bernard introduced him to the two men who had escorted him to the farmhouse. "Georges is the best code man in the Resistance, and Andre is, well, let's just say Andre is a problem solver. He's a lawyer like you, or at least he was until they kicked him out of the Paris bar because he's a Jew."

They sat down at a long table. Bernard poured some wine and raised his glass. "Welcome home, Jean-Claude. I'm sorry it had to be under these circumstances."

They all raised their glasses and echoed the welcome.

Then Bernard spoke. "We don't have a lot of time tonight to get caught up. That will come later. You and Chantal have to leave before dawn, so the farmers don't get suspicious."

Jean-Claude nodded as he drank the wine.

Bernard grew serious and looked at him intently. "For now, here are some basic rules to follow. Only trust those you have been introduced to by us. But if they get arrested they can no longer be trusted. La Milice—do you know what the La Milice is?"

"Yes," Jean-Claude said, "they told me about them in England. It's a branch of the Vichy Police that acts like the SS."

"That's right. They wear brown uniforms and berets and go around hunting Jews and Communists and those of us in the Resistance," Bernard said. "The head of La Milice is Joseph Darnand. I knew him from the last war. He is an anti-Semite, anti-Communist fascist."

The room grew very quiet.

"If they catch you, they take you to the École de Santé Militaire, to the fourth floor where you are tortured until they think you no longer have value," Bernard said through clenched teeth. "Then they take you to the courtyard and shoot you, or if you're a Jew they send you to Drancy in Paris and ship you to the east where you are never heard from again." Anger and hatred came clearly through the tone of his voice and the fire in his eyes.

All this talk about capture and torture made Jean-Claude immediately question his mission. "Anybody have a cigarette?" he asked, needing something to break the tension. Andre handed him one. He lit up. "Papa, I'm no hero. Maybe I'm not cut out to be a spy. I'd rather stay and fight with you and the others. The hell with the mission," Jean-Claude said, feeling overwhelmed at seeing his father and a childhood friend, and not wanting to leave them.

"None of us are heroes," Bernard said unsympathetically. "We all live in constant fear. I know you better than anyone, and I know when it counts, you will do what is necessary no matter what it is." From Bernard's tone, Jean-Claude knew his father had quickly moved past the emotion of the reunion. "London told us your mission is to gather information that will assist the Allies in planning a southern invasion. This is important. Very important. More important than anything you could accomplish with us."

Jean-Claude finished his wine. Chantal refilled his glass.

"I guess you're right. I just got carried away seeing you. They told me in London I was to blend in with the locals and observe. I was told that members of the Resistance would be my contact to get information out. They said I am not to participate in any operations with them and not to have any weapons." He paused and reached into his pants pocket. "I was given this by a friend just before I left. I have it strapped to my leg. Is it too risky for me to keep it?" He pulled the miniature .45 from his pocket and showed it to Bernard.

Bernard turned it over in his hand. "I've seen one like this before. They don't look like much but they can be pretty effective. Keep it. It may come in handy someday. Just don't take your pants off in front of the wrong people," Bernard said with a smile. He handed the gun back to Jean-Claude. "We are going to help you blend in. Chantal will be your primary contact person. She works for the Ministry of Information in Lyon and thinks she can get you on there as a translator. This will give you some cover and allow you to move about the city freely."

Chantal sat across the table from him. They made prolonged eye contact for the first time. She had the same intense look Bernard had. "I have your identity papers to replace those given to you in London. Those are no good, despite what they told you," Chantal said. "You are now Alain Duchon from Villefranche-sur-Mer near Nice. Your story is that you have come from Villefranche, because you don't like the Italians who are occupying the area. I have already told my superior I have a friend who is fluent in English and German who wants a job. He said to bring you by and he would talk to you."

"I'm afraid I might be recognized. This beard may not be enough," Jean-Claude said, frowning.

"Bernard almost didn't recognize you. I didn't recognize you. If I didn't, I doubt anyone else will either," she said. "So don't worry."

He felt somewhat reassured but the thought of going back to the place where he grew up and hoping no one recognized him still concerned him.

"If you get the job, you will be translating English-language documents into French or German. It does not require a security clearance because you are not dealing with classified information. But keep your ears open. Sometimes you hear things. We have a flat for you within walking distance of the Ministry. Any questions?"

"How's Natalie?" Jean-Claude asked.

"So is that the reason you are here?" she asked with some sarcasm.

He shook his head. "I haven't thought about her in years. But seeing you brought back memories."

"She's married with a child. Her husband is in a forced labor camp in Germany. Now she fucks a high-level Gestapo officer who sends messages to her husband. He said he would help keep him alive."

Jean-Claude lowered his head and took a drink. "Can I have another cigarette?"

Michel handed him one and Jean-Claude lit it. He raised his eyes and looked at Chantal, whose determined expression had not changed.

"I'm sorry," Jean-Claude said, saddened over Natalie's situation.

"Don't be sorry. We do what we have to do to stay alive and defeat these bastards," Chantal said with a hard bite to her voice. "The Nazi is a very valuable source of information because he invites her to parties and gatherings with other Gestapo agents and they drink. And when they drink, they talk. He also likes to boast about what he's doing when they are on the pillow. She then passes the information along to us."

This was her sister she was talking about, but it could just as well have been a stranger given how little compassion he heard in her voice.

"Will I ever run into her?"

"I hope not. I don't think she would recognize you. But should you ever see her, you must ignore her. Her life is constantly at risk because of what she is doing, and there is no reason to increase that risk."

"I understand." He paused. "You like to give orders."

"I do not give orders. I give instructions," she said, but even that sounded like an order. "I am your contact. I will also take care of keeping your hair and beard black. You would do well to listen to what I have to say. It could save your life."

Chantal had changed. Always the hell-raiser, but with a good nature, she now seemed hard, driven. She wore little makeup and dressed plainly, but the intensity of her passion made up for what she lacked physically. This alone made her attractive. She had such an air of confidence and spoke with such authority, he knew he should pay attention to her.

Jean-Claude finished his wine and put out his cigarette. He glanced around the room at everyone else. They all had serious expressions on their faces.

"We're here to help you if you get into trouble. Otherwise we probably won't see much of each other," Andre said. "Just listen to Chantal. She will help get you through."

Jean-Claude nodded. There wasn't anything else to say.

She obviously was one they all respected.

In the few minutes they had together before he and Chantal had to leave, Bernard told him he wouldn't contact him due to the increased scrutiny by the Gestapo and the Milice.

"Since the Nazis took over the south this past November, it has become much more difficult to move around and to get information out, especially to the States," Bernard said. "We have increased our operations—assassinations, blowing up railcars, sabotaging rail tracks and roads. We can almost smell the invasion coming. We are beginning to organize armed units to attack the Germans from within Lyon, so we will be ready when the Allies arrive."

Jean-Claude always knew his father was a man of strong convictions, but now he saw those convictions matched with physical courage. But something had changed. His father had changed.

"I want to tell you about a man named Klaus Barbie," Bernard said. "He is the head of the Gestapo in Lyon. He is a man capable of immense cruelty and brutality. His job is to eradicate members of the Resistance and Jews. He is doing this with the assistance of the Vichy government and French police. If I accomplish nothing else, I want to kill him. If I do, I will die satisfied."

To hear his father speak of killing a man disturbed Jean-Claude. He had only once before heard him utter a threat like that and that was after his mother was killed. Now he could almost feel his hatred.

"When this damned war is over, when we have killed all the Nazis and Vichy bastards and have taken control, we will create a place where the workers will determine what happens in their lives, the bourgeois state will no longer—"

"Bernard, knock off the Communist bullshit." Michel's booming voice cut him off.

"Ah, Michel, my friend," Bernard said with a forced smile. "Today we are comrades, but when the war is over and the real struggle for France begins, we will be enemies." Bernard turned to Jean-Claude. "He hates Communism with a passion, but in the meantime, we are on the same side."

At the first light of morning, Chantal said it was time to go. There were no plans to see his father again. He knew in these dangerous times, everything was uncertain. All he could do was hope.

They left on Chantal's motorbike for Lyon.

The ride to Lyon took less than an hour. Because of the noise and wind, it was not possible for them to carry on a conversation, so he held her around her waist and took in the scenery. The landscape brought back memories. It looked the same as he remembered. But as Chantal had warned, this was not the same country he'd left fifteen years ago.

When they arrived in Lyon, she took him to his tiny flat, gave him a key, and said she would pick him up and take him to the Ministry the next morning. She told him to get some sleep. He didn't care whether this was an order or an instruction. He was exhausted. He fell into the bed and slept soundly on his first day back in France.

CHAPTER 3

THE MINISTRY OF INFORMATION

January 1943

T he next morning Chantal picked Jean-Claude up at his flat. They rode on her motorbike to the Ministry of Information, which was housed in the building previously occupied by the Office of Tourism, an agency that no longer had any reason to exist.

Chantal gave him some background on the head of the Ministry, Pierre Lagrange, a career military officer from a prominent family in Lyon. He held the rank of captain. He and his family were anti-Semites, anti-Communist, and strong supporters of National Socialism. Lagrange was also close to Joseph Darnand.

Lagrange and his family believed Germany was going to win the war, and if France was considered a valued partner, she would be able to return to her past glory. That would allow him and his family to regain their rightful place in French society.

Since the Nazis had taken over the south of France in November of 1942, his authority had been diminished, but he was still looked upon as the head of the Ministry. The ultimate power now lay in Berlin and with Klaus Barbie in Lyon.

She described Lagrange to Jean-Claude. He was in his fifties, tall, lean, and well-conditioned. She said she was reasonably certain he was a homosexual, but he was very discreet about it given that Nazis often shipped homosexuals to concentration camps.

Chantal was on good terms with the head of the non-classified division of the Ministry, the one she hoped would be able to give Jean-Claude a job. His name was Paul Du Bois. He had been head of the Office of Tourism before it was taken over. He was proficient in most European languages and English, which allowed him to stay on after the function of the Ministry changed. He was not an ideologue. Privately, he had shared his contempt for the Nazis and the Vichy government with Chantal, but he needed a job and just wanted to survive like so many others.

When they arrived at the Ministry, Chantal told the officer at the front desk Jean-Claude was there to apply for a job. After being waved through, they went to the second floor where Chantal's division was located. She introduced him to Du Bois. After a brief conversation with Jean-Claude in English, French, and German, Du Bois offered Jean-Claude the job. He was happy to get another person in his division with his language skills, since he was constantly being harassed by Lagrange to get information processed faster. Jean-Claude was issued papers that included a photo ID, a most important document as it allowed him to move around the area freely. He also was given verification of employment at the Ministry.

Du Bois then gave him a tour. The lowest level gathered information from all public sources—foreign language newspapers, the BBC, periodicals, radio broadcasts that could be picked up on shortwave. This was a non-classified job and did not require a security clearance. Workers just had to be proficient in the language of the source and be able to translate those parts that might have some intelligence value. This was where Jean-Claude would be working.

Another section dealt with the receipt and translation of dispatches from around the world sent by French and German embassies, or other foreign intelligence gathering sources. This area was classified and required a clearance. The last department, on the third floor, was for the receipt and translation of classified material considered highly sensitive.

Since the Nazis took control of the Ministry, all manner of information flowed through the third floor. Considered a center for highly classified information, only those who had been thoroughly screened worked there.

Jean-Claude was given a desk and a stack of English-language documents and newspapers to translate. He was delighted to read papers from the U.S. and get caught up on all that was going on, especially how the war was going in the Pacific.

He scrutinized everyone working there. He wanted to see if he recognized anyone. He didn't, but that didn't mean someone might not have recognized him, even with his black beard and black hair. The thought would keep him in a state of constant anxiety and high alert every minute he worked at the Ministry.

That evening, he and Chantal drove around the city on her motorbike. The city hadn't changed much from what Jean-Claude remembered, but the atmosphere felt dramatically different. French police, as well as uniformed Milice and German soldiers, were everywhere. People went about their business, but without the kind of vitality he remembered. They looked subdued and weary, and for good reason. They lived in an occupied city, subjugated by their own government that they could not trust, and by the Nazis whom they feared.

Lyon was a perfect city for the operations of the Resistance. Once one left the broad boulevards, the streets were narrow and twisted back and forth with no predictable pattern. Alleys had been used for centuries as ways for people to get to their homes. Unless you knew the way, you could get lost very easily. This was what the Resistance counted on to protect them from the random searches of the Gestapo and police. Numerous bridges crossed over the Rhône and Saône rivers that flowed through the city, and allowed for many ways to leave in a hurry if necessary.

Throughout the evening, they went to several cafés, and Chantal showed him the ones where she would often meet other Resistance members. Café Rouge and Café de L'Arche were places she said could be trusted. She introduced him to the proprietors and some patrons who she knew were active in the Resistance.

Over a glass of wine, they talked about the Ministry.

"This job at the Ministry, is there a chance I can pick up the kind of information I was sent here to get?" Jean-Claude asked.

"Possibly. You will not get much in your current position, but keep your ears open. Sometimes you hear things that could be valuable. That's what I do and I have gotten a few good things. Gossip is rampant around here. Everything that is said is treated as truth and passed on. That's how starved people are for information."

"I'm good at gossip," he said with a smile. Stanley and he had elevated it to an art form.

"The greatest value of the job is having identity papers and a work permit. With them you are free to move about the city and the country, and you can pick up things just by keeping your ears and eyes open. You can never get past a background check, so working in the sections that require a security clearance is out of the question. But things are constantly changing around here, so you never know when an opportunity might present itself."

Chantal drove him back to his apartment. He climbed off the bike. Before they parted she said, "The people I introduced you to can be trusted. At least for now. Things change quickly, and you always have to be careful. Never meet with anyone unless you have cleared it with me first. One day, they're an ally, the next day, after a night at the École, they're an informer. I will introduce you to women who will fuck you when you want sex. They are all women we know can be trusted. We don't want you getting involved with some woman we don't know. Understand?"

"I'm married," Jean-Claude responded somewhat indignantly.

"That's in your other life. In this life you take one day at a time and enjoy it as best you can." She said matter of factly. She then wheeled the bike around and sped off down the dark street. Their time together that day and evening left no doubt in his mind that she was driven to defeat the Nazis no matter the cost or consequences to herself or anyone else.

Jean-Claude spent the next several months getting acclimated to his job at the Ministry and to his life in Lyon as a spy. With the help of the Resistance, he learned where the safe houses were. He also learned how information could be transmitted by radio and how documents could be delivered to trusted couriers, then taken to Switzerland, or transmitted to London.

He constantly thought about how vulnerable he was to discovery. His cowardly side would often take over. His body would grow cold. He lived in constant fear. His apartment, car, and person could be searched at any time for no reason at all. They could find the gun he always carried. Jean-Claude thought about the searches of Japanese homes and property without warrants on thin or no probable cause—the searches he had so strenuously objected to back home. Here, there were no legal protections at all. He was at their mercy. A knock at the door, the sound of a car screeching to a stop outside his building, footfalls on the stairs, a shadow behind him as he walked home—each could be the Gestapo or the Milice coming for him.

Alone at night in his room, he wondered why he ever decided to do this. That's what isolation did to his thinking. He would feel the same old insecurities that had haunted him his whole life. It was also at these times his thoughts turned to Stephanie.

He couldn't help it. In the darkness of his room late at night when the fears came rushing in, the thought of her calmed him down. Time and loneliness had erased any doubts he had about her and in their place was this image of her and his child as a family at home around a Christmas tree, or celebrating a birthday, or the first day of school—images to hold on to, to help him get through the sleepless nights, to help quell his fears.

When he couldn't sleep he would get up and go to a small table, light a candle, and write her a letter. He would tell her how much he missed her and the baby he had never seen, and that he would be coming home soon and they would begin their life together. When he finished, he would hold the letter up to the candle and burn it. He could allow himself the pleasure of writing it, but could not risk the consequences if anybody found it. He performed this writing ritual almost every night.

The good thing was his fears made him more careful. He was constantly on guard for signs he was being followed or investigated. Someone he knew who had been captured and tortured by the Gestapo could turn him in at any time.

He was always mindful of the miniature .45 he had strapped to his leg and his pill he'd hidden in a place where he could reach it easily. He gradually learned to live with his fears, and they eventually subsided until they became a dull ache in his stomach and not the paralyzing sensation he'd felt when he first arrived.

During this time, he also learned much about the Resistance—how factionalized it was. They were made up of anti-Semites and Jews, Gaullists and Communists, deserters from the army, and just regular folk who hated the Nazis. When the war was over, there was going to be a battle for control of France. Bernard and the Communists were going to be in the forefront but many who had been their comrades in the

Resistance were violently anti-Communist and would become their adversaries.

But for the time being, they were united against a common enemy, and the enemy gave them many reasons to hate, especially if you were Jewish.

A virulent strain of anti-Semitism had always existed in French society but even though it was kept under control by a French culture that stressed inclusion, Bernard and Rachel were concerned enough that they decided to raise Jean-Claude in the Catholic faith. With the Nazi takeover it emerged as a powerful force with anti-Semitic laws passed by the Vichy government, enforced by the French police, and implemented by the French court.

Jean-Claude had heard about the deportation of Jews and about Drancy, the dreaded prison in Paris where they were taken prior to being sent to the east, and the brutality of the French police and the Gestapo while rounding them up. But it was impossible to grasp the full magnitude of the brutality and inhumanity that was taking place without witnessing it.

One morning, Chantal showed up at his desk while he was translating documents.

"Come with me," Chantal whispered to Jean-Claude.

Without hesitation, he left the building with her and got on the back of her motorbike. She drove through the tiny back streets of the city until they reached the main rail yard, used for switching trains that arrived from all over Europe. Chantal parked the bike in an area that would not draw attention. Together they walked to the rail yard where they met the railroad worker who had called her to alert her about what was happening.

He'd previously given members of the Resistance information about train departures with critical material and munitions on board, so they could be targeted for sabotage. He had proven a reliable source and a trusted friend. The railroad workers were forced to transport Jews to the concentration camps in the East and most resented it. This was one reason they were so willing to risk their lives by helping the Resistance. Another was they hated the Nazis. As Jean-Claude would learn later, many would be executed as a result.

He led them to an empty boxcar where, using binoculars, they could see scores of people surrounded by armed German soldiers with dogs and a smattering of men in brown uniforms. Jean-Claude couldn't tell from his vantage point if they were SS or members of the Milice.

The civilians were being loaded into boxcars—pushed, shoved, and stuffed into each car, until it couldn't hold any more. Then the doors were slammed shut.

There were children, old people, and all ages in between. He saw a mother carrying a small child trying to climb into the car, but having trouble because she held the child in her arms. A German soldier kicked her from behind causing her and the baby to fall. The baby rolled under the boxcar onto the track. When the mother retrieved the child, Jean-Claude could see the baby's clothes were covered with blood. Two soldiers then lifted her and the baby and threw them into the car and closed the door behind them.

"I'm sure you've never seen a sight like this before," Chantal said through clenched teeth.

Jean-Claude was breathing heavily, almost hyperventilating. It took him a moment to regain his composure. "Not this bad, but similar," he said in a barely audible voice.

"Jews?"

"No, Japanese. Back in the States."

"Mon Dieu." Chantal gasped.

"This is madness," Jean-Claude said, shaking his head in disbelief.

The railroad worker nodded in agreement with a sad expression. "It happens regularly."

Now Jean-Claude understood why Chantal and Bernard had that look of hate in their eyes when they spoke of the Nazis and the Milice. Now he understood why Stanley said he had to go to France. Now he knew what it was to be Jewish in occupied France.

He would never again wonder if it was worth continuing his charade as a spy. He had just witnessed an unspeakable evil and no matter the risk, he would do whatever it took to help destroy it. His hands might grow cold with fear, but his heart would burn with hate.

CHAPTER 4

ENCOUNTER AT THE ÉCOLE

Lyon, May–June 1944

By May of 1944, Jean-Claude had no doubt the Allies would win the war in Europe. He knew it from reading the newspapers from the States and other sources he reviewed daily at the Ministry. He also learned the same thing from Chantal, who kept in constant contact with members of the Resistance who received word from London and the BBC. But there was still no word about the southern invasion.

Things were not going well for Germany. The war on the Russian front was a disaster for them. The German army was in retreat. The Russians were only twenty-seven miles from the Polish border. Bombing runs by the British on Berlin where tons of incendiary bombs were dropped came at a high cost of planes and pilots, but the effect on German industrial capacity and morale was significant.

The Resistance in southern France grew stronger. The reports of Resistance activities, sabotage, assassinations, and bombings were increasing in frequency. So were the reprisals.

Jean-Claude sometimes met members of the Resistance in safe cafés. They told him that their numbers had grown substantially because the Nazis sought to conscript 250,000 Frenchmen to work as forced labor in Germany. Tens of thousands joined the Resistance as a result. Now they stayed hidden away doing whatever they could to hasten Le Jour, the day of liberation.

It was just a matter of time, but how many would die before it ended, and would he become one of them? The end was in sight, but it was still extremely dangerous. The Nazis were increasing their suppression of anyone thought to be a member of the Resistance or a sympathizer, and they were speeding up the removal of Jews. There was no room for error on his part now. One slip, anything to suggest he was not who he said he was, and things could end quickly.

At the Ministry, Jean-Claude had established himself as a proficient translator—accurate and reliable. Du Bois liked him and gave him lots to do, but it was boring work. As the weeks dragged on, he became increasingly frustrated over the indecisiveness of the Allies as to whether there would be a southern invasion at all. There was concern about diluting the strength of the northern invasion forces, and about Churchill's desire to concentrate Allied forces in Italy to push north into Vienna and Eastern Europe and deprive Stalin of a zone of influence over those areas. Until these issues were resolved, the southern invasion was on hold.

His daily life was frustrating too. He worked at his desk all day, had dinner at a local café, and went back to his apartment alone, while Chantal, Georges, Andre, and Michel were constantly engaged in acts of sabotage, or attending clandestine meetings with members of the Resistance. He could only imagine what Bernard was up to, but whenever there was a high-level meeting of Resistance leaders, Jean-Claude was certain he would be in attendance. If there had been a major act of sabotage or an assassination of a major figure of the Milice, Jean-Claude knew that Bernard had something to do with it. For that reason, they did not see each other. Bernard had become toxic, one of the most wanted men in France, and Jean-Claude's identity had to be protected at all costs.

Initially, Jean-Claude was to travel to the area around the Mediterranean to observe, but the chance of detection had increased greatly after the Germans took control of the south. They installed frequent checkpoints on the highway. London decided he should confine his activities to Lyon. It was not his job to question his assignment. He had a mission and he would carry it out as ordered. He would continue to monitor information at the Ministry, and troop and munitions strength in Lyon.

He knew too much to risk being arrested and had doubts how he would hold up under torture. The thought of torture terrified him. He knew he could take a pill or a bullet because they led to a quick death, but physical pain, particularly over a long period of time, made him ill just thinking about it.

By the spring of 1944, Jean-Claude felt secure at the Ministry. No one had recognized him, and so much time had passed, he felt safe from detection. At least at the Ministry.

During the many months he worked at the Ministry, he had only seen Lagrange once, mainly because he stayed in his office on the third floor and rarely came by the station where Jean-Claude worked.

One day, when Lagrange made one of his infrequent stops on the second floor to talk to Du Bois, Jean-Claude became aware of Lagrange frequently looking in his direction. The looks from Lagrange made him uncomfortable. When Lagrange asked Du Bois who he was, Du Bois then introduced them and told Lagrange he was one of the best translators at the Ministry.

Several days later, Du Bois came to his desk. "Captain Lagrange wants to talk to you. Go to the third floor. He is expecting you." Du Bois had a "be careful" look on his face as he delivered the message.

From the way Lagrange had stared at him, he suspected his interest in him was personal, but he was still worried that perhaps he was suspected of something. This is going to be interesting, he thought as he took the elevator to the third floor. He was nervous but under control. If he stayed calm, he believed he could handle anything that came up.

He was shown into the captain's office. It was elegantly furnished, like something one would find in a chateau, not a bureaucrat's office. The captain was, as always, dressed in uniform, neatly pressed and a perfect fit, and sat behind his desk.

"Sit down," he said, pointing to the chair directly in front of his desk. He offered Jean-Claude a cigarette from a silver box on the desk. Jean-Claude accepted and Lagrange gave him a light and lit one himself.

"Du Bois says you are one of our best translators. I asked you to come up here because I am constantly being asked by the high command in Berlin, 'What does this mean, what does that mean,' referring to translations into German from English. They get angry when I don't respond immediately."

"You must be under tremendous pressure. I don't envy you," Jean-Claude said, trying to show empathy. He was relieved that the meeting had nothing to do with his loyalty.

"I am. That's why I could use somebody with your skills in English. It will help me respond faster. There is a small office next to mine. You will be working there from now on. I will tell Du Bois."

Jean-Claude was incredulous. *From the second floor to the third floor with a private office right next to Lagrange's—amazing, but frightening.* He thought about the opportunities this might present. He now knew that Lagrange's primary interest was in him and not his translating skills. He understood it was going to be a balancing act. He wasn't sure how he would handle it. But he knew that while he was going to try and get as much information as he could, he was not going to let it get sexual.

"Here, start with these." Lagrange handed Jean-Claude a sheaf of documents and pointed toward a small room adjacent to his office.

Jean-Claude took the documents and immediately walked into the small office. There was a desk, a telephone, a typewriter, and a mimeograph machine. A quick glance through the documents revealed they were intercepted diplomatic communications. Some appeared to be generated by the military. They were all in English and all were stamped "Classified."

He panicked. He had no clearance and knew if they did a background check they would find out he was not who he said he was. How dumb not to have thought of that, but it was too late now.

"By the way," Lagrange said as he stuck his head into the office, "do you have a security clearance?"

Jean-Claude's heart pounded. "No, sir. I didn't intend to be working at a level where I needed one," he said, trying to conceal the anxiety he felt.

"No matter. It would take weeks to get one and I need help now. Berlin and Paris keep pushing. We'll go without one for now."

He let out a big sigh and lit a cigarette. *He must really be interested in me to take a risk like that.*

Over the next several weeks, Lagrange injected little things into their conversations: "What wines do you like?" "Do you go to the theater?" "Where do you like to dine?" Lagrange asked him to have dinner with him one night. Jean-Claude declined, saying he had a previous engagement, but he realized the invitations would continue, and he would soon run out of excuses.

While Lagrange pursued a courtship with him, Jean-Claude was able to collect some sensitive and important information that he passed on to Chantal. Since the Ministry was a communications hub, he also had access to documents in German originating from Berlin. Some of them dealt with new weapons in development, others with troop strength and allocation. He memorized the content of documents, took notes on tiny pieces of paper, or photographed them with his miniature camera. He then smuggled them out of the Ministry and delivered them to Chantal, who made sure they got forwarded to London.

One day he came across a very disturbing communication Klaus Barbie had sent to Berlin several days before.

The communique read, "In the morning hours the Jewish children's home in Izieu-Ain was closed down. A total of forty-one children ages three to thirteen were arrested. Furthermore, the entire Jewish personnel consisting of ten people, including five women, were also arrested. After transport to Drancy they are to be sent to Auschwitz."

Jean-Claude understood what their fate would be. Now he knew why Bernard said that if he ever got the chance, he would kill Barbie. Jean-Claude vowed that he would do the same. Stanley told him one man can make a difference. This would be his chance to prove his friend right. Killing Barbie would put an end to his mission and himself as well, but it was something he vowed he would do if given the opportunity.

At a restaurant they frequented for dinner, Chantal praised him for the information he passed on to her, and wanted to know how he and Lagrange were getting along. She was curious because she guessed Lagrange was attracted to Jean-Claude, and she suspected that was the reason he had moved him to the third floor.

"He likes to talk about wine and food and the theater," Jean-Claude said in disgust. "I encourage him to talk as much as I can, but he's a bore. I guess I am his protégé."

"Protégé? Don't kid yourself. He's a faggot," she said with a sneer. "He wants to fuck you."

"Well, that's never going to happen. He'll get a bullet first."

Chantal pointed her finger at him. "This is your chance to get some real information. You become his lover. You find out things. He talks on the pillow. You listen."

Jean-Claude shook his head. "You're not serious."

"I am very serious. We do things in war we would never do otherwise." He hadn't heard that kind of intensity in her voice since La Chapelle. "We kill, we lie, we fuck the enemy."

"It's disgusting to think about," he said, even though her words came right out of Major Longacre's remarks that first night at Montague's estate.

"Is it any more disgusting than what Natalie is doing to keep her husband alive and to get information for us?"

"That sex is different. That's natural."

"Natural? Natural?" Chantal exploded. "You think it's natural to fuck somebody you hate? Natural to have to submit anytime he gets the urge? Natural that he can plant his seed in your unprotected body, so you go around terrified you might get pregnant and have to carry that monster's baby? She has told me that if she gets pregnant she will kill herself. That's natural?" At the end of her tirade she was almost yelling. She had attracted the attention of the crowd and Jean-Claude was growing nervous.

"Chantal, keep your voice down. Everyone in the place is looking at us," he said in a hushed voice. She'd made her point, but he still wasn't going to let Lagrange get anywhere near him. He would put up with the man's tedious banter because he was getting access to sensitive material, but he wouldn't have sex with him. He had always been heterosexual and his sexual insecurities made him homophobic. He was prepared to kill Barbie and sacrifice his life doing it before he would have sex with LaGrange. He remembered his vow in the train yard to do whatever it takes, but he hadn't thought about this situation when he'd made that vow.

The next morning began quietly at the Ministry until Lagrange rushed in.

"Come in here." He commanded Jean-Claude to hurry into his office. "They captured a big one last night, and they want me at the École at once. I don't know who they have or what language he speaks, but I want you along in case we need a translator."

To the École? That was the last place Jean-Claude wanted to go.

But before he could come up with a good excuse, they were in Lagrange's chauffeur-driven Citroën entering through the stone gates of the École. They entered the building where an elevator took them to the fourth floor—the dreaded fourth floor, the floor Bernard had told him about. They entered a large room.

In the center of the room stood two bathing tubs left over from its days as a medical facility. Two heating units with big pots on top had steam rising from them. Two other large pots sat on the floor. They looked like they were filled with ice. There were examining tables with leg and arm straps, and pokers rested next to the gas heaters. There were a number of uniformed men inside. Some wore the uniform of the Milice, others the Gestapo. Regular military stood guard around the room.

Jean-Claude's hands grew cold and clammy. He hoped he would not have to shake hands. Fortunately, the Nazi salute had replaced handshakes.

He could hear the sound of boots approaching from the hallway. The room fell silent in anticipation. The door opened and three people entered. Jean-Claude recognized Klaus Barbie immediately as he had seen his photo numerous times. He thought the other man might be Joseph Darnand, the founder and head of the Milice. The third was a woman who had a notepad and appeared to be an aide to Barbie. This was his chance to make good on his vow to kill Barbie. He would now be put to the test. He would find out soon enough if he was up to it.

Barbie wore a tan Gestapo uniform with the red armband and black swastika on the sleeve. He'd tied a white scarf around his neck. He was a short, stocky man with a pale complexion but his eyes were an intense blue. A .45 hung in a holster hooked to his belt. In his hand he carried what looked like a riding whip.

The stories of his brutality were legendary. He would inject acid into bladders, have fingernails pulled out, and burn the flesh with cigarettes. In interrogating women he would strip them naked and have dogs mount them if they didn't talk.

Barbie was reputed to take pleasure from the suffering of his captives. Families of the accused were brought into the room to view their loved ones who were then taken away. Immediately following, a shot could be heard, and the family was informed their loved one had been shot, and if they talked they would be spared. Often they were killed anyway after they talked. This was the reason why Chantal and Bernard said never to trust anyone who had been on the fourth floor.

Everyone in the room came to attention with a crisp salute and a "Heil Hitler."

"Let's get on with it. I didn't plan for this interruption," Barbie snapped.

No one had acknowledged either Lagrange's or Jean-Claude's presence until Darnand came over and whispered to Lagrange, "Who is he?" He nodded at Jean-Claude.

"He's my chief translator. I didn't know what language the captive spoke so I brought him along just in case."

"Tell him to not speak unless he is spoken to," Darnand said, staring at Jean-Claude for what seemed like forever. *Does he recognize me? Had we met sometime in the past?* He didn't think so, but there were dozens of possibilities racing through his head. His legs got rubbery. He could feel his heart pounding.

He put his hand through the hole in his pocket and felt the butt of the pistol strapped to his leg. He also felt for the pill hidden in his jacket pocket. It was there when he needed it.

"Bring him in," Barbie commanded. Darnand turned his attention away from Jean-Claude and toward the door.

One of the uniformed soldiers picked up the phone. "Bring him in."

The door opened. A man was dragged in between two soldiers. His face was bruised. His arms were tied behind his back. The prisoner scanned the room. When he saw Jean-Claude his head jerked slightly, but he did not change his expression.

It was Bernard.

For a second, Jean-Claude's mind went blank. *Oh, God. This is a nightmare.* Except for feeling every muscle in his body tighten, he showed no emotion. He stared at his father, but his father did not look back. An adrenaline rush surged through his body. He kept one hand on the butt of the .45, the other held the pill. He knew he would only have time to fire one shot. Bernard or Barbie? His mind went blank.

Darnand turned to Barbie and pointed to Bernard. "This is Bernard Bonnay, the infamous Bernard Bonnay. I knew him in the last war. Very smart, very cunning. Went to the U.S. after his Jew wife was killed. Very active in the Resistance and responsible for planning many acts of sabotage. He is also a Communist. We broke one of his associates last night and he told us where he was hiding. He should be able to tell us a lot."

Barbie walked forward until he was face to face with Bernard, who stood six inches taller.

"I always like to look into a man's eyes before I question him. I don't see any fear in you. You must be a very brave man." Barbie's ice-blue eyes glared at Bernard, who remained expressionless.

"So, you are a Communist and a Jew lover, and you once lived in the States. Now that intrigues me. Why would you want to leave the comfort of the United States to come back to France?" he asked in an almost conversational tone.

"I came back to finish the job we started in the last war," Bernard said in a firm voice, showing no fear.

"You speak bravely. Your obvious passion is admirable. I like it when a man knows he is facing an extremely painful experience and shows courage. We shall be testing that courage shortly, but first let me ask you: If you and I were to go to another room with comfortable chairs, some wine perhaps, and have a conversation, do you think it would be beneficial to both of us?"

"I would welcome the chance to be alone with you." It was clear what Bernard meant by the tone of his voice.

Barbie slapped him across the face with his whip. "You dare to threaten me," he screamed. "There's no more time to waste. I want the details of your activities since returning to France. I want to know the names of your confederates and where we can find them. I want the locations where transmissions are sent to England. I want to know when and where the invasion is coming. To save a lot of time and you a lot of unnecessary pain, answer me."

"Fuck you," Bernard said in English, sending a message to Jean-Claude that he was going to be defiant to the end.

Jean-Claude marveled at his courage and drew from it.

"What did he say?" Barbie screamed.

Lagrange turned to Jean-Claude. "Translate. Translate into German."

Jean-Claude paused for a second and peered at Bernard who had a slight smile on his face. Jean-Claude translated and said, "Fick dich."

Barbie slapped Bernard again across the face with his whip and nodded to the men who were standing behind Bernard.

They stripped Bernard to the waist, forced him to the ground on his stomach, and tied his wrists to his ankles. They slipped a pole under his arms and between his legs and lifted him over the first tub—the one filled with ice. They lowered him until the pole rested on the sides of the tub, his body submerged completely in the ice water.

Bernard strained to keep his head above water. One of them looked at Barbie, who gave a short nod. They then forced his head under the water. They had obviously done this many times before.

They held his head under for what seemed to Jean-Claude to be forever. When the large bubbles gave way to the small bubbles, the guards jerked Bernard's head out of the water. He choked violently, coughing up water and gasping for breath.

"Who are your associates?" Barbie screamed. "Where can we find them? How do you contact London? When are the Americans coming?"

Bernard said nothing, just gasped for breath.

"Perhaps you don't answer because you are cold." Barbie nodded to the men holding Bernard.

They lifted him out of the tub and lowered him into the adjacent tub, the one that had steam rising from it. Very hot water was constantly being added to keep the temperature high. His head was pushed under by a wooden yoke, because the water was too hot to touch.

The bubbles came instantly. Bernard must have screamed as his head hit the hot water and was submerged. The men manning the baths knew exactly when to pull the victim up from the hot water. Keep him in a second too long and he died. Bring him up at the right time and the pain from the scalding was unbearable. When they brought him up, Bernard screamed, his face bright red.

Jean-Claude trembled. He had seen enough. He reached through the hole in his pocket and grasped the butt of the .45 and started to pull it out. He stared hard at Bernard. Bernard looked at him and screamed, "No!"

Those in the room thought he meant no more torture. But Jean-Claude knew his father was telling him not to use the gun. He relaxed his grip.

Barbie repeated the questions, screamed in Bernard's face. "Who are your confederates? Where are they? Who do you report to? How do you send messages? When is the invasion coming?"

Bernard said nothing. He breathing was heavy.

"Put him back in the ice," Barbie ordered.

Jean-Claude was not going to let this go on. He grasped the pill with one hand and was just about to take the gun from his pocket with the other when the phone rang. It startled everyone. Everything stopped.

The officer who answered the phone told Barbie the call was for him and urgent.

Barbie went over and took the phone. He listened. The expression on his face grew grim and he shook his head from side to side. He put the phone down. "The Allies have landed in Normandy. The invasion has begun." The look of anger and hatred that had shown on his face moments before was replaced with apprehension bordering on fear. "I have to talk to Berlin." His voice grew weaker. "Take him back to Montluc. We will continue this tomorrow. I want to know what he knows about the invasion, so make sure you keep him alive."

The fear of the invasion had been preoccupying the Nazi high command for months. It would now be their entire focus until the end of the war. They needed to find out everything they could about the Allies' plans. That's why keeping Bernard alive was so important.

Barbie left the room. The guards cut Bernard's hands and feet loose and he was jerked to his feet. He was shaky, but he was conscious. Jean-Claude felt a tremendous sense of relief.

"You heard him," Darnand said. "Take him back to Montluc and make sure nothing happens to him."

Jean-Claude glanced at his father as they dragged him out of the room. He had a faint smile on his face. Jean-Claude realized that at least for tonight, Bernard would be safe. He guided the gun back through the hole in his pocket and into its holster. He would not kill Barbie because it would certainly end Bernard's life as well and if there was any chance to save him, Jean-Claude wanted to take it.

Lagrange looked disappointed. "Oh well. We get to come back tomorrow. We must get back to the Ministry."

Jean-Claude followed Lagrange back to the car without a word.

In the car on the way to the Ministry, Jean-Claude told Lagrange he felt he was going to get sick and didn't want to vomit in the car.

"Pull over," Lagrange ordered the chauffeur.

Jean-Claude quickly got out, turned his back to the car, forced a finger down his throat, and vomited.

When he got back in the car he said, "I don't feel very well. I don't think I should go back to the Ministry. Can you take me to my flat?" Jean-Claude didn't have to fake feeling ill. What he had just seen left him pale and shaken.

"I understand the first time you see something like you saw today, it can be upsetting." Lagrange smiled at him in sympathy. "But the more you see, the stronger your stomach. And you were able to watch the master. Not many get to see Barbie himself in action. Let's go to my place, you can rest there. Maybe later when you are feeling better we can go for dinner."

"Thank you. But I feel very weak. I may have the flu. Perhaps another time."

"You're right. I don't want to get sick and miss tomorrow."

Jean-Claude gave him an address two blocks from Michel's apartment and Lagrange gave it to the chauffeur. The car stopped and Jean-Claude got out.

"Thank you. I know I will feel better tomorrow."

The door closed and the car drove away. As soon as they were out of sight he walked quickly to Michel's apartment. If anything could be done to save Bernard, Michel would be the one to put it together.

CHAPTER 5

ESCAPE FROM THE ÉCOLE

June 6, 1944

Jean-Claude entered Michel's apartment building, hoping he wouldn't encounter anyone. While he waited for the elevator, he lit a cigarette and paced. As it descended, he could see it was occupied. He stepped to the side to allow the cage to open. An elderly man he didn't know stepped out.

"Bonjour, monsieur," Jean-Claude said politely.

"Bonjour," the elderly man said and headed for the front door. They had barely made eye contact, but Jean-Claude thought the man might have recognized him. He realized he was paranoid, but who wouldn't be after what he just witnessed.

He stepped into the elevator and pushed the button for the fourth floor. He made his way down the dimly lit hallway to Michel's apartment and tapped on the door.

"Who is it?" Michel called out.

"It's Jean-Claude," he said in a hushed and anxious voice he hoped would let Michel know something was wrong.

The door opened a crack. Jean-Claude pushed his way in.

"I told you never to come here." Michel showed his anger.

"They've got Bernard."

"Who's got Bernard?"

"Barbie, at the École. I just came from there. I watched them interrogate him."

"You were there? You saw this?" Michel said, incredulous.

"There is no time to explain. They plan to take him from the École to Montluc tonight." Jean-Claude spoke rapidly and breathed heavily. "They're going to bring him back tomorrow for more questioning. He'll die tomorrow if we don't do something. I also found out the invasion has begun. The Allies have landed in Normandy."

"Incredible." Michel clapped him on the back. "It has finally begun. All right, calm down. Let me think."

Jean-Claude paced and lit a cigarette.

After a brief pause, Michel picked up the telephone. A moment later someone answered and Michel spoke quickly. "*Oui,* this is Michel. I have a package that is being delivered this evening. I wonder if you would be so kind as to help me pick it up. It is quite heavy. Can you meet me at Café de L'Arche? I can give you the details there." A pause. "*Oui*—Café de L'Arche. Thirty minutes, *merci.*"

Michel turned to Jean-Claude with a fiercely determined look. Jean-Claude remembered Michel's eyes from the night they met at La Chapelle. They had an intensity that burned through him and even through his dense beard Jean-Claude could see his face was flushed.

"Let's go. We have little time," he said and rushed out. Jean-Claude followed right behind him.

Café de L'Arche was within walking distance and right on the Saône. Always crowded, even in the mid-afternoon, this café was one of the relatively safe places to meet.

Michel and Jean-Claude took a table by the window and waited. In a few minutes, Georges walked in. Jean-Claude had not seen him since the farmhouse at La Chapelle. He sat down and motioned for the waiter to come over and ordered espressos for the table.

"Tell him what you told me," Michel said to Jean-Claude with an excitement in his voice that let Georges know something big was happening.

Jean-Claude, still breathing heavily, lit a cigarette to calm down. "I was taken to the École to translate today. They told me they'd captured some high-value suspect the night before, and he was brought there for questioning. It was Bernard." He paused to catch his breath. "Barbie was there. He did the questioning. Then they put him in the tubs. Just when I thought he was not going to make it, the phone rang, and Barbie was told the invasion had begun in Normandy. He had to leave, so he told the guards to take Bernard back to Montluc, but to keep him alive because he wanted to interrogate him again tomorrow to find out what he knows about the invasion."

Michel turned to Georges. "What do you think?"

"Very risky." Georges shook his head and sipped his espresso.

"One person escaped from Montluc, but nobody has ever escaped during transport. The vehicles are too heavily guarded. We considered it once before when they had Jean Moulin, but he was transported before we could attempt a rescue."

"I remember that," Michel said, his jaw clenched behind his black beard. "We waited and when we decided to go, it was too late."

"When we were planning to get Moulin, we did find out about the method of transport," Georges said and leaned in close. "They take the prisoners in a van. There's a driver and a guard in the front, and usually two guards in the back. The prisoners are chained together, but not to the van. We will need a truck to force the van off the road and a car to get Bernard out of there."

"I can get the truck," Michel said.

"Good. I will get a car. Cars are easier to find than trucks," Georges said. "They usually transport after they have had their dinner because the guards like the food at the École better than at Montluc. It's 3:40 now. We will meet at Café Rouge at 6:30. If it wasn't Bernard, I would say the risk is too great. But we owe it to him to try." He looked at Jean-Claude. "You go home. We'll let you know later tonight if we've been successful."

"No. I'm going," he said.

"Our orders are to keep you out of these things. You're too valuable. Go home. You know that's what Bernard would want." He had given an order, one approved by his father.

Georges and Michel left the café. Jean-Claude sat for a while, feeling angry and frustrated that he'd been excluded. He was also exhausted and starved. He got up, left the restaurant, and walked toward his flat.

He stopped at the small café a block away where he regularly dined. He ordered. As he tried to eat he recalled what had happened earlier at the École, and his appetite disappeared. He trembled at the thought of Bernard being tortured. Then he felt a touch on his shoulder that startled him. He looked up. It was Chantal.

"Where have you been?" she asked with concern in her voice. "I've been worried ever since you didn't return from the École. I was afraid you had been found out."

"Lagrange took me to the École. They have Bernard." Jean-Claude began to shake again. "They tortured him, but he was saved by a phone call for Barbie telling him the invasion had begun in Normandy."

"Barbie was there?" Chantal's eyes widened.

"Yes, and so was Darnand."

"Why didn't you kill them both? You had your gun," Chantal demanded, almost yelling at him.

"Chantal, Chantal, calm down." Jean-Claude put a hand on her arm.

She went still, but her eyes blazed with anger. She sat down next to him.

"I swear to you, if the torture had gone on any longer, I was going to kill Bernard and Barbie." Jean-Claude's jaw tightened.

"I've just come from meeting Michel and Georges. They are going to try to rescue him while he is being transported from the École to Montluc."

"When?"

"Tonight."

"Tonight? There's not enough time."

"They plan to take him back to the École tomorrow. If they do, he will die. They are meeting back at Café Rouge at 6:30."

She got up and headed for the door.

"Where are you going?" he called after her.

She didn't answer. She was already gone.

That settled it. He was going.

He hurriedly finished his dinner and went to his apartment to change into clothes more suitable for what might be a rough night ahead. He then made his way to Café Rouge. He arrived around 6:15. He sat at a small table near the front door. The minutes dragged on. There was no sign of either Michel or Georges. By 6:50, he believed they had not been able to put it together—it wasn't going to happen. Just then Georges came through the door and hurried over to him.

"Have you seen Michel?" he asked, out of breath. He didn't even ask Jean-Claude what he was doing there.

"No, and I've been here since a little after 6." Jean-Claude gazed at the big clock that hung over the bar. It was almost 7 o'clock.

"I can't wait any longer," Georges said urgently. "He must have been delayed getting the truck."

"I'm going with you." He left no doubt by his look and his tone that he meant it.

Georges stared at him for a second, and then nodded to him to follow. There was no time to argue.

They climbed into a Peugeot. As they drove across the city toward their destination Jean-Claude's constant fear of being detected left him. It was replaced by the fear of failing—of making a mistake, of doing something that might get his father killed. His heart was racing just as it had before he jumped from the plane into France.

"We'll drive by the École," Georges said. "If we see a truck parked nearby, we'll know the plan is still on. The truck will follow the van when it leaves the École, which is usually sometime around 7:30. Michel will be driving. He will have one person in the cab with him. I'm not sure who that will be. There will be another in the bed of the truck. I hope it's Andre." He checked his mirror to see if they were being followed.

"It's 1.5 kilometers from the École to Montluc. At about 1 kilometer the road narrows, so that it is only wide enough for two cars. When they get to that point, the truck will pull alongside and force the van into the side of the building that's next to the road. When we hear gunfire we will come up behind, and I will help get Bernard into this car. You will then drive him to La Chapelle. Understand?"

All Jean-Claude could do was nod in agreement. Words got stuck in his throat. They drove past the École. About 200 meters from the gate they saw a pickup truck parked at the side of the road.

"The plan's still on," Georges said with relief.

At 7:45 p.m., the gate to the École opened. A large van with the words *Transport Militaire* on the side pulled out. Shortly after, the pickup truck pulled away from the curb with its lights off.

In the Peugeot, Georges and Jean-Claude followed some distance behind the pickup truck. When the two vehicles in front approached the narrow stretch of road, the pickup sped up, pulled alongside, and slammed into the van, forcing it against the wall. The driver of the van made eye contact with the hooded passenger in the truck. The passenger opened fire killing the driver and his escort. The van stopped. Andre, who was in the bed of the truck, jumped out. The rear doors opened and two guards jumped out. Andre gunned them down.

Michel, who had been driving the pickup, ran to the back of the van and helped Andre pull Bernard out. He was barely conscious, but showed signs he knew what was happening.

Fortunately, he was the only prisoner, so no decision had to be made as to whether to take any others.

At the sound of gunfire, Georges turned the Peugeot around, put it in reverse, and backed down the street until he reached the back of the van. He jumped out and helped Michel and Andre half carry, half drag Bernard back to the Peugeot and push him into the back seat.

"Jean-Claude, get going," Georges said. "The rest of us will meet you at La Chapelle."

Jean-Claude nodded. It had all happened so fast he didn't have time to be frightened. He turned and looked in the back at Bernard. His face was still red and he looked dazed, but when he saw Jean-Claude he gave a faint smile. He was weak, but alive.

Just as Jean-Claude was putting the car in gear to drive away, the passenger door opened and a hooded figure with a sub-machine gun jumped in.

"*Bonsoir*, Jean-Claude," the new passenger said, sliding onto the seat next to him and taking off the hood. It was Chantal, breathing heavily and smiling.

CHAPTER 6

THE LIAISON

June 1944

They all made it safely back to the farmhouse at La Chapelle. Bernard was still not fully aware of all that was going on, but he slowly came around, and after several hours was talking and drinking wine. It appeared his most serious injuries were the burns from the hot water, but they were not life-threatening, just superficial. Except for some bruising from the beating and blistering from the hot water, he had not been seriously injured. Apparently the water temperature had not been at the boiling point.

It was almost 5:00 a.m. when Jean-Claude and Chantal got back to Lyon. They discussed not going back to the Ministry and going underground. Instead, they decided much more information could be gathered by staying, despite the risks. Jean-Claude showered, changed clothes, and thought about a story in case Lagrange had come looking for him after he heard about the escape.

When Jean-Claude arrived at his usual hour, Lagrange was already at his desk on the phone. He was frantic. "I have no idea. I don't know. Yes, sir. I will be there." His normally pressed uniform was wrinkled, like it had been slept in. He looked disheveled and needed a shave. He'd obviously had a difficult night.

Lagrange glanced up at Jean-Claude. "Bonnay escaped last night. Four guards were killed. Barbie is furious. I have to go to the École for interrogations. Darnand is rounding up anybody who might possibly have information—suspected Resistance sympathizers, Jews, Communists—anybody. They are both insane with anger."

"Escaped?" Jean-Claude said, trying hard to appear incredulous. "How is that possible?"

"I don't know. That's what we've got to find out. I want you to come with me."

"I'm still feeling weak from the flu. You might get infected." Jean-Claude shook his head.

"This is no time to worry about that. We must go."

Jean-Claude couldn't think of any more excuses, so he followed Lagrange.

Soon they'd arrived at the stone gates of the École and entered the courtyard. Dozens of men stood in a tight group surrounded by guards with dogs.

"Form lines. Form lines," a guard shouted through a bullhorn. Guards used the butts of their rifles to push the men into two parallel lines.

"Silence. Silence," the guards yelled.

The crowd hushed. Only the barks from the dogs could be heard in the large courtyard.

From a balcony overlooking the courtyard, a voice boomed over the loud speakers. Jean-Claude looked up. It was Klaus Barbie.

Barbie spoke in French. "Last night terrorists killed four police officers and helped an enemy escape." His voice echoed through the quiet yard. "We know this was the work of the

Resistance. We will find those responsible. They and many others will pay for what they have done." He raised a clenched fist that held his whip and shook it at the crowd below. "Some of you know who did this. Some of you know where they are hiding. Some of you have information that can help apprehend these criminals. Some of you have information about the invasion. You will tell us or you will die—and not quickly." He paused and then shouted through the bullhorn, "All of you drop your trousers and your shorts."

The scene disgusted Jean-Claude—fifty or so men, their trousers and shorts at their ankles, many shaking from the chill of the morning and fear. It was Barbie's way of combining fear with humiliation.

"Guards. Have one Jew step out of line," Barbie ordered.

A guard pushed one older man forward, so he stood alone in front of the line. He was chosen simply because he had been circumcised and was assumed to be a Jew.

"Jew, tell me what you know."

The man shook violently, clearly terrified.

"Tell me what you know, Jew." Barbie screamed so loud through the speakers that it caused a screeching echo.

The man shook his head side to side, as if to say he didn't know anything.

Barbie probably knew the man didn't have any information, but wanted to make an example of someone.

"Kill him," Barbie shouted.

A man in the tan uniform of the Gestapo walked up behind the man, put a Luger to the back of his head, and shot him. Blood and brain matter shot out from the front of his head as the bullet passed through. He fell to the ground face-first.

The crowd gasped. Jean-Claude looked up at Barbie on the balcony. Jean-Claude did not react with horror like he had when he saw the Jews being loaded into boxcars. He just felt hatred. He had an overwhelming urge to kill Barbie right there, but he was too far away to get a good shot.

"Now you know what will happen to you if you don't talk,"

Barbie boomed. "The next one to be shot will be uncircumcised. I want you to raise your hands if you have information."

Two men from the lines raised their hands.

"Take them to the fourth floor." Barbie shouted out his order over the bullhorn. The sound reverberated throughout the courtyard. "The rest of you will stay standing. If I don't get what I want, I will be back, and one of you will be shot. Then another. Then another. If I have to kill you all, I will. Think carefully while I am gone. Then be prepared to talk when I return."

The guards herded the two men into the building. No one spoke.

He felt a hand on his shoulder. It was Lagrange. "Barbie's a genius, isn't he? Come, let's go inside. I want to show you something."

Jean-Claude followed Lagrange. They entered a large room with a long table at the front. Behind the table were three high-backed chairs positioned like thrones.

"This is where we have the trials," Lagrange said.

Trials? This was the first Jean-Claude had ever heard of trials. "What kind of trials?"

"These are the special military court-martials of the Milice. They were established by legislation in January. There are three judges. Darnand selected me to be a judge," he said proudly pointing to the chairs. "I sit regularly, but anonymously. No one knows I am a judge. We are growing more concerned about the outcome of the war. If we lose, there will be investigations, so our identities are kept secret.

"The accused is brought in, read the charges, then his confession is introduced. The judges meet briefly to discuss the verdict and sentencing. The order for execution is usually prepared in advance as the outcome is rarely in doubt. After the verdict is read, the condemned is taken to the courtyard and executed."

"So there is no defense? No lawyers?" Jean-Claude raised his eyebrows, questioning the process, but asked his question in such a way as to not show his disgust.

Lagrange shrugged. "What's the need? He has already confessed. We do have the power to spare them if we wish."

"This is all based upon some law that was passed?" Jean-Claude asked, wanting to make sure he understood that the government sanctioned these "courts."

"Yes. These are military courts created by the Vichy government."

Jean-Claude made sure he would remember this. "Have you ever spared anyone?"

"No, but there is always a chance. Perhaps today if one of them can provide information about who participated in the escape last night." He shrugged again and said, "Who knows?"

Just then Joseph Darnand entered the room and came up to Lagrange.

"There will be no trials today," Darnand said. "We need to spend our time finding out who did this. Go back to the Ministry and monitor the dispatches from Berlin. I need to know their reaction to Bonnay's escape. Let me know who they are blaming. If we need you, we will call."

Darnand turned to stare at Jean-Claude in a way that made him very uncomfortable. It was a "Don't I know you from somewhere?" look. After a moment that seemed much longer, Darnand turned and left. Jean-Claude could breathe again.

"We've got to get back to the Ministry," Lagrange said as they walked to the Citroën.

On their way, Jean-Claude took a chance. "You said back at the École that you were growing concerned about the outcome of the war. Should I be worried?" he asked Lagrange.

"You heard yesterday that the Allies have landed in Normandy. There are increasing communications from Berlin about a suspected invasion here in the south. They are trying to decide how to allocate their forces to best defend both fronts."

Jean-Claude's pulse quickened. Invasion from the south. Allocation of forces. He had to probe without making it seem obvious. But before he could say anything, Lagrange spoke. "You may be at some risk because of your relationship with me, and you have been to the École to witness an interrogation. I owe you some protection."

Lagrange tapped on the glass separating the passenger compartment from the driver's. "Take me home. I need to retrieve some documents."

In a few minutes, the Citroën turned down a lovely tree-lined boulevard past elegant homes of considerable size and stopped in front of one of them. Number 25, Rue de Bonaparte.

Lagrange motioned to Jean-Claude and got out of the car. "Come with me, I want to show you something."

Jean-Claude's hands went cold. This was just what he had been trying to avoid. Being alone with Lagrange. But now it was unavoidable.

"Wait here. We will be back shortly," he told the driver.

They approached an imposing front door with a bronze doorknocker. He put the key in the lock and they went in.

Once inside, Lagrange smiled. "If there is an invasion, or if Lyon is bombed from the air, I have a shelter for myself and a few others I may wish to include," he said as they walked through the salon into a large library. "Hitler has done this with his bunker in Berlin. This one was constructed many years ago during the last war when my family feared a German invasion. When I became concerned about the direction the war was headed and reprisals for what was being done to the Jews, I made improvements so it would be more comfortable and secure. I could stay hidden for weeks if necessary. Follow me."

Bookshelves lined three walls of the library. On the fourth wall was a large stone fireplace. He walked quickly to the bookcase to the left of the fireplace and moved a book. Jean-Claude couldn't see which one, but it appeared to be on the middle shelf. The bookcase rotated, creating enough space for them to squeeze through. Lagrange took a candle from a table and lit it with his lighter. He entered first, followed by Jean-Claude. They descended a short flight of stairs until they reached another door. Lagrange opened it with the same key he used to open the front door. Jean-Claude's heart pounded.

Inside, Lagrange turned on a light. It was a large room, perhaps 40 square meters. It had a bed, several chairs, an armoire, a toilet, a gas burner, a refrigerator, and a sink. Two of the walls were lined with provisions, including bottles of wine. There was a shortwave radio on a table.

Jean-Claude glanced around, more worried about what was to happen next than about his surroundings.

"Should the Nazis be defeated, I plan to stay here until I can get a sense of which way the political winds are blowing," Lagrange said with a confident smile. He lit a cigarette and offered one to Jean-Claude, who accepted. "If the Communists take over, or it looks like there are going to be reprisals, I will wait for an opportune moment and then leave for Switzerland. My hope, however, is the Gaullists will prevail and all will be forgiven. My family has been prominent in Lyon for decades and that should count for something. But one can never be too careful."

"Quite impressive," Jean-Claude said, keeping as much physical space between them as the room would allow. "As always, you are well prepared."

Lagrange went over to the wall of provisions and took down a bottle of wine. "When we talked at the Ministry, you said you liked good wine. This is a Lynch Bages 1929." He put a corkscrew in the bottle. "An excellent bottle. No matter what the circumstances, you should always keep a good cellar." The cork came out. He put his nose to the end. "Excellent. You have to try this," he said as he poured two glasses.

Lagrange then moved to the shortwave radio. "It's connected to an antenna on the roof. Very discreet, I assure you." He turned it on. "I can monitor broadcasts from Berlin. Music, news, entertainment. I usually have it tuned to music. It helps me relax."

Soon the radio warmed up. Jean-Claude couldn't believe what he was hearing. It was Beethoven's 5th Piano Concerto.

He became slightly disoriented and his head began to spin.

"Ah, the beauty of Beethoven." Lagrange smiled. "It must be Gieseking. I heard he was playing this week. They still have broadcasts of live performances in Berlin, even with all the bombing. Beautiful music triumphs over war." He handed Jean-Claude a glass of wine and held his up for a toast. "To the future. Let us hope the outcome is favorable. Heil Hitler."

Jean-Claude responded, "Heil Hitler."

They each took a sip standing facing each other. Jean-Claude had his right hand in his pocket, his fingers touching the butt of the gun.

Lagrange put out his cigarette and put his hand on Jean-Claude's shoulder. "You know I find you very attractive. I hope that doesn't offend you." He was looking into Jean-Claude's eyes for a reaction. The moment of decision had come.

Kill him, or let it happen and get more valuable information. What was that worth? His manhood? His pride?

Jean-Claude lowered his hand further into his pocket and gripped the butt of his gun. As he did thoughts raced through his mind. He thought about Natalie, who gave herself to a Nazi in hopes of saving her husband. He thought about the Jews being loaded into boxcars. He thought about the children of Izieu whom Barbie had sent to their deaths. He took a deep breath and looked directly into Lagrange's eyes and made his decision.

"No, it doesn't offend me at all," he said in a passive voice.

Lagrange smiled, took the glass of wine from Jean-Claude, and put it on the table. He came back and kissed him and as he did he put his hand on Jean-Claude's crotch and began to massage it. *The gun. I can't take off my pants, or he will see the gun. I have to do something. Think. Think.*

Jean-Claude took his hand out of his pocket and put both hands on Lagrange's shoulders, and gently pushed him to his knees. Lagrange unzipped his fly, reached in, took out his penis and began to orally copulate him. For the moment, Jean-Claude's right thigh where the gun was holstered was of no interest to him.

Come quickly. Come quickly like you always do. Jean-Claude closed his eyes. Disgust gave way to an erotic sensation he could not control. After only a few seconds he felt his shaft swell. He finished.

"You were very excited. You came so quickly," Lagrange said as he stood up and gave Jean-Claude a hug. "It will be better the more we get to know each other. We must go now, so the driver does not get suspicious. We can return soon, and I can promise you we will have more time together."

Jean-Claude took several gulps of wine before they left the cellar, but he still felt shaken and nauseated as they walked out onto the front terrace. Lagrange motioned to him to follow. He walked about five feet to the left of the front door and pointed to a crevice in the wall. "There is a key here. If you ever are in trouble and can't find me, use this key to let yourself in. It also opens the cellar."

Jean-Claude, still trying to regain his bearings, looked in the vicinity Lagrange had pointed and nodded that he understood. He then followed Lagrange back to the Citroën.

On the way back to the Ministry, Jean-Claude thought about how bizarre the experience had been—his favorite piece of music broadcast live from a bomb-battered Berlin while he was being orally copulated by a French Nazi. He wondered if he had lost touch with reality.

Once back in Lagrange's office, reality returned—quickly. Jean-Claude took a risk. "Pierre," he said, calling him by his first name. "I am concerned about an invasion in the south. It could come at any time and it's so close to us."

Lagrange tried to reassure him. "The dispatches I have read from Berlin say that they expect the invasion to land first in Genoa, then push east into the Baltics." He lit a cigarette and offered Jean-Claude one, which he accepted. They both lit up. "They say this is what Churchill wants. He wants to block the Communists from taking over Eastern Europe. I think we are safe for the time being. I will let you know if I hear anything different."

Lagrange gave him a comforting pat on his arm and went to work. "I've got to check those dispatches from Berlin to see who they are blaming. Go see what you can find out from the recent ones on your desk."

Jean-Claude went to his desk hoping for dispatches that would deal with the anticipated southern invasion. As he sat there going over documents he began thinking about what had happened in Lagrange's shelter. He felt disgust over the sexual encounter. He wanted to take a shower, but settled for a trip to the rest room to wash his privates. But he also felt elation over the opportunity to gather reliable and important intelligence. He got a wry smile on his face when he concluded what had happened that afternoon was worth it so long as the sex didn't go any further. But he knew that if he wanted to stay in Lagrange's good graces it would have to continue. He knew the next time he and Lagrange were alone, the sex would progress. He knew that when it did, he would either have to shed his gun or use it.

CHAPTER 7

CHANTEL'S CLOSE CALL

July 1944

C hantel eagerly welcomed the information about the southern invasion Jean-Claude had obtained from Lagrange. He also told her about their liaison. She told him she never doubted he would do what was necessary when the time came. She also told him that it didn't lessen her respect for him as a man. In fact, she said, it enhanced it.

She delivered all the information he had gathered from Lagrange to her contacts in the Resistance who then sent it to London. In it she also told London that Lagrange was sexually attracted to Jean-Claude and that there had been sexual contact and that Jean-Claude feared if he refused to have a continuing sexual relationship, it would raise suspicions possibly leading to his being discovered. She concluded by saying he felt it was too dangerous for him to return to the Ministry. He wanted to go underground and wait for the invasion.

Jean-Claude worried London would take the position that

having sex with the enemy regardless of gender was part of the job and the success of the mission was the most important thing. But to his relief, Chantal delivered a message the next day that said he should do whatever he believed necessary to avoid capture, including leaving the Ministry if he thought it best. London obviously felt he had done a good job and did not want to risk his detection even though he was in a position to obtain more valuable information. They also told him the invasion in the south was going forward and details would be forthcoming shortly.

Chantal and he talked about it and decided he would not go back to the Ministry. His charade had come to an end. They celebrated at a local café with some trusted associates. But their joy was short-lived when they learned about the reprisals. Almost all of the men in the courtyard of the École had been shot the next morning. Any Jews awaiting transport to Drancy instead had been taken to Bron, just outside of Lyon, and shot, their bodies buried in a pit, and then covered with lye.

Chantal knew once Jean-Claude didn't return to the Ministry, she would be questioned because of their relationship. The questioning would most likely take place at the École. As strong as she was, she feared the torture of sexual humiliation more than anything. She decided if it ever was going to happen, she would kill herself first.

After talking to Bernard, Michel, and Georges, they decided both Chantal and Jean-Claude would go to La Chapelle, where Jean-Claude would wait for orders. Georges then drove Jean-Claude to La Chapelle.

Chantal didn't join them because she wanted to go to her apartment to gather up some belongings and some documents she had stolen from the Ministry that were too sensitive to leave behind, and she wanted to travel on her motorbike.

She rushed back to her apartment, threw some clothes in a suitcase, found the documents she wanted to take with her and put them in a big envelope, then hurried down to the street where her bike was parked. She strapped her suitcase to the back, put the documents under her jacket, and left the city, heading south for La Chapelle.

Her mind was racing so fast she failed to notice a checkpoint on the road ahead. When she finally did, it was too late for her to turn around as there was a line of cars behind her and armed guards on the side of the road.

She had gone through numerous checkpoints before without incident, so she wasn't alarmed and she was only five kilometers from La Chapelle.

"Your papers," the officer barked.

Chantal reached for the purse she always carried. It wasn't there. In her haste to leave she had left it in her apartment. She almost panicked, but instead gathered her thoughts and focused on how she might get out of the mess she had created.

"I am sorry. I left them at my flat. I will turn around and retrieve them," Chantal said smoothly without any nervousness in her voice.

"Pull your motorbike to the side," the officer ordered.

"But *monsieur*, I am sorry. I just forgot them. I work at the Ministry of Information in Lyon. You can call."

"You have no identification. I don't know who you are." He called for assistance. His superior officer came over. They were all French police.

"She has no papers," the first policeman said.

"Search her, and if she has nothing let her go."

Her heart pounded, her mouth went dry. Before she had a chance to try to escape they pulled her off the motorbike.

"If you lift your jacket, so that I can see underneath, I will not have to touch your breasts," a policeman said politely.

Bad luck. A gentleman *flic*. Little chance if she offered to suck him, he would let her go.

She unbuttoned her jacket and removed the envelope. "These are documents from work. I work at the Ministry of Information in Lyon. I work on these at home."

The young policeman took them out of the envelope. He looked them over. "Confidential" and "Top Secret" were printed in large block letters across the top of some of the documents. He called for his sergeant to come over. He glanced at them, and ordered the young officer to take her to the local jail for questioning.

The jail in nearby Condrieu, the small wine-making village across the Rhône River from Vienne, was old and used mainly to let drunks sober up before sending them home. When they arrived, she was taken to an office and told sit down and not to move. It was windowless and did not allow for any possible escape. Some time went by. She grew increasingly anxious aggravated by the fact that she had to go to the bathroom.

When they found out she had classified documents taken from the ministry, she would be in serious trouble. She believed she would most likely be taken to the École for questioning.

She had no problem risking her life on a mission and she did not fear death—so long as it was swift. Should she take the pill now? No, that was the cowardly thing to do. It was the ultimate act and not one to be taken unless she was left with no alternative.

She decided to wait. There was always a possibility something might happen to save her. She would keep the pill ready just in case.

The door opened and a ranking officer in the French police entered and barked at her. "Who are you? Where did you get these documents?"

"I have to go to the bathroom now," she screamed.

He slapped her across the face. "Tell me where you got these documents and you can go. Don't talk and you can piss in your pants?"

The only thought she had was to try and buy time. "I will only talk to the Milice. You have no authority. These are important papers and only the Milice will know what to do with the information."

The officer thought for a moment, turned, and left the room. Soon after, two other French policemen came and shoved her down a hall and pushed her into a toilet. When she came out they threw her into a cell. It smelled of urine. The mattress was infested with insects.

Not knowing how much time she had, she quickly surveyed the cell. There was a window at about five feet covered with wooden panels. There were gaps in the wood. The wood appeared very old and was easily removed, but underneath iron bars were deeply grounded in the wall. She removed the wooden panels and used her extended her fingers to measure the distance between the unevenly spaced bars.

The first several were closer together than the others. They had to be far enough apart to let her head push through. The rest of the body had some flexibility. The last bars were the furthest apart. She put her head against them. There might be room, but it would be very tight. The only way to find out was to try.

She yanked the cot against the wall under the window, then quickly stripped naked so there would be less resistance as she tried to fit through the bars. She was perspiring profusely. This was good. Perspiration would act as a lubricant.

She stood on the cot and pushed her head against the bars. It didn't feel like it would fit. She pushed harder. The pain was intense. She had her pill in her hand in case she got caught. She ignored the pain. She twisted and angled her head and pushed harder. Finally her head popped through. She stood on one foot and turned her body sideways. She put one arm through and then the other. Next the shoulders. Very tight. Very painful. Then her chest. Thank God for small breasts.

Her body was wedged between the bars, half in and half out of the cell. Her hips proved the last obstacle. She was on the ground floor, so if she fell she didn't have far to go. It was now dark and a streetlight a short distance away gave off only a dim light. With one arm against the outer wall, she gave a huge push. Her hips popped through. She fell to the ground with a thud.

"Who's there?" a male voice shouted from around the corner. She lay flat against the building and held her breath. Thirty seconds went by. No one came. He must have thought it was a cat or a dog and not worth investigating.

She moved quickly along the old narrow cobblestone street keeping her body next to walls of buildings that hugged the road. When she reached a nearby vineyard, she ran as fast as she could. She was naked, the ground was flat and rocky, but she didn't care. She stayed in the vineyard until she saw a farmhouse and decided to seek help, even though it was risky. Most farmers had stayed away from taking sides and were just trying to survive. She decided to take a chance.

She peered through a window. The farmer's wife hovered over the stove. She rapped on the window. Startled, the farmwife hesitated for a second, then went to the front door and opened it. *"Mon Dieu.* What happened to you, child?"

"The soldiers, they raped me. I ran away," Chantal said, feigning hysteria.

"Come in. Come in. You poor thing."

Chantal hurried inside. The farmer's wife pulled a wool blanket from the nearby couch and wrapped it around her and left the room. She came back with her arms full of clothes that were much too big, but she preferred that to being naked. She then served her some soup. When her husband came in from the barn, his wife told him what had happened to her. The farmer swore at the Germans, sharing that he had fought them in the last war and hated the Krauts.

She was safe. At least temporarily. The Milice would come looking for her when they discovered she had escaped. The farmhouse was not that far from the jail.

Once she had finished the soup, she told them she had to go. Her hands trembled at the thought the Milice could arrive any minute. The farmer and his wife didn't want any trouble, so they did not try to make her stay. She thanked them and left, heading for La Chapelle. She would have to go there on foot, but she knew the way and felt sure she could make it without being detected. The farmer's wife had given her a pair of oversized boots, but they were preferable to bare feet.

La Chapelle was above Condrieu at the top of a steep hillside that had terraced vineyards. Because of the climb and her fear of being detected, it took her several hours to get there, even though it was only a few kilometers from the farmhouse. The heavy clothes and the warm summer night added to her exhaustion from the climb. Plus, she had injured her ribs in the escape and the pain was intense every time she took a breath.

When she finally got to the farmhouse, she pounded on the door. "It's Chantal." Her breathing was heavy. Bernard opened the door. He took one look and began to laugh uproariously. "Look at this, Jean-Claude, a big scarecrow has come in from the meadow."

"Shut up, Bernard," she said and pushed her way inside.

Chantal told them of her escape. After some wine, she began to see some humor in what had happened: a naked woman half in and half out of a jail window, the kind farmer and his wife thinking she had been raped, the bulky coat and clunky shoes. She did look like a scarecrow.

Jean-Claude took a picture of her with his miniature camera. She threatened to kill him if he didn't destroy the photo. After finishing the bottle of wine and taking a bath, she fell asleep and slept for twenty-four hours despite the pain from cracked ribs.

CHAPTER 8

THE RAIL YARD

July–August 1944

Jean-Claude, Chantal, and Bernard waited anxiously at the farmhouse for news of when the southern invasion would begin. The shortwave radio tuned to the BBC kept them abreast of what was happening in Normandy. The Allies had consolidated their landings and continued to advance inland, but they encountered heavy resistance. They expected to take Caen in one day, but it took much longer than anticipated. The Allies, however, were in France to stay. There would not be another Dunkirk. But victory would not come easily, and it was feared the demands of the Normandy invasion might cause the southern landing to be canceled or postponed.

This was the longest period of time Jean-Claude and Bernard had spent together since Jean-Claude had arrived at La Chapelle. Bernard recovered quickly from his experience at the École. He was in good shape for a man 66 years old.

This was a special time for Jean-Claude and Bernard and they spoke about many things. They reminisced about the past and Jean-Claude filled him in on what had happened in his life. He told him about Stephanie and their wedding and how excited he was about the baby, even though he didn't know whether it was a boy or a girl. He left out details about the surprise pregnancy, the anti-Semitic father-in-law, and his doubts about Stephanie's character, all of which had receded into a distant memory.

His father said he was delighted, but his eyes told of a man who had little room left for emotions. "I hope I have a chance to meet her and the baby someday." But Jean-Claude knew his father never expected to be able to fulfill that hope.

There were two things Jean-Claude didn't talk about. Bernard's activities, because he didn't want to talk about the violence, and the bottles of wine and the champagne he had taken from the cellar back in Berkeley.

Jean-Claude told him about the Matsumoto case and Manzanar. Bernard shook his head and said France had gone mad, but he never thought something like that could happen in the United States.

When Bernard talked about the future, he spoke with passion of his hopes for a Communist government after the war. There were scores to settle and inevitable disputes with the Gaullists, but he knew there would be a place in the new France for the Communists, and if he lived, he was going to be a part of it. He would not return to the United States. He'd made up his mind.

It was the first week in August and they were still awaiting news of the southern invasion when Andre came to the farmhouse at La Chapelle, very excited. He had not been back since the escape from the École. They hoped he was bringing word of the southern invasion, but he had other news he was excited about.

Bernard, Jean-Claude, and Chantal, who was still recovering from her cracked ribs, sat down at a table across from Andre. They poured him a glass of wine to help calm him down as he lit a cigarette. "The Germans are moving a lot of heavy armor out of Lyon on flatbed railcars because they have to reinforce their armies in Normandy. We just got word from our railroad workers that this has been happening for the past several days. They said the Germans are working long hours, so they must intend to move out soon."

He drank the wine in gulps and drew heavily on his cigarette. "They said there are tanks, heavy artillery, armored cars, and trucks. And they are going to be on three different trains, but they will all leave from the central train yard in Lyon." He lowered his voice as if telling a secret. "There is a meeting tonight at Monsieur Allard's wine cave in Condrieu. Ledoux is going to be there. So is Michel. Bernard, they want you to come. Ledoux is going to teach us how to blow up the trains."

"What time?" Bernard asked.

"Around 9. We are to meet in his wine cave at the rear of the house. Ledoux said he's taking a risk to come here, but he said he wouldn't entrust the mission to anyone but us."

"You mean there's nobody else around dumb enough to do it," Bernard said. "Half the German army is patrolling the rail yard and they have more dogs than people." He was serious, but from the tone of his voice Jean-Claude could tell he was also excited by the prospect.

"The best thing about the idea is that I will get to see my old friend Pierre, the finest winemaker in Condrieu," Bernard said with a smile.

"I want to go," Jean-Claude said.

Bernard hesitated for a moment then said, "Okay, but for the meeting only, not the rail yard." He pointed his finger to emphasize that the night out did not include the rail yard. "It will be good for you to get out of here for a while."

They had several hours until they were to leave for Condrieu. Jean-Claude and Andre sat in the salon, and he asked Andre about being excluded from the Paris bar. "How could that have happened?"

"Because I'm Jewish. Ten years in the bar and they kicked me out like I was nobody." Andre's voice rose in anger and he clenched his fists as he described what the Vichy did immediately after taking power. "They passed laws defining who was a Jew. You were a Jew if one parent was a Jew, if a grandparent was a Jew, if your wife was a Jew, if she was not, but one of her parents were Jewish, and on and on. It got so bad we joked that if you looked like a Jew you were a Jew. If you are a Jew, you can't hold any administrative jobs in the government; you can't work in the press, the theatre, the cinema.

"After they passed these laws that expanded the definition of who was a Jew they completely wrote Jews out of the civil laws. We have no protection. It's as if we don't exist." He raised his voice as he pointed to Jean-Claude and pounded the table.

Jean-Claude shook his head.

"It's all bullshit," Andre said. "The real reason they passed those laws is that many in the government are anti-Semites, and the rest believed Germany was going to win the war, and wanted to be on the right side when that happened. They didn't do it because the Germans made them do it. They did it on their own, the bastards." Andre's eyes seethed with anger.

"Then they went after the lawyers. They said the number of Jewish lawyers could not exceed two percent of the total number of lawyers in any jurisdiction." He got up and began to stomp around the room as he spoke. "They required the Jewish lawyers who did remain to wear the yellow star on their robes when appearing in the Palais de Justice."

Jean-Claude lit a cigarette. What he was hearing made him angry. Being excluded from the bar because he was Jewish? Stanley would go crazy if he heard this.

Jean-Claude poured them each another glass of wine.

Andre finished half of the wine without stopping. "I was not one of the lucky two percent in the Paris Bar. So they kicked me out. Just like that. So I joined the Resistance. There is no two percent rule in the Resistance. The Resistance takes all kinds, even Jews." He finally calmed down after two more glasses of wine.

"Someday there will be accountability." Jean-Claude said. Andre nodded his head in agreement.

Night came and as it got close to 9:00 p.m., Bernard, Chantal, Jean-Claude, and Andre made their way down the hillside to Condrieu and to the wine cave of Monsieur Allard. When they arrived, Georges was already there. Bernard gave Pierre Allard a big hug. They had been comrades in the last war and were close friends.

The old cave was built into a hillside of solid limestone. It was cool and a bit damp with a slight smell of mold. The only light was from a bulb hanging on a cord from the low ceiling. The casks of aging wine were stacked one on top of the other in racks. They sat on old handmade wooden benches and empty wine casks as they listened to Ledoux.

Ledoux was known as the train wrecker. He had survived being tortured by the Milice, who believed him to be a member of the Resistance. They'd broken his ribs and smashed his face. He had been rescued by fellow Resistance fighters, just before he was to be shipped off to a concentration camp. He then turned his talents to teaching others the art of train wrecking. He was the undisputed expert in the field.

"There are three trains that are going to leave the central Lyon switching yard in the next two days. Each train will have approximately ten flatbeds with heavy weapons on them." He paced as he talked. His voice was high-pitched and shrill, but there was no mistaking its intensity. "There will also be cars with some troops and a car with hostages on each train to discourage us from blowing them up. We know this from reliable sources. If these weapons reach Normandy, it will further slow the Allied advance. They must never get there." He emphasized his point by shaking his fist in their direction.

They all nodded in agreement.

"We have been relatively successful in using plastic attached to the rails, but the Germans are now wise to this and have patrols with dogs that constantly inspect the tracks. We can't count on that being successful in the future."

He reached into a bag he had brought with him. "We have been given a new device by the OSS in London called the Mole. It is really quite ingenious," he said, holding up the device. "We know the most disruptive place to blow up a train is in a tunnel. It takes weeks to clear the wreckage. The Mole is a photoelectric cell. It's light-sensitive, so when there is a significant change in light, it releases an impulse to an amplifier that sends a charge to a detonator attached to the plastic explosives. When a train enters a tunnel, it's plunged into darkness. This sudden change in light is what starts the process." He looked around the cave making sure everyone understood how the device worked.

"The Mole is placed at the front of the car near the rail bed in a place where it can easily detect the change in light. The cord from the Mole runs to the amplifier, taped to the top of the plastic explosives containing the detonator." He passed the device around so each one could have a close look. "The explosives have to be taped above a front wheel on the car's undercarriage and as close to the coupling as possible. The Americans have tested this and said that if these instructions are followed, it will destroy at least several of the cars in the tunnel while not causing fatalities. The tunnel will be clogged and will take weeks to clear."

"There should not be any loss of life, so the hostages will not be hurt. They may be taken off the train and shot, but the wreck will not kill them. The rail yard is heavily guarded, but our friends have given us a location where we can cut a hole in the fence and probably not be detected. They have also mapped the location of the three trains. It should take about fifteen minutes to plant the Mole and the explosives on each car if all goes well."

Jean-Claude listened with rapt attention. This was like the

training he'd received at Lord Montague's estate. As exciting as it was to think about, he realized how dangerous it was going to be.

Ledoux continued with his instructions. "You must make sure the Mole is placed in the undercarriage of the car, so it will not be detected upon inspection. The Germans don't know about this device so they won't be looking for it. Any questions? Now is the time to ask," he said in a commanding voice.

"They must have this place heavily guarded. How do we get in, get the plastic planted, and get out without being seen?" Andre asked.

"We are going to create a diversion," Ledoux said. "As you are cutting the fence, I and two others are going to set off explosives we've already hidden at the end of the yard away from the target cars. We can detonate them remotely. There will be a series of explosions. That should draw the guards to that location.

"In the confusion, we hope you will have enough time to set the Moles. Here are two more Moles." He held up a bag. "There is also a map of the rail yard with the place to cut the fence and the location of the three trains. The guards change shifts at midnight. The diversion will be set off just after the shift change. You should have the fence cut and be ready to enter as soon as you hear the explosions."

"How do we stick the Mole to the car?" Bernard asked.

"Ah. I forgot. The Mole is attached to magnets. You should scrape the surface where you are going to attach it to make better contact. The magnets are very strong and are designed to keep the Mole stuck to the car while it is moving. The rail yard is well lit, so you will be able to see what you are doing. The problem is the Germans will be able to see what you are doing as well unless they are distracted."

Jean-Claude asked the next question. "When do we do this?"

"Tomorrow night. There is little time before the trains depart." He looked around the cave at each of them and asked, "Are you ready to do this?"

They all nodded in agreement. He passed out the two additional Moles and the meeting ended.

As they left, Pierre gave Bernard four bottles of wine. "These are some of the best from my cellar. Good luck, my friend." They gave each other a hug and kissed each other on their cheeks.

"It used to be that you let the wine age, but things are too uncertain these days so I will drink them right away," Bernard said.

Jean-Claude smiled. That sounded familiar.

On the way back to La Chapelle, Jean-Claude said he wanted to go. Bernard said no and reminded him he had his orders. "I am still upset with you for helping with my escape," Bernard said with a smile, "but I will forgive you since you didn't get caught or get me killed."

Michel could not go because he was too big to fit through the small hole in the fence and could not run fast. Chantal was still recovering from her rib injuries sustained in her jail cell escape and had limited mobility, so she would not be going. That left Bernard, Georges, and Andre.

Jean-Claude was frustrated at being left out. He sulked, but didn't say any more about it.

The next night, as Bernard and Andre were getting ready to leave for Lyon, Michel arrived, very upset. "Georges had been detained by the French police for trying to bribe someone to sell him something that was rationed. It doesn't sound serious, but we don't know when he will be free. I can't go, and we can't do the job one man short. One of the trains won't be armed."

"I will go," Jean-Claude immediately spoke up.

"You don't know anything about setting explosives," Michel said.

"Yes, I do. I was trained how to set plastic with detonators. I know how to handle plastic. I listened to Ledoux and understood everything he said. The only thing I don't have experience with is attaching the Mole, but neither do any of you."

"We don't have time to argue. We need to go." Bernard made a quick decision. They needed a third man to complete the mission. He nodded for Jean-Claude to follow. Jean-Claude was surprised at how quickly his father made the decision. It was now very clear everything was secondary to defeating the Germans, and that included his son's safety.

As they drove toward Lyon, the reality of what he was about to do set in. He had never carried out a sabotage operation. Helping Bernard escape was easy. All he'd had to do was drive. This was different, very different. He could die. They could all die. As they got closer to Lyon and the rail yard, his anxiety level increased. The fear of death was replaced by the fear of failure. But the presence of Andre and his father bolstered his confidence. When they reached the fence, he felt he was ready.

The main rail yard in Lyon was huge. It handled switching for trains from all over Europe. Because of its complexity and size, French railway workers still managed it, many of whom were loyal to the Resistance. This was how the maps of the locations of the cars had been obtained.

Bernard and Andre were familiar with the yard, having done surveillance on other occasions, so the map was relatively easy to understand. They recognized the spot where they were to enter. Jean-Claude also recognized the rail yard from the time he and Chantal watched the Jews being loaded into boxcars.

The hard part was locating the three trains. The rail workers said that each train already had a locomotive attached to the cars. While there were numerous locomotives in the yard, only three were attached to flatbed cars with heavy weapons and they were fairly close together. The map Ledoux had given them would help.

At 11:55 p.m., Andre, Bernard, and Jean-Claude crouched at a location next to the fence. Bernard used wire cutters to open a hole so they could crawl through. It was a warm July night and they all perspired heavily, but Jean-Claude's hands were ice cold. He was fueled by adrenaline.

Each man was assigned a train. Jean-Claude was given the

one closest to where they were to enter. It would expose him the least. Bernard took the next farthest, which was about seventy-five meters from the first. Andre had the third, the farthest away.

At 12:05 a.m., a series of explosions boomed from the north end of the yard. Sirens blared. The guards ran in all directions in a frenzied attempt to locate those responsible for the explosions.

The fence cut with relative ease. The yard was well-lit, so they could see the trains, but the searchlights would also reveal them if they were caught in the open. They each took off running in the direction of their assigned target.

Jean-Claude's target was the closest and easiest to spot. He got there quickly and rolled under the first car attached to the locomotive. He placed the explosive on the carriage frame just above the front wheel and about a foot from the coupling. The hard part was to find the best location for the Mole because the wire from the explosives to the Mole had to be concealed, and also because it exposed him to detection. He glanced out from under the carriage.

There was still pandemonium in the yard. He left the Mole on the track just behind the wheel where he could reach it and crawled to the front of the carriage. He lay down between the flatbed and the locomotive and grabbed the Mole. He found a location on the carriage and scraped the rust off the side with a knife. He placed the Mole onto the scraped area. The magnet engaged. He tested the fit to make sure there was a tight seat. It felt secure. Voices could be heard coming closer to his location. He crawled out from under the carriage. This was when he was going to be in maximum danger, but everything was happening so fast he didn't think about it.

He crouched down and ran as fast as he could. A sweeping floodlight came in his direction. He fell to the dirt, tumbled, and rolled just as he had been taught to do. It missed him by a few feet. He got up, raced to the fence, and climbed through.

For the time being, he was safe. He now worried about Bernard and Andre.

Bernard was fortunate. While his train was farther from the fence, it was in a more obscure location off on a spur by itself and out of the direct path of the searchlights. He was able to set his device with relative ease although the magnetic contact would not initially secure, and he had to spend time in an exposed position scraping the rust off the carriage. He finally achieved a seat that he felt was secure. Now he had to get back to the fence. He hopscotched from train to train in order to reduce the time he would be in the open. The sounds of guards and dogs were getting closer, but he made it back to the fence and through. He and Jean-Claude were safe. Now they waited for Andre.

Andre had the hardest and most dangerous train. It was the farthest away and the closest to the concentration of guards. He made it to the flatbed and secured the plastic on the pedestal of the carriage and close to the coupling. He then secured the Mole. He had taken over fifteen minutes because he had difficulty hiding the cord from the Mole to the amplifier. Finally, he succeeded.

The guards continued to search the entire yard for those responsible for the explosion and were getting nearer to Andre's location. Bernard watched as Andre made his way from one train to another, using them as cover, but there were large expanses of open space between the trains. The next run would be the most dangerous because it would expose him for the longest time. He crouched and ran.

"Halt! Halt!" The searchlight had caught him. Andre kept running. There was a burst of machine gun fire. He fell.

Watching from the shadows by the fence, Bernard and Jean-Claude feared the worst. They could see the guards hovering over Andre's body.

"He's dead. There is nothing we can do," Bernard said with

no emotion in his voice. He had witnessed death many times and had learned to steel himself so the experience would not impact him emotionally. At least not outwardly.

Jean-Claude reacted differently. The death of Andre was horrible to watch. He had seen men murdered at Montluc, and it had affected him. But he didn't know them. He felt no personal connection to them. But this was a friend. A man he knew and respected. Now he was gone and he was experiencing the finality of death.

They paused for a moment out of respect for their friend whom they would leave behind, and then ran for the car and drove back to La Chapelle.

On the drive back, Jean-Claude's hands trembled as he lit a cigarette, shaken by the loss of a friend and the close call they all had.

Was it worth it? Would Andre's sacrifice make a difference? These were the thoughts that plagued him as he tried to sleep that night, but was unsuccessful.

The trains left two days later.

A week later, they heard a shortwave broadcast from the BBC that reported two trains carrying heavy weapons had exploded inside tunnels derailing several of the cars and disrupting their shipments to the front for a substantial period. A third train also carrying heavy weapons was not destroyed.

"I'll bet that was mine," Jean-Claude said.

"No," Bernard said. "The report said that when the first two blew up, they stopped the third and took the weapons off. They are now going by land where our planes should be able to get them."

Their mission was successful, but the price was terrible. Andre was dead and Barbie ordered twenty rail yard workers taken to Montluc and shot. He threatened to round up the rest and ship them to the east if he had to evacuate Lyon.

Jean-Claude tried to put the experience at the rail yard out of his mind, but it kept coming back to haunt him. He was counting the days until the southern invasion that would hopefully put an end to all the insanity.

CHAPTER 9

THE SOUTH

August 1944

Good news came from the front—Germany was definitely losing the war.

By the end of July 1944, the Soviets had driven their forces to within eighty miles of the gates of Warsaw. Emboldened by the news, the Resistance took greater risks. Daring acts of sabotage and assassinations became commonplace.

With each passing day, the Nazis became more brutal, reflecting the insanity that was consuming Hitler. There were assassinations by the Resistance, reprisals by the Nazis. It became an all-consuming cycle of violence.

In early August, scores of Resistance fighters were arrested and executed in the area around Lyon as the Gestapo stepped up its efforts to disrupt them in the coastal areas. It became so dangerous that many left for the mountains where they could regroup and train with less fear of being detected.

There they were aided by small squads called Jed teams from operation Jedburgh, organized by combined British and American intelligence in London. Each Jed team consisted of four men: one American, one Brit, one Frenchman—all officers—and one radio operator, an enlisted man. They would parachute into France in uniform. It was their job to arm and train the Resistance fighters, so they would be ready to join the Allies when the invasion began.

On August 5th, Jean-Claude received a coded message from London ordering him to go south to Hyères, a port city about 300 kilometers from Lyon and 30 kilometers east of Marseilles. He was to check into the Hotel La Mer under the name Jacques Carlier and wait to be contacted by a member of the Resistance. He would then be put in touch with members of a Jed unit, who in turn would help him reintegrate into the regular army after the invasion. He was told nothing more.

Chantal had stolen a motorbike to replace the one she'd had to leave behind when she was arrested. She said she would drive Jean-Claude to Hyères and verify the contact was legitimate.

Jean-Claude dreaded saying good-bye to his father, just as he had dreaded saying good-bye to Stephanie. The unspoken thought tormented him. This might be the last time they'd ever see each other.

That night, Bernard walked Jean-Claude down the driveway. He had his arm around his shoulders. Chantal was waiting next to her motorbike. When they reached the bike they stopped.

Jean-Claude's eyes grew moist.

"Be safe, Jean-Claude," Bernard said.

"You too, Papa." His voice cracked. "I love you."

They kissed each other's cheeks and embraced.

Chantal mounted the bike. Jean-Claude climbed on the back. Over the roar of the engine as they drove away, Jean-Claude heard Bernard call out, "*Vive la France.*" He turned and waved, but in the darkness Bernard was too far away to see and he didn't respond.

Chantal and Jean-Claude had become very close—not as

lovers, because they had never been that way, but as two people who had been brought together by the dangers they faced and the mission they shared. He had never met a more courageous woman.

They arrived at the hotel a little before eight at night. Jean-Claude checked in as he had been instructed. They went into the small dining room and ordered dinner. As they ate and drank wine, they talked quietly, mostly about their lives since he had left France fifteen years before. He told her about Stephanie and the baby, then he asked about her.

"How is it that you never married?"

She dropped her eyes, paused, and looked up at him. "I like men and women, but my preference runs to women," she said. "It's probably best since it looks like I was destined to do this work, and a family would have tied me down and made me less likely to take risks." She sounded neither apologetic nor embarrassed. It was who she was and she was not ashamed.

"Anyway, I feel very fulfilled, and if I die, I have lived a life with purpose. If I survive, I will think about finding a lover and settling down." She sat back in her chair with a satisfied look on her face.

He thought about what she said.

Their situation made death an ever-present reality. He made up his mind the night in the rail yard that if he died he would have no regrets. His life too would have had purpose.

The bill arrived for dinner and attached to it was a note that read, "Walk east along the highway outside the hotel tomorrow 8:00 a.m."

Chantal said she knew the waiter. They got up to leave. Chantal glanced at him. "It's safe to follow the instructions on the note," Chantal said. "The contact is legitimate." Then she said, "I'll stay here tonight and leave early in the morning. It will be safer than traveling at night."

Jean-Claude agreed.

The room had one bed. A terrace door opened to the ocean and had louvered panels on both sides that could be closed and still let the wind through. It was August, and the evening was warm. The air smelled of the sea, so they left the door open and closed the panels.

Jean-Claude was thinking about the next day and the impending invasion, and wasn't paying attention to Chantal when she turned out the light and climbed into bed. It was assumed they would share the bed, but what happened next surprised him.

She touched his shoulder and brought her warm naked body next to his. "Make love to me, Jean-Claude," she whispered.

He did not hesitate and pulled her against him. In an instant, he realized that now more than ever, life had to be lived for the moment. Human affection and warmth had been absent from their lives for far too long. The war had made them cold and unemotional. This was a chance to express some feelings.

They didn't speak as he embraced her and kissed her with a passion that was not lustful, but born out of love for someone he cared deeply about. It was a very personal way to say good-bye.

They made love as lovers and as friends. It was as if he had known her body many times. When they finished, she got up to use the bidet. The sheet was damp, not from lovemaking, but from tears.

They went to sleep holding each other. He awoke from a sound sleep to the louvered doors banging in the wind. The bed was empty. She was gone. He wondered if he would ever see her again.

CHAPTER 10

THE INVASION

August 15, 1944

As he had been instructed to do, Jean-Claude walked east on the highway, which ran along the top of a ridge overlooking the Mediterranean. He stared at the sea and wondered how long it would be before the invasion would bring an end to the war. He felt conflicted leaving his father and Chantal and the others behind in Lyon to face an uncertain fate. He had completed his mission. He felt his rightful place was with them. But he had orders.

Just then, an old delivery truck with a sign painted on the side, *Legumes et Fruits*, pulled alongside him and stopped.

"Are you from Villefranche?" the driver asked.

"Yes."

"I used to work at the Café Soleil," the driver replied.

"I know it well."

Café Soleil was the code word for his contact.

"I am François. Get in," the driver said. They shook hands.

"I have heard many good things about you and the work you and your friends are doing in Lyon."

"And I have heard much about what you and your friends have been doing here along the coast," Jean-Claude responded.

François put the truck in gear and the old lorry rumbled down the road. "Each day, I drive from Hyères to Cannes delivering fruits and vegetables. I drive along this highway and I count the ships in the harbor in Hyères and the installations on the beaches. We don't know exactly where the invasion will land, but we think it will be somewhere between Toulon and Cannes. I meet with the others each night and we share what we have learned. One of us then sends the information to the Allies in Italy."

"How great is the risk, now that the Nazis know an invasion is coming?" Jean-Claude asked.

"The risk has gotten much worse. They have begun to arrest anyone suspicious, anyone they believe might be a member of the Resistance. This time before we leave for the mountains will be very dangerous, but I have built up good relations with some of the German military posts along my route. I give them fresh fruits and vegetables. I hope this will be good enough to keep us safe until the invasion."

Jean-Claude began to feel tightness in his stomach that came each time he sensed he was in imminent danger.

"Look there," François said and pointed to the coast below. "See those shafts sticking up from the water? They are attached to an artillery shell that will explode on contact but they are not installed on every beach. We map the beaches that look clean."

Jean-Claude looked and was struck by both the military installation and the beauty of the Mediterranean in the early morning. It was a radiant blue and sparkled in the morning sun.

"And there," François said, pointing to the beautiful villas that dotted the hills overlooking the beaches. "Until the war, they were some of the most expensive real estate in the world. Now the windows are boarded up and many have been fortified and are artillery installations. Look for gun barrels sticking out of the windows."

As they drove, François continued to point out the defenses the Germans had installed in anticipation of the invasion. "Down on the beach, what look like little beach houses and bathing huts are actually bunkers. We map all of them and send them off. By now we have almost the entire coast mapped from Marseilles to Nice. Our job is to keep the maps updated, so the targets can be bombarded once the invasion begins."

Jean-Claude felt like a tourist being shown the landmarks of a famous resort area, but this time they were not beautiful villas or pristine beaches, but rather structures that housed the weapons of war and beaches designed to kill those who tried to cross them.

"Do you think it will ever be the same after the war?" Jean-Claude was distressed by what had been done to the area.

"Nothing will ever be the same," François said sadly, shaking his head. He paused briefly then resumed talking about his surveillance. "We look for troop movement along the highways. Recently large contingents have been moving to reinforce the German army in Normandy and Italy. We think the German defenses along the coast are considerably weaker than they were before. What are left here are not elite units and they don't have much depth. They also don't have the capacity to support the ground troops with air or naval forces. If the Allies can secure the beaches and the paratroopers the high ground, this could be over very quickly."

"We saw the same thing in Lyon. They were sending units to fight in Normandy," Jean-Claude said, lighting a cigarette.

"You will be helping me on my route until we receive orders to take you into the mountains to meet with the Jed team that will help you connect with a unit once the Allies have landed." Jean-Claude nodded to show he understood.

They continued on the road that overlooked the sea, making deliveries to local markets and hotels along the way. Then they stopped at a German outpost in a hotel that had been converted to a headquarters for the units stationed nearby.

"Don't be afraid. I stop here several times a week and give them fruits for free. In exchange they leave me alone and let me make my deliveries without interference. Remember who you are and why you are here. Stay calm and everything will be all right."

The truck stopped in front and François took a basket of fruit from the back. "You wait in the truck."

He walked inside to the dining area of the converted hotel. Groups of German soldiers sat at tables and at the bar. A roar went up when François entered. "The fruit man is here," one shouted.

François put the basket on the bar. "Enjoy, these are the best of the season," he said casually.

Outside, Jean-Claude gazed at the blue Mediterranean through the passenger window when suddenly a voice startled him. "Your papers."

Jean-Claude turned and looked toward the driver's side window. A Gestapo officer in his brown uniform stood outside the car with his hand out. His stomach cramped. But he smiled and reached into his jacket pocket and gave him the ID from the Ministry.

The Gestapo officer looked at the ID then eyed Jean-Claude. "What are you doing down here? You work in Lyon."

Just then François came back and intervened. "He is my nephew come to help me make deliveries. It's the summer season and I am very busy."

"Shut up," the Gestapo barked.

Jean-Claude felt the cold rush of adrenaline. "It's my holiday. August, you know. I'm not expected back for another two weeks." Then he felt pure fear wondering if word he hadn't returned to the Ministry had reached the Gestapo.

The Gestapo officer peered at him for what seemed like an eternity. He then handed the ID back to him and called for a subordinate to come over.

"Take his photograph. Send it to Lyon to the Ministry of Information. Find out if he is who he says he is."

The subordinate obeyed.

"You can go for now. I will check you again the next time you come back," the Gestapo said as he turned around and walked away.

As François returned to his truck, Jean-Claude said, "We've got to get out of here. Once Lyon gets back to the Gestapo, I'm in trouble."

"I agree. I will send word to the Jed unit by pigeon that we are coming tonight." François started up the truck and headed back down the highway to Cannes.

In England he had been instructed on the use of carrier pigeons. He'd felt it was an archaic and rather entertaining part of his training, but of little practical value. Once again what he learned there was proving to be invaluable. It had already saved his life in the rail yard. Now a pigeon might be responsible for extending it.

"I have a flat in Cannes. That's where I keep my birds. We can stay there until it gets dark. Then we will travel north into the low mountains just above the coast. We will go about fifteen kilometers up into the Massif des Maures. You know these mountains?"

"No. I never spent much time in the south," Jean-Claude said, looking up at them. "They're very beautiful."

"They stretch from Hyères almost to Cannes. They are not high like the Alps, but very steep with deep valleys in between. Good for hiking and hiding. They must be controlled once the invasion begins to prevent the Germans from sending reinforcements. There is a camp there where the Jeds are training members of the Resistance. Once there, I will turn you over to the Jed unit. They will take care of you from then on."

When nightfall came, they left François's flat and headed for the mountains. He had not heard back from the Jed unit, but assumed the pigeon had gotten through and they were aware he was coming. After the close brush with the Gestapo, Jean-

Claude felt relieved to finally be given over to friendly hands.

The higher they got into the Massif, the narrower and less maintained the road became. Finally, after over an hour, they turned off the paved road onto one that was dirt. After traveling several kilometers, François stopped the truck. They were in a clearing in a thickly wooded area that was lit only by the truck's headlights.

"Now we wait," François said and sipped from a flask, which he offered to Jean-Claude. Jean-Claude took a swig. It was brandy and it felt very warm as it traveled into his stomach. It relaxed him and relieved the tension he felt over the uncertainties of what lay ahead.

Soon they saw a flashing green light coming from the woods.

"We get out here."

They both got out of the truck and walked toward the direction of the light. "It's François. I have the package with me."

"*Bonsoir*, François, *comment allez-vous?*" a male voice said in French, but with a decided British accent.

"*Bien, merci*," François replied.

A man in a British uniform wearing a red beret stepped from the woods. He nodded to Jean-Claude and said, "Follow me." He led them along a path until they came to an area with a number of tents. The Brit stepped into one of the larger ones. François and Jean-Claude followed. Inside were two officers.

"You must be Bonnay. I am Major Rattner, OSS, and this is Lieutenant La Fleur, French 4th Army, and your escort is Lieutenant Ivory, British RAF."

Jean-Claude nodded. "Good to be here," he said and shook hands with the three officers.

"Welcome," Major Rattner said. "We have been told we must take good care of you. They say you know too much to allow you to fall into German hands."

"That almost happened earlier today. That's why we're here a little bit sooner than planned," François said.

"Yes, your pigeon let us know you were coming." He then

turned to Jean-Claude. "We don't know exactly when the invasion will launch, but we know it's just a matter of days. Once it arrives, we'll get you to a unit."

"François tells me you are training members of the Resistance." Jean-Claude was interested in what the Jed unit did and if he could be of any help until it was time for him to leave.

"We have about 150 men here. They know these mountains and the critical roads between the valleys. They are good fighters and hate the Germans. They just needed some guidance to make them an effective fighting force. We think we've provided that."

He gestured to Jean-Claude to take a seat at the long table that had maps spread out on the surface. "Our job is to secure the high ground and control the east-west roads. We have been told an initial Allied force will come by parachute. The Germans are anticipating an airborne assault and have installed sharp spikes in the open fields to wreck gliders and impale paratroopers. We are clearing as many as we can.

"We are here about 15 kilometers from Draguignan where the German headquarters for this area is located." He pointed to one of the large maps that was spread out on the table. "We are also here to support one of the paratroop units who will drop near there. We have mapped the town and pinpointed where the headquarters are located and where General Neuling, the German commander of the LXII Corps, stays."

He pointed to that location. "It's in an old mansion in a pine forest on the outskirts of the town. It is not particularly well-fortified and with the element of surprise, the paratroopers plan to capture him, or if that's not possible, kill him. But anything can happen to disrupt the mission: weather, poor drops, glider crashes. We have to be ready for anything. Our job is to disrupt the enemy patrols in the area once they become aware there are Allied military on the ground, and to ensure the paratroopers get out okay."

"Sounds like you guys will be right in the middle of things," Jean-Claude said, lighting a cigarette. He was interested in what the major had to say about their mission, but he also studied the map to learn where he was in relation to Lyon.

"Yep. Just the way we like it. Our biggest problem is lack of weapons and supplies. We are expecting a drop tonight. A lot depends on the weather, so we will have to wait and see if they come. If they do, you can help us secure them."

"Glad to be of some help," Jean-Claude said, wanting to make a contribution even though his stay was going to be short.

"I am going back down the hill to take one more ride along the coast to see if there have been any major changes, and then I'll be back to stay," François said and left.

"There's going to be a lot of firepower directed at the coast initially, so we have to keep you out of range," Major Rattner said. "Once the beaches have been secured we will get you to a unit. You're French, right?"

"I was born here, but I have lived in the States for many years. I consider it my home."

"What do you do?"

"I'm a lawyer."

"No kidding. I'm a cop from Milwaukee. Where are you from?"

"California. Berkeley."

"I know the area. I was briefly stationed at the Presidio in San Francisco. Nice weather out there." Major Rattner smiled. "Let's get you some chow and coffee. We have a wait until the birds fly over. A piece of advice. Don't light up outside when it's dark. The glow can be seen from some distance. You have to always be mindful of snipers."

Jean-Claude nodded in agreement and went to the mess tent with the major.

Later on that night, Jean-Claude heard the deep rumble of the C-47's engines. He stood with other Resistance fighters, looking toward the night sky as white billowy objects with crates and boxes attached came floating down. Over the next several hours, Jean-Claude helped retrieve dozens of boxes alongside the other men. They broke them open immediately. They were filled with small arms, mortars, machine guns, ammunition, day rations, and medical supplies.

"This is what we've been waiting for," Rattner said, clearly delighted.

The next day Jean-Claude spent in the camp talking to some of the Resistance fighters. He learned about the horrors many of their comrades had experienced at the hands of the Milice and the Gestapo. He heard about the tens of thousands of Frenchmen who had been involuntarily sent to the east as laborers and how the Vichy government had been complicit in the murder of Resistance fighters and the deportation of Jews to Drancy.

He felt ashamed of his homeland. He now understood how Mas Matsumoto felt about his beloved Japan committing such a heinous act at Pearl Harbor.

He had gone to the command tent and was reviewing maps to make sure he knew where he was in relation to Lyon when at about 2300 hours, Rattner rushed in. Radio had received the code words: *NANCY HAS A STIFF NECK.* They were the code words signaling that the invasion was to begin in a few hours.

The camp exploded in a frenzy of activity. One group was headed to Draguignan to meet up with airborne units who were dropping into the area at that moment. Jean-Claude felt his heart pumping from the excitement of knowing the invasion was actually about to happen.

Major Rattner turned to him. "I assigned one of my best men to watch over you and a driver who knows the back roads. They will take you down the mountain. We should be able to get you to a spot where you will have a good look at the beaches, but out of artillery range. Once the ground forces land, we'll get you hooked up with a unit. We still want to make sure you don't get captured on the way down, but by now things are pretty well set, so, even if you got caught and gave up information, it's too late for it to be of any value."

"So I'm no longer a high-value asset?" Jean-Claude gave the major a wry smile. "Is that what you're saying?"

"Hey, no offense. You're expendable, but I still think you're a nice guy and worth saving. So we'll do our best to get you down safely. You'll leave in a few hours."

This was what he had been waiting for, for over two years. He wondered again what Bernard, Chantal, and the others were doing. He prayed they were safe.

Finally, in the pre-dawn darkness, a twenty-year-old driver who said he had grown up in these mountains was taking Jean-Claude down the mountain in an old four-wheel-drive Range Rover. An older man accompanied them. The Rover bumped along the dirt road until it reached the paved one. The older man said he lived in Hyères and had been a member of the Resistance for over a year, but in the last several months with an invasion imminent, the Nazis had stepped up their hunt for Resistance fighters and it had become very dangerous. That was when he'd gone into the hills and joined the unit. The Range Rover was his.

They stopped on a ridge overlooking the Mediterranean. It was still dark. Jean-Claude strained to see any signs of the armada he hoped was about to land. Down below were beautiful beaches where only a few years before, the rich had sunned themselves and lived in their splendid villas that overlooked the sea. In a matter of hours, the beaches would be a battleground, and the hillsides with the beautiful villas would be pummeled with artillery shells.

They waited on the ridge. An hour before dawn, the planes came. Some carrying airborne units and others dropping tons of bombs on fortified German positions along the coast. For ninety minutes the bombardment continued. Then as the sun came up, Jean-Claude saw the sight he had waited for: the entire horizon filled with ships—thousands of ships—battleships, aircraft carriers, heavy cruisers, and destroyer transports all jammed with ground forces and weapons.

Next came the naval bombardment. For over an hour the coast was pummeled by the heavy guns from the cruisers. Then came the mine sweepers clearing lanes followed by unmanned drone boats that exploded underwater obstacles, and finally the landing crafts.

They first appeared as tiny dots, and then they grew larger as they got closer to the beaches below. As they hit the beaches, thousands of troops poured out, followed by tanks, artillery, and trucks with supplies. It was a show of overwhelming force. There could be no doubt as to the outcome. Jean-Claude knew that the south of France would be under Allied control in a matter of days.

He was elated at the sight, but his elation was tempered by worry. Bernard, Chantal, and the others were constantly on his mind. He was torn. His job here was finished. He had fulfilled his mission. His rightful place was in Lyon with them.

"You stay here," the older man said. "We're going to have a look from the next hill to see if we can locate a safe path down. We will be back shortly."

As soon as they were out of sight, Jean-Claude didn't hesitate. He got into the Range Rover. The keys were in the ignition. He started the engine, took one last look at the flotilla and the invasion taking place on the beaches below, and headed for Lyon. He felt guilty about abandoning his two guides, but they knew their way back, and Lyon was where he wanted to be. That was where he belonged.

CHAPTER 11

RETURN TO LYON

August 1944

It took him hours, but somehow through all the confusion and congestion, all the German troop movements, all the patrols, and all the refugees, Jean-Claude made it back to Lyon. The confusion probably saved him from detection. No one paid any attention to him in the old Range Rover as he made his way into the city.

The German army was in retreat. They realized the Allies would be advancing up the Rhône with little opposition and would soon reach Lyon. The Resistance, now no longer operating in the shadows, confronted the Germans whenever they could and harassed them, delaying their retreat and giving the Allies more time to reach the city.

He went directly to Café de L'Arche looking for someone who could tell him where Bernard, Chantal, and the others were but it was practically deserted. Then he moved to Café Rouge. He approached a waiter he recognized. "Have you seen Chantal or any of the others?" he demanded.

The waiter shook his head.

Jean-Claude went outside to get into the Range Rover to drive to La Chapelle when he heard his name called. It was Georges. Michel was with him. They were in a parked car a short distance away. He ran over and jumped into their car. *What luck to run into them.*

"Where are Bernard and Chantal?" he asked, out of breath.

Michel paused and looked at Jean-Claude. "They were betrayed." His voice was filled with bitterness. "The Gestapo went to La Chapelle two days ago and took them to Montluc. We went to Montluc yesterday to look for them. It's totally deserted. No one is there. No one knows where any of them are." He threw up his hands in exasperation. "The Germans are gone. Barbie is gone. The Milice are in hiding."

Jean-Claude pounded his fist on the back of the car seat. "Where is Lagrange?"

"No one has seen him. He's probably in hiding or on his way to Switzerland," Georges said.

"Start driving," Jean-Claude ordered.

"Where?" asked Georges, who was driving.

"Do you know Rue Bonaparte?"

"Yes."

"Drive there. To number 25."

Georges drove through the nearly deserted streets. When they reached Rue Bonaparte, he slowed the car and drove by the large houses. They all appeared empty. Some had boarded-up windows.

"25?"

"Yes. That's it. Stop here. It's Lagrange's house."

Jean-Claude led Georges and Michel through the iron entrance gate and to the front door.

"You'll never break this down," Michel said, seeing how solid it was.

Jean-Claude went to the wall next to the front door. He wasn't sure exactly where the key was, so it took him a few minutes feeling along the stones until he found it. The key was still there.

"So this was your little love nest?" Georges quipped.

"*Tais-toi*, Georges," Jean-Claude snapped, failing to see the humor in his remark.

It was dark inside. The house seemed deserted.

"There's nobody here," Michel said.

"Just follow me and be quiet," Jean-Claude said.

Jean-Claude led them to the library and turned on a light. He walked to the bookcase next to the fireplace and moved books at random on the middle shelf, not knowing which one was the trigger. He finally found the right one and the bookcase opened. Georges jumped back, startled, and drew his pistol. They squeezed into the narrow opening. Michel had trouble getting through due to his size, but he made it.

Georges flipped open his cigarette lighter to light the way as they stepped cautiously down the dark stairs. When they reached the cellar door, Jean-Claude placed his finger to his lips as he turned the key in the lock and pushed open the door. The room was dimly lit.

Two figures sat up in the bed, startled. It was Lagrange and a young man.

"Get up. Get up," Jean-Claude screamed. The two terrified men jumped out of bed—both naked. "On your knees."

When Lagrange saw who it was, he smiled with relief. "My boy. Thank God, you found the shelter."

"Where are they? Where are they?" Jean-Claude screamed.

"Where are who?" Lagrange replied. Fear showed in his eyes. He started to shake, realizing Jean-Claude was not there for sanctuary.

Jean-Claude got right in his face. "The prisoners that were in Montluc two days ago. Bernard. Where is Bernard?" He was still screaming.

"I don't know—I don't know where they are," Lagrange whined, his voice cracking.

"Let me have a shot at him," Michel said, making a fist and

approaching Lagrange.

Jean-Claude shook his head. "No, I have a better idea. Bring him over to the sink."

Michel and Georges dragged a frightened Lagrange over to the sink.

Jean-Claude turned on the hot water tap. "Now this is your last chance to tell us. Where are they?"

"I don't know. I swear I don't know. No. No, please," Lagrange was trembling, begging, sobbing. "Please, please, I don't know anything."

Georges kept watch on the younger man.

When the sink was filled, Jean-Claude grabbed Lagrange by the hair and pushed his head under while Michel held his arms behind his back. He waited for the small bubbles and pulled his head out. Lagrange choked and gasped for air.

"You like that? You liked it at the École, didn't you? Now where are they?"

"I don't know," Lagrange sputtered. "I was at Montluc two days ago. They said something about taking the prisoners to Saint-Genis-Laval. That's all I know. I left before anyone was moved."

"Get dressed," Jean-Claude ordered.

After they dressed, Michel and Georges tied their hands behind their backs. They all got into Georges' car and drove to Saint-Genis-Laval, a small hamlet a few kilometers outside of Lyon.

The town looked deserted except for an old man riding a bicycle, heading in their direction.

They stopped him. He was shaking, obviously very frightened.

Jean-Claude demanded, "Did you see German soldiers with prisoners here yesterday or the day before?"

The old man didn't answer.

"We are not the Milice. We are friends. We are with the Resistance. Tell us if you saw anything," Georges added.

The old man pointed in the direction from where he had

come. "They went to the mustard fields a kilometer up this road and to the right," he said, still trembling.

Jean-Claude thanked him. Georges drove up the road and after a slight right turn, they knew they had found the right spot. A mustard field fifty meters long and twenty-five meters wide, freshly plowed. An odor arose from the freshly tilled soil. It was the odor of decomposing corpses.

Everyone climbed out of the car and walked to the edge of the field. Now the odor was unmistakable. Tears filled Georges' eyes and he gagged. Jean-Claude still did not want to believe what might have happened there. He walked out onto the plowed surface about ten meters and kicked the loose soil with his boot. It revealed a human hand. He turned and vomited.

He slowly walked back to where Georges and Michel held Lagrange and the young man. Jean-Claude walked over to Georges and extended his hand. Georges did not hesitate. He handed Jean-Claude his pistol. Jean-Claude went up behind Lagrange and kicked his feet out from under him. His hands still bound, Lagrange fell to the ground face first. Jean-Claude pulled him up by his collar and yanked him to his knees.

Jean-Claude held the pistol to the back of his head. Lagrange sobbed and pled for his life—his pants grew wet as he lost control.

Jean-Claude tightened his jaw, his eyes blazing. He had his finger on the trigger. His hand trembled. Seconds passed, but it seemed much longer. Then he lowered his head and relaxed his grip on the trigger. He let go of Lagrange's head and stepped back. Lagrange fell forward, shaking uncontrollably.

He paused, then walked slowly over to Georges and handed him his gun. "Take him back to Lyon. Try him as a war criminal," he said in a tone that reflected the disgust he felt for all that had just happened.

He then turned and headed toward the car.

How easy it would have been to pull the trigger and be done with it. Why bother with a trial? Why not do what Barbie had done many times? Judge him guilty and execute him on the spot. But he couldn't do that. If he had, he would be no better than them. The laws had failed the Japanese in the States and the Jews in France. Killing Lagrange would have just perpetuated the failure. At least this act was a small first step in restoring some semblance of justice.

Suddenly he heard a shot. He thought they had executed Lagrange. He spun around and raced back just in time to see Michel collapse to the dirt. Georges stood over him with the gun in his hand.

"Are you crazy?" Jean-Claude shouted. "What the hell did you do that for?"

Georges had tears in his eyes. "He betrayed them. He was the one who told the Gestapo they were at La Chapelle."

Jean-Claude bent down. Michel was still breathing.

"I am sorry," Michel whispered. "I had to save myself." He struggled for breath. "They were Communists," were his last words.

Jean-Claude turned to Georges. "How did you know?"

"While you and Michel were dunking Lagrange, his boyfriend told me he had been picked up by the Milice and taken to Montluc. He saw Michel there along with a lot of others who were being detained. The boy told the Milice he was a friend of Lagrange. Lagrange came and got him. He didn't think Michel noticed him and he didn't see what happened to him, but several prisoners had already been shot, and he guessed that was going to be Michel's fate as well." Georges shrugged. "I knew once Michel had been to Montluc and survived, he had to be the one who betrayed them. I was going to turn him in, but after seeing this…" His voice trailed off.

They left Michel's body on top of the plowed field, then drove back to Lyon.

An office of the new provisional government had already been established. They turned Lagrange over to them and released the young man.

On August twenty-second, the first Allied forces entered the city. Several days later de Gaulle flew in. On the 3rd of September, Lyon was liberated. Jean-Claude felt no elation. Bernard and Chantal were dead. They hadn't lived to see the victory they had risked so much for, given so much of themselves for, and ultimately died for. He felt as he had after his mother was killed—empty and alone. But then he thought of Stephanie and the baby. That gave him something to live for.

CHAPTER 12

THE LIBERATION OF LYON

September 1944

The southern invasion had gone more quickly than anyone had predicted. There was jubilation in Lyon. The Allies rolled into the city greeted by thousands who had suffered, mostly in silence, for over four years. They had been victimized by a ruthless oppressor and betrayed by a submissive and cowardly French government. But it was finally over.

He found the Allied command post and reported. He expected a court-martial for disobeying orders and stealing the Range Rover. Whatever punishment they were going to inflict would not compare to the emotional pain he was feeling.

After a lot of confusion at company headquarters trying to establish who he was, London finally confirmed his identity. They wondered where he had been and told him there was one pissed-off Frenchman who wanted his Range Rover back, but they also thanked him for what he had done the previous two years. They said he had performed a great service. London said there would be no court-martial.

After the confusion cleared, he met with Colonel White, a high-ranking intelligence officer, who was to give him his assignment.

"I'm Colonel White. London said you did a hell of a job before you went AWOL," the colonel said, smiling.

"Sorry, sir. I had some unfinished family business," Jean-Claude said in a subdued voice.

"They told me as much. I heard your father was killed in the days just before liberation. I'm sorry for your loss."

"Thank you." He had trouble keeping his emotions under control.

The colonel paused for a moment to give Jean-Claude time to regain his composure. "There is a quartermaster unit in the building across the street. They will get you outfitted with a uniform. After you get your uniform, come back here. A member of the OSS wants to debrief you. After that, we will give you your orders. We still need you. This war is a long way from being over, but we've got the Krauts on the run. You will have a chance to pay them back. By the way, you have been given a promotion to captain. Congratulations."

Jean-Claude left company headquarters and headed to the quartermaster's. He was surprised at the turn of events. *Amazing. From a court-martial to captain.* That was something he never would have predicted, but in wartime the unpredictable was often the norm. It picked up his spirits because it validated what he had accomplished during the past two years. It didn't ease the pain of losing his father and Chantal, but it made it more tolerable.

After his visit to the quartermaster, he had two new sets of fatigues, combat boots, a cap with captain's bars, underwear, and a duffle bag with another pair of boots. He put the uniform on. It felt strange. He had never spent much time in uniform before returning to France. The structured life of a soldier was something he would have to get used to. He was relieved to be able to leave his life as a spy behind him. The first thing he did when he got back to his billet was shave off his beard.

He then went to Café de L'Arche hoping he would run into Georges or someone from the Resistance he knew. The café now had a mixture of citizens and soldiers. He sat at a familiar table and ordered a coffee. Next to him were a half dozen GIs who were laughing and having a good time telling war stories.

"Can you imagine those little Japs in those gliders? They didn't know what they were getting themselves into. But those monkeys sure can fight."

Jean-Claude leaned over. "Excuse me, Corporal, did you say Japs? Are we fighting Japs here?"

"No, sir. These are good Japs. These are our Japs. They're with the 442nd. Mostly from Hawaii."

"Are they here in Lyon?" Jean-Claude had a hard time containing his excitement. His first thought was whether Ken might have reenlisted and was here, in France.

"I don't know, sir. They could be anywhere. I just heard that some of them were part of the invasion force."

"Thank you, Corporal." Jean-Claude immediately went back to company headquarters and sought out Colonel White. He now had something to occupy his thoughts other than the loss of Bernard and Chantal. It lifted his spirits.

"Colonel, I have a favor to ask. Back in the States I had a very good friend who is Japanese. I just learned there is a contingent of Japanese fighting here in France and I would like to know if my friend is among them."

"Keeping track of individual soldiers is almost impossible with all that is going on, but he is most likely in the 442nd. I will see what I can do," the colonel said. "Also, I have news for you. Your orders have come in. The 7th Army under General Patch is moving up the Rhône Valley and heading east into the Vosges Mountains. We understand you are very familiar with the area and you are fluent in German. You have been assigned as the intelligence officer with the 36th Infantry Division under General Dahlquist. They are moving out soon."

"Yes, sir. My mother was from Alsace. I know the Vosges region well."

"I will get back to you on the location of the 442nd as soon as I have some information." They saluted each other and Jean-Claude returned to his billet at a large hotel that had been converted to quarters for officers.

With his spirits lifted by the thought of going back to Alsace, where he had spent many summers as a boy, and by the prospect of perhaps seeing Ken, he began to think of life after the war. He knew there was much fighting remaining, but he now felt he had a reasonable chance to survive and be with Stephanie and with the baby he'd never seen. He found a desk in the lobby and sat down to write a letter he was actually going to mail. It would be the first time since his return to France.

> My dearest Stephanie,
>
> I know you have probably given me up for dead not hearing from me for so long. It was impossible given my situation to get any word to you. I am fine. I am in Lyon, which is now free. The end is in sight. It's just a question of how much longer.
>
> I miss you and the baby I have never seen more than you will ever know.
>
> Did we have a girl or a boy?
>
> You can write to me at this address and eventually it will get to me.
>
> I hope we will be together soon.
>
> I'll always love you,
>
> Jean-Claude

He couldn't bring himself to say more. It was too painful to talk about his father or his other experiences. It was best left simple. I'm alive, I love you, and we will be together again.

He addressed the letter to her at her parents' home in Greenwich and left it at the communications center to be mailed.

The next day a corporal tracked him down. "Captain, the colonel asked me to give you this message. The 442nd has been assigned to the 36th Infantry. He said your guy might be with them. You can check it out when you join the unit."

"Thanks, Corporal," Jean-Claude said, elated that Ken might be in the same unit he was assigned to.

In the final day before his unit was to leave Lyon, he met Georges at Café de L'Arche.

They sat at a familiar table, but it felt totally different. No longer were they looking over their shoulders or speaking in hushed tones. They sat and drank wine and smoked cigarettes. It was a bittersweet moment.

"You shaved off your beard," was the first thing Georges said to him.

"I couldn't wait to shave it off. I don't ever want to be that person again."

"You look more like a native without the beard. It shows off your French nose."

Jean-Claude chuckled. "Now that I'm not a spy anymore, I prefer to think of it as my Jewish nose."

They laughed about the shared experiences that had terrified them while they were happening, then lapsed into melancholy and mourned the deaths of Andre, Chantal, and Bernard. Jean-Claude still didn't want to believe they were gone, yet there was no doubt they were buried under the loose soil at Saint-Genis-Laval.

"They're dead," Georges said. "They're never coming back. You have to let it go."

Jean-Claude sadly nodded in agreement.

Georges then described what was happening in the streets. "Mobs are going through the city looking for collaborators, settling old scores. Killing some right on the spot. They found Natalie, shaved her head. They were taking her somewhere, probably to kill her. We found her in time and convinced them she was a partisan."

"What about her husband?"

"He died in the labor camp. He had actually been dead for quite some time, but the Gestapo bastard lied to her so he could continue to have her. She and her child have gone to live with her mother in Vienne. Do you want to see her?"

"No. She needs to get on with her life and so do I. It would just complicate things." He was happy she survived, but saddened because of what she had been through. "If you see her again, tell her she gave me courage at a very difficult moment." He paused as he thought back to that day in Lagrange's bunker.

"Have you found out anything about Lagrange?"

"Yes. He's in Montluc. The provisional government is setting up tribunals to try suspected war criminals. I don't know how much justice he will get. I told them to make sure he had a lawyer. I know that makes you happy."

"Maybe when they readmit Jews to the bar he'll get one," Jean-Claude said, smiling at what an absurd irony that would be.

"I just want to tell you I can't say I am sorry I shot Michel. I know you think that was wrong, but—"

Jean-Claude interrupted him. "I know. I understand. We both did what we thought was right."

They hugged and kissed each other on their cheeks. They said they hoped that someday after the war they would meet again. Just before he left, Jean-Claude reached into his pocket and handed Georges the miniature .45 and its holster. "I traded this in for a big one," he said as he pointed to the side arm on his belt. "I want you to have it. I hope you'll never need it, but it's good insurance."

Georges looked at it, smiled, and nodded in thanks. They hugged again and walked away in different directions and into very different worlds.

CHAPTER 13

THE VOSGES MOUNTAINS

September–December 1944

The 7th Army moved virtually unimpeded up the east bank of the Rhône while the French army did the same on the west bank. They liberated Dijon without much of a fight and then headed northeast into the Vosges Mountains, the gateway to Germany.

During the next month, they advanced 400 miles, took 80,000 prisoners, and linked up with part of Patton's 3rd Army. Now all that stood between them and the Rhine were the Vosges Mountains and a contingent of German troops dedicated to stopping the advance at all costs.

The Vosges Mountains are a series of hills varying in altitude from 1,500 to 4,000 feet with rounded summits called balloons. Sixty percent of the terrain is covered by forests. The remainder consists of meadows, deep valleys, glacial lakes, and steep cliffs.

In peacetime, it was ideal for the kind of bike riding Jean-Claude and Bernard used to do near his grandmother's inn. In wartime, it presented a challenging environment to fight in.

Never before had an invader been able to successfully penetrate an army defending the Vosges. In the fall of 1944, the German high command dedicated themselves to making sure this would not be the first time. The Vosges Mountains were the Germans' Maginot line. At the foot of the Vosges facing Germany is the Plain of Alsace, a broad, flat expanse of land. If the Allies reached the Plain, it was a straight shot to the Rhine.

The seasons had begun to change, and the beech trees were still ablaze in yellow and brown when Jean-Claude reported for duty with the 36th Infantry "Texas" Division, so called because it had originally consisted of members of the Texas National Guard. But fall also brought rain—constant rain—and at the higher elevations, snow. This deprived the Allies of their greatest tactical advantage, air superiority. It also severely limited the use of armored vehicles. It reduced the conflict to individual soldiers fighting small battles in close combat in bad weather that not only exposed them to death from the enemy, but also trench foot, frost bite, and pneumonia.

The Allies established their headquarters in Blâmont, a small village in the Vosges just north of St. Die, 40 kilometers from Colmar. From there, Major General Dahlquist could monitor the actions of the various units, including the 442nd. As the Division Intelligence Officer, Jean-Claude had been assigned the task of interrogating German prisoners and translating classified documents. Upon his arrival at group headquarters, Jean-Claude had been instructed to report to First Lieutenant Wells Lewis, the aide to Major General Dahlquist.

"Bonjour, Captain. Welcome to the 36th Infantry Division. Your office is next to mine. If you need anything let me know and I'll see if I can help you." The young lieutenant addressed him in perfect French.

"Your French is very good," Jean-Claude said.

"I spent a good deal of my childhood in schools on the

continent," Lewis said.

Jean-Claude nodded and asked the question he'd been wanting to ask since he'd arrived. "Lieutenant, I was told there was a combat team made up of Japanese attached to the division. I have a good friend who may be in that unit, and I wanted to see if I could locate him. Do you think you might be able to find out if he's here?"

"What's his name?" Lieutenant Lewis asked.

"Ken Matsumoto."

"There's a lot going on around here and the rosters aren't always current but I'll take a look. Why don't you meet me for chow in the officer's mess at 1900 hours and I'll tell you if I've found anything about your friend."

Several hours later, they found each other among the large group of men who were eating in a makeshift tent lined with long wooden tables.

"I have good news," Lieutenant Lewis began. "Your friend is here. I don't know where exactly because with all the combat they've seen lately, there have been numerous reassignments, and I don't know if he is still alive because the latest casualty figures are still coming in. But if he is alive he's here in the camp somewhere."

"That's great news," Jean-Claude said, relaxing and taking a bite of the food on his tray. "What can you tell me about the unit? The 442nd, I mean."

Lieutenant Lewis shrugged. "I don't know much. It was formed with Japs mostly from Hawaii and some from the detention camps in the States. It's segregated. I guess there was still some distrust, so they wanted to keep an eye on them. But they have fought very well. Better than very well, they have been exceptionally brave. They're really tough."

"How can I locate him?" Jean-Claude asked, anxious to find his friend.

"They have been ordered to take a small village, Biffontaine. They're still up there. Very heavy fighting, but the reports from the front are that the battle is almost over.

"They should be back here soon and when they do return, they are due for some R&R. The bad news is that the casualties are heavy."

"Thanks for checking for me," Jean-Claude said, worried about the prospects of heavy casualties.

"How did you know him?" Lewis asked.

"We were good friends in the States. California. We went to school together. I also know his family. They are probably still in an internment camp. I'm a lawyer. When he was ordered to go to a camp, he refused and I defended him in court. He must have enlisted from there."

"I hope he made it. The fighting has been brutal, like I said." Lewis lit a cigarette and offered one to Jean-Claude.

"Makes me happy I'm the intelligence officer. I don't want to have any part of the fighting. You should be glad you're the general's aide, so you can stay off the front lines," Jean-Claude said as he lit up.

"Unfortunately for me," Lewis said with a look of resignation, "the general often goes to the front and I go with him. I have seen him get so close to the enemy, he can fire his pistol at them. Some have questioned his decision-making, but never his courage." He took a deep drag on his cigarette.

Jean-Claude liked Lewis immediately. Although they were from different backgrounds and experiences, they shared a lot in common. They were both well-educated and could talk about things other than war and death. He learned Lewis's father, Sinclair, had won the Nobel Prize in Literature, and the younger Lewis was a published author himself. Lewis was interested in Jean-Claude's life as a lawyer and his defense of Ken. They talked well into the night over coffee and cigarettes.

At the end of the evening, Jean-Claude had made a wartime friendship. Like the one he'd made with Ian, it was immediate, but of unknown duration.

Early the next morning, Jean-Claude learned those soldiers from the 442nd who survived had returned from Biffontaine in the middle of the night. He rushed out into the street and went up to the first Japanese soldier he saw. "Do you know Lieutenant Matsumoto?"

"Yes, sir," the soldier said. "I saw him just a few minutes ago going into the mess tent."

Jean-Claude thanked him and ran in the direction the soldier had pointed, relieved that Ken was alive and excited to see his old friend. He saw a line of men waiting to go in. Ken was not among them. He stepped inside. The tent was crowded. Jean-Claude walked down the rows of tables. The soldiers looked exhausted, a lifeless expression in their eyes. It was clear they had just been through a terrible experience. Finally, at the end of a long table, on the far side of the tent, he saw Ken.

He had his head down, eating. Jean-Claude put his hand on his shoulder. "Ken, it's Jean-Claude."

Ken looked up, clearly startled, an astonished look on his face. "Jean-Claude? What the hell are you doing here?" He jumped up and they hugged each other.

Ken looked older. He had dark circles under his eyes, and they were bloodshot. His face showed fatigue and weariness. They sat down across from each other. "I can't believe what I'm seeing. At first I thought I was experiencing fatigue and was hallucinating."

"You look exhausted," Jean-Claude said, reaching across the table and grasping his arm sympathetically.

"You'd look this way too if you had been fighting for eight days. These are the first dry clothes I've had in two weeks." Ken shoveled food into his mouth. "I was so tired when we got back last night I couldn't sleep." Ken glanced up at him. "What the hell are you doing here and where did you get those captain's bars? The last time I saw you, you were a lowly second lieutenant."

"This is really a miracle. I mean that you are here, and I am here," Jean-Claude said, just as amazed as Ken at the chance meeting.

"I agree. It's a miracle I'm still alive. I should have been dead a long time ago. So how did you end up in this god-awful place?"

"It's a long story. First, tell me, how are your parents and sisters?"

"As far as I know, my parents and sisters are still in the camps. We don't get mail too often in combat zones."

"I'm sorry to hear that. Life must be very difficult for them."

"Well, things got a lot better at the camp after I saw you. They sent a guy named Merritt to be camp director. Pretty enlightened guy. He wanted to turn Manzanar into a self-governing city. He caught a lot of crap for doing that. Some congressmen said he was coddling us. But he stood his ground for the most part."

"So things changed?"

"It was still a prison, but we were allowed to do a lot of things to improve the camp. We built a lot of the buildings ourselves, schools, a hospital, and an orphanage."

"An orphanage? Why the hell did you need an orphanage?" Jean-Claude asked.

"They sent all the Japanese orphans living in the evacuation zone to Manzanar. They had been in orphanages run by Catholic sisters and the Salvation Army. The sisters pleaded not to have the children removed, but they moved them anyway."

"They forced orphans into the camp?" Jean-Claude was incredulous.

"Yeah, they even sent half-Japanese children living in Caucasian foster homes. But we had to deal with it so we built three buildings for them to live in. The sisters came along to take care of them. It all worked out. They're okay."

Jean-Claude thought about what Barbie had done to the orphans at Izieu. This was a far cry from Izieu, but the Japanese orphans were put in the camp for the same reason as the Jewish children: their race.

"Merritt arranged for Ansel Adams to come down and do a photo shoot of life in the camp to show the country how humane everyone was being treated."

"Ansel Adams, the nature photographer?"

"Same guy. I met him. He said he was going to write a book about the camp to go with his photographs. I don't know whether it ever got published, but he was pretty sympathetic."

"And what about your sisters?"

"When I left, Katy was teaching at the camp school, and Sarah, the nurse, was working in the dispensary. She got married to a guy from L.A. she met in the camp. She got pregnant and has had the baby by now."

"And your mom and Mas?"

"My mom is the same. She takes things one day at a time and makes the best of any situation she finds herself in. My dad feels worthless. Living in the camp has killed his spirit. He has lost his pride. He was such a strong man before…" His voice trailed off. He clenched his teeth. "He still does his bonsais, but he is not the same. I hope having a grandchild has made him happy."

Jean-Claude waited a moment so he could control his anger. "So, did you reenlist?"

"Early last year an order came down saying that if we signed a loyalty oath we could enlist. I told them that was bullshit. I'm a citizen and won't sign any loyalty oath, but my dad convinced me to sign it. If I hadn't, they would have sent me to Tule Lake where all the suspected collaborators were housed, and I probably would never have gotten out. After I signed, I enlisted. It was better than staying in the camp, or so I thought. Merritt said he felt they would give me my commission back and give me a desk job."

He gave a little laugh that was more like a sneer. "They gave me my commission back all right, then told me they were going to put me in the infantry with all the other 'Japs' who came out of the camps. "

Jean-Claude shook his head in bewilderment. An officer who had previously been honorably discharged, a graduate architect, a U.S. citizen, and because he's Japanese they stick him in an all-Japanese infantry unit as cannon fodder because they still have doubts about his loyalty. It made him sick just thinking about it.

"I know. It's insane," Jean-Claude said as he lit a cigarette and remembered their last meeting in Manzanar. "You have a right to be bitter." Ken surprised him by asking him for a cigarette. "When did you start smoking?"

"When I was in a foxhole trying to survive, my buddy next to me gave me one. I think most of us smoke just to take our minds off dying. I know they're bad for me and if I make it back I'll quit. In the meantime, a bullet will kill me faster than these things, plus they give 'em away at the commissary."

"It's fighting with these guys that keeps me from going insane. We are like brothers." Ken took a drag on his cigarette then put it out and resumed eating.

"And there's no question about their loyalty?" Jean-Claude wanted confirmation that disloyalty as a reason for internment was outrageous. But Ken took it the wrong way.

"What kind of bullshit question is that? You still think some are disloyal because we're Japanese?"

"No, no. That's not what I meant. I just wanted proof I was right and there was no disloyalty so if I make it back, I can tell 'em to take their racist laws and shove them up their ass."

"You won't find braver, more loyal men than in the 442nd. But you want to know the real reason we fight? It's not for God and country. There's no God out here and the country has treated us like shit. We fight so we won't let each other or our families down. We don't want to dishonor our families, the same families that are back in the camps. We want to bring honor to our names. 'Live with honor, die with dignity.' Those are the words we live by. We may die but we are not going to embarrass ourselves, our buddies or our families. The problem is too many of us have died."

Jean-Claude thought what he had just been through was tough, but after hearing what it was like from Ken to be in combat constantly, he realized war had many ways to take its toll and destroy lives.

"Have you thought about what you are going to do after the war?"

Ken sneered. "You've seen what this is like. You don't think beyond the next day, sometimes the next minute. All we want to do is survive." He paused and his shoulders slumped as if just talking about his experiences was exhausting. Then he asked Jean-Claude, "So what have you been up to? I thought you were going to be a spy. How did you get those captain's bars?"

Jean-Claude told him about marrying Stephanie and becoming a father, and his life in Lyon as a spy, and losing Bernard and Chantal. The story was hard to tell but he went into a lot of detail. He wanted Ken to know that he too had faced death and suffered the loss of those close to him. He almost broke down when talking about his father and Chantal.

"You've been through a lot," Ken said, shaking his head, "just like the rest of us. I never believed in hell before fighting in this war. But if there is a hell, this place is as close to it as you'll get on earth."

They talked for several hours, until interrupted by the camp loudspeakers. "All members of the 442nd report immediately to the staging area. Repeat. All members of the 442nd report to the staging area immediately."

"What is this bullshit?" Ken asked. "We just got here."

"I'll go find out. Stay here."

Jean-Claude rushed back to division headquarters and found Lieutenant Lewis. "What's up with the 442nd?" Jean-Claude demanded to know.

"We got a mess out there," the lieutenant said. "A battalion from the 36th Infantry Division is surrounded. These guys are from Texas and they're the General's boys. They're in danger of being wiped out. Two other battalions have been unable to get to them. The general wants the 442nd to go and rescue them." He didn't look happy.

"It sounds like a suicide mission. Is the general here?" Jean-Claude asked, looking around impatiently.

"Yes, he's in the next office conferring with battalion

commanders."

Just then the door opened and General Dahlquist stepped out. Jean-Claude was still feeling the emotions of seeing his friend again and spoke without thinking. "General, the 442nd has been in combat for eight straight days. They are exhausted. You can't send them back out there."

"Who are you?" the General asked, looking astonished that a lowly captain would address him that way.

The colonel interceded. "He's our intelligence officer, was with the OSS as a spy for two years. Good man. Has a buddy in the 442nd."

"I'll ignore your impudence, Captain. I suggest you regain your bearings quickly. The next time, there will be consequences," the general said.

"Yes, sir." Jean-Claude reined in his anger and saluted the general.

The general saluted back and walked out. Wells Lewis shot a sympathetic look to Jean-Claude. Lewis knew there was nothing that could be done.

"Those are his boys. No matter what it takes, he's going to get them out. I bet he will be right there next to the guys from the 442nd. That means if he is there, I am going to be there," Lewis said with a look of resignation.

Jean-Claude went back to the mess tent, found Ken, and told him that a battalion of Texans was surrounded and the general wanted the 442nd to rescue them.

Ken looked numb. "You know, Jean-Claude, if it wasn't for the fact the general gets his ass as close to the front line as any general in the army, I'd say he's just sending us in because we're Japs and we're expendable. He's had us going up and down these worthless hills for weeks with no tactical objective we could ever see. But those Texans are his boys, and if they get wiped out, it's his ass. He's the one who sent them up there. He said it was quiet. Not many Krauts. He was wrong again. I don't think he believes we're expendable. I just think he's dumb." Ken looked exasperated and exhausted, but he was a soldier. A

Japanese American soldier. He would do what he'd been ordered to do.

Jean-Claude was frustrated and upset, but there was nothing he could do to prevent his friend from going back into battle. They said their good-byes and like with Bernard and Chantal. He didn't know if this would be the last time he would ever see his friend.

He went to his tent and tried to sleep. He was only partially successful. He was angry. He kept waking up thinking about Ken and Bernard and Chantal. He thought about grabbing an M-1 and joining the fight. He finally gave up trying to sleep as well as any idea of going into combat and went to the headquarters tent to keep track of the battle.

When the 442nd moved out it was raining. Soon the rain turned to snow. The battle conditions were terrible. The fog made it impossible to see the enemy but they fought on relentlessly. Three days into the battle, progress was slow and the outcome appeared very much in doubt. Casualties were heavy. On the fourth day, General Dahlquist and Lieutenant Wells Lewis left for the front to get a firsthand view of the rescue effort.

Late that afternoon, Jean-Claude was in the command tent monitoring reports from the front when he heard the rumble of several jeeps pulling up. He got up to glance outside just as the door swung open and General Dahlquist rushed in, his uniform splattered with blood. He went directly to the rear of the tent without a word. Jean-Claude stopped one of the officers who was following the general and asked if his wounds were serious.

The officer looked grim. "The general wasn't wounded. The blood was Lieutenant Lewis's. He was standing right next to the general when a machine gun burst got him. He fell against the general as he went down. He's dead. The general is really upset," the officer said and followed Dahlquist into the office.

Jean-Claude couldn't speak. A man who had his whole life ahead of him struck down, because he was standing in the wrong place at the wrong time. The searchlight in the Lyon rail yard missed Jean-Claude by only a few feet and he'd survived. Lewis, who was standing next to a general, didn't. War's selection process in choosing who lives and who dies is arbitrary.

He sat down. It took a moment for him to compose himself. The friendship had been short, but the connection had been strong. It left him with that all-too-familiar empty feeling. Ken was right. This was hell on earth.

The day after Lewis was killed, and after five days of close combat where the 442nd slogged, crawled, climbed, and fought, they finally broke through and rescued what remained of the 1st Battalion. The cost in lives was enormous: 800 Japanese wounded or killed. The number of Texans saved: 211. The ratio of losses to those rescued was four to one. The average in similar circumstances was two to one. Ken Matsumoto was not among the 800 Japanese casualties. He had survived.

The stories of heroism during the rescue were numerous. The exploits of the 442nd in rescuing the Texas battalion were widely publicized in the States. The press called it the miraculous rescue of the Lost Battalion. They were hailed as heroes. What the articles failed to mention was that many of the parents of those who'd died as well as those who'd survived were still in the concentration camps.

Jean-Claude was asked to prepare Wells Lewis's obituary for the Stars and Stripes. Based upon what he'd learned from the evening they'd spent together and a review of his personnel file, he wrote the following:

> Wells Lewis born July 16, 1917. Mother, Grace Hegger Lewis. Father, Sinclair Lewis, the first American to be awarded the Nobel Prize in Literature. Graduate of Harvard College 1939, Magna Cum Laude. Author of a favorably reviewed novel entitled *They Still Say No*. Fluent in French and German. Enlisted 1940 as a private. North Africa campaign awarded Silver Star. European campaign

> awarded Purple Heart and the Bronze Star. Battlefield
> commissioned First Lieutenant, 1942. Killed in action
> October 29, 1944, while on the front line of the battle
> to rescue the Lost Battalion in the Vosges Mountains.

He wanted to add, what a waste of a life, of promise and potential. But he didn't. He felt it would not be appropriate to insert his own feelings. He ended the obituary by saying, "Wells Lewis died a hero. His sacrifice, together with that of thousands of others who died in the name of preserving freedom, will always be remembered." But no words he wrote could ever compensate for the loss.

By late November 1944, the Allies successfully pushed the Germans from the Vosges and on to the Plain of Alsace. They were in full retreat.

As his division advanced, Jean-Claude came within a few kilometers of the tiny village near Colmar where his grandparents had their inn and where his mother was buried. He commandeered a jeep. Surely there must be someone still living there. Even though the forests still had pockets of enemy troops, he knew the roads well and felt if he was careful, he would be safe. Given what had happened to Wells Lewis, this was a foolish conclusion, but he could not let the opportunity pass.

As he drove up the familiar road to the inn, he passed the village church with its distinctive dome. He parked in front of the inn and saw an elderly man sweeping the steps. He wore the blue overalls of a French farmer. Jean-Claude recognized him at once. He had been the inn's gardener and caretaker for many years.

"Henri, it's me, Jean-Claude, Bernard and Rachael's son."

Jean-Claude had abandoned his beard and black hair in Lyon after the liberation, so he bore a resemblance to the boy Henri once knew.

"I do not believe what I am seeing. Jean-Claude, Jean-

Claude. It is you." Henri's eyes filled with tears and he embraced Jean-Claude and kissed him on both cheeks.

"Is anyone still here?" Jean-Claude asked with apprehension in his voice.

"The Germans took the inn over for a few years and used it as a retreat for returning troops. Now there is no one here but me. The family is all gone. The Germans took them all. They said they were sending them to the east to work. I have heard nothing since. The inn is empty."

Jean-Claude knew what sending them to the east meant. They were undoubtedly in concentration camps or dead. His shoulders slumped and his excitement turned to despair. He stayed for a while and drank wine with the old caretaker. Sadness overcame him as he thought about the happy days he'd spent at the inn many years ago. He could see his mother playing the piano in the large salon, and his father taking him on bike rides on the trails that crisscrossed the forest just behind the inn.

He drove down the hill to the small cemetery behind the church. He found his mother's tombstone. Rachael Bonnay, October 16, 1887–November 14, 1918. He stood there for several moments as more memories came flooding back. He knelt down and took off his dog tags and laid them on her grave. "Papa's gone," he said softly. "Mamma, I love you. I promise I'm doing all I can to end this." He lingered for a few more minutes then got back in the jeep and left.

He returned to his unit that night, but couldn't fall asleep. He now had his mother's family to add to the list of those he had lost.

By late November 1944, the battle for the Vosges had been won. The 442nd received orders to return to Italy, where they had previously fought with distinction. Another unit, the 522nd Field Artillery, consisting of both Japanese and non-Japanese, was ordered to remain with the 36th Division, which was headed for Germany.

Jean-Claude and Ken met for the last time and said their good-byes.

"Looks like we're headed back to Italy," Ken said. "Where are you going?"

"Paris for a while. Desk job," Jean-Claude said with a smile, having just received his orders the day before.

"You white guys get all the breaks. Just like back in the States," he said without bitterness, but it was still more of the same treatment for Japanese soldiers.

Jean-Claude thought for a moment then asked, "After all you've been through, do you feel the country is worth fighting for?"

Ken paused for a moment. "Mistakes were made, but I still believe in this country. I hope one day people will realize what a mistake it was to lock us up and do something about it."

"I'm not so sure that will ever happen. I've lost a lot of faith in the courts but if I make it back I'll do all I can to make it happen."

"What about you? Do you think France is worth saving?" Ken turned the question around and caught Jean-Claude by surprise.

He thought for a minute. "I don't know. It all depends on what happens after the war. I've seen things I thought I would never see in France. It makes me wonder about the future. I am pessimistic given how things have been handled since the liberation." He remembered what his father had said about the battles that would be fought after the war between the Communists and others for control.

"I think it will come down to whether there's a peaceful transition to a new government but regardless, I think the future of France is very much in doubt."

They hugged each other and agreed to meet in Berkeley after the war. Jean-Claude promised to do everything he could to help Ken's parents reclaim what they had had to leave behind.

There was a sense of hopefulness at their last meeting. The war was winding down, and they knew it would soon be over.

They parted as they had always been; close friends. But they still had to survive. One was going to Paris, the other to Italy.

The odds for survival were not the same.

CHAPTER 14

SUPREME HEADQUARTERS
ALLIED EXPEDITIONARY FORCE PARIS

December 1944–May 1945

A young lieutenant greeted Jean-Claude upon his arrival at the Allied Expeditionary Force headquarters in Paris. "You've been assigned to an intelligence unit here at SHAEF," he said. "The main headquarters are in Versailles, but you will be here in Paris. You will be under the command of Colonel Littleton and will be billeted at the Hotel Crillon. Here's your reservation. Present it at the desk and they will assign you a room. You are to report here to the colonel tomorrow at 0900 hours. I will have someone take your gear over to the hotel for you. Any questions?"

"Wow. Did you say Hotel Crillon?" He was excited with the prospect of staying there. He took the reservation and looked at it to confirm it said Hotel Crillon.

"Yes. But don't get too excited. The hotel was used by the German high command as their headquarters, so it's in pretty rough shape. The most important benefit is that it has heat. At least some of the time."

The lieutenant didn't understand the significance of the hotel to Jean-Claude.

He had known of the Hotel Crillon since his visits to Paris with his father as a child. Bernard had shown him the landmarks of Paris and the Hotel Crillon was a prominent one. It was one of the most magnificent buildings in one of the most beautiful locations in Paris. Built originally as a palace, it overlooked the Place de la Concorde between the Champs-Elysees and the Tuileries Gardens. Marie Antoinette took piano lessons there until she and Louis XVI lost their heads in its courtyard in 1789.

Bernard had said the hotel was an example of bourgeois excess that hadn't been put to its highest and best use since the executions. Jean-Claude didn't care if it was bourgeois or still smelled of Nazis, he was excited at the prospect of staying there.

"Littleton. Did you say Colonel Littleton?" His mind returned to the other fact that had caught his interest.

"Yes. He commands the intelligence unit here. Do you know him?"

"I think so." He couldn't be sure, but it was a pretty safe bet that there weren't two Colonel Littletons who were intelligence officers.

A room at the Crillon and commanded by the officer who had recruited him into the OSS. Finally, something positive was happening in his life.

He walked from SHAEF headquarters to the hotel. It began to snow. The beautiful buildings with their snow-topped roofs didn't appear to have changed much from how he remembered them. But he soon realized this was not the Paris of his youth. It was dark. The streetlights had been turned off. It was not the famous city of lights anymore. The shops were barred or shuttered. The patisseries had cardboard mockups of cakes and bread in their windows because they had nothing to sell. He stopped for a coffee at a café and was served an imitation drink that tasted like chalk. The waiter told him there was no real coffee available, except in those facilities controlled by the military, or in the finer restaurants serviced by the black market.

The waiter went on to tell him that the economy had been virtually destroyed by the Allied occupation. What had emerged in the five short months since the liberation was a flourishing black market that was supplied in part by GIs using their access to everything from fuel to nylons. Those who had been able to secure and preserve their wealth and were not collaborators lived quite well, as did the Allied military and the black market profiteers. Everybody else was freezing and hungry.

Events had created another *Tale of Two Cities*.

Jean-Claude arrived at the Hotel Crillon. It was still elegant—ornate inside as well as out. But at the same time, it had a sterile feel to it, probably because it had been used by the German military for the past five years. Compared to where he had lived since arriving in France, however, it was very comfortable. He slept well his first night in Paris.

When he reported for duty the next day, Colonel John Littleton greeted him. He was the same Colonel Littleton he had met in General Scott's office in Washington.

"Jean-Claude, it is good to see you again. Welcome to Paris."

"Thank you, Colonel. It's a pleasant surprise to be assigned to your command. How is General Scott?"

"He's fine. They have him assigned to a strategic unit planning how to deal with the Russians who want to take over Eastern Europe. The next war, I fear, will be with them. They really believe that Communism is going to sweep the world." The colonel extended his hand. "Please sit down."

Jean-Claude sat in front of the colonel's desk. The colonel lit a cigarette and offered one to Jean-Claude.

Jean-Claude accepted.

"Forgive me for not offering my condolences about your father right away. He was a brave man and made a significant contribution to our successes in France. As did you."

"Thank you." The mention of his father triggered the

thought of Barbie. "Do you know what has become of Klaus Barbie?" He hated Barbie so much, he needed to know.

"Our intelligence has him living somewhere in Germany. We have him identified as a war criminal and a priority to prosecute once this is over. We'll find him."

"I want to be there when he goes before a firing squad. The man's a monster." Jean-Claude didn't hide his hatred.

"That brings me to what you will be doing for us. You have a special combination of talents that can be very valuable. We are beginning to lay the groundwork for war crimes trials. Initially you will be reviewing seized documents, which may detail war crimes, specifically plans to exterminate the Jews. You will also be assisting in the interrogation of captured German military officers, Nazi officials, and members of the Gestapo who might have had a hand in those plans, or knew those who did.

"We know of the atrocities and have been getting word from our sources there are large installations with thousands of Jews and others who were forced to work as slave laborers. We want you to approach your assignment as a lawyer, building a case for a war crimes prosecution with evidence that will stand up in court. That's where you are uniquely qualified, given your language skills, your background as a trial lawyer, and your experiences during the past two years."

"It sounds like an ideal assignment," Jean-Claude said with enthusiasm.

"I'm sure you will make a valuable contribution," Littleton went on. "This war is not over yet, but we are getting close, and when it does end, there will be accountability, but accountability according to law, not vigilante justice. Members of the Resistance are carrying out reprisals, seeking out collaborators and summarily executing them."

"I thought the provisional government here in Paris would step in and bring some order to the prosecutions. I guess that hasn't happened yet."

"Hardly. It has set up what they call *Cours de Justice*. When there are trials," the colonel continued, "the juries consist of members of the Resistance or family members of those who were sent to work in Germany. There is little doubt as to the outcome."

It sounded eerily similar to how Lagrange had described the court-martials of the Milice at Montluc.

"They also shave the heads of women who had relationships with Germans and parade them through the streets. They execute some of them. There's no way to be certain they were guilty, since they are identified by accusation and finger pointing. I'm sure mistakes are being made."

"I know of such a case in Lyon where a mistake was avoided, but just barely," Jean-Claude said softly, his throat tightening as he spoke.

"Well, perhaps an imperfect justice system is better than no justice system at all or what they had under the Nazis." The colonel shook his head. "Without it, there would probably be many more examples of people taking the law into their own hands."

Jean-Claude thought of Lagrange and wondered what happened to him. He felt good about his decision to let him live. Whatever court he faced would provide more justice than a bullet in the back of the head next to the killing field in Saint-Genis-Laval.

"Reprisals just perpetuate violence," Jean-Claude said.

"I agree. But we're not occupiers. The French have to reestablish a justice system that provides real justice. We can't do it for them." Littleton made no secret of his disgust with the way the French were treating suspected collaborators. "Our job is to find and prosecute the German war criminals who committed these atrocities."

"I'll do all I can to help," Jean-Claude said. He then paused. "Colonel, I hesitate to bring this up because it's a personal matter, but I hope you can help me. I have written to my wife numerous times since September and haven't gotten a reply. I realize these letters were written from a war zone and might never have reached her. Would you be able to check on this for me? I'm frantic not knowing anything. She was pregnant when I left and I don't even know if I have a son or daughter."

"I'll do what I can. I'll contact somebody in Intelligence in the States and ask them to track her down. Give me her name and address before you leave today."

"Thank you. This means a lot to me."

The colonel and Jean-Claude ended their meeting on a positive note. They said they looked forward to working with each other. Jean-Claude wrote down Stephanie's name and the address of her parents' home in Greenwich, where she said she would be staying, and gave it to the Colonel.

Ten days later Littleton called him at his office.

"Jean-Claude, I heard back from Intelligence. They have located a Stephanie Stevenson in New Haven." He then gave him her address.

"Thanks, Colonel." Then he wondered. *New Haven? Stevenson, not Bonnay. Maybe it's not Stephanie.* His other letters had not been answered and he was desperate to hear something. He had to take a chance.

He immediately wrote her a letter telling her he was safe in Paris and she could write him there. He said he had written numerous letters since September and had sent them to her parents' home in Greenwich and assumed they were never received. He expressed his love for her and their baby and the hope that the war would soon be over and they would finally be together as a family. He could only trust this letter would reach her.

During the next several weeks, Jean-Claude adapted to the routine of reviewing seized documents for information about possible war crimes. He found it ironic his job closely mirrored the one he'd had at the Ministry in Lyon, with the exception that he did not constantly fear detection.

He also had access to daily news dispatches from the States.

On December 18, 1944, the following came across his desk:

"U. S. Supreme Court Upholds Evacuation of Japanese to Detention Facilities." This was the first he had heard anything about the outcome of the case. The news release said the court found the removal constitutional as a wartime emergency measure, and relied on the military's concern that it was impossible to segregate the disloyal from the loyal quickly enough to secure the region and protect it from attacks from within.

Stanley was right. The Supreme Court had buckled.

The release went on to say the decision was not unanimous. There was a dissent in which one of the justices said, "this was the first time the Court had affirmed a substantial restriction on the personal liberty of U.S. citizens based upon race or ancestry, and what had happened to the Japanese bore a melancholy resemblance to the treatment of members of the Jewish race in Germany and other parts of Europe."

The majority opinion didn't surprise him but he was glad somebody on the court got it right even if it was in dissent. But it did disappoint him. The decision bolstered his belief that in time of war, laws were of questionable value to protect those singled out for blame because of their race or religion.

With the war winding down, he hoped his life could begin to return to some kind of normal and he could put the past behind him. At least he didn't have to live each day as if it were his last. He could begin to have thoughts, realistic thoughts, of going home and being with Stephanie and his child.

On Christmas Eve he returned to the hotel after a party at SHAEF. He was feeling upbeat and looking forward to going to Notre Dame for Christmas Eve Mass. Though not intending a return to his Catholic roots, his spiritual life was sorely in need, and there was no better place to celebrate Christmas Eve in Paris than the cathedral of Notre Dame.

The mood in the city was not joyful, because there were still too many men and women missing or dead or in German labor camps, but the lobby of the Crillon was elegantly decorated and festive. It reminded him of the country club in Greenwich where he and Stephanie had married, but on a much grander scale.

All personal mail was received at the hotel. He checked every day for a letter. That night was no exception even though it was Christmas Eve. The clerk shuffled through a stack of letters and handed him an envelope. The letter was from Stephanie. He stared at the envelope.

Finally. He felt a great sense of relief and joy and anticipation.

He went over to one of the overstuffed chairs in the lobby, sat down, and slowly opened the envelope.

Dear Jean-Claude,

The wonderful news is that you have a beautiful daughter. I named her Nicole. I hope you approve.

When you said you had written many letters since September, I asked my parents if they had received any. I wouldn't know since I have been living in New Haven for over a year. My father said letters had arrived, but he chose not to tell me about them. He said he felt it was best I got on with my life without you. I am very upset he did this, but there is nothing I can do about it now except let you know I didn't ignore you.

When I received your letter I was so relieved to hear you are safe. Jean-Claude, I lay in bed night after night worrying and wondering if you were ever coming home. I was so lonely and afraid. All we heard about were the terrible things that were happening in Lyon. I truly came to believe you would never be coming back.

I didn't want it to happen and I wasn't looking for it to happen, but I met a man who gave me security and comfort and yes, love. He is very good with Nicole and loves her a lot. He loves me too, and I have fallen in love with him.

Jean-Claude's stomach cramped, he felt he was going to be sick, but he forced himself to continue to read the letter.

> Jean-Claude, I know this will be very hard for you, but I felt I had to move on with my life. I decided that if you did come back, I would ask you for a divorce. My father has said he will provide a substantial settlement if you are willing to give up Nicole and let Michael adopt her. He says it would be best for her and would avoid having to deal with the issue of religion as she grows up.
>
> I don't want to return to California. And with you there and me in Connecticut, it would create a difficult situation for you to have contact with her given the distance. You have never seen her, and letting Michael adopt her would also be best for her. Michael is a good person, and he is the only father she has ever known. I promise you she will be loved and cared for. Please consider it. I know you are hurt and probably angry, and you have every right to be. But please give some thought as to what is best for the baby. I will always love you, but this is the way it has to be.
>
> I'm sorry. Please forgive me.
>
> Stephanie

He dropped his hands into his lap and crumpled the letter. He was devastated. Even though he'd had doubts about her when he left, the memory of her and the baby kept him going through many sleepless nights in Lyon when he was alone and afraid and after he lost Bernard and Chantal.

The negative thoughts about her had been erased and in their place he had created a fantasy of what their life would be like as a family when he returned.

All sorts of wild thoughts ran through his head. He would win her back. He would not allow the baby to be adopted. He would fight the divorce. He would agree to move to Connecticut. He would put a knife in her heart the first time he saw her. Then the thought crossed his mind that he should just end all the pain and kill himself.

All he felt was despair and a devastating pain that left him numb. He couldn't think. He knew this was not the time to make any decisions. He needed something to dull the senses, to kill the pain, so he went out and got drunk.

When he woke up, it was Christmas morning and nothing had changed except his head hurt. He felt terrible. He felt only emptiness—abandoned. There was nothing left to cling to.

The first thought he had was the last thought he'd had the night before. He would end it all. He had hit bottom emotionally. He knew he needed help. He turned to the only source he could think of that was immediately available.

He walked from the Crillon to Notre Dame. Because it was Christmas morning the atmosphere on the streets was joyous. The cold morning air and the celebrations going on around him cleared his head.

When he arrived, the church bells were ringing, and the cathedral was filled with worshipers wishing each other a *Joyeux Noel*. He lit candles for Chantal, Bernard, Andre, and Wells Lewis. He took a seat in a pew in the back and bowed his head.

He remembered going to Our Lady of Lourdes in Oakland on the day Pearl Harbor was attacked. He remembered how it gave him peace and helped put things in perspective. The atmosphere in Notre Dame cleansed him. It began to clear his mind of the negative thoughts. Surrounded by worshipers and holiday revelers, he no longer felt alone. He didn't know anybody, but there was a communal spirit he could feel—a connection with all those who had come to the church to pray.

His thoughts returned to the present. The feelings of hate for the Nazis came rushing back to fill the void created by his loss. They were the personification of evil. They had killed his father, Chantal, and Andre. They had murdered millions of innocent Jews. His depression turned to anger, and anger turned to resolve.

Barbie didn't get me, the Milice didn't get me, the German army didn't get me. He became determined to survive, to do whatever he could to defeat them. He had to stop feeling sorry for himself. At least he was alive and free. That was more than millions of Europeans could say.

In the days that followed, he tried not to think about Stephanie and the baby by controlling his thoughts, but it was difficult. No matter how hard he tried, he couldn't escape the fact she had left him, and that his child was going to be raised by another man.

But as the weeks wore on the pain gradually subsided. He was able to get through some days without thinking about them. He kept the letter in a place where he wouldn't see it. He would only read it again before the meeting they were bound to have when he returned. But that day was still a long way off.

He was very fortunate to have Colonel Littleton as his commanding officer. They got along well and he had confided in him about Stephanie.

The colonel received numerous invitations to attend dinner parties and receptions from prominent Parisians who wished to curry favor with the military. Senior officers were often offered the opportunity to dine at Tour d'Argent, the magnificent restaurant overlooking Notre Dame. The understanding was there would never be a bill, but if the chef ever needed anything, he could make a call and someone would take care of it. Jean-Claude was asked to come along as the colonel's guest on several occasions. Littleton felt it would help him get over Stephanie. It didn't help him get over her, but it eased the pain. At a time when most in Paris were eating whatever they could get their hands on, the meals at Tour d'Argent were elegant and the restaurant had a wine cellar with several thousand bottles. On one occasion Jean-Claude asked the sommelier if he had a bottle of 1929 Lynch Bages. Despite the unpleasant experience in Lagrange's bunker, he still remembered how good the wine was and regretted he never had a chance to finish his glass.

While there were lots of attractive women in Paris, Jean-Claude was neither interested nor ready for any kind of relationship, so he resisted those who made advances, most of whom only wanted cigarettes or nylons. He was definitely not looking for something to happen when he attended a reception at the home of a high-ranking French diplomat as the colonel's guest. It was there he met Claudette.

She was attractive, well-educated, and divorced. She was also a Communist.

She'd fled Paris with her two children just before France fell to the Nazis. She left and hid with friends close enough to the Swiss border so she could flee with her children if necessary. Her ex-husband was an active collaborator. She feared that if he found her, he would take the children and have her imprisoned or worse because she was a Communist.

They were introduced by another officer at the party and were attracted to each other immediately. They began to see each other and became friends, then lovers. He told her about Stephanie, and returning to France to find Bernard. She said she had heard stories of Bernard's exploits from her associates in the Party and they considered his death a great loss.

They realized from the start there was probably no future for them. He would be leaving within the year, and she said she would never leave Paris. Her ex-husband had been arrested, and she no longer feared losing her children. It was going to be like his other wartime relationships: strong and intense, but of short duration.

The relationship did lift his spirits, though. It helped him to forget, but not forgive.

Claudette had been an editor of a French magazine that featured prominent artists and authors. It had been shut down by the Nazis, but was just starting to get up and running again. She was excited by the fact that the arts and literature of the city were slowly coming to life.

Hemingway was living in Paris at the Hotel Ritz where he could be seen entertaining Jean-Paul Sartre and Simone de Beauvoir. Picasso was readying his first exhibition since the occupation, with work done before the war, but banned by the Nazis because the art was too extreme and he was a Communist. Claudette made arrangements for them to attend the opening.

Jean-Claude was intelligent, but didn't consider himself an intellectual. Even so he was happy to accompany Claudette to art openings and literary readings. He was taken by her beauty, but also her sophistication. She reminded him of Stephanie. But unlike Stephanie, he believed she was a person of character and integrity. She'd been through a lot and she told him she didn't want to live a life of deceptions and lies. She'd had to do that to survive for over five years, and she never wanted to live like that again.

During the next three months, he analyzed disturbing documents related to concentration camps discovered by Soviet troops as they entered and occupied Poland. One such camp was Auschwitz. The reports told of thousands of starving survivors, mostly Jews, who had been used as slave labor and many thousands more, who had been killed. There were images that gave a graphic picture of the inhumanity that had taken place. It was clearly the type of situation that would warrant a war crimes prosecution, if the architects of the plan could be identified.

One day in mid-April, he received reports that reconnaissance planes had spotted what looked like a massive concentration camp just outside of Munich. Shortly after, Colonel Littleton came to him with orders he was to join the division approaching Munich, and if a camp was located, he was to interrogate any German soldiers, Gestapo, and SS to determine their roles and responsibilities. He was also to interview inmates. He would be attached to the 522nd Field

Artillery Unit, which was already on its way to Munich.

The enemy was in retreat and the Allies met little resistance. When he caught up with the unit, he found it was comprised of a number of Japanese from the 442nd who had fought in the Vosges. He asked if he could ride with one of them.

He was assigned to a jeep driven by a Japanese corporal with another Japanese soldier riding shotgun. They had all been in the Vosges campaign together. Jean-Claude talked with them about the battle to free the Lost R battalion and the heavy casualties the unit had sustained.

Jean-Claude told them Ken Matsumoto was a close friend and asked if either of them knew him.

The driver paused for a moment and looked at Jean-Claude. "Yeah, I knew him. I heard he got it near Seravezza in Italy."

The news sucked the wind out of him. For several moments he couldn't speak. He then reacted angrily. "That's bullshit. You don't know that for sure. Who told you that?" he demanded.

"One of the wounded boys from the 442nd came through on his way home and said Matsumoto was shot when his unit was trying to take a hill. That's all I know, except they said he took out a bunch of Krauts before they got him."

"Listen," the corporal said, admonishing Jean-Claude notwithstanding the disparity in their ranks, "I have lost more buddies than I can count. I know how it hurts. Believe me I know. I'm sorry if he was your friend, but you've got to move on—let it go."

Jean-Claude again fell silent. He couldn't process the corporal's words. He didn't want to believe it. If it was true, everyone he cared most for was now either dead or had deserted him. He thought nothing more could be done to him. In a matter of hours he would be proven wrong.

He finally broke his silence. He had been thinking about Ken and all those Japanese who lost their lives rescuing the Lost Battalion. He thought about their families in the camps back home. It made him angry. He finally asked them, "Do you feel you've been sacrificed because you're Japanese?"

The corporal paused before answering. "I never think that way," he said. "I just do my duty because I don't want to let my buddies or my family down or dishonor their name. That's all that matters." The other soldier nodded in agreement.

A road sign up ahead read Dachau 1000 m. Jean-Claude recognized the name from his reconnaissance briefings as the location of what might be a concentration camp. The two Japanese soldiers had never heard of Dachau or Nazi concentration camps. The only ones they knew were back in the States. Jean-Claude felt his stomach tighten as they approached.

As the convoy drew closer, razor wire could be seen atop the steel fences. Guard towers just like at Manzanar looked over the camp. They slowly drove through a gate into a compound, which turned out to be a satellite of the main camp.

It was April 29, 1945. Soldiers from various units were already inside. The scene was chaotic with prisoners screaming and soldiers trying to maintain order. There was the stench of death—the same odor he remembered from Saint-Genis-Laval.

He saw some soldiers running away from boxcars that were on a siding just outside the main gate. Some were holding rags over their faces. Others wept. He went back to see what was there.

What he saw overwhelmed him. The boxcars were piled high with hundreds of emaciated, decomposing corpses. He ran back inside the gate, staggering, gagging, tears filling his eyes. The sight was unbelievable, an unimaginable human catastrophe.

Back inside the camp, he saw what looked like a gas chamber. Next to it was a crematorium. There were bodies in various stages of decomposition stacked next to the crematorium. Every place he looked, he saw persons barely alive, walking around aimlessly. Their bones protruded from their skin and their eyes were sunken deep into their skulls. They were human skeletons—just barely alive. Those who had the strength hugged the soldiers. Most were too weak to move.

It took several hours for him to get over the emotional devastation. He spent the time talking to fellow officers, sharing feelings, venting anger, and comforting each other while drinking brandy from a flask one of the officers carried with him. He finally calmed down enough to begin his work.

The unit set up a tent for him with a stenographer and a photographer. He debriefed remnants of the SS and other German military still there. The bulk of the German garrison had left the day before they arrived and only low-level personnel remained to face the Allies.

He restrained himself while interrogating the Germans, unlike others that day who let their emotions get the better of them, and took their revenge on the spot. He also interviewed prisoners. He took detailed notes of the degradation and suffering they had experienced. When he found out a film crew had arrived with the rest of the unit, he asked them to film the interviews so they could be used in evidence. He made sure the full magnitude of the catastrophe was recorded, so no one could ever deny what had happened.

He also interviewed witnesses to the shooting of German guards and members of the SS by U.S. soldiers after they surrendered. There were also fatal beatings of Germans by prisoners. He understood why they were killed, just like he understood why Georges killed Michel. The desire for revenge was immediate and visceral. But he kept coming back to the same question: Do we want to be like them?

They too had to be held accountable.

There in Dachau, in the shadow of some of the worst degradation and savagery human history had ever seen, Japanese American soldiers, many drafted out of the camps, were assisting in the liberation of thousands of Jews while their own families were still imprisoned back home. Jean-Claude could only shake his head at the irony. Unfortunately, it did little to remove the images—images that would continue to haunt him for the rest of his life.

The anger felt by the military liberators spilled over to the residents of the nearby towns. Many were forced to come to the camp to view the horror. Farmers' wagons were conscripted to haul corpses away. Many men, some dressed in suits, and ladies in dresses, were forced to help load bodies onto the wagons. Many said they were unaware. Many probably knew, but ignored it. Many got sick at the sight and smell. It was reported there were several suicides of locals who could not deal with the horror they had witnessed.

Jean-Claude compiled enough evidence to clearly establish that war crimes had been committed. His job done, he left Dachau and returned to Paris where the first thing he did was go to the office that kept casualty records. He confirmed that Ken had been killed at Seravezza and was being recommended for the Silver Star. It had been a week since he had been told of Ken's death, but all the pain returned upon seeing it confirmed in print. This combined with what he had witnessed at Dachau left him drained.

Fortunately, he had a job to do. He was to create a file that would stand up in a war crimes trial. It took him a week and when he finished, he submitted it to Colonel Littleton, who was very pleased with the results.

On the morning of May 7, 1945, Germany surrendered, and the war in Europe was officially over.

Parisians did not react with spontaneous joy upon hearing the news that morning. He understood why they didn't feel victorious. While the Germans greeted the Allies as liberators protecting them from the Red Army, the French viewed them as occupiers. The only ones who felt victorious were the Communists.

While they had not gained control of the government because de Gaulle was too popular, they were the most powerful political party in France. They felt the tide of history on their side, and eventually they would be successful in gaining control.

Later as darkness fell, the lights of Paris came on for the first time since the beginning of the war. The streets filled with people and the strains of the Marseillaise could be heard throughout the entire city.

Paris was no longer at risk. She had survived, thanks to the German military governor who defied Hitler's orders to burn the city to the ground, but in many ways, she looked like those who were returning from the forced labor camps in Germany— sad and weak.

Jean-Claude had his moment of reflection. He thought about Ken and how he would have loved the architecture of Paris, and Wells Lewis, who would have been right at home with Hemingway and Sartre at the Ritz, and Bernard, who perhaps could have realized his dream of being a leader in the new France, a Communist France. He thought of Andre, who could have regained his rightful place in the Paris Bar, and finally of Chantal, who, now that the battle was over, might have found someone to love and live out her life with in peace.

Victory had been achieved, but it had come at a great personal cost.

He thought about staying and joining the Party and carrying on Bernard's mission. Perhaps he and Claudette would be able to have a permanent relationship. But in the end, there was too much pain associated with France, and there was unfinished business back in the States.

While the colonel wanted him to stay and participate in the war crimes tribunals that were sure to take place, he acknowledged that Jean-Claude was physically and emotionally tired and wanted to go home. He had done his job. His tour of duty was up, so he gave him the option to stay or go. Three weeks later, he was on a troop ship bound for New York.

CHAPTER 15

COMING HOME

June 1945

During the five days on the troop transport, Jean-Claude thought about what he was going to say to Stephanie, and what he was going to do about the baby. He hadn't read her letter in months, but now he read it over and over. He knew he couldn't win her back and decided she wasn't worth it anyway. He'd always had nagging doubts about her character and the fantasy he had created while in France had been shattered by her letter.

What to do about the baby was the more difficult decision. He had seen lives destroyed by violence. He understood that lives could also be destroyed by non-violent selfish acts. He decided he had to put the baby's interests above his own. That decision marked one of the significant ways the war had changed him.

He wired Stephanie, as they were now allowed to send

and receive personal messages by wire. He informed her he would be in New York City for two days and asked her to come down and meet him at the Palace. She wired back that she would.

He would not hurt her either physically or emotionally. Hurting her would not change anything or make him feel any better. His initial anger was now replaced by resignation. His experiences during the past two-and-a-half years reaffirmed the conclusion he had reached long ago after the death of his mother—life was very fragile and relationships were of an uncertain duration, especially in wartime.

Stephanie had to be forgotten.

He checked into the Palace. He'd chosen this hotel for their meeting because it was the place where they had spent their honeymoon, and he felt it would give the reunion the ironic quality it deserved. They'd agreed to meet in the bar.

He wondered how he would react when he first saw her. It had been two-and-a-half years since they had seen each other. A lot had happened and much had changed.

Jean-Claude arrived early and took a seat at a corner table and waited. He kept looking toward the entrance. He ordered a glass of wine and smoked one cigarette after another.

Then suddenly, there she was. Tall and elegantly dressed, striding toward him with a big smile on her face as if nothing had happened. His stomach tightened. His hands grew cold, just like when he'd faced life and death situations in France. He stood up to greet her.

"Jean-Claude, you look so handsome in your uniform," Stephanie said as she gave him a hug.

Jean-Claude did not hug her back. "Knock off the bullshit, Stephanie. Where's the baby?" Despite his plan to maintain his composure, he reacted with anger.

She drew back a little, her face reflecting the shock at

his reaction.

They sat down across from each other. He lit up.

"Still smoking? You know it's bad for your health," she said in a caring way, obviously trying to break the tension.

"I've experienced a few things in the last two-and-a-half years that were a lot more threatening to my health than a few cigarettes. I appreciate your concern, however," he said with a tinge of sarcasm. "Now, where's the baby?"

"She's in New Haven. I didn't want to confuse her. I felt that if she saw you and we told her you were her father, and then she never saw you again, she would not understand. I wanted to wait and find out what you wanted to do."

Jean-Claude nodded, acknowledging the soundness of her reasoning.

"If you insist on having visits with her in the future, we can set up a time tomorrow to meet her. I hope that's not what you have decided, though."

"Are you certain you're staying on the East Coast?" he asked.

"Yes, I have taken a job at Yale as assistant museum curator, just like the job I had at Berkeley. Michael works in New Haven. That's where we met."

"I really don't give a damn where you two met." Jean-Claude glared at her. "I just wanted to know if you were coming back to the West Coast." His mood changed from question to question.

Her gaze appeared sympathetic, and she made an attempt to reach out to touch his arm. He pulled away.

"Jean-Claude, I know you are hurt and angry. You have every right to be, but we must put the baby first. My father says he will offer a generous settlement if you will allow Michael to adopt Nicole."

Jean-Claude didn't hesitate. He had thought about the

settlement proposal because she had mentioned it in her letter. The last thing he was going to do was let her father buy him off. "You can tell him to take his generous settlement and shove it up his ass. Or better yet, I'll tell him myself."

"Jean-Claude, please calm down. We'll never get through this if we can't be civil to each other." She looked around to see if he had drawn the attention of others in the bar to their conversation.

They were quiet for a moment.

Jean-Claude took a deep breath and leaned back in his chair. She removed an envelope from her purse and pushed it across the table.

"I have filed for divorce. Here are the papers. I am seeking full custody. I know you are a great lawyer and could give me a battle over custody, but I have consulted with the best divorce lawyer in New Haven, who also teaches at Yale, and he says I will undoubtedly get custody." Her demeanor changed to hard and threatening.

A threat to beat him in court. She couldn't have handled it in a worse way. Fortunately for her, he had already made up his mind what he was going to do about the baby if she was going to remain in Connecticut, but he wanted to cool down before telling her.

He paused for a moment and leaned forward in his chair, so they were face to face and looking into each other's eyes. "I've thought about this every minute for the past five days. I have gone from wanting to fight the divorce and custody to just giving up. But in the end I want to do what's right for the baby. It's not fair for me to take out my anger on her. So I am prepared to let you have full custody."

He paused.

She closed her eyes and let out a sigh of relief.

"I won't ask for visitation either, but I will not agree to

an adoption." She instantly opened her eyes. "I'm sure your Yale lawyer told you there is nothing you can do to make me give her up unless I abandon her, and I don't intend to do that. I will pay child support in order to keep my rights. If you don't want child support, we will stipulate that I am not abandoning the baby, but only giving up visitation. We would also agree that at a time in her life when she's old enough to understand, we will tell her who I am and let her know about her heritage. If she wants to see me, it will be her choice. I'm not about to screw up her life, but at some point, she is going to know I am her father. Is that understood?" He was pleased he had thought through what he was going to do about the baby in advance so the emotion of the moment didn't cloud his judgment.

Her relief turned to consternation. She was upset he wouldn't agree to an adoption. She sat back in her chair and crossed her arms, then became petulant. "I think you are being selfish."

"Selfish? Selfish?" he yelled.

"Shh, keep your voice down." She looked embarrassed because he'd drawn the attention of others in the bar to their conversation.

He lowered his voice. "You above all should not be a judge of who's selfish." Jean-Claude paused and sat back, trying to remain calm.

"If you agree," he went on in a calmer voice, "you can have your Yale lawyer send the papers with those stipulations to my office in Oakland. I will look them over. If they clearly state I am not agreeing to adoption and not abandoning her, but reserve the right to have contact with her when she is older, I will sign them. If you don't agree, then I will want regular visitation, and when she's old enough, I will want her to come to California for summers and holidays."

She paused for only a moment. It was as if she was

anticipating this. Perhaps her Yale lawyer had prepared her. "Okay, I will agree. I don't want her shuttling back and forth across the country."

"Good. And if she wants to see me when she's older I am going to tell her about her Jewish heritage."

"Oh, Jean-Claude, you're not serious, are you? You know being Jewish can cause problems."

"I'm very serious." From the tone of his voice and the determined look in his eye, she could not mistake the fact that he meant what he said. "I know better than you can ever imagine how being Jewish can cause problems, but that will never stop me from wanting my daughter to know about her heritage when she's old enough to understand."

"Well, I guess we don't have much more to talk about, do we." It was a statement not a question. She had tried charm, threats, and reasoning, and now she seemed to realize this was the best deal she was going to get. She tried one last time to end on a pleasant note. "I'm really sorry we never got to hear Artie Shaw. He is my favorite."

"He's Jewish, you know," he shot back.

She sat straight up with an indignant look on her face. "I'll have my lawyer send the papers to your office in Oakland." She crossed her legs and glanced away.

"There is one thing more I want to know before you go." It was more of a command than a question.

She turned back and looked at him. "What is it?"

"Did you lie in the Lewis trial?"

She lowered her eyes, paused, and then finally said, "Yes."

He gave her a disgusted look, shook his head, stood up, and walked out. He didn't look back. There was nothing more to say. Later, as he was reflecting on the meeting, he realized she never once asked about Ken or the Matsumoto family or his father. She was a very shallow person. He was glad to be rid of her.

Jean-Claude spent the next day calling his contacts in Oakland and Berkeley to arrange things for his return. He called the professor who was renting his house and told him that even though he was not going to sell it, he didn't want to live in the house when he returned, and the professor could continue to stay there with his family indefinitely. He had decided the house was too big and held too many memories to live in, but it was also his only connection to his past and his father and he didn't want to sell it. His only stipulation was that he would have access to the wine cellar as needed. The professor was overjoyed and agreed.

He then called Irving Stern. He had sent him a letter from France telling him he was coming home.

"Irv, it's Jean-Claude. I'm back in the States. I'll be in Oakland in a few days."

"Great to hear from you, Jean-Claude. I'm glad you made it back safely. Your desk is just as you left it."

"That's good of you, Irv, but I don't know if I'm going to return to practicing law."

"If the issue is getting established again, you can help out with my injury cases until you build up your criminal practice—which shouldn't take too long."

"You're a good friend, Irv. I have some decisions I have to make, but I want you to know that I appreciate your offer."

"Glad to do it, Jean-Claude. I also have a tidy sum in my trust account for the Matsumotos when they return. The tenant was good about paying the rent."

"That's good to hear. I'm going to go and see them and I will tell them they have something to come back to."

After a pause, Irving asked, "Did your father make it?"

"No, he was executed by the Nazis just before Lyon was liberated. Ken Matsumoto didn't make it either."

"I'm sorry about your father. I read about Ken in the papers. Sad news. He was a hero."

"Yes he was. They all were. I'll call you when I get into town. Thanks again for all you've done."

"Thank you for all *you've* done. We owe you and the other soldiers a lot."

He hung up the phone and called his old client to get the status on the Matsumotos' vehicles and his Buick. He reached him at his used car lot. He was still in business. That was a relief. He said they were in good working order, and he would make sure the Buick was ready to go when Jean-Claude got back. After motorbikes, jeeps, and old Range Rovers, he was ready for a nice big comfortable car.

A few days later, he returned to Berkeley and took a room at the Claremont. It felt good to be home. But he still felt very unsteady—not physically, but emotionally. He needed to talk to Stanley to help get grounded, but he had to finalize his discharge first.

The morning after his arrival, he went to the Presidio to get processed out. Sergeant Rizzuto was still there at the same desk.

"Sergeant, do you remember me?" Jean-Claude asked.

"Yes, sir. I surely do. You're the lawyer who defended the Jap. You made captain. Congratulations." The sergeant appeared genuinely happy to see him.

"I'm just thankful that I made it back. Is Colonel Wilson still here? I want to make sure he knows about the bravery and loyalty of the Japanese who fought for us."

"No, sir. He requested reassignment to a combat unit. He was heading to the beach in Normandy when his landing craft took a direct hit. He didn't make it."

"How about General DeWitt?"

"When the Japanese thing calmed down, they kicked him upstairs. He's now Commandant of the Army Navy Staff College in Washington."

Jean-Claude shook his head. "I'm surprised. I never thought he had an intellectual side."

"Is your Jap still in a camp?"

"He reenlisted and was killed in Italy. They've recommended him for the Silver Star."

"See? I knew it. They weren't all bad. There was many more good ones than bad ones. Puttin' all of 'em in camps was bullshit." He waved his hand in disgust. "By the way, there's a colonel here assigned to give out medals to the families of Japs that was killed. He's over in Bravo Company. I'll take you there when we're through here."

"Thanks, I would appreciate that. Did you have to go to Italy?"

"No. They kept me here. Word is my relatives helped the Allies take Sicily. I'm not so sure that's true but that's the family line so who am I to say different."

He completed the paperwork for his discharge. It would take two more weeks before it became final.

Rizutto took him over to Bravo Company's barracks and introduced him to the colonel who was responsible for handing out the medals to the families of those who were killed. He was going to make a trip to Manzanar in two days and asked if Jean-Claude wanted to come along. Jean-Claude immediately said yes. He had planned to make a visit. Now he could be present when the medal was presented to Mas and Mrs. Matsumoto.

Two days later, he and the colonel arrived at Manzanar around midday and were directed to the administration building. It was the same building he'd visited before he left for Europe. They were told the Matsumotos would be sent for.

It was early July and it was hot and dry, but conditions had changed from when he was last there. In place of the barren landscape he remembered, there were orchards of fruit trees, vegetable gardens, the baseball diamond Ken had designed, and flower gardens between the barracks. It was certainly not Dachau.

The thing that had not changed was the ever-present guard towers that stood as a reminder they were in a prison even if the appearance inside the fences looked more hospitable.

Jean-Claude asked the person at the desk how the orchards and vegetable gardens and flowers were able to grow in the desert.

"These Japs really know how to farm. They were able to siphon water from the aqueduct carrying water to LA, and irrigate all that land. They're pretty industrious people. I've grown to really like them. I'll be sorry to see them go."

I'm sure the feeling isn't mutual, Jean-Claude thought as he waited for Mas and his wife to arrive.

There was a look of astonishment on their faces as they came into the room and saw Jean-Claude. Apparently they hadn't been told who their visitor was. They had aged considerably and they looked sad, which was understandable given they had lost their son.

Jean-Claude wanted to hug them, but mindful of their restrained way of greeting, he bowed. They returned the bow.

He introduced them to the colonel and told them Ken was being awarded the Silver Star, the third highest medal for gallantry in combat behind the Distinguished Service Cross and the Medal of Honor. The medal was for his bravery in Italy. The colonel read the citation.

First Lieutenant Kenneth Matsumoto distinguished himself by gallantry in action while his unit was attempting to break through the mountain strongholds of the enemy near Seravezza, Italy. Lt. Matsumoto exposed himself to enemy fire by advancing alone up a hill in the direction of a machine gun position keeping his unit pinned down. When about twenty yards from the enemy position, Lt. Matsumoto hurled two grenades that silenced the enemy's guns. Before the enemy could locate him and retaliate, he advanced further to silence another machine gun position before he was mortally wounded. Lt. Matsumoto's actions are in keeping with the highest traditions of military service and reflect great credit on him, his unit, and the United States Army.

After reading the citation, the colonel handed the medal to Mas Matsumoto. Even though Mrs. Matsumoto didn't fully understand the words of the citation, she wept.

A medal? That's all? No apology. No admission they were wrong. A lousy medal his parents can put on the mantel when they are finally free to go home. That is just wrong Jean-Claude thought. He felt a mixture of sadness and anger, but kept his feelings to himself.

Once the emotions of the moment had calmed, Jean-Claude told Mas and Mrs. Matsumoto he and Ken had met in France, and they had a brief visit.

"We had a good visit. I asked him if he felt this country was worth fighting for after what had happened to you and your family. He said yes and said he hoped that someday the mistakes would be corrected. I told him I would do all I could to make sure that happened. He fought bravely and died a hero." He felt he wanted to say so much more about how he felt about their son, but he couldn't find the words.

Mas looked at Jean-Claude through empty eyes, eyes that appeared like something had sucked the life out of him. Mas then took a folded photo from his pocket and handed it to Jean-Claude. It was a picture of Ken in his uniform. "This is the last picture we have. It was taken the day he left." He paused and looked down, then lifted his eyes and looked at Jean-Claude. "We are proud he brought honor to our name."

Jean-Claude felt a flood of emotion come over him. He fought to hold back tears. He quickly changed the subject.

"I drove by your house and it's still in good condition. Irving Stern has the rent money and the unused portion of the money Ken gave me in his trust account, and the taxes have all been paid. The greenhouse had a lot of broken windows, but they can easily be repaired. You have something you can return to."

He paused to see if that news made Mas feel any better about going back to Berkeley. He remained expressionless.

He turned to Mrs. Matsumoto. "I also checked with the family who agreed to store the boxes with your personal effects in their garage. They are still there and in good condition." He asked Mas to please make sure his wife understood what he'd said about the personal effects. He remembered how worried she was they might be destroyed.

"Are you planning to return to Oakland when you're released?" Jean-Claude asked.

Mas paused. "We are thinking about going home to Japan after the war is over. Like here, mistakes were made by Japan, but someday I hope they will be forgiven and we can live in peace. We still have family there. We come from a beautiful area near Hiroshima and we have always thought about going back someday."

"I hope you don't do that. Don't you want to be with your daughters? Ken told me that one of your daughters has gotten married."

"Yes, I'm a grandfather." When he spoke he finally smiled.

"Don't you want to see your grandchildren grow up?" Jean-Claude asked softly.

Mas didn't answer.

"I remember what you told me about the bonsai, how they give dignity to life, and bring a sense of harmony and well-being and give you strength. Go back to the nursery, to your bonsai. They will give you the strength to start over." He was exhorting Mas to go back and start over, at the same time he was unsure if he could muster the strength to start over himself, or if he even wanted to.

Mas smiled slightly, but still didn't reply.

After a few moments of silence, they said good-bye. Jean-Claude bowed to Mas, but he gave Mrs. Matsumoto a hug like he had done before she entered Tanforan. She hugged him back. He could feel her appreciation. Then he and the colonel left Manzanar for the last time.

By the middle of 1945, most Japanese who had not displayed disloyalty were allowed to leave but many were fearful, especially the older ones. The years of living in the camps made the prospects of return very intimidating. They had become dependent for everything and most had nothing to go back to. In addition, the war in the Pacific was still raging and everyone expected the Japanese would fight to the end to protect their homeland. This would only provoke more hatred. The Mayor of Los Angeles didn't want any Japanese, Nisei or Issei, returning to his city. He said they all should be stripped of their citizenship and all people of Japanese heritage should be shipped back to Japan.

Their plight was much like the Jews who were liberated from Dachau. They had no place to go. They were free, but they were lost.

Jean-Claude waited another day before going to the courthouse to see Stanley. He wanted and needed to talk to him, but he dreaded it. He knew he was going to have to tell him things—horrible things—but he had to see him. Jean-Claude was still suspended between two worlds. He had lived two lives and was coming back to the one he'd left behind while not being able to totally let go of who he had been for the past two and a half years. He needed Stanley's help to ground him.

It felt strange going up the front stairs of the courthouse, walking down the marble halls to the bank of elevators like he had done so many times before. It seemed like such a long time ago. Sometimes time is measured by experiences, not days or years, he thought as he pushed the elevator button.

The elevator opened. It was Percy's car.

"I don't believe what I see. Missa Bonnay. You 'bout gave me a heart attack."

"Hello, Percy." Jean-Claude gave him a big hug and Percy hugged him back.

"I am so glad you made it. We wuz all worried sick about you."

"Thanks. How's the judge?"

"Just as ornery as ever. He's gonna be real glad to see you."

He got off on the fifth floor and walked down the hall to Department Nine. He peeked through the window to see if court was in session. It wasn't. Julie was sitting at her desk when he walked in.

When she saw him, she let out a shriek, jumped up, and came around her desk to give him a big hug as she cried out, "Judge, judge, come see who's here." The door to Stanley's chambers opened and he stuck his head out.

"My God!" he cried in astonishment and beckoned Jean-Claude into his chambers. "Come in. Come in."

It was late afternoon and his chambers were empty.

Jean-Claude sat down. He wasn't quite sure if this was reality or a dream. Even several days after returning to Berkeley, he would sometimes get disoriented and not believe he was back in the States. They both lit a cigarette at the same time.

"You've aged," Stanley said.

"War will do that to you." Jean-Claude looked at Stanley for the first time.

"Well?" Stanley asked in that tone of voice that Jean-Claude knew well. It meant, *tell me everything.* "Was it as bad as I've heard?"

He looked into the old judge's eyes and then lowered his head. "Yes," he said in a barely audible voice.

"How bad?" Stanley asked, his apprehension plainly showing.

Jean-Claude braced himself for what he knew was to come. "Beyond bad."

"How many? Thousands?"

Jean-Claude hesitated, and then spoke. "Maybe millions."

"My God." Stanley paused to regain his composure. "I read in the papers about the camps. That Auschwitz place and Dachau. I didn't want to believe."

"I was there. I was in Dachau. I saw it. It happened." He lowered his eyes. "It happened, and it was worse than you'll read about." He couldn't bring himself to tell him about the children of Izieu or the Jews being loaded into boxcars. Dachau was enough.

There was a long, difficult period of silence as if Stanley was trying to absorb what he had just heard. "What more could I have done?" the old judge cried, looking up as if asking for forgiveness.

"There's nothing more you could have done," Jean-Claude said in a comforting tone. He shook his head.

Stanley's face hardened. "It must never happen again. They're talking about letting the refugees go to Palestine. This is best. They will have a place of their own where they can protect themselves, and make sure it never happens again." Stanley exhaled a big puff of smoke then changed the subject. "What about your father? Did he make it?"

"No." Jean-Claude hesitated and looked down then raised his head and looked at Stanley. His eyes probably revealed the profound sadness he was feeling. "He was executed by the Nazis a week before the liberation of Lyon," he said in a barely audible voice.

"I'm sorry. Did you get to spend some time with him while you were there?"

"We had some good talks and some good times. I have lots of memories. It's still hard for me to believe he's gone." Jean-Claude exhaled smoke and immediately took another drag.

"How are you doing?" the judge asked quietly.

"Well, I could be better. Stephanie is divorcing me. She met another man and she's staying on the East Coast. The more I find out about her, the more I feel it's just as well." Jean-Claude showed none of the emotion he had shown when telling Stanley about Bernard or the fate of the Jews. It was clear he had moved on from Stephanie.

"I don't think I had a chance to tell you before I left that she got pregnant. I found out about it the day I was leaving. I have a daughter I've never seen. I'm going to let her have custody because that's best for the baby, but I'm not letting her be adopted. Someday I'll meet her when she's old enough to understand who I am." Jean-Claude took a breath. "And I will tell her about her grandmother."

"You should have married a nice Jewish girl." Stanley shook his head and smiled.

"I'll remember that if there's a next time." Jean-Claude returned the smile. "You will be happy to know I feel more like a Jew than when I left. I have to. There aren't many of us left."

Stanley didn't smile, only nodded. He took a deep puff and exhaled. "I read about Ken Matsumoto getting killed in action. It made the local papers. They said he died a hero."

Jean-Claude stubbed out a cigarette and lit another. "You won't believe this. I ran into him in France." Jean-Claude was more animated emotionally as he spoke of Ken and their wartime meeting. "We were able to spend some time together before he shipped out to Italy. He and his buddies were brave soldiers and their loyalty was never in doubt. Putting them in camps was a disgrace. What happened to them is an example of why laws meant to protect people like Ken and his family aren't worth a damn in wartime."

"That's exactly what I told you," Stanley said but not in a self-satisfied tone.

"I just got back from Manzanar seeing his parents. They gave him a medal. And listen to this. I entered Dachau with a bunch of Japanese soldiers from the camps here. They were freeing Jews while many of their parents were still in the camps back home. Is that the ultimate irony, or what?" Jean-Claude stood up and began pacing back and forth feeling the emotion from all they discussed. His hands were cold and he was chain-smoking.

The old judge shook his head in disbelief, and sat back in his chair. He had regained his composure, but his face was gray, his shoulders slumped forward, and his eyes had the look of profound sorrow. "That's enough for today. I can only take so much." He leaned forward. "So what are you going to do?"

"Irv has kept my office for me, but I don't know if I want to go back to practicing. I used to think I could make a difference. You taught me that." He glanced at Stanley. "Now I'm not so sure. Maybe the Communists might make a difference. Bernard was a true believer. I might go back to France and join the Party, or work for the war crimes tribunals they are setting up. I just don't know. I'm pretty confused right now."

"Don't be a *putz*. The Communists are just as bad as the Nazis. Stalin is as bad as Hitler. This stuff about the freedom of the workers is all bullshit. It's just a way to keep power. Don't do it." Stanley made a fist and pounded his desk. "Listen, it's not perfect here. Sure, we messed up with the Japs, but it's still the best of the worst."

"I've seen the worst. But the same thing could happen here. Just let some crazy like Hitler take control and the Constitution becomes a scrap of paper just like McCloy said. Germany was no backward country. They had laws. They had culture. But they became barbarians. The French prided themselves on their civilization and their culture. But they became barbarians. It doesn't take much to turn men into monsters and laws can't stop them."

"You have learned well what I have taught you," Stanley said. "But I've also taught you that you can't quit. You can't give up. You can make a difference just like you did in France."

Jean-Claude opened his mouth to protest, but closed it.

Stanley leaned forward. Their faces were only a few feet apart. "Remember, it was racism behind all the insanity. If we are never allowed to forget what happened to the Jews or the internment of the Japanese, we may be able to keep it from happening again. You and the others must never let it be forgotten."

Jean-Claude slumped in his chair. "Like I said, my head's pretty messed up right now. I don't know what I'm going to do."

"You go home. Get some sleep. When you wake up, you come here to court tomorrow morning. You come to my chambers just like before. Understand?" It was spoken like an order. Like an order Chantal would have given.

"I'll think about it," Jean-Claude said, and then fell silent.

Finally, he reached his emotional limit. "Stanley, I've got to go. Sorry I had to be the one to tell you all this."

As Jean-Claude stood, Stanley got up from behind his desk. "I'm old. My time is short. Yours is not. Don't waste it. Don't let all the sacrifice mean nothing. Never let them forget. Never let it happen again," he said in defiant tone. He then turned around to the bookcase behind his desk and took the bonsai down from a shelf and handed it to Jean-Claude, who had been so preoccupied with what he and Stanley were talking about he hadn't noticed it. "I watered it every day." He shook his head. "Well, that's not quite true. Julie watered it every day."

No matter how hard he tried, he couldn't hold back the wave of emotion that swept over him. The bonsai was the last straw. The tears finally came. Years of bottled up emotion poured out.

Stanley put his arm around him. "Take the tree. You told me it gives you peace and makes you strong. This is what you need now."

Jean-Claude took a deep breath and tried to stop sobbing. All he could say was, "Thanks." He was exhausted. He needed to get some air, clear his head, and stop crying. He didn't want to be seen in the courthouse with a tear-stained face.

He went into the men's room, which was just outside Stanley's chambers, and washed his face. Ten minutes later, having left his visible emotions behind, he walked down the hall to the elevators with the bonsai in his hand.

The door opened. It was Percy's car, but Percy didn't say anything. It immediately became clear why. The only other occupant was Judge Kelly. They glanced at each other. Kelly glanced at his uniform and then the tree.

"I want to thank you for your service," Judge Kelly said as he stuck out his hand. "I hope to see you back in my courtroom soon."

Jean-Claude shook his hand and nodded. As Kelly got out of the elevator, he peered at Jean-Claude. "And when you do come back, try to be on time."

Some people never change. He's still an asshole.

He walked out of the courthouse through the big bronze doors that opened up to a view of the lake. The fresh air cleared his head. It felt good to be in the courthouse again, but he realized the war had changed him.

After all he had been through, he wondered if he could ever lead a normal life? Had he been permanently damaged? Could he ever stop thinking about all the horrible things he'd seen? The hand coming up from beneath the dirt at Saint-Genis-Laval, the horrors of his father nearly drowning in the tubs at the École, the Jews being loaded into boxcars, the Matsumoto family being treated like criminals, and, finally, Dachau.

He had lost those most dear to him. His wife had left him.

He no longer trusted that the laws could protect the innocent. Could he ever be an effective lawyer again? Could he ever commit to a relationship again?

Even if he tried to control his thoughts, he knew the images would remain, haunting him. He could never forget. Maybe Stanley was right. Maybe it was up to him and the others who had witnessed these horrifying things to keep the memory alive so no one would ever forget. Maybe he could make a difference. Maybe.

These were the thoughts that were going through his mind as he looked out across the lake from the courthouse steps. He could see the Regillus. He smiled and lit a cigarette. *Maybe I'll go over there tomorrow and see if they have any vacancies.*

As he walked to his car he tossed his cigarette, hesitated a moment, then reached into his pocket and took out the rest of the pack and threw it in the trash can that was on the sidewalk.

He got into the Buick and as he pulled away from the curb, he turned on the radio. Artie Shaw was playing. The sun was shining. It wasn't raining like it was that day a lifetime ago.

EPILOGUE

JAPANESE AMERICANS

In *U.S. v. Korematsu* 323 U.S. 214 (1944), the final decision in the Japanese internment cases deciding the constitutionality of the exclusion order was handed down by the Supreme Court on December 18, 1944. In a six-to-three decision, they upheld it.

Justice Hugo Black wrote for the majority:

> Korematsu was not excluded from the Military Area because of hostility to him or his race. He was excluded because we are at war with the Japanese Empire, because the properly constituted military authorities feared an invasion of our West Coast and felt constrained to take proper security measures, because they decided that the military urgency of the situation demanded that all citizens of Japanese ancestry be segregated from the West Coast temporarily, and, finally, because Congress, reposing its confidence in this time

of war in our military leaders—as inevitably it must—determined that they should have the power to do just this.

Justice Frank Murphy dissented. Though lengthy, it merits being quoted almost in its entirety because of its eloquence and its thorough repudiation of racism as the basis of enacting and upholding a law.

> This exclusion of all persons of Japanese ancestry goes over the very brink of constitutional power and falls into the ugly abyss of racism. Individuals must not be left impoverished of their constitutional rights on plea of military necessity that has neither substance nor support. That this forced exclusion was the result in good measure of this erroneous assumption of racial guilt rather than bona fide military necessity is evidenced by the Commanding General's Final Report on the evacuation from the Pacific Coast area. In it he refers to all individuals of Japanese descent as "subversive," as belonging to "an enemy race" whose "racial strains are undiluted," and as constituting "over 112,000 potential enemies...at large today" along the Pacific Coast. In support of this blanket condemnation of all persons of Japanese descent, however, no reliable evidence is cited to show that such individuals were generally disloyal. Individuals of Japanese ancestry are condemned because they are said to be "a large, unassimilated, tightly knit racial group, bound to an enemy nation by strong ties of race, culture, custom and religion."
>
> Studies demonstrate that persons of Japanese descent are readily susceptible to integration in our society if given the opportunity. The failure to accomplish an ideal status of assimilation, therefore, cannot be

charged to the refusal of these persons to become Americanized, or to their loyalty to Japan. And the retention by some persons of certain customs and religious practices of their ancestors is no criterion of their loyalty to the United States.

The need for protective custody is also asserted. This dangerous doctrine of protective custody, as proved by recent European history, should have absolutely no standing as an excuse for the deprivation of the rights of minority groups.

The military necessity which is essential to the validity of the evacuation order thus resolves itself into a few intimations that certain individuals actively aided the enemy, from which it is inferred that the entire group of Japanese Americans could not be trusted to be or remain loyal to the United States. No one denies, of course, that there were some disloyal persons of Japanese descent on the Pacific Coast who did all in their power to aid their ancestral land. Similar disloyal activities have been engaged in by many persons of German, Italian and even more pioneer stock in our country. But to infer that examples of individual disloyalty prove group disloyalty and justify discriminatory action against the entire group is to deny that under our system of law individual guilt is the sole basis for deprivation of rights. Moreover, this inference, which is at the very heart of the evacuation orders, has been used in support of the abhorrent and despicable treatment of minority groups by the dictatorial tyrannies which this nation is now pledged to destroy. To give constitutional sanction to that inference in this case, however well-intentioned may have been the military command on the Pacific Coast, is to adopt one of the cruelest of the rationales used by our enemies to destroy the dignity of the individual and to encourage and open the door to discriminatory actions against other minority groups in the passions of tomorrow.

No adequate reason is given for the failure to treat these Japanese Americans on an individual basis by holding investigations and hearings to separate the loyal from the disloyal, as was done in the case of persons of German and Italian ancestry. It is asserted merely that the loyalties of this group "were unknown and time was of the essence." Yet nearly four months elapsed after Pearl Harbor before the first exclusion order was issued; nearly eight months went by until the last order was issued, and the last of these "subversive" persons was not actually removed until almost eleven months had elapsed. Leisure and deliberation seem to have been more of the essence than speed.

Moreover, there was no adequate proof that the Federal Bureau of Investigation and the military and naval intelligence services did not have the espionage and sabotage situation well in hand during this long period. The Final Report, p. 34, makes the amazing statement that, as of February 14, 1942, "The very fact that no sabotage has taken place to date is a disturbing and confirming indication that such action will be taken." Apparently, in the minds of the military leaders, there was no way that the Japanese Americans could escape the suspicion of sabotage.

I dissent, therefore, from this legalization of racism. Racial discrimination in any form and in any degree has no justifiable part whatever in our democratic way of life. It is unattractive in any setting but it is utterly revolting among a free people who have embraced the principles set forth in the Constitution of the United States. All residents of this nation are kin in some way by blood or culture to a foreign land. Yet they are primarily and necessarily a part of the new and distinct civilization of the United States. They must accordingly be treated at all times as the heirs of the American experiment and as entitled to all the rights and freedoms guaranteed by the Constitution.

Another dissenter in *Korematsu* was Justice Robert Jackson, who, shortly after writing this dissent, was appointed by President Roosevelt to be the chief American prosecutor at the Nuremberg war crimes trials of the major war criminals. His words are prophetic:

A military order, however unconstitutional, is not apt to last longer than the military emergency. But once a judicial opinion rationalizes such an order to show that it conforms to the Constitution...that principle then lies about like a loaded weapon ready for the hand of any authority that can bring forward a plausible claim of an urgent need.

In 1946 during a ceremony on the White House grounds after a special parade honoring the 442nd on their way home, President Harry S. Truman told them "You fought for the free nations of the world along with the rest of us. I congratulate you on that, and I can't tell you how much I appreciate the privilege of being able to show you just how much the United States of America thinks of what you have done. You are now on your way home, but you fought prejudice—and you won. Keep up that fight, and we will continue to win—to make this republic stand for what the Constitution says it stands for: 'The welfare of all the people all the time.' "

He could have added "… and to make it more than just a scrap of paper."

In 1952, with the passage of the McCarran-Walter Act, Japanese immigrants were finally allowed to become naturalized citizens of the United States.

Earl Warren, attorney general of California at the time of Pearl Harbor, supported the removal of all Japanese to the interior. He later became Chief Justice of the United States. Long after the event he said, "It was wrong to act so impulsively, without positive evidence of disloyalty, even though we felt we had a good motive in the security of our state. It demonstrates the cruelty of war when fear, get tough military psychology, propaganda, and racial antagonism combine with one's responsibility for public security to produce such acts."

In 1981, a report by the Presidential Commission on the Wartime Relocation and Internment of Civilians concluded that the relocation and incarceration of the Japanese Americans was not justified by military necessity. It stated that the broad historical causes that shaped these decisions were race prejudice, war hysteria, and failure of political leadership. Racism, they concluded, played a major part in the decision to imprison those of Japanese ancestry. The failure of the justice system should be added to the list.

Korematsu's conviction for evading internment was overturned on November 10, 1983, after he challenged the earlier decision by filing for a writ of *coram nobis*. In her ruling, U.S. District Court Judge Marilyn Hall Patel of the Northern District of California wrote,

There is substantial support in the record that the government deliberately omitted relevant information and provided misleading information in the papers before the Supreme Court.... The judicial process is seriously impaired when the government's law enforcement officers violate their ethical obligation to the court. Korematsu remains on the pages of our legal and political history. As historical precedent it stands as a constant caution that in times of war or declared military necessity our institutions must be vigilant in protecting constitutional guarantees. It stands as a caution that in times of distress the shield of military necessity and national security must not be used to protect governmental actions from close scrutiny. (*Korematsu v. United States* 584 F. Supp. 1406) (1984)

On August 10, 1988, President Ronald Reagan signed the Civil Liberties Act of 1988, which provided for a onetime payment of $20,000 to each surviving Japanese American who had been interned during World War II and offered a formal national apology.

In 1998, President Clinton awarded Fred Korematsu the Presidential Medal of Freedom. President Clinton, in awarding the medal, told Korematsu, "In the long history of our country's constant search for justice, some names of ordinary citizens stand for millions of souls—*Plessy, Brown, Parks*. To that distinguished list, today we add the name of Fred Korematsu."

The all-Japanese 442nd Regimental Combat Team became the most decorated military unit in U.S. military history. It also suffered the highest casualty as a percentage of its total population.

Twenty-two members of the 442nd who demonstrated extreme bravery in combat were given the Distinguished

Service Medal, despite deserving a higher award. In 2000, President Clinton, in recognition of their bravery and dedication, recognized this and awarded all twenty-two the Medal of Honor. Of the twenty-two, ten had been killed in action and only seven survived to personally receive the award.

AFTER THE HOLOCAUST

A French High Court was convened soon after the war and tried 108 defendants charged with Nazi collaboration. It handed down eight death sentences. Joseph Darnand was convicted and executed by firing squad on October 10, 1945. Pierre Laval, prime minister of the Vichy government, was tried and executed by firing squad on October 15, 1945. Marshall Phillipe Petain, who had been installed as president of the Vichy government, was tried and condemned to death, but was spared due to his age. He died in 1951 at the age of ninety-four.

Klaus Barbie fled to Germany where he was arrested by units of the American armed forces. He was turned over to U.S. Army Intelligence, who concluded his value as an informant outweighed any need for punishment. Communism had now replaced National Socialism as the number one enemy, and Barbie was considered to have valuable intelligence about members of the Communist Party in France.

The Counter Intelligence Corps (CIC) of the U.S. Army then assisted his escape to Bolivia. He lived there until 1983 when a team of French Jewish Nazi hunters tracked him down and forced his extradition to France.

When he arrived in France, he was informed of the charges against him and advised of his rights to an attorney. By the time his case went to trial, he was represented by Jacques Verges, a noted attorney famous for representing dissidents and radical causes, and nicknamed the "Devil's advocate." The trial lasted four months. Verges turned what was to be a prosecution of a war criminal into an indictment of France and its participation in the persecution of the Jews and its own atrocities in Algeria and Vietnam. The whole ugly period was laid bare.

Barbie was convicted in 1987 of crimes against humanity and sentenced to life in prison. France had abolished the death penalty by that time. One of the counts of conviction related to the roundup, torture, and deportation of French railway workers in August 1944. Another dealt with the deportation and murder of the children of Izieu. Both of these events are recounted in this book. In the end, he received something his victims or the Japanese Americans never did: due process. In 1991, he died in prison at age seventy-seven. A video history of his activities can be found in the Historical Notes section that follows.

On December 5, 2014, the *Wall Street Journal* reported that France has agreed to pay $60 million in reparations to Holocaust survivors in the U.S. and other countries as part of a deal that shields the country from legal action in the U.S. The payment seeks to compensate non-French Jews who were among the tens of thousands of people France deported to German death camps when the country was under Nazi occupation.

Abraham Foxman, the National Director of the Anti-Defamation League and a Holocaust survivor, said, "There is no amount of money that could ever make up for the horrific injustice done to these victims and their families."

Rights once lost don't come back quickly, if ever. The fact that it took over fifty years to finally set the record straight regarding the Japanese internment is evidence of that.

Horrific wrongs done in the name of a French government that willingly enacted laws resulting in the deportation and ultimately the deaths of French and non-French Jews can never be remedied. Money cannot compensate for moral transgressions. We can only try to learn from them.

There will come a time again when our system of laws will be tested. If we remember what happened to the Jews in Europe and the Japanese in the United States and reread the words of Francis Biddle and Justice Murphy, we may be able to prevent or at least minimize injustice. If we do not, the specter of Dachau looms and the likes of Klaus Barbie stand ready to take control.

HISTORICAL NOTES

BOOK 1

Immediately after Pearl Harbor, Francis Biddle, the Attorney General of the United States, issued a statement that not only assured the Japanese Americans they would not be victimized but also stood, and still stands, as a testimonial to American values. Unfortunately his noble words did nothing to stem the tide of anti-Japanese sentiment that was to sweep the West Coast. His words are worth repeating.

> War threatens all civil rights; and although we have fought wars before, and our personal freedoms have survived, there have been periods of gross abuse, when hysteria and hate and fear ran high, and when minorities were unlawfully and cruelly abused. Every man who cares about freedom, about government by law—and all freedom is based on a fair administration of the law—must fight for it for the other man with whom he disagrees, for the right of the minority, for the chance for the underprivileged with the same passion of insistence as he claims for his own rights.

> If we care about democracy, we must care about it as a reality for others; for Germans, for Italians, for Japanese, for those who are with us as those who are against us. For the Bill of Rights protects not only American citizens, but all human beings who live on our American soil, under our American flag. The rights of Anglo-Saxons, of Jews, of Catholics, of Negroes, of Slavs, Indians—all are alike before the law. And this we must remember and sustain—that is if we really love justice, and really hate the bayonet and the whip and the gun, and the whole Gestapo method as a way of handling human beings. (Francis Biddle, Attorney General of the United States, December 10, 1941)

The lofty words of Francis Biddle soon gave way to war hysteria and the racism that had always existed against the Japanese. It culminated several months after Biddle's remarks when President Roosevelt issued his executive order that allowed for the removal, and ultimately the imprisonment, of 120,000 Japanese Americans. It read:

> Now, therefore, by virtue of the authority vested in me as President of the United States, and Commander in Chief of the Army and Navy, I hereby authorize and direct the Secretary of War, and the Military Commanders whom he may from time to time designate, whenever he or any designated Commander deems such action necessary or desirable, to prescribe military areas in such places and of such extent as he or the appropriate Military Commander may determine, from which any and all persons may be excluded, and with respect to which, the right of any person to enter, remain in, or leave shall be subject to whatever restrictions the Secretary of War or the appropriated Military Commander may impose in his discretion.

> I hereby further authorize and direct the Secretary of War and the said Military Commanders to take such other steps as he or the appropriate Military

Commander may deem advisable to enforce compliance with the restrictions applicable in each Military area hereinabove authorized to be designated, including the use of Federal troops and other Federal agencies, with authority to accept assistance of state and local agencies. (Franklin D. Roosevelt, The White House, February 19, 1942)

THE TRIALS OF THE FOUR CASES THAT REACHED THE SUPREME COURT

The trial of Ken Matsumoto depicted in the novel is a compilation of facts and circumstances taken from the four cases that went to trial and ultimately ended up in the Supreme Court.

The scene where Ken Matsumoto is taken into custody in the courtroom is taken from Fred Korematsu's account of his trial as told to Peter Irons and recounted in his seminal work on the internment cases, *Justice at War*.

The cross examination of Ken by the Judge is taken from the trial of Min Yasui. (Yasui v. United States 320 US 115 (1943). The trial took place in Portland, Oregon and began on June 12th 1942. It was presided over by United States District Court Judge James A. Fee. The cross examination of Ken Matsumoto depicted in the book closely parallels that of Judge Fee's cross examination of Mr. Yasui at his trial.

The legal arguments regarding the importance of the *Milligan* case, the infamous Harvard Law Review article and the stacking of the courtroom with uniformed JAG officers came from the trial of Mitsuye Endo. Her case was tried in San Francisco before United States District Court Judge Michael J. (Iron Mike) Roche. It is set out in detail in Peter Irons treatise and in Bill Hosokawa's book *Nisei—the Quiet Americans*.

The language in the Judge's ruling on Matsumoto's habeas petition challenging the legality of the curfew and removal orders came from the trial of Gordon Hirabayashi in Seattle before United States District Court Judge Lloyd D. Black. It is a distillation of the Judge's written opinion in the case taken from the account in Peter Irons' *Justice at War.*

In the electronic version CLICK on CTRL and LEFT CLICK on the link. In the print version, go to julesbonjour.com and click on the links.

MANZANAR

Manzanar was one of ten concentration camps in the western United States hastily established to house the 120,000 Americans of Japanese descent who were ordered to leave their homes in 1942. At its peak Manzanar housed 10,000 men, women, and children. This YouTube video begins with the government's reason for the forced relocation but then shifts to a contemporary documentary that graphically shows what life was like in Manzanar and the demoralizing effect it had on its residents. https://www.youtube.com/watch?v=ac19C-rfMp8

In the autumn of 1943, Ansel Adams was invited to Manzanar by the camp director Ralph Merritt to take photographs of the facility and the Japanese who were being forced to live there. The photographs and the book he wrote about his experience at Manzanar entitled *Born Free and Equal* were first exhibited at the Museum of Modern Art in 1944. The photographs depict the internees as non-threatening human beings and the camp as a place run in an orderly and humane way. The public, used to seeing Japanese depicted as threatening and monstrous and wanting to see them punished, reacted negatively to the photographs and the book. Many of the photos were taken down from the exhibit and many of the books were destroyed. The link below is to the photographs. http://twistedsifter.com/2012/02/ansel-adams-life-on-japanese-internment-camp/

The book *Born Free and Equal* is available through Amazon and other booksellers. http://amzn.to/1nHFmE9.

OAKLAND/ALAMEDA COUNTY COURTHOUSE

http://www.davidsanger.com/images/oakland/S5-60-3398.courthouse.m.jpg

UNITED STATES DISTRICT COURT

Courtroom no. 1 circa 1942
Location of the Matsumoto trial in the book and actual courtroom for the Korematsu trial.
http://en.wikipedia.org/wiki/File:James_R_Browning_Courthouse_Courtroom_1.JPG

REGILLUS APARTMENTS

OAKLAND, CALIFORNIA

http://upload.wikimedia.org/wikipedia/en/f/fc/Regillus_entrance.jpg

http://www.homesintheeastbayhills.com/wp-content/gallery/past-listings/200-lakeside-ext.jpg

http://photos3.zillowstatic.com/p_d/ISx26mlmlfre03.jpg

THE CLAREMONT HOTEL

http://4.bp.blogspot.com/_xYUmbleMHrQ/SIa21jeFtlI/AAAAAAAAb4/nTosk_7KbSA/s400/Hotel%2BClaremont.jpg

http://www.mtc.ca.gov/images/ta01-0201/ClaremontResort.jpg

http://www.claremontresort.com/images/p-history.jpg

BOOK 2

THE LIBERATOR PISTOL

www.youtube.com/watch?v=62jtMEgtBL0

BEETHOVEN'S 5TH PIANO CONCERTO PLAYED ON SEPTEMBER 4, 1944, IN BERLIN

Walter Gieseking was a brilliant pianist in the middle decades of the 20th century. The reference to listening to Beethoven's 5th piano concerto in Lagrange's bunker is based on the fact that he performed the concerto in September of 1944 in Berlin. It was broadcast live over Berlin radio and recorded in what is believed to be the first stereo recording ever made.

Despite the environment in which it was performed, a noted critic has called the recording brilliant. If one listens closely one can hear the sounds of anti-aircraft fire in the background.

Gieseking was the son of a German doctor and spent most of his adult life in Germany. Ironically, he was born in Lyon.

It is available on CD. The adagio from this recording can be listened to by going to the following link, which contains a picture of Gieseking and a bombed-out Berlin.

https://www.youtube.com/watch?v=EY7lvuVjjX4

KLAUS BARBIE: A VIDEO IN FOUR PARTS
Klaus Barbie – part one of four
https://www.youtube.com/watch?v=XoO555_xiKQ

Klaus Barbie – part two of four
https://www.youtube.com/watch?v=XajjEnbqnco

Klaus Barbie – part three of four
https://www.youtube.com/watch?v=nQ4AMMOJ5mQ

Klaus Barbie – part four of four
https://www.youtube.com/watch?v=_NGt6r_fR_s

THE ESCAPES

Bernard's escape while being transported from the École is taken from an account of the escape of Raymond Aubrac planned and carried out by his wife, Lucie, and members of the Resistance. Her life and the escape are recounted in the 1997 film Lucie Aubrac, and in her biography, *Outwitting the Gestapo*. She died at the age of ninety-four. Raymond Aubrac lived to be ninety-seven.

The escape of Chantal is based upon the experience of Marie-Madeleine's and her escape from a jail cell as recounted in her autobiography *Noah's Ark*.

THE MOLE

The description of the use of the Mole device used to blow up trains came from a training film prepared by the Office of Strategic Services (OSS) in 1942. It is available on YouTube. https://www.youtube.com/watch?v=9cipyPJJdnM

THE LOST BATALLION

The rescue of the "Lost Battalion" by members of the all-Japanese 442nd Regimental Combat Team is fact. The rescue was given wide publicity in the States but with little mention of the families still in the camps. The link is to newsreel coverage of the rescue.
https://www.youtube.com/watch?v=S8JbenmTD-A

DACHAU

Japanese members of the 522nd Field Artillery Team were some of the first to enter a satellite camp of the main camp at Dachau. They helped liberate thousands of Jews. This link contains graphic photos. http://bit.ly/1Fh5lEz

WELLS LEWIS

The way Wells Lewis was killed is accurately portrayed in the novel. He led a short, but remarkable, life. A documentary entitled *Wells Lewis: Lost Heir to a Minnesota Son,* is interesting and compelling in that it discusses his life growing up as the son of a Nobel Laureate and his own achievements. It is also heartbreaking given that a life full of promise was extinguished so abruptly. This is a link to the video.
https://www.youtube.com/watch?v=1Fts1dT_SV8

As was said in the novel, war chooses its victims arbitrarily.

HOTEL CRILLON

http://palacehotelsoftheworld.com/wp-content/uploads/paris-hotel-le-crillon-logo.jpg

http://www.luxuryhotelexperts.com/images/showcase/luxury_hotels_920/hotel_de_crillon_02.jpg

ABOUT THE AUTHOR

Jules Bonjour has been a criminal defense attorney in the San Francisco Bay area for forty nine years. In this, his first novel, he draws upon his many years defending those who have suffered discrimination and prejudice to write about the injustices that Japanese Americans experienced after Pearl Harbor and the Jews suffered in Vichy France after France fell to the Germans in 1940.

He has a B.S. from Northwestern University, a Masters Degree from U.C. Berkeley and a J.D. from Berkeley Law (U.C. Berkeley) He has three children and eight grandchildren and lives in Berkeley near the UC campus and the Claremont Hotel with his wife of forty four years. He is still an active criminal defense attorney.

ACKNOWLEDGEMENTS

It is with sincere gratitude that I acknowledge the following persons who read the manuscript and made constructive suggestions, many of which were adopted. I have listed them in alphabetical order.

Bella Barany, Lincoln Bergman, David Billingsley, Jim Brosnahan, Hon. Carol Brosnahan, Beth Chapmon, Kevin Cragholm, Paul Dorroh, Susan Farrow, Patricia Golde, Ivan Golde, Matthew Golde, Clair Green, Tran Ha, James Hermann, Hon. D. Lowell Jensen, Hon. Ken Kawaichi, Alyson Madigan, Jim Rothe, and Michael Thorman.

I owe a special debt of gratitude to the late Barclay Simpson, founder and retired CEO of Simpson Manufacturing, who was my friend for almost fifty years. He read the first rough manuscript and encouraged me to push on. He also fought in World War II, and helped preserve our way of life, which made it possible to correct the wrongs that were done to Japanese Americans.

I am indebted to Peter Irons, who wrote the book *Justice at War*. It is the most comprehensive work on the internment cases ever written, and it was from his work that I was able to piece together the events that occurred during the four cases that went to trial.

Special thanks to Beth Barany and Carol Malone, my editors. Special thanks to David Roth and Boris who proofread the first printing, and to Ezra Barany who designed the cover.

And finally to my wife, Monique, who read the manuscript as an editor, proofreader, and partner. She also allowed me the freedom to spend countless hours writing and researching, to the exclusion of her and the many things we could have done together.

Jules Bonjour

Berkeley, California

April 2015